PRAISE FOR *REMEMBER WHEN:*

"Remember When is a richly textured book that deeply touches the heart. I was enthralled from the very first page. Robin Lee Hatcher has outdone herself."
> —Debbie Macomber, author of *One Night*

"Ms. Hatcher fills *Remember When* with dimensional characters handling realistic conflicts and, at the same time, keeps the magical essence of love alive on every page. Tender and touching, this poignant tale tugs at your heart. An impressive read!"
> —*Rendezvous*

"A talented storyteller, Robin Lee Hatcher writes a charming, heartwarming story that makes the reader yearn for those simpler days of long ago. Reserve a place on your keeper shelf next to the other two books of Hatcher's *Americana Series!*"
> —*Love Letters*

STOLEN KISSES

"No one need ever know what happened here, Sarah. You didn't know what you were doing. I'm all to blame. But if we say nothing, there'll be no harm to your reputation."

Her eyes widened.

Jeremiah continued, his voice even more harsh. "You're engaged to my brother. The two of you are to be married in a week. Is it necessary for us to cause him grief over something that was an accident? It meant nothing to either of us. We weren't thinking straight. Desire can make people forget what is right. It meant nothing."

She took a quick step back, staring at him as if he'd struck her.

He flinched inwardly, seeing he'd hurt her, loathing himself for it. Loathing himself more because he knew he was lying. It hadn't meant nothing to him. For a moment, he'd felt…he'd felt something fill the emptiness of his heart.

Remember When

ROBIN LEE HATCHER

LEISURE BOOKS   NEW YORK CITY

*To those special schoolteachers of my youth
who allowed my imagination to take wing,
and to all those who dare to dream.
Don't be afraid to reach for the stars!*

A LEISURE BOOK®

November 1994

Published by

Dorchester Publishing Co., Inc.
276 Fifth Avenue
New York, NY 10001

Printed in the United States of America.

My heart was a habitation large enough for many guests, but lonely and chill, and without a household fire. I longed to kindle one! It seemed not so wild a dream.

—Nathaniel Hawthorne,
The Scarlet Letter

Remember When

Prologue

Cuba, July 1898

The Stars and Stripes fluttered in the hot breeze above the captured trenches of San Juan Hill.

Jeremiah Wesley, his thigh bleeding, sank onto the ground beside the other Rough Riders and doughboys, all of them panting and sweating. Numbly, he looked back at the way they'd come.

The wounded and dead cluttered the slope. Everywhere, Spaniards and Americans lay in pools of their own blood. A gray haze hung over the earth, and Jeremiah's nostrils burned with the acrid scent of gun smoke. A humming sound buzzed in his ears. Eventually, he realized it was the moaning of the

11

wounded, more than a thousand of them.

He saw the colonel standing over a dead Spaniard's body and knew that Roosevelt was reveling in both the victory and the gore. Jeremiah had expected to feel the thrill of battle, too. He didn't. He just felt empty, the same haunting emptiness he'd felt for years.

A sweet, familiar voice whispered in his heart, *Go home, Jeremiah. It's time you went home.*

Maybe she was right. Maybe it was time to go home.

Chapter One

Homestead, Idaho, December 1898

Bundled against the frigid winter day, Sarah McLeod hurried along the boardwalk toward the station. Tom was due to arrive today, and she was eager to be there when her younger brother stepped off the train. He'd been away three years now, but it seemed longer. And come spring, he'd be off to Boston where he would continue his schooling. The next time he returned to Homestead, he would be a doctor.

Sarah was so proud of her brother, she could just about burst. He was young—only eighteen—and already he was on his way to achieving something wonderful, something he'd dreamed about for years. She couldn't help but envy him, at least a little. But only a little. Mostly, she felt a bubbling joy and pride.

When she stepped up onto the depot platform, she saw Doc Varney standing close to the building, out of the icy wind that stung her cheeks. She raised her hand and waved.

Dr. Kevin Varney was a distinguished-looking man with glasses, gray hair, and a bushy beard. It was he who had encouraged Tom to become a physician. Many were the nights when her brother, only thirteen or fourteen at the time, had gone over to Doc Varney's home and studied the medical books that lined the shelves, staying up long past his bedtime, asking the doctor question upon question. The elderly physician had been so impressed by Tom's intelligence and eagerness to learn that he'd gone to great lengths to help Tom get admitted to the Elias Crane Science Academy for Boys in San Francisco.

"I didn't know you'd be here," Sarah said as she stopped beside the older man.

"Not come and welcome Tom home?" His eyes twinkled. "You know me better than that, young lady." His expression sobered. "How's your grandfather?"

Sarah gave a slight shrug. "Ornery as ever. It was all I could do to make him wait at home. He kept saying a little fresh air was good for a man."

"Catch pneumonia is what he'd do." The

14

doctor tugged at the collar of his coat. "I can't say the two of us won't be doin' the same."

She nodded in agreement, then gazed down the length of track that stretched toward the southeast end of the valley. She hoped the train would be on time. If it were even a few minutes late, her grandfather was likely to disobey her orders and come down to the station himself.

Sheriff Hank McLeod at seventy-four was as strong-willed as he'd ever been. It was his body that had changed. At one time a tall, barrel-chested man, he was now much thinner and somewhat bent with age, and he lacked the energy that used to carry him through each day. Still, he stubbornly held on to his position as sheriff, and no one in Homestead had the heart to tell him he should retire, especially after he'd lost his wife of fifty-one years last summer. Sarah had been after him for months to at least hire a deputy, but so far, according to him, he hadn't found anyone suitable.

It had been a constant strain on Sarah, trying to make sure her grandfather got the rest he needed. Perhaps he'd be better behaved while Tom was home. After all, her brother would be a doctor one day. Grandpa would have to listen to him.

"There she comes," Doc Varney said, interrupting her perplexed thoughts.

Sarah focused her gaze once again on the

ribbon of track. She saw the billowing cloud of soot shooting up into the air moments before the train itself came into view. Her excitement surged to the fore once again.

"Do you suppose he's changed much?" she asked as she rose on tiptoe, her eagerness making it difficult to stand still.

"I imagine he's become a man while he was away."

Doc Varney was right, of course. Tom McLeod *had* become a man. He'd changed so much that Sarah almost didn't recognize him when he stepped down from the train a few minutes later.

She rushed forward and threw herself into his arms. "Tommy!" She gave him a kiss on the cheek, then stepped back. "You're taller . . . and you've grown a mustache!"

"Like it?" he asked with a cocky grin, turning his head so she could view it from another angle.

She frowned as she looked at him. "I'm not sure. You look so . . . so different."

Doc Varney stepped up behind her. "Well, I like it, young man. Gives you a look of distinction." He held out his hand. "Welcome home."

"Thank you, sir." Tom shook the older gentleman's hand as he met his solemn gaze.

"I've heard good reports about you," the doctor continued, his voice oddly gruff.

"I've tried to do my best, sir."

"I knew you would." Doc Varney cleared his throat as he released Tom's hand and stepped backward. "Well, I won't keep you. It's too blasted cold out here to stand about, and your grandfather's anxious to see you. When you get settled, come over to my office and we'll have a long visit."

"I'll do that," Tom replied.

Sarah slipped her arm through her brother's as the doctor walked away.

Tom looked at her again, and his grin returned. "You got prettier while I was gone. No wonder Warren's been pestering you to marry him for so long." He shook his head. "It's hard to believe you'll be a married woman in a couple of weeks."

It was hard for her to believe it, too, and she'd rather not think about it now. Thoughts of her impending wedding always left her feeling restless and confused.

Tom tapped the end of her nose with a gloved finger. "And I always thought you'd wait for that English lord," he teased.

She playfully slapped his arm, then smiled as she tugged him forward. "Let's go home. Grampa can't wait to see you, and I've got lunch all ready. I made all your favorites. I know you must be hungry."

Unnoticed, Jeremiah watched the interchange from the step of the passenger car. He saw the lovely blond woman kiss the young man's cheek. Her blue eyes—even from where he stood he could tell they were blue—glittered with exuberance and joy. Her happiness spread a glow over the entire platform. Even he felt warmed by it, and he was merely an observer.

A short time later, the couple walked away, arm in arm, oblivious to anything else around them. He knew what that kind of absorption was like. He'd felt it himself a long, long time ago.

The empty feeling in Jeremiah's chest intensified, and the cold returned, blasting his cheeks with its icy breath. Hunching his shoulders inside his coat, he stepped down to the platform, walked the length of it, then stared toward the center of town.

Homestead had changed in the years he'd been away. He shouldn't have been surprised, but he was.

Instead of just one street, the town had several. New houses and businesses had sprouted up. There was a second church at the opposite end of town from the one he remembered. There was even a hotel and a bank. It was all very different from the town of his memories, and yet, it was very much the same.

It was home, and he was back. For the first time in years, he felt he'd done something right.

He turned toward the train and went after his belongings. There wasn't much. He'd been able to pack everything he owned into a couple of carpetbags. He picked them up, one in each hand, and headed into town.

Snow crunched beneath his boots as he made his way toward the center of town. His first destination was Barber Mercantile. It had been a letter four years ago from Stanley Barber, the proprietor of the mercantile, that had brought Jeremiah word of his father's death. He'd been deeply saddened by the news, realizing it was forever too late for him to find a way to please his father, to prove himself to Ted Wesley. Perhaps that was why the rest of Mr. Barber's letter had surprised him. His father's will had left the farm solely to Jeremiah. It was still difficult for him to believe, especially after the way they'd parted company all those years ago.

Jeremiah had always wanted to personally thank Mr. Barber for his kindness, for taking the time to track down his whereabouts and write to him. But there was also another reason, he admitted to himself, for going to the mercantile. Emma Barber. He remembered Stanley's wife and knew she would be able to tell him about his father and brother and the farm in the years he'd been away. Mrs. Barber had always known everything about everybody in the valley.

A bell chimed over his head as he opened the door to the store. He felt a wave of nostalgia at the familiar sights and smells. Nothing had changed in all these years. He could have been a kid again, stopping by the mercantile on his way home from school. He knew just where the pickle barrel would be and the jar of licorice, too.

A woman behind the counter turned from the shelves she'd been stocking. She was too young to be Emma Barber, yet there was something familiar about her. "Hello. May I help you?"

He set his carpetbags on the floor near the door, then removed his hat as he strode forward. "I'm looking for Stanley Barber."

"I'm sorry," she said with a slight shake of her head. "Mr. Barber died almost two years ago. Is there something . . ." She stopped and stared at him a moment. "Why, you're Jeremiah Wesley."

He stared back at her, wondering who she was.

"I'm Leslie. Leslie Barber. Well, it's Leslie Blake now. I don't suppose you remember me at all. I was just a girl when you went away. How long has it been?"

"Close to fourteen years," he answered.

"Land o' Goshen! Is it really? I can hardly believe it. Why, you must not even recognize the town. Homestead isn't like it used to be when we were children. The railroad's come through and we've got our own hotel and that new Methodist church. The school's just about bursting at the seams, what with all the children everybody's got. I was just sayin' to Annalee . . . You remember my sister, don't you? Well, I was just sayin' to her how much everything has changed since we were children. Of course, we've watched it happen. It must be a real surprise to someone who's been away as long as you."

It wasn't so much that he remembered Leslie as that she reminded him of her mother. Plump and warm-natured, Emma Barber had loved to chatter and gossip whenever someone was in the store, just as Leslie was doing now.

Suddenly she stopped speaking. With a shake of her head, she said softly, "I'm real sorry about your wife. And your pa, too. I've lost both my parents since you went away. I know how it feels."

The door joining the living quarters to the mercantile opened at that moment, drawing both their gazes.

"George, come here," Leslie called. "There's someone I'd like you to meet." As soon as the man was close enough, she reached out and took hold of his left hand, then faced Jeremiah again. "This is my husband, George Blake. George, this is Jeremiah Wesley, Warren's big brother. We knew each other when we were in school, only I was too little for him to remember."

George shook Jeremiah's hand. "Howdy."

Jeremiah nodded his own greeting.

"Tell us what you've been doing all these years," Leslie urged, her eyes glittering with interest.

This was one reason why he hadn't come

back before now, he realized. There would be questions to answer. He'd have to dig into old memories he would just as soon forget. Maybe he'd been wrong to return. Maybe it was all better left alone.

In silence, he watched George Blake drape his arm over Leslie's shoulders. The gesture was casual, yet lovingly possessive. Leslie glanced up, giving her husband a smile, a smile rife with affection and understanding.

Jeremiah felt a tightness in his chest.

"Are you home to stay?" Leslie persisted, her attention returning to Jeremiah.

"Don't know for sure."

She grinned at him. "Jeremiah Wesley, you haven't been gone so long you've forgotten the determination of the Barber women, have you? My ma would've had every detail of the last fourteen years out of you before she'd've let you out of this store." Again she exchanged a glance with her husband, before continuing. "I'm a lot like my ma that way. If you don't tell me where you've been or what you've been doing, I'll simply burst with curiosity."

He subdued a sigh of exasperation. He might as well get used to it. Leslie Blake wouldn't be the last person to ask him about the past. Steeling himself, he looked her straight in the eye and said, "After Millie died, I moved around a lot. I worked cattle, did some bartending, even spent some time with the railroad before going to work in a

factory back in New York City. Last couple
of years, I was in the army."

"The army? Were you in the war?"

Scenes of the battlefield flashed, unbidden,
in his head. "Yeah. I was in the war."

"I noticed you had a bit of a limp when
you came in. Were you hurt bad?"

"No." He put his hat back on. "Listen, I'd
better get over to the livery and see about
renting a rig. Warren's not expecting me, and
I need to get out to the farm before dark."

Leslie shook her head. "You won't find
Warren out there. He's workin' in town. He's
got himself a shop right down the street."

"A shop?"

"Makin' furniture. He's real good at it, too."
She paused, then added, "He's going to be
real surprised and glad to see you."

Jeremiah nodded without comment, then
turned and left the store.

As the mercantile door closed behind him
with a rattle of glass and the bell jingling
overhead, he thought she was probably right
about his brother being real surprised to
see him. He wasn't so sure about Warren
being glad.

Chapter Two

Warren Wesley ran his fingers over the smoothly sanded surface of the table, enjoying the feel and smell of the wood. He was taking particular pleasure in making this piece because it would be used in what was to be his new home. The old table that currently stood in the dining room of the McLeod house was scratched and marred, the wood and craftsmanship of poor quality. He would be glad when he could make firewood of it and this new table would take its place.

As he moved the sandpaper over the dark cherry wood, his thoughts drifted toward his wedding day. He'd waited a long time for it, and now it was almost here. It was nearly five years since he'd first asked Sarah McLeod to be his wife. It hadn't been easy to convince her to marry him. She'd had her head in the clouds for as long as he'd known her, always dreaming about places and things beyond her reach. She'd long since passed the age when she should have forgotten such nonsense and settled down with a husband.

With *him*, he thought with a satisfied smile.

He felt a tightening in his groin as he considered the delights of their wedding night. Sarah had never allowed him more than an occasional chaste kiss, but it wouldn't be long before he would have the right to do more. Only two weeks and Sarah would be his. He'd been patient a long time. He wouldn't have to be patient much longer.

The shop door opened, letting in a cool gust of air. He turned from his workbench, squinting as he looked toward the sunshine spilling in through the windows on either side of the door. It took his eyes a moment to adjust before he could make out the tall figure of the man who'd entered.

"Hello, Warren."

He frowned, wondering who the stranger was, wondering how he knew his name.

"Have I changed so much?"

His eyes widened. Was it possible?

Jeremiah gave a humorless chuckle. "Yeah, it's me. You've changed, too."

"I didn't think I'd ever see you again." He hadn't *wanted* ever to see him again. His brother had never been anything but trouble. Everyone in Homestead had known it. Yet, in the end, he'd still been their father's favorite son.

Jeremiah's gaze traveled around the shop. "A business of your own. Dad must have been proud of you."

Dad was never proud of me. "I didn't have the shop before he died." He took a step forward, wishing the sun weren't so bright at his brother's back, wishing he could see Jeremiah's face more clearly. "What brought you back?"

His brother was silent a long time before answering. "It was time to come home." He paused again, then asked, "Is there room for me out at the farm or is the place full of a wife and kids?"

Warren felt a tightening in his gut. Was it possible Jeremiah didn't know that he, not Warren, had inherited the farm? Of course he didn't. Dad hadn't answered any of his letters. If Warren didn't tell him, Jeremiah would be none the wiser. Maybe he'd just leave again.

He spoke carefully, trying to disguise the tension he felt. "The house is empty. I'm livin' in town now." He drew a deep breath. "I've got the farm up for sale."

Jeremiah didn't respond immediately. Instead, he set his carpetbags on the floor, then walked slowly around the shop, stopping to run his fingers lightly over the tables and bedsteads and chairs that filled the room.

When he'd gone full circle, he turned to face his brother again.

"The farm's mine, Warren, and we both know it. Dad left it to me."

Warren's temper flared. "So what if he did? You weren't here. You never came back, never wrote. For all I knew, you were dead. That made it mine," he snapped. "Besides, I need the money. I'm getting married in a couple of weeks."

Damn Jeremiah for coming back, just now when everything was going right in his life.

Sarah carried the dish of steaming vegetables into the dining room and set it in the center of the large table. "I'm sorry Warren couldn't join us for lunch, but he'll be here tonight for supper."

"I don't mind having you to myself." Tom chuckled. "Or the food either. You don't know how much I've missed your cooking, Sarah. They didn't serve meals like this at the academy. I can promise you that."

She smiled, pleased with his compliment. "Well, you won't know if it's delicious until you taste it." She settled onto her chair. "Why don't you say grace, Tom?"

He nodded, then bowed his head. "We thank you, Father God, for bringing us back together. Bless this food you have provided from your bounty. In Jesus' name. Amen."

"Amen," Sarah whispered.

"Amen," Grampa echoed.

Tom glanced up at his sister and grandfather, then reached for the platter of roast beef. "I'm starved."

Sarah laughed aloud, reminded of when her brother was little. He'd always been hungry. He'd been forever pestering their grandmother for something to eat. The moment he arrived home from school, he'd be in the kitchen.

I'm starved, Gramma. What's there to eat?

She continued to smile as she watched Tom heaping mashed potatoes onto his plate and smothering them in gravy. He might not be a little boy any longer, but he certainly hadn't lost his boyish appetite.

"Did I tell you Dr. Crane visited me at the academy and told me all about the institute?" Tom asked their grandfather as he passed the gravy boat.

Grampa shook his head. "No, you didn't tell us that yet."

"I've never met anyone like him. He's so dynamic. Truly brilliant. He's the best teacher of medicine in the country. No matter what you ask him, he never makes you feel foolish for asking. All these years at the academy, I've heard others talking about him with such awe. Now I know why. I can't believe I'm actually going to be studying under him. There were so few selected from my class. I can't believe I was one of them."

Sarah watched her brother's animated expression, only half-listening to what he was saying. She was thinking what a handsome man he'd become. He looked surprisingly like their father when he was close to the same age—hair as black as ink, eyes the same lead gray as his father and grandfather. Not that she remembered their papa. Not really. But she did have the photograph taken of her parents on their wedding day. Except for the mustache, it could have been her brother in the photograph standing beside their mother on that long-ago day.

How proud Tom and Maria McLeod would have been of their son, she thought, watching as her brother gestured expressively with his hands. A doctor's hands. Hands that would be used to soothe and heal. Yes, her parents would have been proud of Tommy.

She wondered what her parents would think of her if they could see her now. Would she be a disappointment to them? She was nearly twenty-one and unmarried while most of her friends had already started families of their own.

Not that Sarah hadn't had the opportunity to marry. Warren Wesley had first proposed to her when she was just sixteen. She'd turned him down, telling him she couldn't marry him because she was going to travel the world one day. She was going to be a famous stage actress and then she was going to marry someone rich and important, someone like a president or an English lord or a European count.

29

Undaunted, Warren had proposed again when she was eighteen, but again she'd refused. She'd decided to study medicine, like her brother. She was going to be a nurse and work with Tom, she'd told him. How could she get married? There was so much she still wanted to see and do.

When he'd asked her again on her nineteenth birthday, she'd told him maybe. By that time, she'd realized she didn't want to be an actress or a nurse. She wasn't sure of anything anymore. She'd been told so often that her dreams were foolish, she hadn't known what she wanted anymore. But she'd known her grandmother had hoped she would say yes.

"You're grown up now, Sarah," Gramma Dorie had said. "It's time you were settled. I'd like to see you married before I'm gone. Warren Wesley is a fine young man. You'd be lucky to be his wife."

And so, when Warren had proposed once again on Sarah's twentieth birthday, she'd agreed to marry him, making her grandmother a happy woman, although Doris McLeod hadn't lived to see the wedding.

Her wedding . . . The thought caused a flutter of nerves in her stomach.

Then she smiled to herself. Tom was right. She had been waiting for that English lord—and lots of other exciting things, too. She supposed her gramma had also been right. They had been foolish, her dreams of travel, of meeting fascinating people and seeing extraordinary things, but she didn't care. They'd been *her* dreams. Oh, how very much she'd wanted to . . .

"What do you think, Sarah?"

Her brother's question brought her attention abruptly back to the present. She was surprised to realize the two men were leaning back in their chairs, their lunch plates now empty. How long had she allowed her thoughts to wander?

"I'm sorry. I . . . I . . ."

Tom laughed. "Daydreaming, weren't you, sis?" He glanced at their grandfather and winked. "Remember when we used to go fishin' at your favorite spot on the river and she'd sit on those rocks and stare off into space, dreaming about the Eiffel Tower and Buckingham Palace and pretending she was royalty or something? She's got that same look on her face now."

"I remember," Grampa said, turning a fond gaze on Sarah. "And I wish I could've made all those dreams come true for her."

She felt a sudden tightness in her chest. Her grandfather looked so old and frail, so unlike the man who'd raised her. Whatever would she do when he was gone?

Shaking off those melancholy thoughts, she put on a smile and said, "If they'd come true, you'd have to call me *my lady* whenever you visited me in my castle."

Tom hopped to his feet, swept off an

imaginary hat, and executed an elaborate bow. "My lady Sarah, how kind of you to allow your lowly kinfolk to join you for lunch in your beautiful castle."

"Do sit down, my good fellow," she responded, sticking her nose in the air as she sent him a censuring glance. "The servants shall be clearing the table soon, and you're liable to trip them."

Both men laughed aloud.

She grinned as she rose from her chair and reached for the nearly empty meat platter.

"I'll help you," Tom offered as he picked up more dirty dishes. "And I promise not to trip any of the servants."

Sarah felt a sublime contentment as she led the way into the kitchen.

Jeremiah shoved more wood into the stove, thankful for the plentiful supply he'd found stacked against the side of the house. There might even be enough to see him through the winter, if he was frugal.

But firewood wasn't his most pressing problem. He could always go up into the mountains and cut some wood himself if he needed to. No, the real problem was money.

Before he'd left Warren's furniture shop, he'd told his brother he would pay him half the price he was asking for the farm. He supposed he'd done it out of guilt. Although Jeremiah legally owned the place, even he had to wonder about his father's bequest. Ted Wesley had never approved of Jeremiah. Everything his oldest son had done had been wrong. Everything. Jeremiah couldn't understand why his dad had left him the farm. Their angry parting words still played in his head as clearly as if they'd just spoken them.

"You're a fool, Jeremiah. You'll never amount to anything if you do this."

"I know what I'm doing."

"You can't provide for a wife. You'll probably both die of starvation before you're through. And what kind of wife can she be? She's just a child."

"She's no child. I love her. I'm going to marry her."

"Not and live under my roof."

"To hell with your roof. And to hell with you, too."

Turning from the stove, he shook off the memory as he glanced around the main room. Except for a layer of dust, it was difficult to believe that no one had been living here for so long. It seemed as if, any moment, his dad could come walking through the door. The place was exactly as it had been fourteen years ago. His dad hadn't changed a thing in all those years, hadn't moved so much as a chair.

Actually, Jeremiah wasn't surprised. Ted Wesley had been a man of habit and routine.

"You'll find, son, that there's great comfort in the familiar."

He sank onto a chair and stared at the flickering orange flames inside the black belly of the stove. He supposed that was why he'd come back. He'd wanted—needed— to be surrounded by the familiar. It was time to come home, to lay old things to rest at last. It was time he made peace with himself, if with no one else.

Outside, the wind whistled through the trees, a lonely wail in the darkness of a winter's night.

Jeremiah closed his eyes, listening to the crackling in the stove and the wailing beyond the walls, contrasting sounds, one friendly, one not so. He listened and felt the isolation surround him.

"Well, I'm back, Millie," he whispered. "Now what?"

But silence was his only reply.

All through supper that evening, Sarah had the feeling that something was troubling Warren, but she didn't know what and he didn't let on.

Of course, that was like Warren. He didn't like to "worry your little head about things," as he always put it. Sometimes she wondered what on earth they would talk about when they got married and spent even more time together. What if they found they had nothing to talk about at all?

She looked at her fiancé across the table, wishing for once she would feel that quiver of excitement she thought she should feel. But maybe she was wrong. She supposed nobody really felt that way. It was probably only the stuff of novels. Maybe it was just another one of her foolish dreams.

That had to be it. After all, there was nothing wrong with Warren. He wasn't tall or dark or mysterious—all the things she'd dreamed about when she was a girl—but he was pleasant looking and hardworking. He was certainly patient or he never would have waited so long for her to make up her mind about marrying him. Everyone said what a fine husband he would be, and she knew it must be true. Of course, he could be a bit condescending at times, but was that such a serious flaw?

Heaven only knew what all he would have to put up with when he was married to her!

When supper was over, Sarah cleared the table and washed the dishes while the men retired to her grandfather's study for a smoke and a glass of whiskey. By the time she'd dried and put away the last plate, the three of them had returned to the living room and were waiting for her to join them.

Warren sat beside her on the upholstered tapestry sofa her grandmother had ordered from the Montgomery Ward catalogue a few years ago. He took hold of her hand and squeezed lightly.

"I've got some news," he announced without preamble, his gaze sweeping over the others in the room. "My brother's returned."

"Jeremiah?" Grampa asked.

Warren nodded. "He's staying out at the farm."

"Well, I'll be . . ." Hank muttered. "I never expected him to come back to these parts."

"Anybody care to fill me in?" Tom asked, looking at Warren. "I didn't even know you *had* a brother."

Sarah felt nearly as much in the dark. She'd known Warren had an older brother named Jeremiah, and she supposed she'd even met him when she was a child, although she didn't remember it. For some reason, she'd never asked Warren about Jeremiah. She'd always intuitively avoided doing so, suspecting her questions would be unwelcome.

Grampa stared up at the ceiling, as if that would help him recall the facts. "Let's see. Jeremiah must've been about seventeen when he and Millie Parkerson ran off together. Back in . . . oh"—he was silent for several moments—"about 'eighty-five, that was. It was spring. Just time for plantin'. Millie was barely sixteen. I remember that much for certain." He looked at Tom. "You'd've been no more'n five at the time."

"They eloped?" Sarah didn't say it, but she couldn't help thinking it sounded terribly romantic, two young people so much in love they'd defied the world to be together. She wished she could remember them.

"Hmmm." Grampa nodded. "Caused a bit of a ruckus around these parts, too. Mrs. Parkerson took it real hard, havin' her only child run off like that, and she wasn't ever the same till the day she died." He frowned thoughtfully. "Seems to me we heard Millie died back in . . . let's see . . . must've been about 'ninety-two, maybe 'ninety-three. Her an' the babe she was carryin' at the time. That's the last I heard of Jeremiah."

"How terribly sad for him," Sarah whispered. She looked at Warren. "Has he come back to stay?"

"He plans to keep the farm. He says he's going to buy out my share."

"But that's wonderful, Warren. Now both our brothers have returned. We must do something to make Jeremiah feel welcome."

Warren's hand tightened on hers. "It's not all that wonderful. I can't sell the farm, and I was counting on that money to pay for the wedding trip I promised you."

She felt a sting of disappointment. No trip to New York and Philadelphia. She would never see The Assembly, not even from the outside. All her plans . . . Then she silently scolded herself. How selfish of her! Jeremiah Wesley had lost his wife and unborn child. Now he'd come home after all these years. He should be welcomed, not resented.

"Well, then we shall just have to wait to

take our trip," she said with determined cheerfulness. "Having your brother home again is so much more important."

Warren turned a dark look in her direction. "I want you to stay away from Jeremiah," he said, his voice low and stern.

"But—"

"He'll only cause trouble. He's always caused trouble. Stay away from him, Sarah. I mean it."

Chapter Three

Jeremiah returned to the mercantile the next day with a list of supplies he needed. When he mentioned he was looking for a job, George Blake brought up the town's need for a new deputy.

"Our last deputy moved away last spring and Sheriff McLeod's gettin' pretty old. To be honest, he can't handle the job anymore."

"McLeod's still the sheriff? *Hank* McLeod?"

George nodded. "You know, with your experience in the army and the war and this being your hometown and all, you're probably just the man for the job."

A sheriff's deputy? It had a nice, respectable ring to it. But was he the right man for the job? Besides, he'd come back to farm the land.

As if he had read his thoughts, George said, "Why don't you go talk to McLeod while we fill your order? He can tell you more about the job than I can. He'll answer any questions you've got."

A lawman? A deputy? He wasn't sure. Folks in these parts had never thought too highly of him. He'd been in more scuffs and scrapes than he cared to remember. They probably wouldn't think him a good choice for the job.

"The pay's pretty good," George added, as if knowing what Jeremiah needed to hear.

"I'll talk to McLeod." He said the words before he could change his mind. After all, he'd made a promise to buy out Warren's share of the land. He couldn't do that without a job.

"Good." George grinned. "You remember where the McLeod house is? It's over on North Street. Easy to find. It's the biggest house there."

"I'll find it. Thanks."

From her second-story bedroom window, Sarah stared across North Street at the idle waterwheel attached to the side of Homestead Lumber. In the spring, summer, and early fall, the wheel turned rapidly, forced into action by the cold water filling Pony Creek, but in the dead of winter, when the water in the creek was low—or frozen as most of it was now—the wheel stood silent and still.

Rather like the McLeod home now that Tom and Grampa had gone for a visit with Doc Varney, she thought with a smile.

It was amazing how much life Tom had brought back to the house in a mere twenty-four hours. She hadn't realized how empty their home had seemed while he'd been away. And he would be gone again so very soon. Not that she begrudged his going. He was doing what he'd always wanted to do. He was studying to be a doctor. He was following his dreams.

How lucky he was.

She sighed as she turned her back to the glass and settled onto the window seat. She tucked her legs up beneath her skirt, drawing her knees toward her chest, then reached for the well-read issue of the *Ladies Home Journal* that lay nearby. The magazine fell open to an illustration of dancers swirling about a chandelier-lit ballroom. She knew most of the words by heart, but she read them anyway.

During just one hundred and fifty years the entrance into "society" in Phila-delphia has been through the door-way of "The Assembly." The manag-ers of the functions of that annual court of honor have been foremost in regulating the social sovereignty of the city. Nowhere else in the United States is there a dynasty which has held longer or more nearly uninter-rupted sway.

It was easy for Sarah to imagine just what it would be like to walk through those doors on the arm of some dashing escort, perhaps a mysterious European count. Her gown would be made of satin and lace, and she would wear a tiara in her hair. He would be dressed in a suave black dress suit. He would also be tall and dark and incredibly handsome. Heads would turn, and people would whisper, wondering who she was, who he was, who they were.

Indeed, the City Dancing Assembly of Philadelphia was in existence before the aristocracy of Charleston had begun their Cæcilia, and even before the far-famed Almack's was founded as the seventh heaven of the fashionable set in London.

The orchestra would play waltzes for hours and hours, and Sarah would dance nearly every one of them. She would laugh softly and politely at her escort's jokes, but she would not allow him to presume she felt more for him than was proper.

She would . . .

A loud rapping at the front door disturbed her pleasant daydreams. Immediately, she felt a rush of guilt. She should be imagining herself waltzing with Warren, but try as she might, she'd never been able to do so. Warren was so . . . so . . . *Warren*.

The caller knocked again.

With a sigh, she set aside the magazine and hurried from her room. While she was still on the stairs, the visitor knocked a third time, this time more loudly.

"Just a moment," she called, quickening her steps.

She pulled open the door, expecting to find a familiar face, but instead there stood a stranger—a very tall, very dark, very handsome stranger. A stranger who could have easily been a mysterious European count had he been wearing a full-dress evening suit and silk hat.

"Excuse me," he said as he touched the broad brim of his Metropolitan with two fingers. "I'm looking for Sheriff McLeod. I thought this was his house."

His accent was nothing like she imagined a European count's would be, but his voice had a deep, pleasant resonance that caused something to curl inside her. She would have sworn she heard the stirring notes of "The Blue Danube" playing in the background.

One dark eyebrow arched slightly as the stranger stared down at her. She thought for a moment she should know him, that perhaps he should know her.

"I thought I would remember which house it was," he said, "but everything's different. If you could tell me where he lives—"

43

"I'm sorry," she said quickly, shaking off the daydream she'd been weaving about him. She felt a blush rushing to her cheeks. "This *is* Sheriff McLeod's home, but he isn't in at the moment. I'm his granddaughter, Sarah McLeod. Perhaps I can help you."

He shook his head. "No, it's the sheriff I need to see. Would you tell him Jeremiah Wesley was by and wanted to talk to him?"

"Jeremiah?"

This was Warren's brother? But they didn't look anything alike. Jeremiah's hair was as blue-black as a raven's wing, his eyes the color of coal mixed with soot. His features were chiseled, masculine, powerful, and he was a head taller than his brother.

She realized she was staring at him and fought back another blush of embarrassment. "Do come in." She opened the door wider. "Please. Grampa won't be much longer. He and my brother just went over to see the doctor for a short visit. They'll be back soon."

"Well, I—"

"Please. You've come all this way into town, and it's too cold to just stand about waiting."

He hesitated only a moment longer before pulling his hat from his head and stepping through the open doorway. "This is very kind of you, Miss . . ." He paused, as if not knowing what to call her.

"Please, call me Sarah. Miss McLeod sounds so formal."

44

He nodded but said nothing.

"Come into the sitting room and warm yourself by the fire. I'll get you some coffee."

"Don't go to any trouble."

"Oh, it's no trouble. The coffee's already made."

She left him in the living room and hurried into the kitchen. A hundred questions raced through her head as she snatched two cups from the cupboard and filled them to the brim with hot, dark coffee. In no time at all, she was carrying a tray back into the living room.

Jeremiah rose from his chair and waited while she set the tray on a low table near the sofa and seated herself; then he sat again.

"Do you take cream or sugar?"

"No. Just black, thanks."

She held out the china cup and saucer toward him. When he reached for them, their fingers touched briefly. Sarah felt that odd curling sensation in her stomach again. Quickly, she pulled her hand away, then stared down at her own cup as she added both sugar and cream to her coffee.

"My own brother just arrived home yesterday, and now you're here, too," she said to fill the silence. "You were on the same train and didn't even know it. Isn't that a strange coincidence, Mr. Wesley?"

No answer.

"I suppose, since we'll be family soon, it would be proper for me to call you Jeremiah. Do you mind if I do so?"

When he didn't reply, she looked up to find him watching her with a questioning gaze.

"You'd rather I didn't?" she asked, feeling disappointed.

"I'm afraid I don't understand, Miss McLeod."

"But surely, he . . ." She straightened. "Warren didn't tell you?"

His dark brows drew together.

"Warren and I are engaged to be married. I thought you knew."

Chapter Four

She was exquisitely beautiful, his brother's intended, and there was an unmistakable innocence in her sky-blue eyes that made Jeremiah feel old and jaded. He remembered the way she'd welcomed that young man— her brother, she said—at the train station. He remembered the look of utter joy and the warm glow her happiness had cast all around her.

Warren was a lucky man.

"Congratulations, Miss McLeod," he said.

"Please, you really must call me Sarah." She set her cup on the table, then braced the palms of her hands on the edge of the sofa and leaned forward. He could see an excited glint in her eyes as she said, "I've always wanted to travel. It must be wonderful, seeing so many different places, meeting different people. I've dreamed for ages of going to Philadelphia and New York City and London and Paris." She sighed wistfully. "Would you mind terribly telling me where you've been?"

"There's not much to tell."

"Oh, surely there is—"

The front door opened, letting in a blast of cold air along with Sarah's grandfather and brother, effectively cutting off whatever she'd been going to say.

Jeremiah rose from his chair, glad he'd been able to avoid being rude to her. And he would have been rude. He didn't want to talk about himself or his past. Especially not to his brother's fiancée. He didn't want to say where he'd been or what he'd seen or what he'd done. Perhaps because he'd seen and done too much.

Besides, he didn't want to be the one to disabuse Miss Sarah McLeod of all her romantic notions of the world beyond Long Bow Valley. It was plain to see she was a young woman with a head full of dreams and illusions.

Jeremiah, in contrast, had no illusions left.

Sheriff McLeod paused in the entry to the front living room. His body had shrunken with age, and he was no longer the physically threatening sheriff of Jeremiah's memory.

However, Hank McLeod's gray eyes were just as steely as Jeremiah remembered, and they assessed him with a quick but thorough glance before Sarah could introduce them.

Apparently, the sheriff didn't need any introductions. "Welcome back, Jeremiah," he said as he stepped forward, offering his hand.

"Thank you, sir."

"Jeremiah's been waiting to speak to you, Grampa," Sarah interjected.

"Have you now? Well, that's fine. Just fine." Hank stepped back and turned toward the younger man waiting behind him. "I don't suppose you remember my grandson? Tom, this is Jeremiah Wesley."

It was her brother's turn to step forward and shake hands with Jeremiah.

Tom was a darker version of Sarah. He was of average height and handsome, his gray eyes revealed quick intelligence, and his smile was warm and friendly. "Pleased to meet you, Mr. Wesley."

"Call me Jeremiah." He returned his gaze to Hank McLeod. "I wonder if I might have a word with you, sir. George Blake told me the town's looking for a deputy to work for you. I'm interested in the job."

"Is that right? Well, come with me to my study." The sheriff led the way.

Hank's study was a small, cluttered room at the back of the house, filled with an oak desk and lined with bookshelves. A brass spittoon was placed just beneath the window. The room smelled of leather and smoke. A man's domain.

Hank closed the door. "Have a seat." He motioned to a leather-upholstered chair, then walked slowly around to a matching chair behind the desk and sank onto it. His eyes closed momentarily, and Jeremiah wondered if he was nodding off to sleep. But before he could say anything, Hank opened his eyes and stared across the desk at him. "So, you're interested in being the town's new deputy?"

"Yes. Yes, I am."

"You never struck me as the deputy sort, Jeremiah. If my memory serves, you caused more trouble than you ever stopped." The words were softened by an amused glint in his eyes.

"Yeah, I guess I did, at that," Jeremiah concurred, then said, "I'll be honest with you, McLeod. I've never been a lawman. Never even thought about it bein' a possibility."

"So tell me what experience you've got."

He drew in a deep breath. "I've done a lot of things since I left Homestead. Farmed a little place back in Ohio for a few years. After Millie . . . after Millie died, I didn't care to stay on there so I moved around. Did some mining, some bartending, worked cattle on a ranch in Montana for a while. Spent a few months with the railroad, laying track and blasting through rock. A few years back, I went to New York and worked in a factory, assembling motors. After that, I joined the army." He paused a moment, then shook his head. "I'm not sure what kind of a deputy I'd be, or if I'd even take to it," he said quietly, adding, "but the truth is, I need the job."

The sheriff nodded slowly, as if digesting what Jeremiah had just told him. Finally, he asked, "Ever been in trouble with the law? Real trouble, I mean. Not the set-downs I gave you when you were a boy."

"No."

"I expect you know plenty about usin' a gun after bein' in the army."

A muscle in his jaw flinched, but he answered, "Yes."

"I heard you were wounded in the war. Your leg bother you any?"

He'd forgotten how quickly news traveled in a small town. He guessed everyone knew he was back by now, along with everything else he might have told Leslie Blake. "Not much," he answered. "My leg's sound. The wound just left me with a bit of a limp."

Hank glanced out the window. "Homestead's always been a nice, quiet town. Had a bit of serious trouble back eight or nine years ago, but mostly bein' the deputy here means lettin' somebody sleep off a bit too much whiskey in the jail, breakin' up a fight at the saloon now and then, collectin' taxes that aren't paid on time, issuin' licenses, occasionally looking for rustlers, that sort of thing." His gaze returned to meet Jeremiah's.

"Not very excitin' work for someone who's seen the country like you have."

"I'm not looking for excitement."

Hank leaned against the back of his chair. "Care to tell me what you did in the war?"

No, he didn't care to tell him. "I did whatever I was told to do by my superior officers."

"Where'd you serve?"

"Texas, Florida . . . Cuba."

"I see."

Did he? Jeremiah doubted it. He doubted that anyone could understand what war was like unless they'd been there. The boredom. The heat. The flies. The stench. The sickness. The blood. The young boys, their bodies bloating, lying open-eyed on the battlefield.

"What brought you back to Homestead, Jeremiah?"

"It was time," he answered firmly. "And, I suppose," he added, "because I had nowhere else to go."

"Do you plan to stay?"

"Yes."

For a second time, the sheriff turned his gaze out the window, staring at the back door of Carson's Barbershop and Bathhouse. "I got to know your pa pretty well over the years. Ted Wesley was a good man. Honest. Hardworkin'. God-fearin'. He was mighty proud of you."

The last surprised Jeremiah. He couldn't remember his dad ever being proud of him for anything. He could only remember how often he'd been told what a disappointment he was, how he'd never amount to much.

"He missed you a lot." Hank looked at him again. "I expect a man like Ted Wesley would've raised a son who'd make a darn good deputy." He stood and held out his hand. "You've got the job if you want it. You think on it overnight and tell me tomorrow. You come have Sunday dinner with us. Don't bother to say no. We'll be expectin' you."

Sarah heard the men's voices in the hall and rose from the sofa in expectation of their return to the living room. A moment later, she heard the front door open and her grandfather bidding Jeremiah a good day. The door closed before she even reached the entry.

Disappointment rushed through her. She hadn't had a chance to ask him *anything*.

"Nice young man," Grampa said as he entered the room, walking slowly past her to his favorite chair near the fireplace.

"Did he tell you where he'd been all these years?" Sarah asked. "Did he give you any idea what he's been doing?"

The old man shook his head. "Not really."

"Didn't you ask him?"

Grampa looked up at her with a solemn gaze. "Isn't any of my business, princess, nor any of yours. A man's got a right to his privacy. Don't be pryin' into his affairs."

She knew he was right. Nobody liked a busybody. But if she didn't ask, however was she going to find out all the things she was dying to know?

"Well," her brother said from behind her, "is he going to take the job as deputy?"

Grampa nodded. "I think so. I invited him to have Sunday dinner with us so we can talk about it some more. Hope you don't mind, Sarah."

"No, of course not," she answered. "I don't mind at all."

"What about Warren?" Tom interjected. "After what he said yesterday, he's not likely to be keen on the idea."

Sarah tilted her chin upward. "I'll speak to Warren. They're brothers. They should make peace with each other."

As Jeremiah guided the rented horse and sleigh down the street, he heard the shouts of the schoolchildren as they played tag in the schoolyard. At the corner of West and North Streets, he paused for a moment to watch them, and his thoughts drifted back through the years to his own boyhood.

He remembered when that schoolhouse was first built. Miss Adelaide Sherwood had been the teacher then. Miss Sherwood with her fiery red hair and friendly smile. No, he guessed she'd been Mrs. Will Rider by the time they'd built the new school. There'd been plenty of excitement over the books and desks and chalkboards, all of them as brand-new as the building itself. He remembered the smell of wet wool as coats and scarves and mittens hung on hooks on the back wall and the way the single room felt in winter, either too hot or too cold, depending on how far away a desk was from the fat black stove.

Good memories for a change, he realized. He hadn't thought about any of it in years.

With a shake of his head, he turned the horse right on West Street. The runners on the wagon bed slid across the hard-packed snow with a steady *whoosh*ing sound. As the sleigh crossed the bridge over Pony Creek, Jeremiah glanced to his right at the lumber mill and thought of his dad.

Ted Wesley had gone to work at the mill as soon as he and his sons settled in the valley. He'd done the farming after his regular mill shift. Yet Jeremiah couldn't recall ever hearing his dad complain about how hard life was. He'd simply accepted it as it was.

Suddenly, he missed his dad as he'd never missed him before. He wished he could talk to him again. He wished he could tell him he was sorry he'd disappointed him. He'd like to say he regretted all the things he'd done that had caused his dad grief. His hot temper. His impatience with school. His fighting. His running away. The money he'd taken. He wished . . .

"Get up there," he called as he slapped

the reins against the horse's rump, at the same time shoving away his troublesome thoughts.

He managed to keep from consciously thinking anything for quite some time before the image of Sarah McLeod's innocent blue eyes crept into his head. Eyes that looked at the world as if it were wrapped in a bow, just waiting for her to open it. Eyes clear and guileless and unafraid.

Actually, he pictured more than just her eyes. He saw her lovely face with its milky complexion and tiny, turned-up nose and heart-shaped mouth, soft and pink. He remembered the smooth sweep of her gossamer hair, the silvery-blond tresses dressed high and loosely brushed back from her forehead. He recalled the pleasant shape beneath a simple yellow shirtwaist and brown skirt.

Then he remembered she was engaged to marry his brother. If it was peace he was seeking in Homestead, he'd best keep himself and his thoughts clear of Miss Sarah McLeod.

Chapter Five

Tom held the squalling newborn as Doc Varney attended to the mother. His pulse raced with the excitement of what he had just seen, of what he had just done. He'd never expected when he'd arrived in Homestead yesterday that he would be helping to deliver a baby before nightfall today.

"Well, let's see to that boy," Doc said as he took the infant from Tom's arms. "Why don't you tell Mr. Jones it's safe for him to come in now." Doc grinned and winked as their eyes met.

Tom went to the bedroom door and opened it. "Mr. Jones," he said to the pale-faced man seated in the rocking chair near the fireplace, "you can come in now."

"My wife, is she—"

"She's doing fine. And so's your son."

Yancy Jones rose from the rocker. "It's a boy?" he asked breathlessly.

Tom nodded. "Come see for yourself."

The tall, lanky rancher hurried past him into the bedroom. He glanced at the dresser where Doc was attending to the baby, then crossed to the bed. He knelt on the rag rug covering the wood floor and reached for his wife's hand.

Lark Jones, looking pretty despite the lengthy labor, smiled weakly. "You've got a son, Mr. Jones," she whispered.

"I know." He squeezed her hand. "I was gettin' as worried as a duck in the desert. Katie didn't take nearly so long gettin' here. If I was t'lose you, I—"

"There wasn't any danger of that." Lark's eyes drifted closed. "No danger at all."

Tom knew her words weren't entirely true. It had been a difficult delivery. Without Doc Varney, she might not have survived. Tom prayed he could be even half the physician Doc was. If so, he'd consider himself fortunate.

Doc Varney finished his care of the newborn, then wrapped the squalling infant in a small blanket and carried him to his mother. "Why don't you see if he'll nurse? May quiet him down."

Lark glanced toward Tom, then blushed as her gaze fell away.

Doc cleared his throat. "Tom, would you

carry my bag out to the sleigh? I'll join you directly."

He did as he was asked, bundling himself up tightly in his warm coat and fur-lined hat and gloves before stepping outside. Night had fallen, but a full moon spilled a pale light across the frosty landscape.

By the time Tom had stashed the doctor's bag beneath the seat and pulled the blanket from the horse's back, Doc Varney appeared in the doorway.

"You come for me if there's any change," Doc told Yancy. "Otherwise, I'll be by in a couple of days."

"I'll do that. And . . . thanks, Doc."

Doc Varney grinned and patted the new father on the shoulder. "I did the easy part. You've got to raise him." Turning toward the sleigh, he said, "Let's get home. Your sister's going to be frettin' something fierce."

As soon as they had the lap robes wrapped snugly around their legs, Tom picked up the reins and slapped them against the horse's backside. Bells jingled merrily as they headed toward Homestead, the moon lighting their way.

"Why do you suppose it suddenly bothered Lark to have me there?" Tom asked after a spell of silence.

"I expect 'cause she remembered she went to school with you and your sister, and now you've helped deliver her baby. She doesn't think of you as someone studyin' to be a doctor. You're just Tommy McLeod, the mischief maker who was always *needin'* a doctor."

Tom nodded as he considered the older man's answer. "What about when I return from Boston? Are others going to have trouble thinking of me as a doctor? Or will I always be the kid who fell out of trees and broke his arm and skinned his knees?"

Doc Varney chuckled. "A few crusty old souls my age might think you're still wet behind the ears, but you'll steer them right in no time. I've got great faith in you, young man. You've got a special way of makin' people trust and listen to you. It's a gift; that's what it is."

As usual, his mentor's praise warmed Tom.

"This valley needs you," the doctor continued, his voice more somber. "I'm getting too old to be traipsing around the countryside on a night like this. It's time I got to stay home with Betsy and stare at the fire in the evenings. It's time a young man like you took on the doctoring needs of Homestead. You won't get rich practicing medicine here like you might in a bigger city, but you'll get rich in other ways. I promise you."

Tom clucked at the horse, then said, "Never much cared about bein' rich, Doc."

"I know, boy. I know."

Jeremiah tossed more hay over the stall gate to the sorrel gelding. Tomorrow, he'd decided, he was going to return the rented rig and horse to the livery, and he was going to buy a mount of his own. Sort of a celebration for getting the job as the town's new deputy.

He shook his head. He hadn't really believed that Hank McLeod would hire him. After all, the sheriff had known him since he was a boy. Hank knew what kinds of trouble he'd gotten into all the time. There hadn't been many in Homestead who'd thought Jeremiah Wesley was headed anywhere except down a road straight to hell. He'd been told so often enough by his father.

Millie had been one of the few who'd believed in him, who'd believed there was something good to be found in him. Right up to the bitter end, she'd kept on believing.

"You're a good man, Jeremiah," she'd told him time and again. "Don't you pay no mind to what your pa says. I know the good in you."

With a shake of his head, he picked up the lantern and left the barn, making his way across the snowy barnyard to the house. Closing the door, he listened to the silence, a silence broken only by the crackling fire.

He'd believed Millie once. He'd believed he was good. He'd believed he could do anything, be anything, because she'd believed. But the truth was, the only thing good about him had been Millie.

He glanced about the empty, silent house

and wondered why he'd ever thought Millie wanted him to come back here. It didn't make any sense to him. It just didn't make any sense.

Sarah lifted the curtains and stared out at the moonlit street. "Do you suppose the baby's arrived by now, Grampa?" she asked.

"Could be. Never know about these things. Your ma always had a difficult time."

She turned from the window, pulling her shawl a little tighter around her shoulders. "What was she like?"

Grampa smiled. "A lot like you, princess. She made your pa mighty happy. Dorie always said God gave her another daughter to love when Tom married Maria."

"Tell me more." She sank onto the rug beside his chair and leaned her arms on her grandfather's thigh as she gazed up at him.

Hank stroked her hair. "This was their house. Your pa built it when he and Maria first came here. They wanted a house full of children. They were always so disappointed when your ma would lose a baby. And then you came along." He lightly pinched the tip of her nose. "You wrapped us all around your little finger from the very start."

Sarah laughed, but she knew it was true, at least about her grandparents. Doris McLeod had seldom been able to say no to Sarah and her little brother, no matter what mischief they got into. And there'd been plenty of mischief, at least where Tommy was concerned. He'd been a grand one for thinking up ways to make trouble.

"He's going to make a wonderful doctor, isn't he?" she asked softly.

Grampa didn't seem the least bit surprised by the turn her thoughts had taken. "Yep, Tom's gonna be a wonderful doctor."

Sarah laid the side of her head against her grandfather's thigh and closed her eyes. They remained that way for a long time, only the crackling fire disturbing the silence.

Sarah straightened the moment the front door opened. "He's back," she said as she rose to her feet.

Tom entered the living room, his cheeks red from the cold, his eyes shining with excitement. "It's a boy," he announced proudly.

"And Lark?" Sarah asked.

"She's fine. Mr. Jones, too." He pulled off his coat and hat as he spoke, then disappeared into the entry to hang up the winter garments. When he returned to the room, he asked, "Any coffee made? I'm about frozen clear through."

"I'll get you some." She headed toward the kitchen, pausing to give her brother a quick kiss on the cheek. "Come with me. I want to hear all about it."

Tom glanced at their grandfather.

Hank flicked his wrist, as if shooing away

a pesky fly. "Go on with your sister. I'm ready to turn in for the night anyway. We can talk in the morning."

Sarah had already filled two cups with coffee and was setting them on the table by the time Tom caught up with her. They sat down on opposite sides of the table, and she watched him fold his hands around the hot cup and drink down about half the coffee before setting the cup back on the table.

"There," she said, "you're warmer. Now tell me everything you learned tonight."

"I don't think that's a subject I should discuss with an unmarried female."

She kicked him under the table, only half in jest.

"Ouch!" He leaned down to grab his shin.

"Don't you dare say such a thing to me, Tommy McLeod," she scolded. "I know a good sight more than you think I do."

"Only about ballrooms and the peerage of England," he muttered, then grinned at her as he straightened once again. He leaned forward, his arms braced on the table. "It really was the most amazing experience I've ever had, Sarah. Plenty hard on Lark . . . I mean, Mrs. Jones, but to see life begin like that . . ." He fell silent.

Sarah's gaze dropped to his hands which were once again cradling the warm coffee cup. For the second time in as many days, she thought about how he meant to use those hands, how he meant to bring healing to their friends and neighbors. A lump formed in her throat and tears burned her eyes.

"I'm so proud of you, Tommy," she whispered. "I hope you always know that."

"Sure, sis. And I'm plenty proud of you."

Sarah thought how very lucky she was to be his sister.

Fanny watched her sister, Opal, lean toward the whiskeyed-up fellow at the bar, giving him a generous view of her equally generous breasts. Opal's laughter could be heard above the noise of the piano as Quincy pounded out another lively, if off-key, tune.

Her stomach tightened and rolled. She wondered if she'd be sick again.

Turning her head, she saw Grady O'Neal watching her with a frown. Grady owned the Pony Saloon, and it was because of him she had a warm place to stay this winter. She hadn't known what else to do when her ma died except write to Opal, like her ma had told her. She hadn't known her older sister was working in a saloon. But then, they'd never been very close. Thirteen years separated the two of them, and Opal had left home by the time Fanny was five.

"She can stay here," Grady had said when Opal dragged her into his office right after she'd arrived in Homestead, "but she'll have to earn her keep, just like the rest of you girls."

"She don't know nothin' about such things,

Grady. Just look at her," Opal had protested. "You can't expect her to—"

"She can serve drinks and smile. She don't have to do any more'n that . . . for now."

Fanny's stomach lurched again. The bile burned her throat and tears stung her eyes as she fought the nausea.

She didn't understand how Opal could do it. Night after night, her sister painted her face and put on one of the fancy gowns that showed her bosom and a good deal of her legs, then came downstairs to flirt with the men who frequented the Pony Saloon. And some of them ended up in her bed, too. Fanny knew 'cause she was locked out of the room they shared until there weren't any more "visitors."

Once again, Fanny swallowed the sickness. Her head pounded and her ears rang. She felt hot and cold at the same time and knew there was a film of sweat above her lip. She wanted to go to bed, but it looked as if Opal would be using the room soon.

She closed her eyes a moment and drew in a deep breath, willing herself to feel better. Grady had said she had to earn her keep. That meant serving drinks to the customers and smiling and parading around in a dress that made her feel awful and look even worse, if anybody wanted her opinion. She also swept up in the morning and washed the glasses and mugs and did anything else Grady told her to do.

"Well, hello there, sweet thing."

She opened her eyes to find a grizzled fellow dressed up in a dark suit and string tie standing right in front of her. His hair was slicked back and his beard had been recently trimmed, but from the smell of him, he hadn't bothered to use the bathhouse before putting on the suit. His eyes showed signs of the alcohol he'd already consumed, and he swayed slightly as he looked at her.

"You're new since last time I was in Homestead. Why don't ya come si'down with me?"

She shook her head. The motion made her dizzy.

"Whatsa matter? Ain't I good enough for ya?"

"I'm sorry. I . . . I—"

"Come on." He grabbed her by the arm and yanked her toward him.

At just that moment, she lost control of her sickness. The vomit splattered over the man's suit coat and pants. She grabbed her stomach, leaned forward, and continued to heave. She heard someone shouting angrily, but she couldn't make any sense of the words.

Someone pulled on her arm again. He—at least it felt like a man's hand—smacked her across the cheek, making her ears ring and the room spiral.

She dropped to her knees and threw up some more. Tears stung her eyes. Her throat burned.

Grady O'Neal would send her away for

certain now. Opal wouldn't want her around neither. What would she do then? Where would she go if Grady threw her out?

Maybe she was dyin' like her ma. Ma hadn't been able to keep nothin' down toward the end. Fanny felt like she was dyin'. She almost wished she was. At least dead she wouldn't have to worry no more.

Tiny colored dots danced against her tightly squeezed eyelids, the dots growing larger and larger. The sounds around her grew more faint until she didn't hear anything at all.

Chapter Six

It had been years since Jeremiah had
attended church, although he'd heard preach-
ers say parting words over the recently
departed more often than he cared to
remember. Knowing how long it had been,
he was surprised by the familiar feel of the
pew in the Homestead Community Church.

Thinking back, Jeremiah knew it would
have been hard for him to come up with more
than a half a dozen times when Ted Wesley—
and therefore, his sons—had missed Sunday
services in the years Jeremiah was growing
up. Today, after nearly fourteen years, he'd
walked to the same exact pew where the
Wesley family had always sat, just as if he'd
been doing it every Sunday of his life.

Of course, there were some things that

were different. When he was a boy, he'd listened to Rev. Pendroy preaching from the pulpit. These days the church was pastored by Simon Jacobs, a portly man of average height who gave his sermon in a reed-thin voice with precise articulation. And although Jeremiah tried to listen attentively, he soon found his thoughts wandering as he surreptitiously glanced about the church.

Many in the congregation were strangers to him, but there were plenty of familiar faces, too. Some had been students with him when he was in school. Now those former schoolmates had families of their own. Others had grown old while he was away. Some were noticeably absent. Like his dad, they had passed on and would remain forever as he remembered them from his youth.

He recognized pretty Rose Townsend. Except, Leslie Blake had told him yesterday, she was Rose Rafferty now. She sat next to her husband, Michael, the town's mayor and owner of the Rafferty Hotel. Two youngsters, a boy and a girl, were seated on either side of them. The girl had inherited her dark gold hair from her father. The boy's hair was the same chestnut shade as his mother's. They made a handsome family, the four of them. The mayor and his wife and their children. Homestead's leading family. At least, that's what he'd been told. Remembering Rose's bully of a brother and drunkard of a father, Jeremiah found he was pleased for the way things had turned out for Rose.

Michael Rafferty leaned over and whispered something in his wife's ear. Rose smiled, a smile that made her cheeks dimple. Jeremiah glanced away. There was an intimacy in the way they looked at one another, and he was reminded of how alone he was.

His gaze moved on.

Old Doc Varney sat in the pew in front of him and to the left. The doctor had grown a bit heavier over the years, but he looked as hale and alert as ever. His salt-and-pepper hair and beard were appropriately dignified for the town's doctor.

While Jeremiah watched, Doc Varney leaned to his side, much as Michael Rafferty had done with Rose moments before, and whispered to the woman at his side.

Doc has a wife? The idea of the old bachelor being married surprised Jeremiah, but it seemed to be true.

George and Leslie Blake were across the aisle and one row up from him, and he recognized Leslie's sister, Annalee, sitting beside them. Between Annalee and the man Jeremiah guessed to be her husband—another stranger to him—were three children, the youngest no more than a year old.

Jeremiah's thoughts, as well as his gaze, stopped wandering when he came to Sarah McLeod's profile. He vaguely remembered he'd decided yesterday that he needed to give this young woman a wide berth, but for the life of him, he couldn't remember why at the moment. A more attractive vision he couldn't remember ever seeing.

She was dressed all in blue, the same sky-blue shade as her eyes. Her matching felt hat, trimmed with feathers and ospreys, perched atop her gossamer hair at a jaunty angle. Her attention was riveted upon the reverend, and it was apparent that she was engrossed in the words of the sermon, completely unaware of anyone or anything else around her.

She was very much aware that he was watching her.

Sarah knew that Jeremiah Wesley was no mysterious count from Europe. He was merely an ordinary man, returning home after a long sojourn. Warren's brother, for pity's sake.

But knowing he was watching her, staring at her, made her pulse quicken and her breathing grow shallow. She could almost swear, if she turned her head and looked at him, she would discover him sitting there in a black suit and silk hat. She expected he would smile at her mysteriously—as all mysterious European counts were known to do.

It was absurd. Warren was right. She *did* have her head in the clouds. It was time she started acting her age. After all, she would be twenty-one in just over two weeks. Her birthday was the day after her wedding day,

when she would stand in this church as Warren's bride.

Warren's bride . . . That was what she
should be thinking about. She should be
filled with excitement about her upcoming
wedding. There were a hundred and one
things which needed her attention. If she
couldn't focus her thoughts on the sermon,
she could at least let her mind rest on something of importance.

Of course, it might have helped things if
Warren were seated beside her this morning, but he hadn't shown up for church. She
suspected she knew why. He was angry with
her. When she'd told him her grandfather
had invited Jeremiah to Sunday dinner, he
had been unreasonably perturbed.

"I told you to keep away from him, Sarah,"
he'd said.

"Grampa invited him. Not me."

"Well, don't expect me to sit down to eat
with him."

"Warren, he's your only brother. Shouldn't
you try to get along?"

"You don't understand, Sarah . . ."

She subdued a sigh. No, she didn't understand, and it would be difficult for her to
do so as long as Warren clammed up and
refused to talk about it.

Once again, she tried to concentrate on
what the reverend was saying, only to realize
that Jeremiah was still watching her. She'd
never had anyone stare at her so hard or
for so long. She wondered if her hat was

crooked or her collar unbuttoned. Or perhaps she had a smudge on her cheek. Whatever the reason, she wished he would stop.

Why *did* he keep staring at her that way?

Jeremiah suddenly remembered why he shouldn't be staring at Miss Sarah McLeod. She was engaged to marry his brother. She was going to be Warren's wife.

Wife . . . For Jeremiah, Millie had defined the word. She hadn't been beautiful, he supposed, not like Sarah McLeod, but she'd had a beauty of the soul. Whatever she'd touched had become beautiful, too, and Jeremiah had been blessed because of it. She'd always been able to read his heart and usually his mind, too. He knew just how lucky he'd been to know and love her. He didn't suppose many men ever had the opportunity to have what he'd had, even for a brief period of time.

He focused his gaze on Sarah again. He wondered if Warren would find what Jeremiah had had, what he'd lost when Millie died. Would he be lucky enough to be loved without reservation? Would Sarah and Warren find joy in each other?

He found the questions strangely disquieting.

Jeremiah returned his attention to the pulpit just as Rev. Jacobs' sermon came to a close. The congregation rose to their feet to sing one last hymn, and then the service was over. He started to turn, but Hank McLeod's voice stopped him.

"Wait a moment, Jeremiah," the sheriff called. "Before we head over to our house for dinner, you'd best let me introduce you around. Folks're mighty eager to make your acquaintance."

Jeremiah turned—and looked directly down into the tiny pieces of sky that were Sarah's eyes.

The poetic turn of his thoughts was completely out of character for Jeremiah. It made him uncomfortable, which, in turn, made his voice abrupt. "Mornin'."

"Good morning, Jere . . . miah." The catch in her voice as she said his name left him with a strange feeling in his chest.

Then Hank began introducing him to other members of the congregation. Jeremiah had to concentrate on the names and faces, as he figured any good deputy would do. Miss McLeod was quickly enough forgotten.

All but her eyes. Those blasted innocent blue eyes.

Tom stood beside Sarah at the back of the church, watching as Grampa introduced Jeremiah Wesley to others. "I like him," he said. "Grampa does, too. I think Mr. Wesley will make a good deputy for Homestead."

When his sister didn't respond, he glanced down at her. She was watching Jeremiah with a faraway expression on her face. It was an expression Tom knew well.

He leaned close to her ear. "What are you doing, sis? Making a prince out of our new deputy?"

"What?" She turned her head so swiftly they bumped foreheads. Sarah's cheeks flared with color.

Tom knew two things. One, he'd guessed something uncomfortably close to the truth, and two, he'd better not say anything more about it. Sarah seldom lost her temper, but when she did, she was mad clean through.

"Look," he said, changing the subject. "Doc and Mrs. Varney are waiting for us. Let's walk home with them. Grampa and Mr. Wesley can catch up later." Before she had time to think about his suggestion, he took hold of her arm and steered her toward the older couple.

"Don't you look lovely today, Sarah," Betsy Varney said as they approached. "It's so nice of you to invite us for Sunday dinner."

Sarah's smile returned quickly. "You're always welcome. You know that, Mrs. Varney."

Tom observed his sister. *Had* she been making a prince out of Jeremiah? Tom might be only eighteen, but even he knew that daydreaming about another man wouldn't bode well for Sarah's marriage to Warren Wesley.

His sister turned her head and looked up at him, her smile sweet, her anger completely forgotten. "Shall we go?" she asked as she slipped her hand into the crook of his left elbow.

He had to be mistaken, he decided. Sarah would never take notice of another man, especially not Warren's own brother. It just wouldn't cross her mind.

The four of them walked out of the church, pausing briefly on the landing before starting down the steps, Doc and his wife leading the way. Just as Tom and Sarah reached the bottom, a woman wrapped in a drab coat and wool scarf stepped away from the side of the church and quickly approached the doctor.

"Excuse me, sir," she said as she stepped into his path. "Can I have a word with you, Dr. Varney?"

Tom heard Betsy Varney's quick intake of breath even as he felt his sister's fingers tighten on his arm.

"I don't suppose you remember me. M'name's Opal." Her eyelids were painted a bright purple shade. Her lips were as red as cranberries. "Opal Irvine. I work over at the Pony Saloon. You saw to me when I was ailin' a few years back."

"Of course, Miss Irvine. I remember. What can I do for you?"

"I've come about my sister. She's real sick, and I think she's needin' a doctor."

"What seems to be the matter with your sister?"

"She can't keep nothin' in her stomach.

77

Not even water. And she feels real feverish to me."

Doc Varney tenderly removed his wife's hand from his arm. "You go on with Sarah, my dear. I'll join you as soon as I'm finished with Miss Irvine's sister." He glanced behind him. "Tom, would you go to my office and bring my medical bag to the saloon, please?"

"Right away, sir."

Without a backward glance, Tom hurried off in the direction of the doctor's house, his concerns about his sister forgotten.

Sarah was still standing in the church-yard with Betsy when her grandfather and Jeremiah came out of the church.

Remembering her brother's teasing question, she looked at Hank McLeod's new deputy and was relieved to find she saw nothing more than a man in a dark, slightly worn suit wearing a broad-brimmed Metropolitan hat. He was definitely not a prince—nor that confounded count either.

What a relief! Maybe now she could become friends with the man who would soon be her brother-in-law. Then she would have two brothers. She couldn't think of anything nicer. And she was certain Warren would eventually come around. He couldn't continue to be unreasonable forever.

"Where's Tom and Doc?" Grampa asked as

he carefully descended the steps, Jeremiah keeping pace with him.

Betsy's pinched mouth made her look as if she'd been eating an unripened persimmon. "He's attending to one of *those* women in the saloon."

"Well, I suppose they get sick, too," Grampa said mildly, as if commenting on the inclement weather.

The doctor's wife wasn't mollified. "It's their evil ways that cause their sickness. God's punishment, I say. They should all be driven out of the valley."

Sarah thought Betsy's attitude was somewhat unreasonable. Other people got sick all the time, and it wasn't blamed on sins and evil ways. Still, she wished Doc hadn't asked Tom to go into that dreadful place. Trouble came out of the Pony Saloon more often than not. She hadn't lived with the sheriff all these years without learning that much.

"Come along, Mrs. Varney." She took hold of the other woman's arm. "We've dinner to put on the table. Doc and Tom will catch up with us as soon as they can."

They started walking, the two men following silently behind them.

"You don't understand," Betsy continued unabated. "You're too young. You don't know the temptations a place like that provides, but you'll understand as soon as you're married. No God-fearing woman can rest easy, knowing that saloon and those women are there, tempting our husbands."

Tempting their husbands? Sarah tried to imagine the elderly, dignified doctor carrying on with the likes of Opal Irvine, but even she didn't have that good an imagination. The notion almost made her laugh aloud.

She felt Betsy take a deep breath and knew the woman was prepared to continue her oratory on the evils of the Pony Saloon and all who entered its doors.

"Smells like we're gonna get another snow," Grampa announced loudly from behind them. "What do you think, Jeremiah? Is it gonna snow?"

There was a moment's hesitation, followed by, "I think you're right, Sheriff. It does smell like it could snow. Temperature's dropping, too."

Sarah glanced over her shoulder and winked at the two men, silently letting them know she understood their game—and was thankful for it.

Chapter Seven

Tom watched Doc Varney's every movement, observing the way he checked the patient's eyes and throat, felt her pulse, and listened to her heart. He made note of Doc's air of quiet assurance and wondered if it came from years of practicing medicine or if it was a gift he'd been born with. He suspected it was a combination of the two.

Tom shifted his gaze to the girl on the bed. Except for a nasty bruise on the right side of her face, she was as pale as a bleached sheet. She lay as still as death while the doctor examined her, her breathing so shallow it was barely discernible to Tom's naked eye.

"Mind telling me what happened here?" Doc asked the woman standing behind him, touching the bruise on the girl's cheek.

Opal shrugged. "Fanny got sick on one of the men downstairs. He hit her." She said it matter-of-factly, as if it weren't anything unusual or even unacceptable.

What an awful life this must be, Tom thought as he returned his attention to the patient.

"How old is she?" Doc inquired.

"Sixteen."

"Could she be with child?"

Tom glanced quickly at Opal.

She shook her head. "No, sir. She don't have men visitors. She just serves drinks and sweeps up."

Tom felt a sense of relief. He couldn't imagine the waiflike girl cavorting as a prostitute. Again he thought how dreadful her life must be, living and working in this place. It seemed so unjust.

As if in reply to Tom's reflections, Opal said, "Our ma died this year, and Fanny didn't have nowhere else to go. We got no other family." She sighed softly. "Is she goin' t'be all right?"

"It's nothing serious, Miss Irvine." Doc rose from the bedside and handed Opal a small, dark bottle. "Give her a spoonful of this four times a day. Keep cool rags on her forehead to help bring the fever down. This evening, try giving her sips of water at regular intervals. If she keeps it down, tomorrow you can try some beef tea, as much and as often as she would like it.

Stewed prunes would be good, too." He picked up his bag. "I'll be back to check on her tomorrow evening."

"Thanks, Doc." She glanced at Tom, then back at the physician. "Fanny's not like me. She's a good girl with a good heart. I'd have done better for her if there was any way I could."

Doc Varney patted her shoulder. "I'm sure you would, Miss Irvine." He turned toward Tom. "We'd best be on our way."

Tom nodded and followed the doctor from the room. Once the two men reached the street, he said, "Poor kid. Doesn't seem right."

"No, it surely doesn't."

"She looked younger than sixteen. It's a shame she has to live like that. Is she really going to be all right?"

"I'm as sure as any doctor ever is. There are few certainties in medicine, Tom. The best anyone can do is study and learn all science can teach us, then pray that God will give us insight when it's most needed." Doc draped an arm over Tom's shoulders. "Now, let's get home to that meal your sister's got ready or she's likely to skin the hide off us."

Jeremiah kept remembering Sarah's wink throughout dinner. It didn't matter that he knew she'd really been winking at her grandfather. It intrigued him.

She intrigued him.

83

She talked about the most unusual things. She seemed to have read books about every country in the world, and she quoted the oddest facts. Effortlessly, she guided the conversation from one topic to another, smiling when she should smile, laughing when she should laugh, expressing sorrow or dismay when she should. And yet, he knew with a certainty that she had no idea she did any of it. Her emotions and reactions were honest and truly felt.

My brother's a lucky man, he thought.

Then, I was lucky once, too.

The thought lingered in his head, and after a moment, he realized he didn't feel the bitter guilt he'd felt for so long.

Yes, he'd been lucky. He'd known the warmth of love. Life hadn't been easy for him and Millie, working that piece of land in Ohio, but they hadn't minded. They'd been too blasted young to mind, he supposed. Besides, they'd had each other. It had been enough.

His attention drifted back to Sarah McLeod. She wasn't anything like Millie. Sarah was as fair as a summer's day. Millie had been more like autumn with her chestnut hair and hazel eyes. Sarah was friendly and quick to laugh. Millie had been soft-spoken and shy. Sarah was . . .

A knock sounded at the door, interrupting his musings. Tom McLeod went to answer it, and when he returned, Warren was with him.

His brother's gaze found him instantly. Jeremiah caught the look of enmity in his glance just before Warren flashed a smile at the rest of the group. "Hello, everyone. Sorry I'm late. Couldn't be avoided." He walked to the empty place across from Sarah and sat down.

Sarah knew she was feeling unreasonably cross with Warren. He had, after all, apologized for being late. And he didn't completely ignore his brother as she'd expected him to. But it did seem to Sarah that the spark left the table at the same time Warren sat down.

A half hour later, when everyone was finished eating, the men retired to her grandfather's study while the women cleared the table and washed the dishes. Shortly thereafter, Doc and Betsy Varney thanked the McLeods for their hospitality and left for home. Tom said he was going along with them to get some of Doc's medical books. Her grandfather announced he was feeling tired and intended to lie down and leave the young folks to themselves. After he'd gone upstairs, Jeremiah said it was time for him to leave as well, using the excuse that it was a long, cold drive back to his farm.

Sarah kept the door open just long enough to watch Jeremiah stride down the street toward the church where his patient horse awaited him; then she closed the door. Turning around, she found Warren standing in the entrance to the living room, watching her with a strange expression.

"I don't know why you're so unreasonable about your brother," she said without thinking. "I find him a very nice person and quite delightful company. In fact, I was extremely sorry to see him go."

It would have been hard to describe the emotions that played across her fiancé's face, but she knew she'd upset him. She was instantly contrite. Heaven only knew what had caused her to say such a thing.

"I'm sorry, Warren." She hurried to him, resting her palms against his chest. "I know you aren't close to Jeremiah, and I guess, from what you've said, you'd just as soon not have anything to do with him. But he *is* your only living relation, and now he's going to be Grampa's deputy. Couldn't you try to make amends with him? I think it's what he wants."

His response was sudden and unexpected. His hands grasped her upper arms, and he yanked her quickly to him. Then his mouth was pressed against hers. She tried to pull back, but he wouldn't let her. His grip only tightened, and his mouth became more insistent upon hers.

Eyes open, she felt a terrible panic, as if he were stealing the air from her lungs, suffocating her. In some corner of her mind, she knew she should be enjoying Warren's kisses, but she couldn't. Not while she felt as if she couldn't breathe.

When he let go of her, she stepped quickly back from him. She swallowed quick gulps of air, one hand pressed against her rapidly beating heart.

"Sarah—" he began.

What was wrong with her? There wasn't a reason in the world to feel afraid of Warren. Why, he was the most harmless man she knew. He was patient and soft-spoken. He went to church every Sunday. He was generous with his neighbors. He wouldn't hurt a soul. She'd never even seen him truly angry until his brother returned. Certainly, he wouldn't hurt her. He was "exceptionally fond" of her, as he'd told her on numerous occasions over the past five years.

But fear was the only word she could think of to describe what she was feeling.

He sighed. "I . . . think I'd better go."

She knew she should insist he stay. She knew she should invite him back into the living room for coffee. She knew there were several things she should do or say, but she didn't do or say any of them.

Warren opened the door, then glanced over his shoulder. He looked as if he would say something, but in the end, he only nodded before going outside and closing the door behind him.

Sarah wandered back into the living room

and sat on the divan near the fireplace. She stared into the flames as she tried to sort through her confusion, but for the moment, nothing made any sense at all.

Warren wished it weren't Sunday. If not, he could have gone to the Pony Saloon and had a drink. But Warren wasn't one to flout convention, so he went home instead.

Home, for Warren, was a small room in the back of his furniture shop. It wasn't much, but he didn't need much. After he and Sarah were married, he would move into the McLeod house. The old man planned to leave it to Sarah when he died, which suited Warren just fine. He had lots of plans for the place. He would make it into a showplace for his furniture. His craftsmanship with wood would be seen in every room. It would become the finest house in all of Idaho.

Dropping down onto the edge of his bed, he mulled over what Sarah had said about Jeremiah. She thought it was time for him to make amends with his brother. Of course, he couldn't expect Sarah to understand the things that stood between the Wesley brothers. His past was too complex for Sarah to grasp. He wasn't sure he understood it all himself, so how could he explain it to a girl like Sarah?

Still, she was right about Jeremiah being back to stay. It did appear he would be the new deputy, although that was something else Warren didn't understand. How could folks who'd known Jeremiah as a young man decide to make him a deputy? Only Warren seemed to remember the way his brother had been—rebellious, unruly, trouble. Not exactly deputy material.

But with Jeremiah working in Homestead, their paths were going to cross frequently from now on. It would make life simpler if they were to call a truce, as Sarah suggested.

Damn! Why did Jeremiah have to pick now to come back to Homestead?

Warren lay back on the bed and stared up at the ceiling as old memories played through his mind. He'd tried so hard to please his father. From the time he was just a little tyke, he'd done everything Ted Wesley asked of him. He'd followed all the rules. He'd worked hard in school. He'd never shirked his chores. Unlike Jeremiah, who'd never done what was expected of him, Warren had toed the line.

And where had it gotten him?

After all those years he'd helped his father on the farm, hating it as he always had—the dirt and the dust and the rain and the mud . . . After the months he'd taken care of his sick and dying father, never once complaining, never once not being there to make Ted Wesley more comfortable . . . After all the ways he'd tried to please and all the things he'd done, his father had still left everything to Jeremiah. He'd left everything to the son who'd run off years before and had never come back, and Warren would never understand why.

No, Sarah didn't know what she was asking of him. It wasn't that simple. It just wasn't that simple.

Chapter Eight

Jeremiah was sworn in as the new deputy shortly before noon on Monday. After a few more words of congratulations and expressions of confidence in the job he would do, the mayor and the sheriff left him alone in his new office.

Deputy Sheriff Wesley . . .

What would you think of this, Millie? Back a couple of days, and they've made me the law.

He turned away from the door and surveyed the room.

Off to his right was a scarred desk, its top littered with papers. In front of the desk were two buckeye arm chairs with cane seats. Behind the desk was a large-armed chair with a high back and a swivel seat.

In the far corner, behind and to the left of the desk, was a gun rack which held several Winchesters and two Colt rifles. A couple of paintings—one of bright sunflowers, the other a watercolor of a couple picnicking beside a stream—hung on the wall. Jeremiah suspected Hank's granddaughter had placed the paintings there.

At the back of the room, near the door leading to the two jail cells, was a Windsor wood stove which was belching heat into the room. A blue-speckled coffeepot that had seen better days sat on top of the stove beside the chimney pipe. Nearby was a narrow sideboard where coffee and a few other amenities were stored, and next to it was a wood box, filled to the brim.

Jeremiah stepped over to the sideboard and took one of the cups from the nook, then filled it with coffee. He took a sip. The brew was dark and bitter, and he wondered when the pot had last been washed. But he'd had worse, especially in the army.

Carrying the cup with him, he turned and looked into the second room. Black iron bars formed two sides of the small cells. Inside each stood one cot with a thin tick mattress, a pillow, and a brown wool blanket. There was also a wooden bucket and a slop jar in each cell. A narrow, barred window provided the only light in the cramped quarters.

Jeremiah turned away from the cells and walked over to the desk. The sheriff's desk.

Yes, his brother was a lucky man, Jeremiah thought as he listened. He wondered if Warren knew just how lucky he was. Women like Sarah didn't come along every day. She must love him a great deal to go to all this trouble.

Sarah found that looking into Jeremiah's sooty-black eyes was a rather disconcerting experience. Her mind went blank after a while, and she couldn't remember what had brought her to his office. She couldn't even remember what she'd been saying to him. Her stomach was unsettled and fluttery.

Jeremiah shook his head. "I wish I knew how to fix things, Miss McLeod."

"Sarah," she corrected softly, enjoying the way his mouth moved when he spoke, thinking it a quite wonderful mouth.

His voice softened, too. "Sarah."

Her heart skipped a beat.

He cleared his throat as he glanced down at the food spread on his desk. "Warren and I weren't ever close. When we were younger, I think it was just the difference in our ages, but later on . . ." He looked up at her again. "I guess he's got reason enough to resent me. He never took to farming the land like I did, but he's the one who ended up here, keeping the place going. God only knows what Dad was thinking when he left the place to me. I never thought . . ."

Sarah felt a tiny pull in her chest. There was a world of sadness in his eyes. She felt the need to comfort him but was at a loss about how to do it.

She straightened in her chair, reminded suddenly why she'd come to see him. It was for Warren. She was here to help Warren. Her fiancé. The man she was pledged to marry in just two weeks.

Drawing a quick breath, she said, "I'm sure, with a little effort, you could change things. Won't you try? Please? You've come back to Homestead to stay. Wouldn't it be better for you both if you could at least be friends?"

"Yes, I guess it would."

Sarah immediately brightened. She brought her hands together. "Oh, I'm so glad, Jeremiah. Then we can be friends, too."

Tom followed Doc Varney to the small room on the second floor of the Pony Saloon. Doc tapped lightly on the door before opening it, then entered the stuffy, windowless room.

Fanny Irvine opened her eyes as the doctor approached her bed. Bracing her hands beside her, she tried—and failed—to push herself up on the pillows at her back.

"Well, I can see you're feeling better, my girl. There's some color in your face today."

Tom thought Fanny still looked gray. The only color he could detect was the purplish bruise along the side of her face.

"Mind if my young associate here has a look at you?" Doc asked as he motioned for Tom to come closer. Then he opened his black leather bag and pulled out the stethoscope. "Give a listen and tell me what you hear."

Tom accepted the instrument. Nervously, he stepped around the bed, knowing Doc was watching his every move. What if he did something wrong? Doc would be disappointed in him if he bungled something as simple as this.

At that moment, he looked into the patient's eyes. Brown eyes, too big for her face. Fanny reminded him of a lost puppy caught in the rain. He forgot all about his mentor.

"Don't worry," he told her. "You're going to be fine." As he spoke he took hold of her fingers and gave them a comforting squeeze.

She attempted a smile, and something odd happened in Tom's chest.

He pulled his gaze away from hers, pressed the chest piece over her heart, and concentrated on the sounds coming through the stethoscope. A steady heartbeat. Perhaps a little fast but nothing abnormal.

He straightened. "Sounds good," he told Doc.

"And her temperature?"

Tom checked that, too. "Almost normal."

The elderly physician nodded, then glanced down at his patient. "Tell me how you feel."

"Better." Her voice was a hoarse whisper.

97

She cleared her throat, then repeated, "Better."

"You've been eating your beef broth?"

She wrinkled her nose and nodded.

"Then I think you might try eating some solids tonight. It wouldn't hurt to put a little meat on your bones, young lady."

Fanny dropped her gaze to the blanket covering her. She plucked at a loose thread with a finger and thumb. "I don't think I could keep down Grady's cookin' just now. It's mighty greasy."

Doc glanced across at Tom, then back down at the girl. "I imagine Mrs. Potter has something from the restaurant that will appeal to you. I'll have Tom here bring it to you."

Her eyes widened as she quickly looked up. "I don't have the money for no restaurant food. Opal'd skin me alive if I—"

"You let me worry about it, Fanny." Doc patted the back of her hand. "I'm the doctor, remember. You must do what I tell you."

Fanny glanced anxiously toward the door, then back at Doc, and finally over at Tom. "Opal ain't been havin' visitors 'cause of me bein' sick in bed, and I ain't been able to do my chores either. If Grady knows I—"

"All the more reason for you to follow my instructions," Doc interrupted again, more firmly this time. "Now, I'm going to have Tom bring you a light meal, and I want you to eat every last bite. Tom, you're to remain with Fanny until she's done as I've told her."

Fanny's brown eyes flooded with helpless tears, causing a tightening in Tom's chest. What right had anyone to make a girl like Fanny afraid to eat decent food? He had a good mind to tell Mr. Grady O'Neal just what he thought of him and his like.

"I'll be back soon," he told her. Then he offered a teasing smile. "Don't you go anywhere."

Sarah felt wonderfully lighthearted when she left the sheriff's office. She had succeeded in her mission. Jeremiah had agreed to make an effort with his brother. Now, if she could only get Warren to make the same concessions, all would be well.

She frowned thoughtfully, her lightheartedness dissipating as she followed the uneven boardwalk down Main Street toward Warren's furniture shop. Sarah knew from experience how stubborn Warren could be. Once he'd made up his mind, it was difficult to get him to change it.

Warren, she knew, was a creature of habit. He ate his supper with the McLeods on Wednesdays and Saturdays and joined them for dinner on Sundays after church. On Tuesdays, he and Sarah ate lunch at the Rafferty Hotel. Warren always ordered the fried chicken. Always.

Warren worked in his furniture shop from precisely eight o'clock in the morning until

precisely six o'clock at night, six days a week.
Except for Tuesdays, he allowed himself no
more than thirty minutes for lunch. On Tuesdays, when they went to the hotel restaurant,
he allowed a generous forty-five minutes.

Warren Wesley was boring. Why hadn't she
admitted it to herself before?

In fact, Warren was frightfully boring at
times. He never wanted to do anything out
of the ordinary. She couldn't imagine him
eloping with her, couldn't conceive of him
being so in love he would defy convention.
His entire world revolved around his business and his precise schedule.

Boring. Boring. Boring.

Oh, but it wasn't fair to think about him
only that way, she knew. Warren had many
good qualities. He was an upstanding member of the community. He was fair and honest in all his business dealings, scrupulously
so. He was kind and always willing to lend
a helping hand. He never forgot her birthday. He always gave her a gift for Christmas
and again at Easter. He was industrious and
would certainly be a good provider for his
wife and family.

And Warren was eager for a family. He
wanted several children. He'd told her so
more than once. A shiver that had little to do
with the cold ran up her spine as she remembered Warren's kisses and her reaction to
them. She knew that more than kissing was
needed for the begetting of children.

"Love grows the longer you're with a man," her grandmother had told her. "Give yourself time. Your feelings for Warren will get stronger."

But what if she never felt differently about Warren's kisses? What if . . .

Suddenly, or so it seemed, she was standing in front of Wesley's Furniture Emporium. She stared at the lettering on the glass pane in the door. *Warren Wesley, Proprietor.*

Nerves. That was all it was. She was simply nervous because of the upcoming wedding and all the details still to be seen to in so little time. She'd never thought of Warren as boring before.

Had she?

The door opened before her.

"Sarah, what are you doing out in this cold? You'll catch your death." Warren took hold of her elbow and drew her into the shop.

The air smelled of fresh-cut wood. Shavings littered the floor near Warren's work bench.

"You shouldn't be standing about on a day like this," he scolded gently. "It's well below freezing out."

"I wanted to talk to you."

"Couldn't it have waited until tomorrow when we have lunch at the hotel?" He gave her one of his tolerant, you-should-know-better smiles.

She felt anything but tolerant. "If I'd thought it could wait, I wouldn't be here,

Warren." Even in her own ears, she sounded waspish. What on earth was the matter with her lately?

"Well, then . . ." He sighed. "I suppose we should sit down so you can tell me what's on your mind." He led the way across the shop to a pair of saddle seat chairs.

Had he always treated her like a mindless child? she wondered as she followed him. Surely not. Warren was simply concerned for her welfare. He cared for her and always tried to make certain she was protected.

She pulled off her gloves and shoved them into the pockets of her Mackintosh, then removed her coat and placed it over Warren's waiting arm. She sat down, watching as he carried the coat to a rack near the door.

He was so unlike his brother, she thought—and immediately felt her cheeks grow warm.

Warren had an ordinary face, not unpleasant but not striking either. His light brown hair was already thinning at the temples, and she imagined he would be noticeably bald by the time he was thirty, just four years away. He was average in height, perhaps a bit less than average since he was only a few inches taller than Sarah herself.

So different from Jeremiah Wesley.

Unable to prevent herself, she envisioned the deputy in his office—his black hair needing a trim; the badge, pinned to his shirt, looking so right on a man with such broad shoulders; the way he'd watched her with his dark eyes; the slightly crooked curve of his mouth.

Again her cheeks infused with heat, and she turned her gaze guiltily toward the floor, not wanting Warren to read her thoughts.

"So, now tell me what was so important it couldn't wait until tomorrow." Warren sat down in the chair beside her.

Sarah drew a quick breath, then glanced up. "I came about Jeremiah."

His mouth thinned.

"He was sworn in as deputy this morning. He's going to be carrying out most of the sheriff's duties in Grampa's place."

"So I heard."

"Warren . . . he's your only family, your brother. That makes him my brother, too. Almost, anyway. Please, if not for yourself, do it for me."

"It's not that simple."

That was when she lost all patience with him. "Of course it's that simple, Warren Wesley! And stop treating me as if I haven't two pennies' worth of sense between my ears." She rose from her chair. "You can be as stubborn as you like, Warren, but I intend to make Jeremiah feel welcome. He shall be included with the family, and I shall treat him exactly as I treat my own brother."

With that, she stormed to the coatrack, grabbed her Mackintosh, slipped into it, and left the shop without buttoning it closed.

*   *   *

Fanny felt terribly self-conscious with Tom McLeod sitting beside her bed, watching her eat. She didn't have much of an appetite to begin with, and his being there didn't help things.

Still, she knew she would hate it when it was time for him to go. She'd never had anybody treat her as nicely as Doc Varney and Tom McLeod.

While she ate, Tom told her about his life at boarding school. She didn't understand a lot of what he said, but she liked to hear him talk anyway.

"I came awfully close to being expelled because of the frog escapade. If it weren't that Doc was an old friend of the headmaster . . . Well, let's just say I learned my lesson. I got serious after that. I want to be a doctor too much to lose my chance over a bunch of silly pranks." He pointed at her idle fork. "More," he stated. "Doc said you're to clean your plate."

"But I'm full."

He smiled as he shook his head and wiggled his finger at her fork again.

He's got the nicest smile I've ever seen. "Really," she whispered. "I couldn't eat another bite."

He leaned toward her. He smelled good. Like bay rum and fine milled soap. She'd never been near a man who smelled so good. He spoke in a whisper, saying, "You won't tell Doc I let you disobey?"

Fanny shook her head.

"All right then. Just this once." He took the tray from her lap and set it on the floor beside his chair. "I suppose it's time for me to go so you can rest."

"Will you come with Doc tomorrow?"

"Sure. I'll be here. I guess Doc made you my patient now, too. That means I've got to look in on you, just like he does."

Fanny felt better than she had in months.

Chapter Nine

Jeremiah was just reaching for his coat, his destination Wesley's Furniture Emporium, when the door to the sheriff's office opened and his brother stepped inside. Their gazes met. Neither spoke at first.

Finally, Jeremiah motioned toward his desk and the chair beside it. "We might as well sit down."

Warren nodded, and when they were both seated—Jeremiah behind the desk, his brother across from him—Warren said, "I understand Sarah came to see you."

"Yes, she did."

"It seems very important to her that we make peace with one another."

"Yes, it does."

Warren glanced around the office. "I never

pictured you as a deputy. Especially not in Homestead."

"Me either."

"It wasn't fair, you know. Dad never should have left the farm to you. I was the one who stayed. The farm should have been mine." His gaze returned to meet Jeremiah's. "I was the one who helped him till and plant and harvest all those years you were gone."

Softly: "I know."

Warren's voice was filled with bitterness. "I hated farming. I always hated it, but I did it because I was the one who was here. But it didn't matter what I did for him. It was always you he was thinking about. Even when we were little, it was always you. You were always his favorite."

Jeremiah said nothing.

"He scrimped and saved so you could go to college, but there was never any money for me, for what I wanted to do." He leaned forward. "I was glad when you ran off. I thought maybe . . ." He let his words die away.

Jeremiah looked back across the years but couldn't see what Warren saw. Jeremiah remembered a father who'd constantly reminded him of what a disappointment he was, not one who favored him. He remembered the lectures he'd received, the whippings he'd gotten. His dad had reminded him often that Jeremiah was expected to make something of himself, then reminded him how unlikely it was he would succeed.

His memories were of a man who never showed affection, whose only emotions were anger and disapproval.

He looked at his brother, wondering whose memory was right.

They'd been so different, the two of them, right from the very start. Warren had hated farming, but he'd always liked working with wood. Jeremiah had forgotten until now. It seemed most of his memories of Warren were of him carving things out of wood. Come to think of it, his brother had made the table in the Wesley house when he was only about ten years old.

But Jeremiah had loved the land. From the time he was a little boy, he'd liked to work in the fields. Ted Wesley had farmed out of necessity, as a way to feed his family. But Jeremiah had loved the look and the smell of the earth when it was freshly turned. He'd loved watching the green sprouts come up through the dark soil. He'd loved harvesttime when a man could see what his hard labor and nature's blessings had wrought.

Lord, he'd forgotten how much he had loved farming the land. He'd stopped loving it when Millie died. At least, he thought he'd stopped loving it. Maybe he'd been wrong about that, too.

"Did you know Dad sent the rest of your college money to Millie's grandmother in Ohio, to help you two along? He didn't keep one red cent of it for us. Not a penny."

Jeremiah's eyes widened as he stared at his brother.

Warren nodded. "It's true. As soon as he found out where the two of you had gone, he sent what money you didn't take with you when you left."

"I didn't know. Grandmother Ashmore never told me." He paused, then added, "I'm sorry, Warren. I . . . I never knew."

His brother rose from his chair and walked to the opposite end of the office, then back to the desk. "Sarah is a wonderful girl. I expect she'll make me a fine wife. Her family has always been well respected in Homestead. She does take some silly notions into her head, and I suppose it will be my duty, as her husband, to see she doesn't get carried away with them." He sat down again. "However, I think, in this instance, she may be right. You now represent the law in this town, and I run a business here. We should do our best to appear cooperative, if nothing more."

"I'm willing if you are, Warren."

They rose in unison, then shook hands. Their gazes held, and Jeremiah found himself wondering if this was why Millie had wanted him to return. Maybe he'd needed to put things right with his brother.

It was Warren who broke the silence by withdrawing his hand. "I'd best get back to the shop. I've got an order to fill by Friday." He walked to the door, stopped, and looked back at Jeremiah. "Sarah will expect you to join us for supper on Wednesday evening."

"I don't want to intrude."

"You'd best plan on it." Then he opened the door and left the sheriff's office.

Jeremiah sank back onto his chair and felt a small portion of the peace he'd sought fall into place.

Rose Rafferty held her coat close about her as she walked toward the hotel. Her heart was racing furiously, and her feet felt as if they had wings.

She was going to have a baby.

It's true! It's true! It's true!

She'd nearly given up hope after so many years. Benjamin had been born before she and Michael had celebrated their first wedding anniversary. Sophia had arrived almost a year to the day later. But it had been nearly seven years since Sophia's birth, and Rose had begun to fear she would never get pregnant again.

Michael had always said he wanted a houseful of children. That was why they'd built the big house they'd moved into five years ago. So they'd have plenty of bedrooms to fill. Now, at last, they'd get to use the nursery.

She entered the hotel through the front doors.

Paul Stanford, the hotel clerk, glanced up from the ledger. "Good afternoon, Mrs. Rafferty."

"Good afternoon, Paul," she returned with a brilliant smile. "Is Michael in his office?"

"Yes, ma'am."

"Is he alone?"

"Yes, ma'am."

She stopped at the door and composed herself, doing her best to hide her buoyant mood. A long time ago, she'd been able to hide her feelings, but that had been before she met Michael. He'd changed all that for her.

Still, she would dearly love to surprise him.

Drawing a deep breath, she opened the door part way and poked her head inside. "Are you busy?" she asked.

Michael rose from his desk. "Never too busy for you." He strode toward her.

As the door swung closed, he drew her into his arms and kissed her the way she liked to be kissed, slow and sweet. When he let her go, she was breathless.

"So what's brought you here in the middle of the afternoon?"

"Oh, nothing important," she lied as she moved away from him, wandering over to peek at the papers on his desk, trying her best to appear nonchalant. "I had some errands to do in town." She touched the hat perched on her head. "Do you like my new bonnet?"

Michael cocked his head slightly to one side. "It's very fetching," he replied, but she could tell he was beginning to suspect something.

"I thought so. Mrs. Gaunt made it especially for me. You know, that woman is a remarkable seamstress. She nearly has my new gown finished already. I don't understand it. I've always been all thumbs with a needle and thread."

Michael walked toward her. "Rose, is there something you need to tell me?"

"Tell you?" She widened her eyes. "Whatever makes you think so?"

His expression was stern. "Because you're beginning to chatter like Sophia when she's nervous."

"Well . . ."

Michael took hold of her arms and drew her toward him. His blue eyes were filled with worry and concern. "What is it, Rose?"

"I should tell you that I've placed a rather large order at the mercantile."

He raised an eyebrow, waiting for her to go on, his fingers tightening slightly on her arms.

"Really, all of Sophia's baby things are so old, I just felt like buying all new things." She smiled.

"All new—" He stopped abruptly.

She bobbed her head up and down in answer to his unspoken question. "Next July."

"A baby!"

Suddenly she was in his arms, her feet off the floor, and he was spinning her around in circles. When he set her down again, he pulled her close for another kiss.

Rose wondered if any woman had ever been as sublimely happy as she.

"Care to tell me what's troublin' you, princess?"

Sarah turned in the window seat and met her grandfather's gaze. She let out a heavy sigh, then lifted her shoulders in a futile shrug. "I quarreled with Warren."

Grampa entered her bedroom and sat on a nearby chair. "Serious?"

She shrugged. "I suppose not. I just think he's being unreasonable about Jeremiah."

He nodded. "That's all?"

No, she wanted to say. *No, that isn't all. I'm confused. I don't know what I want or what I think or what I feel. When I look at Warren, I don't feel what I should feel. Everything's all mixed up inside my head.*

"That's all," she said, not wanting to worry him, and reached out to lay her hand on the back of his.

"Then why don't you come downstairs with me and beat me at a game of checkers? Now that I've got a deputy who can do all the work, I don't know what to do with myself. I'm as good as retired now. Won't be long before I give up the badge altogether."

"Do you mind terribly?" She slipped off the window seat. "Retiring, I mean."

Hank stood and put his arm around her shoulder as she slid hers around his back.

"No, I reckon I don't mind much. Just seems strange, that's all."

"Maybe I should teach you how to cook."

He chuckled. "Not if you don't want the house burned down around your ears."

A half hour later, Sarah was giving her grandfather a thorough thrashing at checkers when the front door opened.

"It's me," her brother called from the entry. When he appeared at the living room doorway, he said, "Look who I brought with me."

Sarah looked up to find Jeremiah standing beside Tom, her wicker picnic basket in one hand.

"Thought I'd better return this." He offered a half grin. "The food was great."

She rose from her chair. "I completely forgot I'd left it with you." She walked forward and took the basket from him. "Thanks for returning it."

Jeremiah glanced toward Sarah's grandfather, then back at her. "Would you mind if I spoke to you a moment? Alone."

She felt a strange sensation in her stomach as she looked up into his dark eyes. "Of course." Her reply came out in a broken whisper. She drew a quick breath. "Why don't we step into Grampa's study?"

She led the way, not bothering to look behind to see if he followed. She knew he did. His presence was like a physical touch.

She walked into the study and over to her

114

grandfather's desk before turning around. As she did so, Jeremiah closed the door. Her heart began to beat at an abnormal pace.

He took a step forward but stopped while there was still plenty of distance separating them. "I . . . I just wanted to thank you for what you've done, Sarah."

"What I've done?" she repeated.

He was so darkly handsome, so tall and strong. His raven-black hair was a little long but clean and shiny. A stray lock fell across his forehead, and she had the absurd desire to brush it back with her fingertips.

He really *could* be a European count.

"Yes, for Warren and me."

It was a bit like falling into Pony Creek in the spring when the water was chilled by melting snows. Her wayward thoughts came abruptly back to the present.

"Warren and you?" She sounded like an idiot, repeating everything he said.

"He came to see me this afternoon. We . . . well, I think things will be better between us in the future. Thanks to you."

Drawing a deep breath, she moved around her grandfather's desk and sat on his chair. "I'm glad I could be of help. It's the least I could do for a brother." She looked up and met Jeremiah's fathomless gaze, and her heart began its rapid beating again.

Jeremiah's voice was low. "I've been thinking how lucky Warren is."

She found it hard to breathe when he

looked at her that way. As if he could see inside of her while hiding his own thoughts and emotions completely.

"Warren's waited a long time to marry you. But then, a special love's worth waitin' for."

"Did Warren say that?"

He shook his head, and a smile tweaked the corners of his mouth. "No. Small-town gossip. I heard it from Leslie Blake."

She nodded in understanding. She supposed most folks did think Warren had waited because he loved her, but she knew him better than that. He'd waited because he thought she would make him the best wife. It was a practical decision. Warren was always practical. Sarah suddenly longed for something different from mere practicality.

She stifled a sigh. Warren would never understand the strange yearnings she felt, but she instinctively knew that Jeremiah would.

"You loved your wife very much, didn't you?" she asked softly.

His face became a stoic mask.

"Someday, I hope you'll tell me about her."

He acted as if she hadn't spoken. "Well, I'd better head on back to the farm. It'll be dark before I know it." His departure was quick.

Sarah stared toward the empty doorway for a long time, wondering about Jeremiah, wishing she understood him, feeling a need to know and understand him.

"What brought you back to Homestead, Jeremiah?" she whispered.

Chapter Ten

Jeremiah awakened two days later to a sharp wind whistling around the corners of his little farmhouse. He left his bed and crossed to the window. The early morning sky had been obliterated by dark clouds. They roiled and churned across the heavens, bringing with them the promise of more snow.

He'd have to do it, he realized. He'd have to move into town, at least until the spring thaw began. He couldn't keep riding back and forth between town and the farm in weather like this. What if there was a real problem in Homestead? What if folks couldn't get out here to tell him he was needed or he couldn't get into town to do whatever was required of him as deputy? He was being paid to do a job, and it wouldn't be fair for him to shirk his duties, then blame it on the weather.

He let the plain cloth curtain drop over the window, hoping to keep out some of the cold that was blasting through the glass, and turned toward the wood stove.

It wouldn't be for long, he assured himself as he stoked the fire. Once fair weather arrived, he'd be able to return to the farm, at least most nights of the week. Until then, he'd just have to make the barren storeroom above the jail into something habitable.

As soon as the chill was gone from the air, Jeremiah washed and shaved. After he'd dressed, he fixed himself a quick breakfast, his thoughts remaining upon his move into town.

He'd need a bed and a table and a chair. He supposed Warren could help him out with those items. He only needed the bare necessities, just enough to get by. He wouldn't worry about cooking. He could take most of his meals at one of the town's two restaurants.

Except Wednesdays and Saturdays. He was expected at the McLeod house for supper on those nights.

The memory of Sarah McLeod as she played hostess was a pleasant one: her silvery-blond hair swept up from her slender neck, loose tendrils coiling at her nape; her blue eyes fringed by thick, golden-brown lashes; her tiny, turned-up nose; her womanly figure.

It's the least I could do for a brother.

He frowned as he recalled her words. Sarah's brother? He wasn't thinking about her like a brother.

His frown became a scowl. Just what *was* he thinking? That he was attracted to her? That would be a disaster, considering she would be marrying Warren soon. Besides, he knew the kind of woman who was right for him. A woman like Millie. Quiet, shy, a woman of simple needs. He'd been happy with Millie. Their love had been gentle and solid. He didn't pretend to expect he'd ever find that kind of love again. But then, he didn't want to find it. He didn't want a woman to depend on him ever again.

Besides, Sarah was nothing like Millie. There was a vitality about Sarah McLeod that was almost palpable. He didn't need to know her well to see that she looked at the world through rose-colored glass. She expected every cloud to have a silver lining. He felt a bit sorry for her. One day, she would be forced to see the world as it really was.

Well, none of that was his worry. She was his brother's fiancée. Let Warren worry about her and her head full of silly, impractical dreams.

He shoved back his chair from the table as he raked the fingers of one hand through his hair. He'd better get a move on if he wanted to get to town before the snow started to fall.

"Good gracious!" Madeline Gaunt exclaimed as Sarah entered the dress shop along with a blast of frigid air. "Hurry and close the door, my dear, before we both catch our death of cold."

The tiny, birdlike woman bustled forward, put her arm around Sarah, and hurried her toward the back of the shop where a stove was spreading its warmth over the room.

"You take off your coat while I get you some tea to warm you."

"I'm all right, Mrs. Gaunt. Really."

"It's weather like this that makes me wonder what I was thinking to come here," the woman muttered as she filled a cup from the teakettle. "An old woman like me belongs in milder climates."

"You're not old," Sarah protested with a smile. She had a similar conversation with the seamstress nearly every time she came into the shop.

"'Course I'm old, and don't you deny me the right to say so, young lady. I worked hard to get to this age." Madeline held out the teacup as she waggled a finger at Sarah with her free hand. "Now, you drink this before we begin."

Sarah accepted the cup, then sat on a small wooden chair near the stove and obediently sipped the tea.

"My dear, you won't believe how much I've accomplished these past two weeks. This is going to be my most beautiful creation ever." As she spoke, the seamstress entered a second room. When she came out, she was carrying Sarah's bridal gown across her arm. "Thank heaven you decided on a long engagement, dear. Sewing on these iridescent beads has been the most difficult task." Madeline glanced at Sarah. "Well, come along. Your wedding day is nearly upon us. Let's see how this fits."

A short while later, Sarah was staring at her reflection in the looking glass. The *princesse*-style gown, complete with a lengthy train, was made of the finest satin. The bodice had a high neck, and a lacy fichu that was caught at the waist with a silver pin. The three-quarter sleeves had enormous puffs that seemed to broaden her shoulders and narrow her waist.

"Oh, my!" Madeline Gaunt breathed as she pressed her palms together in front of her mouth. "My dear, I had no idea. You were so right about making this new gown. As lovely as your mother's old wedding dress is, this is breathtaking, even if I do say so myself. What a beautiful bride you shall be."

Sarah had the ridiculous desire to burst into tears. She'd never worn anything so lovely in all her life, nor had she ever felt so miserable.

Madeline went to get her pins. "You just

let me make a few more adjustments. A tuck here and there is all it needs. Now don't move. I don't want to poke you."

Tom left Zoe's Restaurant with a plate of hot food. He knew it wouldn't stay hot long in this weather, so he hurried his steps on his way to the Pony Saloon. He ignored the sullen glance of the proprietor as he walked toward the stairs and along the hallway with its gaudy red wallpaper.

He rapped softly on the door. "Miss Irvine, it's me. Tom McLeod. May I come in?"

Hearing a soft, affirmative reply, he turned the knob and opened the door.

Fanny was sitting up, her back braced by pillows. Her brown hair had been brushed and was caught at the nape with a ribbon. She was wearing a purple bed jacket—several sizes too big—that made her look rather sickly, but Tom knew she was greatly improved over when he'd first come here with Doc on Sunday.

"I've brought your lunch. Doc's orders."

She smiled wanly as she watched him with her enormous brown eyes. She reminded him of a wild doe caught in a cruel trap. One wrong move, and she would break her neck in her efforts to escape.

"Let's see. What do we have today?" Tom sat on the chair beside the bed and removed the cloth from the plate. "Mmmm. Chicken pie. One of my favorites." He set the plate on her lap. "So what stories would you like to hear today for your dining pleasure?"

Fanny dropped her gaze to the plate of food. "Whatever you'd like t'tell me, I guess," she said softly. She glanced quickly up at him, then away again. "I like all your stories, Mr. McLeod."

Why, she was almost pretty when she blushed like that, Tom thought, surprised to discover it.

He pulled the fork from his pocket. "Here. You'd best eat while it's still warm."

Fanny reached for the utensil without looking at him. He wished she would look. He liked her eyes.

Mentally, he chastised himself. That wasn't the sort of thing a doctor should be thinking about his patient. Doc Varney had put Tom in charge of Fanny's care, and his concern needed to remain on her recovery.

He cleared his throat and settled back on his chair. "Have I told you about the time we accidentally set Professor Hurley's lab on fire?"

Hank McLeod was staring out the window of his second-floor bedroom when he saw his granddaughter turn the corner into North Street. He felt a catch in his heart. She looked so sad, so despondent, so unlike the burst of pure sunshine that was usually Sarah.

"Ah, Dorie," he said aloud, "I wish you

123

were here." His wife would have known what to do for Sarah. Hank just felt helpless.

It was Doris McLeod who had always been certain that Warren was the right man for Sarah, that his levelheaded approach to life was just the right counterbalance for Sarah's dreaminess. It was Sarah's grandmother who had told Hank time and again, "Watch. You'll see. Warren's a good catch. Sarah will come to her senses." And she'd been right, too.

If only Dorie were here now. She'd know what to do. She'd know how to get Sarah to talk to her, to pour out what was weighing so heavily on her heart. All Hank wanted to do was wrap his granddaughter up in a bear hug and hold her until whatever was troubling her went away. But he knew that was no answer. Not really.

He shook his head. He knew Sarah's worries were caused by more than a mere quarrel with Warren. Besides, the couple seemed to have patched things up. Sarah had gone to lunch with her fiancé yesterday, just as she had every Tuesday for the past year. She'd told Hank that things were just fine between the two of them.

No, whatever was bothering Sarah was something more than a lovers' tiff. He just didn't know what.

Hank turned and left his room, taking the stairs slowly—and cursing each and every one of them while he was at it. He hated the way his body had betrayed him by getting old. Except for an injury now and again, like the time he was shot back in 'ninety, he'd hardly been sick a day in his life. To wake up one day and discover he'd become an old man had caught him unprepared.

"How's Mrs. Gaunt coming with the dress?" he asked Sarah as she entered the house a few minutes later.

She looked up and feigned a smile. "Just fine. The gown is lovely. Almost completed." She removed her Mackintosh and hung it on the coat hook. "Where's Tom?"

"Out with Doc, I suppose. At this rate, he won't be needin' that fancy institute back in Boston. Doc's going to have him all schooled and ready to start practicin' medicine before the year is out."

Sarah crossed the entry hall, pausing to stand on tiptoe to kiss Hank's cheek. "Let's see if we can't make him stay home a little more. His visit will be short as it is. He doesn't need to spend all of his time with Doc Varney."

"Well, I notice he never misses supper," Hank replied with a chuckle and a wink.

Sarah's smile was genuine this time. "Speaking of which, I'd best see to it or supper will never be ready. I wouldn't want to disappoint my dear brother."

She headed for the kitchen, and soon Hank heard the banging of pots and rattle of pans as Sarah got the meal under way. Whatever was troubling her, she wasn't going to tell him. At least, not yet.

Sarah blamed her tears on the onions. Chopping them always made her eyes water. And that was exactly what she told Tom when he found her standing at the counter, knife in hand, tears rolling down her cheeks.

"If *you* didn't like them so much," she said with a sniff, "I'd leave them out entirely."

Her brother looked unconvinced. "Why don't you tell me what's made you so sad, Sarah? Maybe if you do, I could do something to—"

"Here. Chop these." She set the knife on the counter, stepped to one side, and motioned him forward.

With a shrug, he did as he was told.

Sarah walked over to the stove, wiping her eyes with her apron as she went.

Whatever is the matter with me? She'd never in her life acted like this. It wasn't like her to go all weepy over the slightest thing.

She drew in a deep breath, determined to put a stop to this nonsense. Then she checked the bread in the oven before tasting the stew that was simmering on the stove top.

"Needs more onions, right?" Tom asked as he came up behind her.

She sniffed, then smiled. "Yes."

"Thought so." He dropped the diced onions into the pot. "Tell you what. I can keep an eye on the bread. Why don't you run upstairs, wash your pretty face, put on one of your best dresses, and we'll make a party out of tonight."

Tears threatened again. She swallowed quickly. "I love you, Tommy," she whispered, then hurried out of the kitchen to do just as he'd suggested.

Chapter Eleven

Tom did manage to turn the evening into a party. He regaled everyone with a recitation of his escapades at boarding school. Time and again, the dining room rang with laughter, and by the time Sarah served dessert, she was feeling much better.

She had so much to be thankful for, she reminded herself. She had a grandfather and brother who adored her, and she had a fiancé who was an upstanding member of the community. She had never known want, and if she were brutally truthful, she'd have to admit she'd been spoiled by everyone in her family.

Oh, certainly her dreams of travel abroad—and of meeting dukes and earls and counts and so forth—would never come true, but those had all been the dreams of a young girl. She was nearly twenty-one. It was time she put such childish things aside.

Yes, she felt better. Much better.

"So, Jeremiah," Hank said, interrupting Sarah's thoughts, "tell me how you're takin' to this deputy sheriff business. You gonna like the work?"

"I'm getting the hang of it." Jeremiah paused, then added, "I've decided to move into Homestead for the winter. I'm staying in the room over the jail. Unless you object, sir."

Her grandfather nodded. "Excellent idea. Be glad to have you closer at hand, in case you're needed."

"The old storeroom," Tom said thoughtfully. "Behind the false front. I'd forgotten it was even there." He glanced at his sister. "Remember when we hid up there because we'd eaten all the cakes Gramma baked for the church supper, and we knew we were going to be in a world of trouble?"

Sarah smiled at the memory. "The whole town was out looking for us for hours. I thought Gramma would skin us alive when we finally came out of hiding. She made Grampa put a lock on the door after that." She moved her gaze to Jeremiah. "That room's not a very suitable place to live, as I recall."

"I don't need much."

There was something in the black depths

of his eyes that told her he'd lived in worse places. Places she wouldn't even be able to imagine. For just a moment, she seemed able to see beyond his eyes and into his heart. She saw pain and loneliness, and she felt it as if it were her own pain and loneliness. And then the window into his heart slammed closed, and she could see only his eyes again.

She lowered her gaze to her plate, an odd ache in her chest stealing her appetite. She wondered if he knew what she'd seen in his eyes and if he cared that she'd seen it. She wondered what had caused the pain and why a man like him was lonely. She wondered . . .

The scraping of chair legs on the floor drew her gaze back to the man who held her thoughts captive.

"I'm afraid it's time I checked around town before it gets any later." Jeremiah rose from his chair. "Supper was delicious. Thanks for having me."

"You're always welcome, Jeremiah." She wished she could say more. She wished she could say something that would take away his hurt, whatever the cause.

Warren stood. "It's time I was going, too. Mind if I walk along with you?"

Jeremiah shook his head. "If you want."

Warren stepped over to Sarah and reached down for her hand. He squeezed her fingers gently. "Good night, Sarah."

She thought for a moment he might bend

to kiss her cheek. But Warren never tried to kiss her when anyone else was around. Such public shows of affection would never be acceptable.

He straightened, his gaze sweeping over Tom and settling on Hank. "Good night, sir. Night, Tom."

Sarah sat very still while the two brothers were shown to the door by Tom, staring with unseeing eyes at the dirty dishes cluttering the supper table.

I don't love Warren.

Why did that come as a surprise to her? She'd never told him she loved him. She'd only said she was fond of him. Gramma had said fondness was enough at first, and Sarah had believed her. She'd been willing to give love time to grow.

I don't want to be his wife.

Warren was a good man. Oh, certainly he could be irritating. But wasn't everyone from time to time? Warren had many fine qualities. She was lucky he'd asked her to marry him. Everyone said so. And he'd been so patient with her. He'd been willing to wait. That should tell her how much he cared for her.

But I should love him and I don't. And I don't want to marry him.

Whatever was she to do?

Jeremiah and Warren walked side by side in silence for a while before Warren said, "She's a wonderful young woman, isn't she?"

Jeremiah glanced sideways at his brother. "Sarah? Yes, she's wonderful, all right. You're a lucky man."

"I guess I've known I wanted her for my wife since she was about fourteen. I never doubted it for a moment. She comes from a fine family, of course. Everyone respects the McLeods, which is something a businessman, such as myself, must think about when he takes a wife. I've waited a long time for our wedding, but I believe Sarah is worth the wait."

"Mmm."

Warren stopped suddenly. Jeremiah took a couple more steps, then stopped, too, turning to look at his brother with questioning eyes.

"Sarah's going to be my wife in about ten more days. She'll always make you welcome in our home because you're my brother. So will I. I . . . I just thought you should know that." He shoved his hands into the pockets of his coat and started walking again.

Jeremiah didn't know what to say. He didn't know if there was anything *to* say. He fell into step beside his brother, shortening his stride to match Warren's.

"We're going to live in the McLeod house after we're married," Warren continued. "I want a large family, and that place has room for us to grow. I've got plans for some changes I want to make." He glanced sideways. "What about you, Jeremiah? You plan to make any changes to the house out at the farm?"

"Hadn't thought about it." He glanced down the shadowed alley that cut behind the buildings on Main Street. It was empty, as far as he could tell.

"You ought to. The place'd be worth more with a bigger house on it."

"I'm not planning to sell, so it doesn't much matter what it's worth."

"Well, what about if you marry again? It's not big enough for a wife and family."

Jeremiah looked over at the darkened school building. "I don't plan on marryin' again," he said abruptly.

He heard Warren draw in a breath, as if preparing to say more, but in the end, he didn't. When they reached the furniture shop, they bid each other good night. Then Warren unlocked the door and went inside while Jeremiah headed down Main Street.

A light burned in the parlor of the boardinghouse run by Virginia Townsend. Across the street, the Rafferty Hotel looked festive with two bright red ribbons on its front doors, a reminder that Christmas was coming.

Carson's Barbershop and Bathhouse was darkened for the night. Jeremiah checked to see if the door was securely locked. Finding it so, he moved on.

He could hear music coming from the

Pony Saloon. Glancing through the window, he saw several men playing cards, more standing at the bar, nursing their whiskeys and beers. A couple of fancy women with painted faces and low-cut gowns mingled with the male patrons.

He thought of the women he'd known since Millie died. They'd all worked in places like this. He shook his head and moved on, not wanting to dwell on the memories.

About a half hour later, after checking the other businesses and the Methodist Church, Jeremiah made his way up the outside stairs to the old storeroom over the jail. He stoked the small stove, thankful that someone in the past had thought it necessary to install a source of heat in the storage room, then tossed his hat and coat aside, stripped down to his long underwear, and crawled into the bedroll he'd spread on the floor earlier in the day.

But before he could fall asleep, Warren's question came back to torture him. *What about if you marry again?*

He couldn't expect Warren to understand. He wasn't sure he understood himself. How could he marry again? Millie had given him everything he could have hoped for. She'd made him believe in himself, believe that anything was possible. She'd shown him a better way of living. She'd changed him. Changed everything around him, and he'd loved her more than life itself. When she'd looked at him as if he were ten feet tall, as if he were a hero, he'd believed it, too. Millie had made him a better man.

But that better man had died the day Millie died.

No, it wouldn't be right, him marrying again. He didn't have anything to offer a woman, not anything that mattered. Look at him, living in an empty storage room over the jail. Even with the farm, there wasn't much he could call his own. He'd be lucky to feed himself for the first few years. The land was going to take a lot of work.

He rolled onto his side and pulled the blankets up around his ears, prepared to go to sleep. Then, unbidden and unwanted, the image of Sarah McLeod drifted through his mind. Sarah with her silvery-blond hair that invited a man's fingers to caress it. Sarah with her eyes like pieces of sky. Sarah with an innocence that was at once frightening and provocative. Sarah . . .

He squeezed his eyes more tightly closed. If he'd wanted proof the better man inside him had died, this was it. A better man wouldn't be thinking this way about his own brother's bride.

"What am I doing here, Millie?" he whispered into the darkness.

But the sweet voice that had spoken to his heart so often through the years remained silent. It seemed that even Millie had deserted him.

Chapter Twelve

"Ma, when do we get to go for the Christmas tree?" Benjamin Rafferty asked.

Rose glanced down at her son. "Tomorrow afternoon, your pa said."

"Yippee!" The boy raced out of the kitchen. "Sophie, we go for the tree tomorrow!"

Rose chuckled softly. "Every year, it's the same thing," she said over her shoulder to Sarah McLeod. "They can't wait to go cut down the Christmas tree." Still smiling, she returned her attention to the pie crust she was rolling out.

"I remember how much fun it was when I was a little girl, going after our tree with Tom and Grampa. I loved riding in the sleigh, the horses prancing through the snow, the bells on the harness jingling merrily. The air was always so cold I thought my nose would drop off before we got back."

Rose turned her head to look at Sarah. The younger woman had paused in her cookie-cutting, and she was staring off into space, lost in favorite memories.

"Gramma always had lots of hot chocolate waiting for us at home." She smiled as she looked at Rose. "I know just how Benjamin and Sophie feel."

"Why don't you come with us, Sarah?"

"Oh, I couldn't—"

Rose stepped toward the table in the center of the kitchen where Sarah was working. "Please say you will. We can bring back a tree for your house, too. One more won't make a difference to us. Your grandfather's health certainly won't let him do it, and from what I hear, Doc is keeping Tom busy from dawn to dusk. Besides, I wouldn't mind your help with the children. I tire so easily these days." The last was added softly as a smile lifted the corners of her mouth and her hands cradled her stomach.

She hadn't meant to say anything just yet. She hadn't told anyone except Michael. And for a moment, she thought Sarah wouldn't understand. After all, Sarah was unmarried, and had never had children of her own. She probably wouldn't recognize the significance of what Rose had said.

But Sarah did understand. "Rose, are you going to have another baby?"

She nodded, her tender smile blossoming into a joyful grin. "Yes."

Her friend wiped her flour-covered hands on her apron as she skirted the table, coming over to give Rose a tight hug. "How wonderful!" Sarah took a step backward. "But are you sure you should go on such an outing? Maybe you ought to stay home this year. Tom and I could go with Michael to get the trees."

"I wouldn't dream of not going. I went when I was pregnant with both Benjamin and Sophia, and I was much further along with them than I am with this one."

"When's the baby due?"

"In July."

"That seems so far away." Sarah gave Rose's arm a quick squeeze. "Oh, dear," she muttered suddenly, turning toward the oven. Quickly she removed a sheet of cookies before they could burn.

Rose watched as the younger woman scooped the baked cookies off the pan to cool. After a moment, she said, "July does seem far away now, but I know from experience it will come faster than expected." As she spoke, she turned back to the counter and lined the pie tin with dough, carefully shaping the crust, then trimmed the excess dough with a knife.

"It's strange how time goes so fast when you don't want it to," Sarah commented, "and drags when you wish it would fly."

Before replying, Rose filled the pie crust with the finely chopped mixture of venison, raisins, apples, spices, and cider. Then she said, "I imagine you're wishing away the days until your wedding." She covered the mincemeat with the top pie crust and sealed the edges.

"Not really," came Sarah's soft answer.

Surprised, Rose glanced over her shoulder.

Sarah smiled weakly. "There's so much still to do. I don't think it was wise to plan the wedding so close to Christmas. And Grampa really needs me these days. If Tommy weren't here . . ." She shrugged. "I don't dare wish time would go more quickly."

Rose couldn't help wondering about the younger woman's response. There seemed to be something Sarah wasn't saying. But Rose wasn't one to pry. "Well, if there's anything I can do to help, you need only ask."

"Thanks, Rose. I will."

"You can't stay in bed forever, Fanny," Opal warned as she stared into her dressing table mirror. "Grady's not gonna put up with it much longer."

"I've been sick."

Opal twisted on the stool. "Yeah, you been sick. And now you're not. What d'you think's gonna happen? That boy ain't gonna fall into bed with you. And if he does, he's not gonna look back when the door slams behind him after he's got what he's come for. You know as well as I do what that is, Fanny Irvine."

Fanny swallowed the lump in her throat. "I don't want him in my bed."

"Sure, you don't. I've seen the way you been lookin' at him."

"I ain't—" She stopped herself, then continued in an even voice. "I'm not going to make my livin' that way."

Opal laughed as she turned back to her pots of cosmetics. "You too good for that? Well, don't go thinkin' any man's gonna want you for nothin' else. You ain't much t'look at, ya know, an' you sure as hell don't come from a proper family. If it's marriage you're hankerin' after with that McLeod boy, you might as well forget it right now. I hear he's set to leave Homestead come spring."

Fanny blinked back hot tears as she rolled onto her side, her back to her sister. As much as she hated to admit it, Opal's words cut deeply into the delightful dreams she'd been weaving around Tom McLeod. She'd been imagining he was sweet on her—and more. She'd been wanting things that could never be, could never come true. Her sister was right.

A few minutes later, Opal got up from the stool and slipped into one of her flamboyant gowns. Then she splashed on a heavy dose of her favorite cologne.

"Fanny, you get out o' that bed an' be ready to leave if I come up with a visitor," she said as she crossed the room, pausing at the door, "or I guarantee you, Grady's gonna be in here demandin' that you pack up and get out for good."

The door closed soundly behind her, and Fanny was left alone with the cloying fragrance of lilies of the valley.

She made no sound as she cried. She'd learned to do that a long time ago, cry without letting anybody know. It was habit now. But what she really wanted to do was scream and rage. Only that wouldn't do any good either.

Finally, she got out of bed and walked over to her sister's dressing table. She stood there, staring at her reflection in the glass.

Her brown hair hung limply down to her shoulders. Her milk-white skin was marred by a smattering of freckles across her nose. Her eyes were too big; her mouth was too small. She was skinny and flat-chested, without any sort of curves. She'd always been glad of it, especially when she had to work downstairs serving drinks. Why would any man take a look at her when he could have one of the dolled-up hurdy-gurdy girls with their bosoms hanging half out of their dresses?

And why would Tom McLeod take any notice of Fanny Irvine either? He was going to be a doctor. He'd be finding himself a girl from a fine family, a girl with an education and good manners, a girl who could talk

141

properly, a pretty girl with shiny hair and nice clothes, a girl who was all the things Fanny wasn't.

She sank onto the stool as tears ran down her cheeks a second time.

It hurt. It hurt real bad.

Jeremiah tromped through the new-fallen snow on his way back from the telegraph office. He was finding there was plenty of paperwork a deputy had to see to, even without any kind of trouble in town. He'd been amazed to learn he actually didn't mind the paperwork. In truth, he found it kind of interesting. It was a whole lot better than assembling motors in a factory or laying railroad track or living in an army tent in the tropics.

He opened the door to the sheriff's office, then stamped his feet a time or two to shake loose the snow before stepping inside. When he looked up, he found Sarah sitting near his desk, the familiar picnic basket with its red-and-white-checkered cloth on the floor beside her.

"Hello," he said, surprised. For some reason, he hadn't expected her to deliver his lunch today as she had every other day this week.

Or maybe he just hadn't wanted her to bring it after the images that had haunted his thoughts last night.

"I brought your lunch."

He shrugged out of his coat and hung it on a hook. "So I see."

"I . . ." She rose from her chair, looking as lovely as he'd ever seen her. "I'm to tell you Grampa wants you to have one of the mattresses we've got in the attic. And a lamp, too."

"That's kind of him."

She picked up the basket and set it on his desk. "It's just cold sandwiches again and a jar of peaches. And a few of the cookies I made for the Christmas social at the church on Saturday."

"You really don't have to do this, you know." He crossed the room. "Bring me lunch, I mean. I could eat over at the hotel or at Zoe's Restaurant."

"I want to do it." Sarah glanced up and their eyes met. Her cheeks looked flushed, her eyes bright. "After all, you took this job just to pay Warren for the farm." Her voice softened. "I know you didn't have to do it. I know your father left the farm to you, not to Warren."

Jeremiah shrugged. "I needed something to keep me busy till the thaw comes. Besides, it's only fair Warren gets half. You two will need it to help get you started after you're married." He sat down behind the desk.

"I suppose."

He thought of the years he'd struggled to make the tiny farm in Ohio succeed. "Trust me." He reached for one of the sandwiches. "You will."

"Warren only wants the money so we can take a wedding trip back east. Philadelphia and New York." Sarah sank onto the chair opposite Jeremiah. "It seems rather selfish, making you take a job just so we can travel."

He met her gaze once again. "You don't want the trip?"

"I thought I did," she replied in a hushed tone.

He was strangely disquieted by the look that passed over her face. He dropped his gaze to the food. "I never found much to my liking back there myself." He took a bite of his sandwich.

"I've always wanted to go to those places. Philadelphia and New York, I mean. The *Ladies Home Journal* has so many stories about those cities and the people who live there. It all seems so . . . so exciting and wonderful."

"Mmm." Even if his mouth hadn't been full of food, he wouldn't have said anything. What could he say? That she was sorely mistaken about how exciting and wonderful those cities were? That most people never saw the swells of society? That most people lived in closed-in, rat-infested tenements, worked in factories where they roasted in the summer and froze in the winter, and died without hardly anybody knowing or caring they were dead?

Let her have her dreams, he thought, purposely keeping his gaze trained on the food set before him.

"Jeremiah?"

He kept chewing.

"Haven't you any good memories about the years you were away?"

He couldn't stop himself from looking up any more than he could stop himself from answering her. "Yes . . ." He pictured Millie in his head. "I've got a few."

Her expression was soft, caring. "Tell me about her. I'm sure I must have known Millie when I was little, just as I must have known you. But I don't remember. Tell me about her."

His appetite was gone. Of all people, he didn't want to discuss Millie with Sarah. He couldn't say why. He just knew it was true.

He wrapped the rest of the sandwich in the cloth and set it back into the basket, followed by the unopened jar of peaches. "I've got work to do, Sarah. I'd better get to it." He rose from his chair, leaving no doubt that she was being dismissed.

When he would have handed her the basket, she waved her hand. "No, you'll be hungry later. Just keep it here." She, too, rose from her chair. As she pulled on her cloak, she said, "I'm sorry for prying, Jeremiah. I . . . didn't mean to."

"I know," he admitted.

Like a coward, he remained behind his

desk as Sarah walked across the room and let herself out.

As she disappeared from view, Jeremiah realized why he didn't want to talk about Millie with Sarah McLeod. Because Sarah had opened a door in his heart that had stayed closed for many years, a place only Millie had ever entered, a place that had been empty and cold for far too long. Sarah had opened the door, but she could not come in because she didn't belong there.

She belonged with his brother.

Chapter Thirteen

Friday dawned with a light cloud cover and the first temperatures above freezing the valley had enjoyed in over two weeks. It was a good day for the annual trek to find the perfect Christmas tree.

Bundled in her warmest, fur-lined cloak, a hood covering her head and her hands tucked into a fur muff, Sarah left the mercantile and hurried along the boardwalk toward the hotel. She was just passing the livery stable when the oversized door opened and Jeremiah rode out astride a large buckskin gelding. He reined in when he saw her.

The horse snorted and bobbed his head impatiently, his breath making tiny clouds beneath his nostrils.

Sarah's heart did a tiny skip at the sight

of man and beast. They seemed such a well-suited pair, both of them powerful and restive. She hadn't realized it until now, but she'd been hoping to see him, watching for him as she'd walked through town. In fact, it seemed he'd been in her thoughts more often than not. Certainly more often than was proper.

"Morning, Sarah." He touched the brim of his hat. His words were polite, but his tone was cool, distant.

She offered a tiny smile. "Good morning, Jeremiah. Are you on your way out of town?"

It was a ridiculous question. Where else would he be going on horseback? She'd asked it only to have a reason to stand there and talk to him. She wondered if her motives were as obvious to him. She hoped not.

"Out to the farm," he answered. "I need to bring back a few more things."

She tried to think of something else to ask him but failed. Finally, she said, "The Raffertys are taking me with them to bring back our Christmas trees. We'll go right by your farm on our way to the mountains. Perhaps we'll see you on the road."

She started forward again, then paused, suddenly remembering what she wished to know. She looked up at him a second time. "We'll see you at the Christmas social tomorrow night, won't we?" When he didn't answer immediately, she added, "You'd be missed if you weren't there."

He stared down at her, his eyes unreadable, his expression unfathomable. When he answered, he sounded more resigned than anything. "I'll be there."

I'm glad. I'd miss you.

There. She'd admitted it. At least to herself. She was the one who would miss Jeremiah if he didn't come. It didn't really matter to her if others missed him or not. *She* would miss him. *She* wanted him to be there.

Perhaps he would ask her to dance. Perhaps he would take her in his arms for a waltz while an orchestra played Tchaikovsky or Strauss. She could almost see a glorious chandelier overhead, ablaze with light. She could imagine Jeremiah wearing a fine suit and gloves. She could see herself in a satin gown with a long train and . . .

"Sarah!"

She heard Warren calling her name, but she was reluctant to turn away from Jeremiah, reluctant to give up the pleasant daydream she'd been spinning in her head. She wanted to savor these strange, unfamiliar feelings that coursed through her. She wanted to keep looking at Jeremiah, this private enigma of a man. She wanted to keep feeling the things that just looking at him made her feel. She wanted . . .

"Sarah!"

Containing a frustrated sigh, she turned around.

"Couldn't you hear me calling you?" Warren asked as he hurried toward her.

"No, I'm sorry," she lied. "I couldn't."

Warren glanced toward Jeremiah and gave him a quick nod of acknowledgment, then returned his gaze to Sarah. "You'd better come along. The Raffertys are ready to leave. They're waiting for you."

"You're not coming?" She was ashamed of the sense of relief that washed over her.

He shook his head. "I got a new order in from Boise today. I can't waste my time on Christmas trees when there's an important order to fill."

Jeremiah nudged his horse forward. "I'd better be on my way. Have fun, Sarah."

"I will."

Warren took her arm and propelled her along the boardwalk, scolding mildly. "You know, you really should try to be on time, Sarah. Benjamin and Sophia are anxious to be under way. You know how impatient children can be, especially this time of year."

She swallowed an irritated retort.

"I do have some exciting news to share with you," he went on, not reading her mood. "I've received a telegram from Mr. Kubicki. He's made me an offer to form a partnership. He'd like me to come down to Boise City to talk to him and discuss the terms."

"How nice." She wanted to turn and look

behind her. She wanted to watch Jeremiah as he rode out of town.

"Sarah, you don't understand what I'm telling you. A partnership in Boise. We could live right in the capital city. My business would double, triple. We could have a fine house right in town. It's an opportunity of a lifetime."

She looked at him. "Leave Homestead?" she asked, incredulous. "But you've never mentioned such a thing before."

"What's to keep us here? It's an opportunity too good to pass up. You'd learn to like it in Boise."

What's to keep us here? What about her grandfather, her brother, her home? "What about all your plans to fix up Grampa's house? I thought you wanted to live there and turn the house into a showplace for your furniture." She paused, then asked softly, "Isn't this something we should decide together, Warren?"

"Don't worry. I'll let you know what I think we should do as soon as I get back. You'll have plenty of time to pack for a move to Boise beforehand."

She was stunned into utter silence. He didn't care what she thought. He didn't care what she wanted or didn't want to do. *He* would make the decision, and *she* was expected to follow.

"A woman must learn to live with a man's peculiarities, Sarah. Remember his

good points and don't dwell on his bad. Warren will be your husband, and your place will be at his side."

She remembered her grandmother's advice, but this time she couldn't heed it. Not with Warren. Not when she didn't love him. Not when it was another man who filled her thoughts.

Perhaps she would have said something right then and there if Michael Rafferty hadn't hailed them.

"Mornin'!" he called. "Have you decided to join us after all, Warren?"

"Afraid not. Too much work to do. But I've brought Sarah along. I found her talking to my brother over near the livery. Lord knows when she would have arrived if I hadn't gone after her."

It was all Sarah could do to keep silent, but now wasn't the time to say the things she knew must be said. Not with Michael and Rose and their children listening.

She would wait and call off the wedding in private.

It didn't take Rose long to sense Sarah's unhappiness. She suspected that Sarah and Warren had had an argument, and from the look on Sarah's face, it had been a serious one.

Determined to make her young friend forget her problems and enter into the spirit of the occasion, Rose carried on a lively, if one-sided, conversation. She talked about Lark's new baby boy, then mentioned the possibility of the Raffertys going to San Francisco for a month in the spring, followed by all the latest gossip she'd learned during her last visit to the mercantile.

"Leslie tells me our new deputy has set up housekeeping over the jail," she said as she leaned forward to tuck the lap robe more tightly about Sophia's legs. "It can't be very comfortable, but I suppose Jeremiah's used to making do."

Sarah turned to look at Rose. "Was his life very hard before?"

"I'm not sure what you mean."

"Well . . ." Sarah seemed to consider her words carefully, then continued. "I guess what I really want is for you to tell me what you remember of Jeremiah—and Warren—when they were boys."

"What I remember? My, it's so long ago." She searched her memory for some stories she thought would interest Sarah, but there seemed so few. "Warren and I were in school together. He was simply one of the boys. You know how it was in school. The boys kept to themselves, the girls to ourselves. At least until you get old enough to want to be noticed." She smiled. "But Jeremiah . . . He left Homestead so long ago."

"Do you remember his wife?"

"Millie?" Rose smiled. "Yes, I remember Millie. She was the sweetest person, but very shy. I remember how surprised folks were when Jeremiah started courting her. He had always been the sort to get into trouble. Smoking behind the school outhouse. Skipping school to go fishing. That sort of thing. Nothing serious. Just pranks, but the kind that got him into more than his share of trouble." She shook her head. "Nobody would have ever thought Millie Parkerson would take a shine to Jeremiah, but she did."

"They eloped?"

"Yes. If my memory serves, they wanted to get married and settle here, but his pa wouldn't hear of it. Millie's widowed ma wasn't too keen on the notion either. Millie was only sixteen, and Mrs. Parkerson wanted them to wait. Next thing everybody knew, they ran off together."

Sarah turned to look at the passing landscape, and her words were muffled by the wind. "She must have loved him a great deal."

"Yes, I'm sure she did."

Sarah was silent for some time before returning her gaze to Rose. "Tell me more about Lark's new baby," she said, changing the subject abruptly.

Rose was happy to oblige. She loved talking about babies, especially now that she knew she would be holding one of her own before summer's end.

*   *   *

Jeremiah built a fire in the stove and stood near it until the room began to warm, his thoughts on a golden girl in a silver-gray cloak, white fur framing her pretty face. And in his mind, he slowly removed the cloak, slowly pulled the pins from her hair. In his mind, he drew her close and savored the sweetness he knew he would find in her soft, pink mouth.

He swore beneath his breath. Was there nothing decent left in him? Could he sink any lower than this? How long after Warren and Sarah were married would he continue to lust after his brother's wife?

He swore a second time and turned away from the stove. How had this happened? It was such a short time since he'd first arrived in Homestead and had felt the rightness of his decision to come back. And now he wondered if he'd be able to stay.

His gaze moved slowly over the room.

What do I do now, Millie?

He no longer expected an answer, that familiar, quiet whisper in his heart, but it was habit to ask after so many years. He listened, hoping he would find some words of wisdom to guide him.

There were none.

Sarah joined the children on the bobsled while Rose watched and Michael chopped down the first of two trees they'd selected. The hill wasn't terribly steep, but it was swift. Sarah screamed and laughed right along with Benjamin and Sophia as they swooshed down the slope, snow blowing up in their faces. When the sled came to a halt, she was panting as if she'd run a race.

"Let's do it again," Sophia said as she scrambled to her feet.

Benjamin grabbed the rope at the front of the sled. "Yes, let's."

"I'm willing," Sarah replied, starting up the hill even as she spoke.

A flake landed on her nose, and she glanced upward, surprised to discover it was beginning to snow. She had thought it too warm to snow today.

By the time the bobsled had carried the trio to the bottom of the hill the second time, large flakes were falling steadily. After their third run, the snowfall had become so dense it was difficult to see the horses and sleigh at the top of the hill. The temperature dropped fast as the wind rose in a sheer whistle.

"Come along," Sarah said to the children as they started to trudge up the hill. "I think we'd better get back to your mother so she doesn't worry."

They found Michael dragging the second tree to the sleigh. Sarah hurried to help him load it onto the bed and tie it on. She saw his concern as he glanced upward.

"We'd better hurry," he said as their gazes met. "This looks like it could turn into a bad one."

In a matter of minutes, everyone was back

in the sleigh, lap robes wrapped tightly about them, but by then it was difficult for Sarah to see two feet in front of her face. She felt a thrill of alarm as she wondered how the horses would ever find their way safely down the mountain.

Warren rose from his workbench to stretch his muscles. When he turned, he was surprised to see snow falling outside. Surprise turned to concern when he saw the intensity of the storm. He crossed the shop to stand before the window, peering outside. He could hear the wind beginning to rise.

Damn, if this turned into a real blizzard, the train probably wouldn't make it up this way, and he'd have to postpone his trip to Boise City.

He started to turn back to his workbench when a second thought occurred to him. Sarah and the Raffertys were out in this. He leaned toward the glass. He couldn't even see the hotel across the street.

He hoped they were on their way home. If they were still up on the mountainside . . .

Tom McLeod had his nose buried in a medical journal when his grandfather knocked on his bedroom door. He removed his reading glasses as he looked up.

Hank's face was furrowed with concern. "Have you looked outside?"

"No." He turned his head and gazed at a

sheet of white. "Wow! I haven't seen snow like that in years." He rose from his chair and walked to the window. "Whew! It's a real Idaho blizzard."

"Sarah's out in it."

Gads! He'd completely forgotten.

Tom turned to meet his grandfather's gaze. "She's with Mr. Rafferty. He'll take care of her."

He turned as his grandfather stepped up beside him, and both of them stared outside at the driving snow.

Jeremiah wasn't sure how long he'd slept. He remembered lying down on the bed, not because he'd been physically tired but because he'd been mentally worn out by his troubled thoughts. He'd thrown an arm over his eyes, as if to shut out the world. Sometime after that, he'd fallen asleep.

He was surprised by the darkness in the room when he awakened. Upon looking outside, he discovered why and knew he wouldn't be going back to town until the storm had blown itself out.

Sarah. Had she and the Raffertys returned to town before the storm began? If they were still up on the mountain in this . . .

For a moment, he considered going out to look for them, but he knew immediately how foolish the idea was. He couldn't see his own outbuildings in this blizzard. He would be lost before he made it fifty yards.

Besides, Michael Rafferty had impressed Jeremiah as a sensible man. Michael would know what to do to protect his family and Sarah. They most likely were all back in Homestead, seated beside a nice, warm fire. He was worrying needlessly. Sarah was fine.

Like a banshee, the wind wailed down out of the mountains. The snow was blinding, stinging their faces and eyes as they huddled together in the sleigh. When the horses refused to move, Michael got out to lead the team.

"I'm scared!" Sophia cried to her mother, clutching at her coat.

"I know, honey," Rose shouted close to her daughter's ear, "but we're going to be all right. Your pa will make sure of that."

Sarah was just about to add her own words of reassurance when the sleigh suddenly tipped sideways, pitching her out into a world where there seemed to be no earth or sky. Only snow. Everywhere snow.

Her hands reached out to grab hold of something, anything. She slipped and tumbled and rolled, helpless, out of control. Down and down and down she fell.

And then, an eternity later, she stopped with a jarring *thump*. She waited several moments to collect herself, drawing long, deep breaths into her lungs. Finally, her legs trembling, she struggled to her feet.

"Michael!" she shouted. "Rose!"

The wailing wind was her only reply.

Chapter Fourteen

"Rose!" Michael scrambled frantically toward the overturned sleigh. "Rose! Sophie!" He slipped, fell, got up again. "Ben! Sarah!"

"We're here, Michael. We're all right. The children are with me."

He couldn't see them. He couldn't see anything. But now he could hear Sophia crying.

"Be careful," Rose called as he drew closer.

The ground fell out from under him even as she spoke. He grabbed hold of the sleigh just in time to save himself from sliding down the mountainside.

"Are you hurt?" He felt his way forward on hands and knees.

"No. No, I think we're all right."

He reached his huddled family. Squinting his eyes against the blinding snow, he touched his wife's cheek with his fingertips. "The baby?"

"I'm fine, Michael, but what about Sarah? I don't know where she is."

"Dear God," he whispered. The moaning wind caught his prayer and whipped it away. He raised himself up on his knees and cupped his hands near his mouth. "Sarah!" he shouted. "Sarah!"

He waited, listening, straining to hear a response, but there was nothing.

He looked back toward his wife and children. "Sit still while I get the sleigh righted. Don't move until I say it's all right. We've got to get off this mountain."

"Michael! We can't leave without her."

"We don't have any choice. I've got to get you and the children to safety."

"I won't go without her," Rose returned stubbornly.

Michael was torn. He didn't want to tell her they were likely to all freeze to death if they didn't get out of the storm soon. He didn't want to frighten Rose and the children. On the other hand, she was right about Sarah. If they left now, they might not find her until the spring thaw.

He winced at his negative, if realistic, thought. If Sarah were hurt and unable to answer, she would probably die before anybody could find her. But Michael Rafferty knew his wife. She said she wouldn't budge and she probably wouldn't, not if he didn't at least try to find Sarah.

"Sit still," he repeated.

He crawled back to the sleigh, then stood up. Working blind in the driving snow, he freed the ropes that bound the pine trees to the bed. After dragging them free of the vehicle, he threw his weight against the over-turned sleigh, pushing until it righted itself.

He grabbed one of the ropes and tied one end to the sleigh, the other end around his waist. That done, he turned and made his way back to his family.

"Come on. Let's get you away from this hillside."

"Michael, I—"

"It's all right. I'm going to look for her. Now come on." He drew Sophia out of Rose's arms and held his daughter against his side. Then he reached down for his wife's hand. "Hold onto Ben and stay close to me," he said as he pulled her to her feet.

Slowly, carefully, they made their way back to the sleigh. Michael set Sophia on the seat, then lifted his son up beside the girl.

"Wrap up in those lap robes," he told them. Then, turning to his wife, he said, "You'd better go up with the horses, keep them calm. I'm going to lower myself down the side of the mountain. I'll go as far as the rope will allow. But, Rose, if I don't find her soon, we've got to go without her. There's nothing else we can do." He leaned forward and pressed his cheek against hers, saying, "If anything happens to me, you get the children to safety. Do you hear me? You don't come after me. Just take care of yourself and the children."

Battered by a wind that seemed to fly at her from every direction, Sarah stumbled forward. Time and again, she fell into deep drifts. The hem of her skirt was encrusted with ice. It dragged at her legs like a heavy weight, making every step more difficult than the last. She hugged herself, desperate for warmth and trying not to think about how cold she was.

She couldn't tell where she was. For all she knew, she was walking in circles. But her only hope was to find shelter, and so she kept moving, silently praying that God would guide her steps.

Tom hurried to answer the banging on the door. The moment he did, Warren stepped inside, covered from head to foot with snow.

He whipped off his hat. "They're not back. Nobody's seen hide nor hair of them."

Tom stared outside a moment, then closed the door. "It's going to be dark in a few hours. Shouldn't we be forming a search party?"

"To do what?" Warren asked. "We'd all

get lost in this. It's the worst storm I can remember."

Tom resented Warren's calm logic. He glanced over his shoulder at his grandfather who stood at the entrance to the living room. Hank's expression was grim. His lined face looked older than it had that same morning.

"Grampa?"

"I'm afraid Warren's right. It'd be suicide to go out in this now. We'll have to just sit tight until the storm lets up."

Tom paced angrily back into the living room. He walked to the window and stared out at the freezing tempest. He hated this feeling of helplessness. He wanted action. He wanted to do something. Sarah was out in this storm. Sarah, who had loved and spoiled him all the years they were growing up. If anything happened to his sister . . .

Hank crossed the room to stand beside him. He placed a hand on Tom's shoulder, squeezing lightly with his fingers. "Not much more we can do for now but pray, boy."

"But . . ." He glanced at his grandfather.

Tears shone in the old man's gray eyes. "I know, Tom. I know."

Rose could scarcely feel her fingers inside her gloves. She held them beneath the horse's nostrils, hoping the animal's breath would warm them, if only slightly.

But worse than the cold was the icy fear that taunted her. Where was Michael? Why hadn't he come back? Had the rope broken? Had he become separated somehow? Was he wandering away from them even now, blinded by the storm? Or worse still, was he lying somewhere, hurt, maybe dying?

She wanted to leave her place in front of the team of horses. She wanted to go pull on the rope. And what of the children? She couldn't see them. Couldn't hear them above the wind. Were they all right?

Calm down, Rose.

Taking a deep breath, she followed her own order. She refused to panic. Michael had never let her down. Never once in all the years she'd known him. He'd be back. He'd get them all safely home.

As if in answer to her thoughts, he appeared suddenly beside her.

"Michael!" She threw herself into his arms. "Oh, Michael, I was so frightened." She leaned back to look at him. His face was covered with snow. Icy crystals clung to his eyelashes and eyebrows.

"There's no sign of Sarah anywhere," he said, holding Rose tightly against him. "We can't wait any longer. We've got to get out of this or die."

"I know. I know."

She felt like crying, but she held back the tears. She had to think about Michael and Benjamin and Sophia. She couldn't let anything happen to her beloved family.

God, watch over Sarah, wherever she is.

*   *   *

Sarah wanted to lie down and rest, just for a moment. She was so tired. So very, very tired. But she knew that if she did, she might never get up again.

She'd left the mountains and trees behind her some time before. She wasn't certain if that was good or bad. It seemed the wind and snow blew even harder on the valley floor. Although the land was flat instead of rugged, the drifts were deeper and the air was colder.

If she could only reach one of the farmhouses . . .

Helplessness nearly overwhelmed her. She could have already passed one, maybe more. She could have walked within a few feet of a front door and never known it. She couldn't see. She couldn't see anything.

Tears welled in her eyes. They were warm, she thought. How could her tears be warm when everything else about her was so bitterly cold?

Suddenly, she tripped and fell face first into a deep drift. She tried to get to her feet, then fell again.

"I can't," she choked. "I can't do it." Turning her face up toward the sky, she shouted at the heavens, "I can't do it!"

Her anger had stolen the last of her strength. Giving up, she meekly accepted her fate as she curled into a ball and let the snow blow over her.

*   *   *

Holding on to the rope he'd tied between the house and the shed, Jeremiah went to check on his horse. He noticed that the snow drifts were nearly halfway up to the roof on the west side of the small barn, and there was still no sign of the storm abating.

He paused in the barn doorway and glanced in the direction of the mountains. Had she made it down before the storm? he wondered. Was Sarah safe at home even now?

He shook his head, driving away his troubled thoughts as he entered the barn, closing the door behind him.

He tossed more straw into the stall, then brought the buckskin some oats. "We may be here awhile, fella," he said as the horse buried his muzzle in the bucket and chomped contentedly, unconcerned by the blizzard raging beyond the protective walls of his humble shelter.

When the horse was finished eating, Jeremiah broke the ice that had formed in the water trough. Finally, having done all he could to protect his horse, he pulled the collar of his coat up and yanked his hat down tight over his ears before venturing back into the storm.

He didn't know what caused him to stop before he reached the house. He didn't know what made him turn and stare off into the blinding snow. He couldn't see anything. He couldn't even see the barn he'd left only moments before.

Sarah.

He shook his head. He must be getting cabin fever. There was nothing out there but wind and snow. Michael had cut his Christmas trees and taken Sarah and the others back to Homestead. There was no reason for him to be thinking about her now.

He started forward, then stopped again. He knew he was just imagining it, but he could've sworn it had sounded like a woman crying.

The wind. Just the wind.

Once again, he started toward the house, and once again, he thought he heard crying, soft, gentle sobbing. Impossible. He couldn't have heard anything above the noise of the storm. He stopped and gazed off into the blowing snow.

But what if it wasn't just the wind? What if Sarah and the Raffertys hadn't gotten off the mountain before the storm? What if she was out there, alone and in trouble?

Unable to prevent himself, he returned to the barn for another rope and tied it to the fence post near the corner of the barn. Holding on to the other end, he headed blindly forward.

"Hello! Is anybody there?"

He held an arm up to shield his face as he peered into the storm. He walked as far as the rope would allow.

"Hello! Can you hear me? Is anybody there?"

Only the wind replied.

He turned, ready to retrace his steps back to the house. Something tripped him, and he nearly lost his grasp on the rope as he dropped to his knees.

And that was how he found her, curled tight against herself, unmoving, as still as death. Somehow he knew, before he brushed the snow away to reveal the silver-gray cloak, that it was Sarah. Something in his heart had told Jeremiah she needed him.

Jeremiah carried Sarah back to the house, his heart pumping furiously in his chest. Once inside, he took her over to the stove and laid her on the floor, as close to the heat as he could safely put her.

Was she alive?

He brushed the snow from her face. She looked so pale and still. She didn't move at all. He leaned his head close to hers. For a moment, he feared the worst. Then he felt the warmth of her breath against his cheek.

"Thank God," he whispered as he straightened.

He shucked off his coat and set to work. He had to get her out of her wet things. He had to get her warm and dry. Every minute, every second, counted.

He pulled off her gloves and took a moment to rub her hands between his. Next he raised her torso off the floor, cradling her head against his chest as he maneuvered her out of her cloak. After that, he moved to her feet.

He cursed the laces on her boots, but eventually he managed to loosen them. He removed the sodden, ice-encrusted shoes and tossed them toward the stove. Her stockings were damp and stiff. Working quickly, he shoved her frozen skirts upward, then rolled her stockings down her legs. As he'd done with her hands, he rubbed her feet and ankles, stimulating the blood, hoping to warm her more quickly.

She'd begun to shiver by this time, and as the moments passed, the shivering became more violent. He knew he had to get her warm, and he had to do it quickly.

There was only one thing he could think to do.

With deliberate swiftness, Jeremiah re-moved the rest of her clothing, right down to her chemise and drawers. Then he hesitated.

Was he certain what he was doing? he wondered.

He glanced at her face. She was deathly pale. Her teeth rattled as shivers shook her body. Touching her skin was like touching ice. That made up his mind. The last of the cold, damp garments were added to the pile of discarded clothing. Then he lifted Sarah into his arms and carried her to the bed.

As soon as he'd laid her down, he removed his own boots, shirt, and pants. Clad in his long underwear and socks, he crawled into the bed beside her, pulled the layers of blankets over them both, and cradled her against him.

Several times during the long night that followed, Jeremiah rose and added wood to the stove, keeping the fire hot and the house as warm as possible. Then he returned to the bed and gathered Sarah once again into his arms.

It had been a long time since he'd held a woman in his arms this way, wanting nothing from her, wanting only to shelter, protect, comfort. He hid his face in her cloud of silvery-gold hair and willed her to be well. It would be unthinkable for Sarah not to get well. Sarah was too beautiful, too full of life, to have it all taken away from her.

As the minutes and hours ticked by, Jeremiah felt the loneliness of his existence like a stab wound in his chest, and holding Sarah was like a salve to that wound. There was a small part of him that wished the storm would go on forever, a small part of him that wished he could stay in this bed, holding Sarah in his arms, for an eternity, keeping the wretched loneliness at bay.

He knew that keeping her with him was an impossibility. She belonged to Warren. Jeremiah had no right to hold her against him, to feel her softness, to smell the clean scent of her hair. If she hadn't become lost in a blizzard, he wouldn't be holding her now.

But for this one night, while she remained asleep and unaware, Jeremiah allowed himself to admit how wonderful it would be to have the right to hold Sarah as he was holding her now.

As the night stretched on and still she didn't awaken, Jeremiah became afraid. Nothing he was doing, nothing he had done, had made any difference.

"Sarah," he whispered into her hair, "you've got to fight. You've got to live."

That was when he began to pray.

Jeremiah had given up praying after Millie died. God hadn't listened to the frantic prayers of a young husband for his wife and unborn child. Jeremiah had watched Millie suffer. He'd watched her die. He'd buried her. And he'd decided the Almighty didn't care.

Now there was another young woman who needed Jeremiah, and he was just as helpless as before. There was nowhere else to turn.

So he prayed, begging God's mercy for the still, cold woman in his arms while beyond the walls of the house the storm raged on.

Chapter Fifteen

Sarah dreamed of angels with flowing white gowns and enormous ivory wings. She dreamed they swept down from the heavens and carried her out of the cold and into a place of warmth. It was a lovely dream.

Still in a state of half-sleep, she realized at last it wasn't a dream. At least, not all of it. She *was* warm. She could hear the shrieking of the wind, but it seemed distant, faraway, unable to touch her while she was surrounded by such delicious warmth. She snuggled closer to the source, not wanting to awaken just yet, not caring what was reality or what was merely illusion.

And then she felt the touch of a hand upon her back, moving slowly along her spine.

She held her breath, coming abruptly and completely awake but not daring to move, not daring to open her eyes. She listened, first to the wind outside, then to the steady breathing beside her.

Memories of her ordeal in the blizzard returned. She remembered the hours of looking for shelter. She remembered the moment she'd given up and lain down in the snow, not caring if she lived or died. That was the last she remembered.

She felt the hand continue to move up her back, then change direction and follow the same path down. Fingertips upon bare skin. A *man's* fingertips on her bare skin.

She opened her eyes slowly.

The anemic light of early morning, dimmed further by the falling snow beyond the window, revealed a small bedroom. She was in a house. But whose house?

Her pulse raced and her heart pounded in her chest. She feared that its thundering would awaken the man who held her so close in his embrace.

What had happened? How had she come to be here?

Moving with care, she tipped her head back until she could look at him. A tiny gasp escaped her lips at the moment of recognition.

Jeremiah's hand stilled as he opened his eyes. Their gazes locked, but he said nothing. They simply stared at

174

each other for what seemed an eternity.

His face was darkened by the shadow of a beard. His black hair was disheveled, wild and untamed. Looking at him, she felt a strange quickening inside her.

She should have known it would be Jeremiah who would rescue her. From the first moment she'd seen him, standing in the doorway of her home, she had felt a connection with him, as if she'd known him forever. It was as if he actually were her imaginary count come to life.

That thought made her smile.

In response, Jeremiah's arms tightened around her. She watched his mouth drawing near but felt no anxiety. She waited, hoping beyond hope his kiss would be all she'd dreamed a kiss could be.

It was even more.

His mouth plied hers with tenderness, but her reaction was earth-shattering, completely beyond anything she'd ever expected. Her entire body was afire from it.

There was no panic, no feeling that she couldn't breathe as she had always felt with Warren. She didn't want to pull away or escape. She wanted only to feel more, to do more. This was exactly what she'd been longing for. *This!*

Sarah tilted her head slightly to better receive the ministrations of his mouth upon hers. The kiss deepened, and a small moan vibrated in her throat. She reveled in the taste of him, the smell of him, the feel of him. She took strange pleasure in the sounds he made, soft, urgent, unintelligible sounds.

Rocked by a thousand foreign sensations, she clung to him with a fierceness she'd never known. She heard the soft voice of conscience bidding her to have a care, to stop before she did something she would later regret.

But she ignored the warning.

Jeremiah knew that what he was doing was wrong.

All through the night, he had held Sarah, offering her the heat of his body and nothing more. There was nothing sexual in his actions. When he'd touched her bare back, he'd thought only of keeping her warm, making her well. He hadn't expected everything to change so abruptly. He hadn't planned to kiss her, nor had he expected this sudden and overwhelming flare of desire when he did.

Where rational thought still existed, he recognized he was being unfair to Sarah. She was too innocent to know what she was doing, but he knew. He knew he should break the kiss, take her arms from around his neck. He knew he should get out of the bed.

Now. Before it was too late.

But he couldn't. He couldn't stop himself from tasting the sweet nectar of her mouth, from teasing her lips with his tongue until they parted for him. He couldn't stop himself from tangling his fingers in her silken hair. He couldn't stop himself from pressing his body against hers, from feeling her move instinctively against him.

She stirred emotions within him that had slumbered much too long. It was more than just a desire to couple with a woman. Much more.

He began to stroke her back with his hand again. He'd done it throughout the night in an effort to drive away the cold that had threatened her life. But she didn't need to be warmed any longer. Her skin felt heated, as did his own.

He shifted, rolling her onto her back and turning himself on his right side, supporting his weight with his elbow. He released her mouth and trailed kisses down her neck to the most tender part of her throat. He laved her skin with his tongue, pressing against the pulse point, feeling the wild beating of her heart and knowing that his own beat in unison with it.

When she wriggled, he drew his left hand across her stomach and brought it to rest on her breast. She gasped in surprise. He rose up on his elbow again and looked down into her eyes.

She was young and naive and inexperienced. If he proceeded . . .

She ran her tongue across her lips and

pressed her body closer to his, undoing him completely, chasing his reason and conscience back into hiding.

Sarah felt the thrill of his mouth upon hers again, and when his hand began to knead her breast, she found the sensation to her liking as well.

Tentatively, she placed her left hand against his chest, wishing she could touch his skin rather than the fabric of his long underwear. She felt a wild and reckless need to get as close to him as possible.

He broke the kiss with an abruptness that alarmed her.

"Tell me to stop, Sarah," he whispered hoarsely. "Please. Tell me to stop now."

She shook her head, unable to speak. She didn't care if what they were doing was wrong. She only cared that Jeremiah never stop. She'd been waiting for him all her life. She didn't want him to stop now.

"Forgive me," he murmured as he sat up and turned his back to her.

She thought he was leaving her, and she felt a chill far worse than anything she'd felt in her hours of wandering, lost in the blizzard. But he didn't leave her. In what seemed no more than the blink of an eye, he shed his underclothes and returned to gather her into his embrace.

She knew a moment of panic as flesh pressed against flesh. She felt the differences in their bodies and was both frightened and intrigued by them.

And then he began to kiss her again, to caress her again, and she forgot her fears and uncertainties. She cared for nothing but the way he made her feel. She cared for nothing but this man.

Jeremiah . . .

When her passion had built to a crescendo and she thought she could take no more, Jeremiah covered her body with his own.

"Forgive me," he whispered again.

At the moment of their joining, she felt an unexpected pain. She cried out softly, and he stilled inside her. Then she discovered it was she who could not remain still. She had to move. She could not help herself.

Slowly but steadily, as he kissed and caressed and moved within her, her desire raged hotter and hotter until she thought she could bear no more. Finally, it seemed as if she were exploding from within, and somehow she knew it was happening to him, too.

Joy and passion infused her, tearing from her lips a cry of pleasure. Then, clinging to Jeremiah, she toppled off the ends of the earth.

Some time later, Jeremiah stared down at the sleeping young woman in his arms.

What have I done?

But he knew good and well what he had

done, and it couldn't be undone.

He slipped free, rose from the bed, and dressed. Then he left the bedroom. He added more wood to the dying fire to chase the increasing chill from the house. When the flames burned hot once again, he turned and walked to the window and stared outside.

The storm hadn't let up at all. Drifts of snow were piled high against the house. If it kept up like this for another twenty-four hours, they wouldn't be able to get out the front door.

He'd taken his brother's promised bride into his bed.

He closed his eyes, feeling shame wash over him.

He'd taken her innocence, her virginity.

Disgust at his lack of self-control overwhelmed him.

And she'd made him feel more alive than he'd felt in years.

How was he supposed to put things right?

"Jeremiah?"

He turned from the window to find her standing in the doorway, wrapped in a blanket. Her pale hair fell about her shoulders in enchanting disarray. Her blue eyes watched him with shy uncertainty and something else he couldn't quite read.

He wanted to tell her he was sorry, but the words stuck in his throat, in part because he felt an unexpectedly fierce jolt of desire. It took all his concentration to remain where he was when what he wanted most was to cross the room, carry her back to his bed, and make love to her again.

She dropped her gaze to the floor. "How did you find me? Out there, I mean."

He still couldn't answer. Besides, what would he tell her? That he'd sensed she needed him? That he'd been looking for her, wondering if she was safe? Maybe it was fate. Or perhaps it was mere chance. What difference did it make? He'd found her. He'd brought her into his house. He'd taken her into his bed.

He'd let her get close to his heart.

"You saved my life." She looked at him again, moving forward. "I'd given up hope, but you found me." She stopped, just a few feet away, her blue eyes unwavering as she stared up at him.

Once before, a girl had looked at him like that, with utter trust, believing he was something he wasn't. He recognized that look, and it struck a fear in him much worse than anything he'd been feeling already. Whatever nebulous thoughts of the future he might have entertained fled in terror. He could never be the man she thought he was, and he had to make it clear to her now, before it was too late for everyone.

He raked the fingers of both hands through his hair, then said in a cool voice, "No one need ever know what happened here, Sarah. You didn't know what you were doing. I'm all to blame. But if we say nothing, there'll be no harm to your reputation."

Her eyes widened.

He continued, his voice even more harsh. "You're engaged to my brother. The two of you are to be married in a week. Is it necessary for us to cause him grief over something that was an accident? It meant nothing to either of us. We weren't thinking straight. Desire can make people forget what is right. It meant nothing."

She took a quick step back, staring at him as if he'd struck her.

He flinched inwardly, seeing he'd hurt her, loathing himself for it. Loathing himself more because he knew he was lying. It *hadn't* meant nothing to him. For a moment, he'd felt . . . he'd felt something fill the emptiness of his heart.

He'd felt *Sarah* fill the emptiness of his heart.

But he was not the man she thought him. He could never be that man. Even more importantly, she belonged in another man's heart. She belonged to Warren.

He turned his back to her and stared with unseeing eyes at the wintry world beyond the glass. An eternity later, he heard her walk away, and finally the bedroom door closed, leaving him alone and empty once more.

Chapter Sixteen

The blizzard blew itself out after nearly twenty-two hours, and Tom had the search party organized before noon. By one o'clock, twelve men on snowshoes set out from Homestead to look for the Rafferty family and Sarah McLeod.

Holding the tattered remains of her pride about her like a shield, Sarah left the sanctuary of the bedroom, this time clad in her own clothes instead of a blanket. She held her head high, determined not to let Jeremiah see the pain in her heart.

He was standing at the window, just as he'd been when she'd left him several hours before. He turned when he heard her approach.

"The storm's broken," he said.

She nodded.

"It's time I took you home."

"Yes."

A lengthy silence stretched between them before Jeremiah asked, "How did you get to my place, Sarah? What happened to the Raffertys?"

"I don't know. The sleigh overturned up on the mountain, and I was pitched out. I couldn't find them again. I looked and looked and kept calling for them, but . . ." She glanced past him at the frozen landscape. "Do you think they're all right?"

"They may have found another farmhouse. Just like you ended up here." His words offered a bit of hope, but his expression belied it.

Sarah closed her eyes and felt the oppressive weight of guilt. When she'd been lying in Jeremiah's arms, reveling in the things he was making her feel, the Raffertys might well have been dying—and she hadn't even given them a thought. "I should have told you where they were as soon as I awakened. We should have gone after them."

"We couldn't have gone out in that storm. We'd've been lost before we'd gotten out of the yard."

Her gaze flicked toward the window. "Well, I'd like to go look for them now." *I don't care where we go as long as we leave here. I can't stay and have you look at me that*

184

way, as if you can't wait to be rid of me.

"You've been through a lot. I should take you home first. You shouldn't try to—"

"I'm going to look for them." She lifted her chin defiantly. "They're my friends. They need help. There's nothing wrong with me to keep me here. I'm perfectly fit and capable of going out to find them. I can't just leave them out there if . . . if that's where they are."

Jeremiah didn't attempt to dispute her wishes. "All right. I'll fix us something to eat; then we'll go." He gave her a hard glance. "But if we don't find any sign of them in the next couple of hours, we start back for Homestead. No arguments. Understood?"

Reluctantly: "Understood."

He pointed through the bedroom doorway at the chest of drawers. "You'll find some men's clothes in there. If we're going traipsing around the mountain, I want you dressed in something besides skirts and petticoats. Put on several layers. It's still plenty cold out."

Obediently, she crossed the room, then paused in the doorway and glanced over her shoulder. She hated to verbalize her fears, but she couldn't seem to help herself. "Do you think there's any chance they're alive?"

His expression softened. "I hope so, Sarah. I truly hope so."

The search party found the Raffertys in an abandoned shack at the base of the mountains. They were cold, but otherwise unharmed.

Sarah wasn't with them. Michael told Tom how she'd become separated from them the previous day. It wasn't said aloud, but no one believed she would be found alive. Not even her brother.

Jeremiah gave the buckskin a generous helping of oats before setting out with Sarah. He wouldn't be riding anywhere today. He and Sarah needed to move fast, and a horse sinking up to its belly in fresh, powdery snow would only hinder them.

Using the snowshoes he'd found in the shed, he led the way, shortening his strides to accommodate Sarah. They didn't talk. After all, what could they say to each other? He told himself over and over it would be better if they both forgot about last night, if they both pretended it had never happened.

But it was difficult to follow his own advice. Time and again, he pictured the way she'd looked in his arms, the way she'd felt, the way she'd moved and sighed, even the way she'd tasted. There had been a naturalness about her lovemaking that had delighted and excited him. There had been a rightness in their joining.

No! It hadn't been right! Nothing about it had been right, and he couldn't allow himself to think so, even for a moment. She was pledged to marry Warren. She *had* to marry

Warren, for both their sakes.

He remembered the way she'd looked at him when she'd followed him out of the bedroom, wrapped in that blanket. It was the starry-eyed look of a woman who saw only what she wanted to see, not what was really there. It was a look that struck terror in his soul. He wasn't that man. He never had been, and he never could be.

Millie had looked at him that way. Was it because he had been her first and only lover? Was that what made a woman look at a man as if he were bigger than life? As if he were a hero? Was that what made a woman trust a man with her heart, with her very existence?

Well, he had quickly disabused Sarah of the notion that there was anything noble or heroic about him, and he'd done it for her own good.

Six men left the search party to take the Raffertys back to Homestead. The other six—Tom McLeod, Warren Wesley, George Blake, Vince and Paul Stanford, and Chad Turner—pressed on up the mountain, calling for Sarah as they went.

She heard her name from a great distance. She stopped and listened. Yes, there it was again.

"Jeremiah, did you hear that?"

The look he gave her was blank, as if he'd been deep in thought.

"Someone's calling for me. Hurry. It must be Michael. They must be all right."

She moved ahead of him as quickly as the awkward snowshoes would allow, jogging across the snowy terrain, huffing and puffing as she went. For the moment, she forgot the torment of her heart. She stopped berating herself for the reckless things she'd done with Jeremiah and concentrated only on finding her friends.

Please, oh please, let them be all right. Let them be alive.

"Sarah!" The cry was closer this time. "Sarah!"

"I'm here!" she shouted. "Michael, I'm here! I'm all right!"

Her eyes searched the mountainside, trying to find some sign of Michael and the others.

"Sarah!"

This time she realized it wasn't Michael's voice she heard. It was Warren who was calling her name.

She stopped abruptly, turning her head to look behind her. Jeremiah was there. She could see by the grim expression on his darkly chiseled face that he, too, had recognized his brother's voice.

I don't love Warren, she told him with her eyes. *But I could love you, if only you'd let me. I could love you forever.*

He looked away from her, staring up the mountainside. He cupped a hand near his mouth and shouted, "She's here! Warren, she's here!"

And just like that, he gave her back to his brother.

She heard responding cries.

"She's found!"

"Over this way!"

"She's alive!"

Minutes later, she saw several men appear in various places along the mountainside, hurrying in her direction. Tom was in the lead.

She was sobbing by the time her brother reached her. He grabbed her in a tight embrace and held her close to him. She wept softly against the scratchy wool fabric of his coat, clinging to him with clenched fingers.

"We've been looking all over for you," Tom said as he rubbed her back, offering what comfort he could.

She sniffed as she pulled away from him. "Rose and Michael? The children?"

"They're safe. All of them."

Fresh tears began, and once again she pressed her face against Tom's coat.

Jeremiah spoke up. "I found her last night in a snowdrift near my farm. If I hadn't gone out to feed my horse when I did . . ." He let his words drift away, his meaning clearly understood.

Warren arrived just then. "Sarah?"

She looked up. "Hello, Warren."

"You had us worried half to death." He reached out as if to pull her into his arms, but instead merely patted her shoulder.

"I'm sorry."

"I knew I should have forbidden you to go," he muttered before giving her a perfunctory kiss on the cheek, all he had ever done in the company of others, all he would ever think to do.

She suddenly envisioned Jeremiah, gloriously nude, his body well muscled, his chest lightly covered with hair as black as that on his head. She thought of Jeremiah's kisses and the way his body had moved against hers.

But Jeremiah didn't want her. It had been only a rash moment of insanity. He would keep her terrible secret. He wanted her to marry Warren.

She fought a fresh onslaught of tears. "I'd like to go home," she managed to say, her throat painfully tight, her eyes burning.

"Of course." Warren looked from her to his brother. "It seems I have much to thank you for, Jeremiah."

She couldn't help herself. She turned to look behind her. For just a moment, their gazes met and held. She felt a new wave of confusion and pain washing over her.

Tom took hold of her arm. "Come on, sis. We'd better get you home."

*   *   *

Jeremiah decided not to return to town with the others. He made an excuse about going back for his horse. He would return to Homestead in the morning, he told them.

"There's gonna be plenty of celebratin' tonight," George Blake told him. "You'd best change your mind. Folks're gonna want to thank you for savin' Sarah's life. You'll be a hero 'round here for that."

A hero? Not for what he'd done. Not very damn likely.

Several of the other men echoed George's sentiments. Including Warren.

Jeremiah shook his head. "Sorry. I need to think about my horse."

He purposely didn't look at Sarah again. He wasn't sure he could stand it, seeing her tear-streaked cheeks, knowing how he'd hurt her.

As he walked home, his slight limp exacerbated by the bitter cold, he cursed himself for being every kind of fool. Hero? He'd rescued an innocent girl, and then he'd taken advantage of her. She hadn't known what she was doing. She hadn't been thinking straight. He should be shot for what he'd done. And if Hank McLeod ever found out, he didn't doubt he would be shot.

When he entered the house some time later, he halted immediately inside the door, his gaze locked on the entrance to the bedroom. He remembered the way Sarah had looked, standing there, wrapped in the blanket.

He remembered, and he cursed the day he'd returned to Homestead.

As night blanketed the valley, Sarah lay alone in her bedroom, the final farewells of the well-wishers ringing in the night air as they headed for their homes. She drew a ragged breath and let it out slowly. Beneath the blankets, her hands were clenched into tight fists, her nails biting into the flesh of her palms. She knew she had to hang on to her control just a little longer, just until her grandfather came to bid her good night.

Sure enough, she heard his soft rap on the door just before it creaked open, spilling golden lamplight across the floor.

"Are you still awake, princess?" he whispered.

"I'm awake, Grampa."

He entered, walked over to her bed, and sat on the edge beside her. He reached out with a gnarled hand and brushed strands of hair from her forehead. She could feel his quivering through his fingertips.

Hot tears burned her eyes and a thick lump formed in her throat. "I . . . I love you, Grampa." Her words were barely audible.

He remained silent for a long time before saying, "You'd tell me if you were feelin' poorly, wouldn't you, Sarah?"

"Doc said I'm fine, Grampa. I'll be up

in no time, just like he said. I'm fine. Really I am."

"Then is somethin' else troublin' you? You've looked so sad all day."

She shook her head, unable to speak the lie aloud. How could she tell Grampa what she had done? He was old and in poor health. Telling him would only serve to break his heart. He would be so disappointed, so ashamed of her.

"All right then. I won't mention it again. Just remember, I'm here if you need to talk." He leaned forward and kissed her brow. "You get plenty of rest, princess. You've been through quite an ordeal. Tom and I can shift for ourselves till you're up and around."

She nodded.

Her grandfather patted her shoulder, then rose from the bed and left the room, whispering, "Good night," before he closed the door.

Good night, Grampa, she mouthed, her throat too thick with tears to speak it aloud.

Rolling onto her side, she covered her face with her hands and gave herself permission to cry, while promising herself that, after tonight, she would not cry again over what had happened.

Then, as exhausted tears carried her toward sleep, she whispered, "Good night, Jeremiah," and left him with her heart.

Chapter Seventeen

Sarah remained in bed throughout the following day. Tom and Grampa pampered her outrageously, bringing her hot tea and tempting her with delicious food. She did her best to please them by drinking and eating whatever they provided, but she tasted little that passed her lips.

Warren came to see her after church. He sat in a chair beside her bed, reaching forward to take hold of her hand. "I'm very grateful nothing happened to you out there, Sarah."

She wanted to die.

"I know I'm no good with words, Sarah, but I want you to know I was deeply concerned for your welfare. You're important to me. Our marriage is important to me."

Perhaps she would die.

He was silent for quite some time before speaking again. "I'm taking the train down to Boise City tomorrow to talk to Mr. Kubicki about his offer. I expect to be away several days." A small frown creased his brow. "I do hope Mr. Kubicki and I can come to an agreement. I think this move would be wise for us." He rose from his chair, leaned down, and kissed her on the lips.

She tried to feel something. She tried to summon all those wild, tumultuous sensations she knew she should feel.

She felt nothing except a desire for it to stop.

Warren straightened. "I'll call upon you as soon as I return. See that you get your rest. It wouldn't do for you to be sick for our wedding."

She nodded as she closed her eyes, feigning weariness, not opening them again until she heard the door close behind him.

Later in the afternoon, Tom told her Jeremiah had returned safely to town. "Grampa's gone over to the sheriff's office. He wants to thank Jeremiah for what he did for you."

"He would have done the same for anyone he found in a snowbank," she said, pleased that her voice sounded normal.

"Well, we're just glad it was you, sis. We don't know what we'd do without you. Any of us. Grampa, me, Warren. We'd all be lost without you."

After her brother left, she pondered his statement. Would they be lost without her? Grampa, perhaps. He was old and needed her help. But Tom was a self-reliant young man with a great future before him. He would be leaving Homestead in the spring. He would confidently make his own way in the world. He loved her, but he wouldn't be lost without her.

And Warren? What about him? He'd said she was important to him. But what exactly did that mean? He'd never professed to love her, and his displays of affection were always carefully controlled. He was certainly more apt to criticize than express approval. He belittled her daydreams. He thought many of her actions foolish or childish or both. He was irritated by her tardiness. He had never been interested in her opinions. Why, she wondered, did he want to marry her if all these things were true? And why had none of these things seemed so apparent to her before?

She should have told him she'd decided to call off the wedding. Two days ago, she'd been ready to tell him. She didn't love him, and whatever it was Warren felt for her, she was quite certain it wasn't love.

But Jeremiah didn't want her. He'd sent her back to Warren without a backward glance. His rejection of the love she had to offer him had left her confused and uncertain. She didn't know what to do anymore. She didn't know what to feel or what to say.

Lying there, overrun by troublesome thoughts, she recalled something Warren had said to her long ago. "It's important for a successful man to have an attractive, well-mannered wife. A businessman is often judged by the woman he marries. I'm sure you'll never disappoint me, Sarah."

She rolled onto her side, facing the wall, as visions of Jeremiah once again intruded. Visions of the way he'd touched her. *A well-mannered wife.* Visions of the way she'd responded to his touch. *I'm sure you'll never disappoint me, Sarah.*

"I've already disappointed you," she whispered, but the longing in her heart wasn't for Warren. It was for his brother, a man who didn't want her at all, and Sarah felt smothered beneath the weight of her own guilt and shame.

Hank McLeod had tears in his eyes. "I just came to say thanks for savin' Sarah's life."

Jeremiah shook his head as his gaze dropped to his desk. "It was pure luck I stumbled onto her. I didn't do anything but bring her in out of the cold." The lie seemed to burn his tongue.

"Well, Tom and I are mighty grateful you were there, no matter how it happened. I know you kept her from dyin'. That's all that matters to me." The old man held out his hand.

Jeremiah had no choice but to take hold and shake it. But he heard the accusing voice of his conscience calling him a hypocrite as he did so.

"We'll be expectin' you for supper Wednesday night, but I reckon Sarah'd be glad if you came by before then, so she can thank you, too."

"I'll do my best."

A few minutes later, the sheriff bid Jeremiah farewell and left the office. He was relieved Hank hadn't seemed inclined to linger. He'd been afraid of what Sarah's grandfather might say to him, afraid of the lies he might be forced to tell.

Jeremiah walked over to the stove and poured himself some bitter-tasting coffee from the battered coffeepot.

I reckon Sarah'd be glad if you came by . . .

If he closed his eyes, he could almost smell the soft lavender fragrance she wore. He could almost feel the silkiness of her silvery-gold hair. He could almost taste the sweetness of her lips and hear her soft cries in the darkness. He could almost see the expression of wonder on her face as they discovered the uniqueness of each other.

He swore angrily and set his cup beside the pot. He didn't need coffee. What he needed was a stiff drink.

*   *   *

"Well, Doc?" Michael asked as Doc Varney stepped out of the bedroom.

"I found no reason for you to worry. Rose seems to be completely unaffected by your experience. I'm as certain as I can be that this baby will be hale and hardy, just like your other two were when they were born."

Michael breathed a deep sigh of relief. The doctor had said the same thing yesterday after checking them all over, but he'd wanted to be absolutely certain.

"What about Sarah?" he asked as he watched the doctor drop his stethoscope into his black bag.

Doc frowned. "There's nothing wrong with that young woman physically, other than some exhaustion. But . . ." He shook his head. "But something's wrong. I just can't put my finger on it. Maybe she was simply frightened by the whole ordeal, but . . ."

Michael raised an eyebrow.

The doctor gave a shrug. "She's going to be just fine. We've got the good Lord to thank for keepin' you all safe. It's a miracle any of you survived the storm."

After the doctor left, Michael went to the bedroom he shared with Rose. His wife was sitting up in bed, her thick, chestnut-colored hair falling in a mass of waves over her shoulders. He thought how little she'd changed through the years. Looking at her, he lost his heart all over again, just as he always did.

"How're you feeling?" he asked as he crossed the thick Persian carpet that covered the floor of the spacious bedroom.

"Ridiculous. I don't need to be in bed, and I certainly didn't need to see Doc again today."

He sat on the bed beside her and drew her into his embrace. "Humor me."

"Mmmm." She laid her cheek against his chest. "Where are the children?"

"With their grandmother."

"We've got the house all to ourselves?" She slanted a glance at him.

He grinned, recognizing the mischievous look in her gold-flecked eyes.

She laughed low in her throat. "Maybe I do need to stay in bed a *little* longer."

"Maybe you do, Mrs. Rafferty," he said, echoing her laughter. "Maybe you do."

Jeremiah had intended to buy a bottle of whiskey and take it back to his room above the jail where he could drink it alone. But the moment he entered the Pony Saloon, he was surrounded by well-wishers, and all of them seemed intent on keeping him there.

Three times he told the story of how he'd gone to the barn to feed his horse and had thought he heard something. He told how he'd kept hold of the rope and gone to check and had stumbled over Sarah, her body barely visible beneath the blanket of snow covering her. He told how he'd carried her into the cabin and laid her by the fire to get warm.

And that was where he stopped telling the truth.

He downed another shot of whiskey, feeling the slow burn as the liquid made its way to his belly. He'd like to get drunk, good and drunk, but he didn't suppose the deputy sheriff was supposed to do that.

He cursed softly, damning himself for ever coming back to Homestead, damning himself for taking the blasted job as deputy, damning himself for being the no-good, worthless sort of man he was.

"Why don't you fellas go away and let this man have some peace?"

He looked up at the woman standing beside him. Her hair was dyed a bright red, and she wore a generous application of face paint. At one time, he supposed she'd been considered pretty. If he were fair, she wasn't all that bad-looking now. Only he wasn't interested.

She chased the rest of the men away, then sat down at the table across from him. "Hi, honey. My name's Opal."

He poured himself another glass of the amber-colored whiskey.

"Everybody in town's been talkin' 'bout how you rescued the McLeod girl. You're a real-life hero in these parts. We don't get many heroes in this saloon."

He emptied the glass in one long gulp.

Opal reached forward and covered his hand on the bottle when he moved to pour himself some more. "Why don't you let Opal congratulate you?" She glanced toward the bar, then back at Jeremiah. She leaned forward, her breasts nearly spilling over the top of her bodice. "I won't charge you the regular," she added with a wink.

He considered taking her up on it. Maybe that was one way to forget what he'd done. But he knew he couldn't do it. He knew he'd find no pleasure in Opal's bed. Not now. Not after Sarah.

Chapter Eighteen

In the days following the blizzard, Sarah kept herself busy with all the preparations for Christmas. She tried her best not to think about Jeremiah and what they had done in his house at the farm. She vacillated wildly between being certain she loved him to being certain she despised him. She wavered between blaming herself for what had happened in that old farmhouse and blaming him for everything that was wrong with the world.

Night was the most difficult time, when she lay in bed and everything was so silent. Night, when she closed her eyes and felt Jeremiah's arms around her, felt his lips upon hers. Night, when she remembered all those things about Jeremiah Wesley that she had no right to know, all the things she wanted desperately to forget.

She was grateful for Warren's absence. She wasn't ready to face him just yet. She feared he would look at her and know the truth. Regardless of what he might guess when they saw each other again, she would have to tell him she couldn't marry him. But she didn't know exactly how to go about it, especially right now when her thoughts were so confused.

Five days after Sarah's return to Homestead, Rose Rafferty paid a call at the McLeod house. Sarah was alone in the parlor at the time, her brother off with Doc Varney, as usual, her grandfather lying down for his afternoon nap.

"I'm sorry I didn't come sooner, Sarah," Rose said as she settled onto the chair beside the sofa, "but Michael hasn't wanted to let me out of his sight. Doc keeps telling him the baby and I aren't in any danger, but Michael worries all the same."

"I don't blame him. I was worried, too."

Rose leaned forward, her expression sober. "Michael feels the accident was his fault. If anything had happened to you . . ." She glanced down at her hands, folded in her lap, as her words faded away.

"But nothing *did* happen." Sarah heard the waver in her own voice as she spoke and was certain the falseness of her words would be obvious. Forcing herself to smile, she added, "We're none of us the worse for wear."

"Thank God Jeremiah found you."

A knot formed in her stomach. "Yes."

Rose's face brightened. "Well, you're right, of course. We're none of us the worse for wear, and there's no point dwelling on what might've happened. Let's talk about happier subjects, shall we?"

For nearly an hour, the two women chatted amicably about Rose's children, about their friends and neighbors, about the Christmas social which had been postponed from the previous Saturday because of the blizzard. In truth, Rose did most of the talking, and she didn't seem to notice how little Sarah said. For her part, Sarah was grateful for the diversion her friend had created. It was a relief to think of something other than herself and her own problems.

But in the end, Rose turned the conversation in an unwelcome direction. She asked about Sarah's wedding preparations, then said, "Mrs. Gaunt tells me your dress is all but finished, and she's waiting for you to come in for your final fitting."

Sarah tensed. "Yes. I . . . she sent word to me. I guess I really must go in soon."

"Is that a note of nervousness I hear?" Rose offered an understanding glace. "It's only normal to be nervous, you know. Every bride is. Especially just before the wedding. But I promise you, there's no call to worry."

Sarah shifted her gaze toward the window, uncertain what she should say, not wanting to lie about what was bothering her but unable to tell the truth.

And in her mind she saw Jeremiah, gathering her into his embrace, kissing her, caressing her, touching her so intimately. Her cheeks flooded with warmth.

Rose joined Sarah on the sofa. She took hold of Sarah's hand. "It just occurred to me. You must be wondering about . . . well, about the . . . the intimate relationship between a man and his wife. Did your grandmother ever . . . ever tell you what to expect?"

Sarah felt her blush deepen as her gaze dropped to a worn spot on the carpet.

"You haven't anything to fear, Sarah. It can be the most wonderful thing in the world."

She knew that. She knew it too well.

Occasionally stumbling over her words, Rose proceeded to explain the act of love between a married couple. It took all of Sarah's fortitude not to squirm in her seat. She couldn't look at her friend. She was certain her own personal knowledge would reveal itself in her eyes.

"The ultimate joy, of course, is knowing your union has created a baby," Rose finished, her free hand settling on her abdomen in a gesture of protection and love.

"A baby?"

Rose nodded. "If a woman is lucky."

Sarah went cold all over. Their union could have created a baby? She'd never considered such a thing. She hadn't known. She hadn't thought. What if . . .

Rose's fingers squeezed her hand. "There really isn't anything to fear. I promise you. I'm sure Warren will be a very thoughtful husband."

"It . . . it isn't that," she managed to say. "I . . . I just don't think I want a baby right away."

Rose's smile was gentle, reassuring. "You needn't worry about that, Sarah. A baby isn't always the result. If it were, I'd have dozens of children already." She blushed and turned her gaze out the window. "Oh dear. I can't believe I said that."

But Sarah scarcely noticed the other woman's discomfort. She was too busy feeling awash with relief.

Tom stepped through the door of the saloon, pausing as it closed behind him. His gaze found Fanny almost at once. She was setting a beer on a table and collecting payment from a customer.

He hadn't seen her for a week. Doc had proclaimed her fit to return to work, and then there'd been no excuse to look in on her. With the blizzard and his worries about Sarah, plus his studies and his work with Doc, he hadn't had much time to give thought to Fanny, but today he'd felt the need to see her, to make sure she was doing all right.

The dress she wore was too large for her, emphasizing how thin and frail she looked. She was wearing her hair up on her head, and a gold ostrich feather decorated the coiffure. She looked like a little girl playing dress-up with her mother's clothes.

At that moment, she glanced up and saw him standing there. He felt a catch in his chest at the sadness in her large, doelike eyes.

He forced a smile as he started forward. "Hello, Fanny," he said when he reached her.

"Mr. McLeod." Her chin nearly touched her chest and her gaze was directed down toward his shoes.

"I came by to see how you're feeling."

She glanced toward her boss, standing behind the bar. "I . . . I'm fine."

"Mind if we talk a minute or two?"

"Well, I . . . I'm supposed to be working."

He looked toward Grady O'Neal, then back toward the girl before him. "Isn't part of your job to make the customer feel welcome?"

Color infused her pale cheeks as she nodded.

"Fine. Then let's sit down right over here"—he took her arm—"and have us a visit." As soon as he sat down, he placed eight bits on the table. "That's for Mr. O'Neal so he won't feel he's being cheated."

"You don't have to do that," Fanny whispered.

No, he didn't have to do it, and he didn't have to be there, involving himself in her squalid little life. But it seemed he just couldn't help himself.

"Fanny, would you like to get out of this place?"

"Oh, I couldn't. Grady'd have my hide if I missed any more work."

Tom shook his head. "No, I don't mean for a few hours. I mean for good."

"I don't have nowhere t'go."

"If I could find you another job and a place to stay, would you leave here?"

Her eyes widened. "Why would you go'n do a thing like that?"

Why? He wished he knew himself, but he didn't. He just knew he wanted to help her, and this seemed the best way. "Would you leave if you had another job and a different place to live?"

"Yes." Her reply was soft but filled with hope.

"Then I'll see what I can do." He rose from the chair. "I'll let you know." He turned to leave.

"Mr. McLeod?"

He looked back over his shoulder.

"Why're you doin' this for me?"

He shrugged. "I just want to."

She smiled. Again, he thought there was something almost pretty about Fanny Irvine. And again, the thought surprised him.

*　　*　　*

Jeremiah rubbed the crease in his forehead with the fingers of one hand as he laid the telegraph on his desktop. He had a pounding headache, making it difficult to concentrate on the legal mumbo-jumbo in the report from the sheriff in Boise City.

He left his chair and went to pour himself some coffee, then decided what he needed was something to eat. He hadn't gone out for food today, hadn't wanted to. Like every day since Sunday, he'd done his best to avoid folks. He didn't want to be congratulated and thanked. It made him too uncomfortable. And it made him think of Sarah.

Jeremiah grabbed his coat from the hook and shoved his arms into the sleeves.

Damn it! He didn't want to think of Sarah McLeod.

He slammed his hat on his head.

There wasn't a single blasted thing he could do to change what had happened out at the farm.

He pulled on his gloves.

He'd done what was best for both of them, telling her she should keep silent and marry Warren.

Jeremiah reached for the door and stepped outside into the blustery winter's day. With a quick glance down Main, he crossed the street and entered Zoe's Restaurant. Luckily, at three o'clock in the afternoon there weren't any other customers.

The swinging half-door into the kitchen opened, revealing a plump, gray-haired woman. "My goodness," Zoe Potter said. "It's a surprise to see you, Mr. Wesley. I thought you'd given up eating here."

"No, ma'am." He removed his hat and set it on the chair next to him. "Just been busy."

"Well, that's good to hear. What can I get for you?"

Jeremiah glanced at the menu on the chalkboard near the door. "Have you got any of your roast beef left?"

"You're in luck."

"Then that's what I want."

"I'll bring it right out."

Just as she disappeared into the kitchen, the restaurant door opened again. Jeremiah felt his appetite leave him as Sarah entered the room.

She didn't notice him at first. She set a basket—the one she'd used to bring his lunch every day last week—on a table, then pushed the hood of her cloak from her head. That was when she saw him.

He saw the look of surprise, followed by dismay, dart across her lovely face. He saw the sudden stiffening of her proud shoulders, the infinitesimal lifting of her chin.

"Hello, Jeremiah."

There was something different about her eyes. He wondered what it was.

"Sarah."

"I heard you'd returned to town."

The innocence was gone. That was what was different.

"Had to get back to work."

She glanced toward the kitchen. "Of course."

What was he supposed to say to her? Sorry I acted like a cad? Sorry I'm not who you thought I was? Sorry for using you like a cheap dance hall girl?

She picked up the basket from the table. "I was just bringing some things to Mrs. Potter for the Christmas social tomorrow night."

He remembered the way she'd looked almost a week ago, standing on the boardwalk, as she'd talked to him outside the livery stable. She'd looked up at him, her pretty face framed by the fur trim on her hood, her hands tucked into her muff.

We'll see you at the Christmas social tomorrow night, won't we? You'd be missed if you weren't there.

He noticed she didn't ask if he was going to the social this time. She probably didn't want him there. He didn't blame her.

Sarah's gaze fell away from his. "Well, I'd better take these things into the kitchen. Good afternoon, Jeremiah."

He didn't reply.

She took a few steps, then turned to face him once again. She chewed on her lower lip, as if contemplating an important decision. Finally, with an abrupt nod of her head, her decision obviously made, she crossed the room to stand beside his table.

"Jeremiah." Her voice was low. "You . . . I . . ." Again, she chewed on her lower lip. "I believe I . . ." She let out a frustrated sigh; then the words came out in a rush. "We should try to at least be friends."

Before he could even think of anything to say in response, she whirled about and disappeared into the kitchen, leaving only the still swinging half-door as evidence she'd ever been there at all.

Sarah's heart was still racing madly when she slipped out the back door of the restaurant. With hurried steps, she followed the alley behind the livery and saloon, then turned onto the short path leading to the back door of her house.

Once inside, she shut the door behind her and leaned against it, her eyes closed, her lips pressed together in a solemn line. She'd known it would be awkward to see Jeremiah again, but awkwardness didn't describe the swirl of emotions she'd felt when she drew close to Jeremiah and looked down into his dark gaze.

She'd felt the sudden urge to comfort him. Her heart had ached for him. She'd wanted to tell him that what had happened between them wasn't his fault but hers. She'd wanted it to happen. It had been her choice. She'd wanted to hold him and kiss him and . . . and so much more.

She wanted to tell him she loved him.

No, it couldn't be love. Love took time to grow. That was what she'd always been told. No, she wasn't in love with him. She couldn't be. She'd simply been carried away with . . . with the unfamiliar passions he'd aroused. And passion was a fleeting thing, so she'd been told. She would get over it. It wouldn't last.

Friends. That's what she'd said she wanted them to be. Friendship was something that lasted.

But would friendship be enough?

Chapter Nineteen

"You can't miss the Christmas social, Jeremiah," Warren insisted. "Folks will be coming in from miles around. You're the new deputy. They'll want to meet you if they haven't already." He clapped Jeremiah's shoulder. "Besides, most of them have heard how you rescued Sarah. That sort of news travels fast, even when folks are snowed in. You're a mighty important fellow 'round these parts now."

Jeremiah turned away from his brother and shuffled some papers on his desk. "You'd think they'd all have better things to do. A week ago, most of 'em were buried under all that snow. A lot of them lost livestock. It's going to take some a long time to come back from that storm." He grunted his disapproval. "Seems to me they ought to stay home and forget this blasted social."

"Maybe so, but they'll all be there anyway. Listen, Jeremiah. I've got a pretty important announcement to make tonight. I'd like my brother to be there."

He turned around. Warren had no idea what he was asking of him. But what could he say? *I'm sorry, Warren. I can't come. I bedded your fiancée and would prefer not to see her.*

He cursed silently, then asked, "You can't just tell me now what your announcement is?"

"No." Warren grinned. "You're my only family. You should be there."

Jeremiah didn't think he'd seen his brother this animated since he was a little boy. Especially, he'd never seen Warren acting this way toward him, as if he truly wanted their relationship to improve. If what Warren wanted was so important to him, how could Jeremiah refuse?

Especially now. After what he'd done.

"All right, I'll be there."

Again Warren patted him on the shoulder. "Thanks."

After his brother left, Jeremiah sank onto his chair and cradled his face in his hands, his elbows resting on the desk. How had he let this happen? How could he have done this to Warren? How could he have done it to Sarah?

*   *   *

Addie Rider whisked off her apron as she cast a satisfied glance over the interior of the Homestead Community Church. Will and Preston, her husband and their seventeen-year-old son, had moved the pews from the center of the room, shoving them against the outer walls. Where the pulpit usually stood there was now a long table, covered with a festive red cloth, a large punch bowl in its center. Later, the table would be laden with all kinds of food, and the crystal bowl would be filled with a sparkling punch.

"Mother," Lark's voice interrupted, "where do you want Yancy to put the tree?"

Addie turned. Her eldest daughter, Lark, stood near the doorway, cradling Addie's infant grandson in her arms. The sight made Addie's heart sing.

"I think over there," she said, answering Lark's question. She pointed to the corner of the room farthest from the wood stove, behind the table.

A moment later, her son-in-law carried in a beautiful pine tree, along with a good measure of snow. The church room was immediately filled with the pungent scent of pine.

"Thank you, Yancy." Addie watched as he stood the tree in the designated corner. "You chose a perfect tree."

"It's not hard to do when you've got a forest of 'em right behind your house. Besides, I had Katie's help." He glanced behind him at his six-year-old daughter. "You picked it out, didn't you, sugar?"

Katie nodded. Her smile revealed her two missing front teeth. "Yeth, I picked it out."

"Will you help me decorate it, Katie?" Addie reached for the box containing the red velvet bows as she called to her younger daughter, "Naomi, I need your help, too. We're running out of time. Folks will be arriving soon."

Fifteen minutes later, Yancy claimed his wife and children and took them over to the hotel to get ready for the Christmas social. Will waited by the door with Preston and Naomi while Addie gave the room another quick glance.

"You'd better get a move on, Addie," her husband prompted.

"I know," she replied, but she still didn't turn to leave.

Will stepped up beside her, placing his hand against the back of her neck.

"I was thinking," she explained softly, "how many years now we've decorated the church for the social. Preston was just a toddler that first year. Remember?" She turned her head to gaze at her husband.

Will's hair was graying near the temples, but he was still the handsomest man in town as far as Addie was concerned. Even after eighteen years of marriage, she was still sometimes surprised he had chosen her to be his wife when he could have picked any number of young women far prettier than Addie Sherwood, the spinster schoolmarm from Connecticut.

He leaned over and kissed her forehead. "I remember. And every year, you get sentimental about all the years that've gone before." His smile was gentle, loving. "Now let's get you over to the hotel so you can put on that pretty green dress you've been savin' for this occasion. I've been looking forward to dancing with you when the music starts."

"You've outdone yourself again, Mrs. Rider," Sarah said an hour later as she looked at the pretty Christmas decorations that brightened the church house.

Already the room was full of people who'd come to Homestead from all across the valley to share in this night with their neighbors. Near the tree, musicians softly played a Christmas carol. Older folks lined the benches along the walls. Married couples and young singles stood in bunches, visiting about whatever had happened since last they'd seen one another. Children darted hither and yon and occasionally swiped cookies from a plate near one end of the long table.

"I enjoy doing it," Addie replied with a smile. Then she asked, "Where are your grandfather and brother?"

"Grampa's feeling a bit tired tonight. Tom

stayed home with him. They both thought I should come and wish everyone merry Christmas."

"We're glad you did. Give Sheriff McLeod my best wishes, will you, Sarah? And tell him I hope he feels better soon. Things aren't the same when he's not here."

"Of course. I'll tell him."

Warren returned from hanging up Sarah's wrap. "Would you like some punch?" he asked her after bidding Addie hello.

Sarah shook her head without looking at him. She felt guilty for even coming with Warren tonight. If she'd known he would be returning from the capital city today, she would have been prepared to talk to him, to tell him she was calling off the wedding, breaking their engagement. But she hadn't known and he'd caught her totally unprepared when he'd shown up at her front door just a short while ago.

I'll tell him when he takes me home, she told herself. I'll tell him I can't marry him. I won't let the charade continue a minute longer than that.

"Well, I'm thirsty." Warren took hold of her arm as he excused them from Addie Rider, then guided her through the crowd toward the punch bowl. He filled two cups and handed her one, acting as if he hadn't seen her tell him she didn't want any.

Sarah tried not to be irritated. After all, it was Warren who had every right to be angry with her. Even to hate and despise her. He just didn't know it yet. She hoped he would never know the complete truth.

"There's Jeremiah." He lifted his arm to wave at his brother.

Sarah's stomach dropped, and her breath caught in her throat. She didn't turn to look across the room, didn't want to see him for herself. Instead, she looked at Warren and felt the guilt bearing down harder upon her shoulders. Only a short time ago, he'd barely been cordial to his brother. Now he was grinning and eagerly urging Jeremiah to join them.

Sarah had tried to help these two men become a family, to mend whatever differences had driven them apart years ago. And in one night, in one reckless act, she might have destroyed their newfound friendship for good.

Her eyes misted over as she dropped her gaze to the cup in her hand. Why had she done it? What had come over her? She couldn't blame her actions on the blizzard. She couldn't blame Jeremiah for his attempts to keep her warm. She couldn't blame anything or anyone other than herself. She'd known that what she was doing was wrong. She could have stopped him. He'd *asked* her to stop him. Why hadn't she listened?

She looked up and saw Jeremiah walking toward them, and her answer was there in her heart. *Because I love him.*

It was true, and she couldn't deny it any longer. From almost the first moment she'd laid eyes on him, she'd loved him. It didn't matter whether or not it made sense. It didn't matter that love wasn't supposed to happen this way. It didn't matter if she knew so very little about him. She knew him in her heart, *with* her heart. She loved him.

"I'm glad you came, Jeremiah," Warren said as he reached out to shake his brother's hand.

So am I, Jeremiah. But the thought brought no joy, only sadness and confusion.

Their gazes met, and she thought she saw her own guilt mirrored in his dark eyes.

Jeremiah saw something besides guilt in Sarah's gaze. He saw the look that had so frightened him out at the farm. The look of a woman who wanted him to be something he wasn't. He hardened himself against it, hardened his heart against her.

Warren grinned. "Told you everybody'd come into Homestead for this. We won't have elbowroom in another thirty minutes."

Jeremiah merely nodded as he glanced around the room, glad for a reason not to look at Sarah any longer.

"I'd like to introduce you to some people," his brother said.

Sarah spoke up softly. "I think I'll join Rose and Lark. Excuse me." She slipped away before Warren could say anything.

Warren frowned slightly as he watched her

moving away, but when he turned back to Jeremiah, he merely shrugged his shoulders. "Come on. I'll do the honors. I kind of like havin' a hero for a brother."

Jeremiah winced inwardly, knowing the truth and despising himself for it.

Nearly two hours later, the food had disappeared and the punch bowl was nearly dry. Three men played music on a fiddle, guitar, and mouth organ. The crowd had thinned a little, leaving room for a few couples to dance in the middle of the room.

Sarah had managed to slip away from Warren and Jeremiah a second time and was now seated with several older women. She wasn't listening to what they were saying. No matter how hard she tried, her thoughts continued to return to Jeremiah. Even when she didn't lift her eyes, didn't turn her head, she seemed to be aware of exactly where he was standing in the room. It was agony, knowing.

"Sarah?"

She glanced up, surprised to find Warren standing beside her.

"Will you come over here for a moment?"

The urge to refuse was nearly overwhelming, but when he put his hand under her elbow and drew her to her feet, there was little she could do except follow after him. He led her across the room to where Jeremiah stood near the potbelly stove. With a deft motion, Warren moved her to stand between the two brothers, then turned his back to the stove as he faced the crowd.

The moment there was a break in the music, Warren called out, "Folks! Can I have your attention, please?"

Little by little, the conversations came to a halt. Everyone's eyes turned toward the trio. Sarah felt terribly conspicuous, standing between the two men—the one she was supposed to love and the one she did love.

"I've got some news I'd like to share with you all."

Sarah's heart began to thump in her chest. An ominous feeling of dread seeped through her veins.

"Some of you have probably heard I've been down to Boise City this week. You might find it interesting that they've got no snow on the ground at all."

There was a murmur of voices.

Warren raised his hands to recall their attention. "For those of you who haven't been down that way in a few years, I can tell you the capital is really thriving. It's an exciting place." He glanced over at Sarah. "That's why I've accepted Mr. Kubicki's offer to form a partnership. You've all heard of Kubicki & Company. Well, the name is now Kubicki, Wesley & Company. We'll be making fine, affordable furniture to be shipped everywhere in the country. Sarah and I will be moving to Boise right after the wedding next week. I've already made arrangements to buy our new home."

Sarah turned her head to stare up at him, unable to speak.

And then there was no more opportunity to say anything to him. Townsfolk gathered 'round, everyone congratulating Warren on his success, expressing their regret at seeing him and Sarah leave Homestead.

At some point, Sarah glanced up and met Jeremiah's gaze. *It's for the best,* she could almost hear him say, just before he turned and walked away.

But Sarah knew it wasn't for the best. She also knew she wasn't going to go to Boise City with Warren.

Not when everything she wanted was right here in Homestead.

Chapter Twenty

"You're awfully quiet," Warren commented as Sarah opened the front door of her house.

She glanced up, dreading the moment she now faced. "I think you should come inside."

"Are you sure? It looks like your grandfather and Tom have already turned in for the night."

"I'm sure. We need to talk." She moved into the entry hall, her fingers already working to unbutton her cloak.

As soon as the door closed, Warren stepped up behind her and lifted the cloak from her shoulders, hanging it on the coat rack, then doing the same with his. Sarah didn't wait for him but continued on into the parlor. She took the poker and stirred up the fire in the fireplace, then added some wood to the flames.

When she straightened and turned, she found Warren standing just inside the parlor doorway. "Come in and sit down, Warren," she told him as she sat on an overstuffed chair.

He frowned. "You've been acting strange all evening, Sarah. Is there something you haven't told me? Has your grandfather's health worsened more than you've let on?"

"This isn't about Grampa. It's about us."

"About us?"

This was even more difficult than she'd expected. It was true she'd never loved Warren, never pretended to love him, but she'd always been fond of him. She recognized all his good qualities, all the things that had seemed, combined with her grandmother's urgings, to be enough for a happy marriage. She knew now they weren't enough, but she also knew saying so would hurt him.

Warren sat down on the sofa across from her. "I'm listening, Sarah."

She drew a deep breath. "I'm not going to Boise with you."

"But of course you're going." He spoke in the tone of an adult explaining something to a child. "A woman's place is with her husband, and a man's place is where he can best provide for his family."

She clenched her hands in the folds of her

skirt. "I'm not going to be your wife."

In stunned silence, he stared at her.

Sarah dropped her gaze to the floor near his feet. "I . . . I'm sorry, Warren. I thought I could marry you, but I can't. I would make you a very poor wife. I've known it for some time. I just haven't known how to tell you."

"You can't mean to do this," he said incredulously. "The wedding's only three days away. I've told everyone we're going to Boise to live. What will they say?"

She looked up again. His expression had changed, grown hard and unforgiving. She thought of the anger and resentment he'd harbored against his brother for so many years, and she knew he would feel far worse toward her now. His pride was too wounded to forget or forgive. He would resent her forever.

"I can't help what people will say," she replied at last. "I only know it would be a mistake for me to marry you. I . . . I would make you unhappy, Warren. I'm not the sort of woman you need."

He jumped to his feet. "How do you know what I need? I chose you because I wanted you, because I knew you'd be the perfect wife for me. I've waited for five years for you."

But you don't love me. "I know," she whispered.

"I've been tolerant." He began to pace the length of the room. "I've been understanding. I haven't pressured you in any way."

"Warren . . ."

Suddenly, he stopped before her and pulled her up from the chair. "I've wanted you for too many years to let you go now. You're mine." He kissed her harshly, ignoring her muffled protests.

Sarah pushed at him, panic rising as his grip on her arms tightened painfully.

He broke the kiss as abruptly as he'd begun. "I won't let you do this, Sarah. I won't let you embarrass us both this way. You're going to be my wife and you're going to come with me to Boise."

"No. No, I won't. I don't love you, Warren, and I won't marry you."

"There are other things more important to a marriage than love."

Her voice rose in anger. "Not to me. I'll marry the man I love or not marry at all."

Warren released his hold on her arms and stepped back from her. The expression on his face altered as he continued to stare at her, changing from irritation to frustration, then to the dawning of understanding, and finally to disbelief. "Good Lord," he whispered.

She turned her back toward him and walked over to the fireplace. She touched the mantel with the fingers of one hand and looked down into the low-burning fire. Why didn't he just leave? she wondered. Why did he refuse to simply accept her decision? He didn't love her any more than she loved him. He thought it an unimportant emotion. She didn't.

"It's Jeremiah, isn't it?" Warren asked, his voice void of emotion.

Jeremiah's image appeared in the flames, and her heart ached for Warren even as she shook her head, unable to speak the denial aloud.

She didn't hear Warren's approach, and his hand on her shoulder, spinning her about, caught her by surprise. "You think you're in love with Jeremiah, don't you?" Anger raised his voice to a near shout as he once again captured her upper arms in a tight grasp. "What happened between you two out at the farm last week?"

She felt her face flush as she said, "Nothing." She lifted her chin defiantly, hoping he couldn't read the truth in her eyes.

He stared at her for a long time before suddenly letting go of her as if burned. "I'll kill the bastard," he ground out through clenched teeth, and she knew he'd seen what she'd most wanted to hide from him.

Sarah reached for him. "Warren, wait!"

But he ignored her as he spun about and strode toward the door, slamming it behind him as he left.

Jeremiah sat on the side of his cot and stared across the room at the red coals in the belly of the stove. The lamp on the stool was turned down so only a faint light illuminated his sparsely furnished room.

She was leaving. She was going away with Warren. It was the best thing for all of them. He wouldn't have to see her with Warren, wouldn't have to remember all the things he needed to forget—the way she'd felt in his arms, the way her mouth had tasted, the sweet smell of her hair, the sweet joy of her smile.

No, it was best that Warren was marrying her and taking her away. Best for everyone. Certainly, it was best for Sarah. Jeremiah had nothing to offer her. Nothing.

Sarah . . .

He raked the fingers of one hand through his hair and cursed softly. In all the years since Millie had died, he hadn't given more than a passing thought to the women he'd met. Why was it the one who belonged to his brother who had to change the familiar pattern?

He heard footsteps on the stairs leading up to his room and glanced up just as the door burst open.

"You sonuvabitch!" Warren shouted as he lunged across the room.

Warren's fist connected with Jeremiah's jaw before he had a chance to defend himself. Jeremiah was knocked off the cot by the blow. On his hands and knees, he looked up at his brother.

"Get up!" Warren demanded.

"I'm not going to fight with you."

"Get up, you no-good, lying bastard! Get up and let me give you what you deserve!"

Jeremiah eased himself back onto the cot, warily watching his brother's clenched fists. He didn't speak. What could he say in his own defense? He knew he deserved Warren's rage.

"It wasn't enough you were the only one Dad thought about, right up until the day he died? It wasn't enough you got the farm when it was rightfully mine for all those years I stayed and worked it? That wasn't enough? You had to take Sarah away from me, too?" He swung at Jeremiah again.

Jeremiah managed to dodge the blow, but he didn't bother to rise from the cot. His silence seemed to infuriate his brother even more.

"Damn you!"

Jeremiah held out a hand, silently begging Warren to listen to reason. "I don't know what Sarah told you—"

"She didn't tell me anything except she's not going to marry me. She didn't have to tell me anything more than that. I guessed the rest."

Cautiously, Jeremiah rose from his bed. "Listen, Warren. Maybe it isn't as bad as you think." How easily the lie slipped from his lips, he thought, but he shoved away any feelings of guilt as he continued. "Maybe if I talk to her, she'd listen to reason. I'm sure you're wrong about her feelings. She probably doesn't know what she's doing. She's just getting nervous. She—"

"Damn you to hell! Are you going to tell me you don't want to marry her after what you've done?"

A telling silence filled the room before he answered, "No, I don't want to marry her."

Warren hit him again, this time catching him just below his eyebrow.

The whole side of Jeremiah's head throbbed. He covered his left eye, ignoring the black spots that filled his remaining vision. He fought to control his anger, knowing he'd reached the end of his patience. "Don't try to hit me again, Warren," he warned. "That's the last one you're allowed."

His brother stepped backward as he drew in an audible breath. Then he shook his head, his shoulders slumping in defeat. "You're right, Jeremiah. She's not worth fighting over, is she? All these years I've waited, thinking she'd make me the perfect, virtuous wife, and it turns out she's no better than one of the girls in O'Neal's saloon." He turned on his heel. "To hell with her," he muttered. "To hell with you both."

"Sarah?"

She looked toward the doorway and the sound of her brother's voice.

"What are you doing, sitting here in the dark?" he asked.

Was it dark? She hadn't noticed. When had the fire died?

Tom entered the parlor, crossing to the fireplace where he stirred up the coals, bringing life back into the fire and throwing light across the carpet, chasing away the shadows that had filled the room only moments before.

Her brother straightened and turned. "What's wrong, Sarah?" he asked as he approached her.

She shook her head.

He knelt on the floor and took hold of her hand within both of his. "You can tell me."

She met his gaze. "I've broken my engagement with Warren."

"But . . . why?"

Again she shook her head.

"Sarah, you can tell me."

No. No, she couldn't tell him. She couldn't tell anyone. It was all too mixed up in her own head, her own heart. She didn't love Warren; she loved his brother. She had given herself—her body and her heart—to a man she scarcely knew, to a man who didn't want her to love him. She was ashamed and heartbroken. And she couldn't share her pain with anyone else. Not anyone.

Tom squeezed her hand gently. "Is there something I can do to help?"

"No," she whispered, her throat feeling suddenly tight. Then she realized there were tears streaking her cheeks.

Tom pulled her toward him. Sarah slipped off the edge of the chair and down to the floor where her brother gathered her into his embrace, her cheek pressed against his chest as he smoothed her hair with his hand and uttered soothing phrases, telling her everything would be all right.

This time, Sarah didn't believe him.

Chapter Twenty-one

Sarah's depression lasted about another thirty-two hours. She stayed in her room and cried until she had no tears left. She felt completely sorry for everything she'd ever said and castigated herself for each and every thing she'd done, almost from the day she was born.

But when she awakened early on Christmas morning, her natural optimism intruded on her misery, and she began to see things more clearly.

She was right to have broken off with Warren. She was and would always be sorry she'd hurt him, but even if Jeremiah had never returned to Homestead, it would have been wrong for her to marry Warren. She would have made him a poor wife, and she would have been as unhappy as he. She should have realized it much sooner. Perhaps she had. Perhaps that was why she'd insisted upon such a long engagement. In fact, she was certain that was why.

As for Jeremiah, he didn't know she loved him. They'd been wrong, of course, to share the intimacies they'd shared, but that didn't have to mean they could never set things right. He might very well come to love her in return if only she afforded him the chance.

Slipping from her bed, Sarah knelt beside it, clasped her hands, closed her eyes, and bowed her head. She searched her heart for words that would explain what she felt, what she wanted. "Forgive me. Make it right. Please, God, make it right. I love him so." She started to rise, then added, "Thank you for not granting my prayers about going to Europe like I always thought I wanted. Thanks for keeping me here. And, Lord, if you will, let Jeremiah love me, too. Amen."

She opened her eyes as she got to her feet, feeling a great . . . expectancy. As if something wonderful were about to happen. And why not? Christmas was a time of miracles. Anything could happen. Absolutely anything. Even love.

She grabbed her wrap and put it on as she poked her feet into her carpet slippers. Then she ran a brush quickly through her hair before catching it back at the nape with a ribbon.

Leaving her bedroom, she hurried down the stairs and into the kitchen where she stoked the banked coals in the stove. She hummed a Christmas carol as she set about preparing breakfast, and her heart lightened even more.

As she worked, she enumerated the many things she had to be thankful for. Grampa was still with them and still able to get around. Tom was home, his schooling was going well, and he was destined for a brilliant career as a doctor. She had many wonderful friends, a warm house, a loving family. Her life was full of good things.

And, of course, there was Jeremiah. Love was the greatest thing to be thankful for, both loving and being loved. She was filled with love for him and full of hope that he would love her in return.

"Well, this is a change," Tom greeted her as he stepped into the kitchen.

She glanced over her shoulder. "Merry Christmas, Tom."

He crossed to stand beside her, one eyebrow raised as he perused her. "I guess it must be a merry one, judging from the look of you." He kissed her cheek. "Merry Christmas, Sarah. Glad to see you're feeling better."

"Me, too." She laid several strips of bacon in a frying pan.

He reached for a biscuit, hot out of the oven. "Care to tell me what's brought about this astonishing change in mood? Have you decided to marry Warren after all?"

"No," she answered seriously. "I think I've just done some growing up." She pushed a few stray wisps of hair off her face with the back of her hand as she looked at her brother. "I did the right thing in breaking off with Warren. I should have done it long ago." She shook her head. "No, I never should have accepted his offer of marriage in the first place. I always knew we were unsuited to each other."

He looked relieved. "Then I guess it won't bother you to learn he took the train down to Boise yesterday? I hear he's gone for good."

"So soon?"

"Are you sorry?"

She considered the question a moment. "Only that I hurt him." Thoughts of Jeremiah intruded, but she pushed them away. "If I had it to do over . . ." Again she shook her head. "I wish I hadn't hurt Warren, but I know I did the right thing. So does he, deep down."

Tom lightly punched her shoulder. "Going to start looking for that prince again?" he asked with a teasing wink, trying to coax a smile from her.

"No." She turned away, not wanting him to read her private thoughts.

No, she didn't want a prince or a wealthy financier from New York City or even a mysterious European count. She wanted a deputy, a farmer, a tall man with sooty eyes and ebony hair and a chiseled jaw. She wanted Jeremiah Wesley, and she was going to do her darnedest to make him see he wanted her, too.

Homestead was quiet when Jeremiah did his morning check. All the businesses were closed except for the saloon, and when he glanced inside that establishment, he found it empty. It seemed the good folks of Homestead—even the sort who normally frequented the saloon—were at home with their families that morning, opening gifts, preparing sumptuous Christmas dinners, celebrating the day and what it stood for.

But not Jeremiah. Jeremiah was alone.

His footsteps slowed as he approached Wesley's Furniture Emporium. Unconsciously, he rubbed his jaw, as if it still ached.

Warren had left town without seeing Jeremiah again. If not for Leslie Blake, Jeremiah wouldn't have known his brother was gone.

He'd sure made a mess of things, he thought as he walked past the shop without glancing through the windows. His brother had resented him for years, but the resentment had been for things Jeremiah had had no control over. But what had happened with Sarah was different. That was something he could have prevented. What had happened with Sarah was completely his own fault. He deserved every rotten name his brother had called him. He deserved that and much more besides.

Jeremiah trod across the hard-packed snow to the schoolhouse where he checked both doors, finding them locked and secure. As he turned around to continue on his rounds, he saw all the tiny footprints left in the snow by small boots and shoes. There were three snow angels placed side by side and two good-sized snowmen, and he remembered watching the children making them while on recess last week.

Sam would've been six. He would have been in school.

That thought—and the corresponding stab of pain it brought—were completely unexpected. He sat down on the school steps, drawing a deep breath of cold air into his lungs.

The old memory smote him like a blow in the solar plexus. He saw them so clearly, himself and Millie, snuggled together in their bed in that drafty, two-room farmhouse, planning the future of their unborn child. He remembered Millie, tiny and fragile, her brown eyes so large and trusting. He'd wanted a daughter just like Millie. She'd wanted a fine, strapping son, just like his dad, and had insisted on calling the baby Sam.

Samuel's a good, biblical name and fittin'

with yours, Jeremiah. Sam'll grow up to be as good a man as his pa. You'll see.

"Ah, Millie, I'm sorry."

He'd failed her. Time and again, he'd failed her, and still she'd gone on trusting him, believing in him.

"Why'd you want me to come back here, Millie? Why'd you tell me it was time to come home?"

It's time, Jeremiah.

He couldn't help the bittersweet smile from curving the corners of his mouth. "Where've you been?" he asked the familiar, inaudible voice. Then his smile faded. "I've made a real mess of things, Millie. Got any answers?"

But as quickly as the voice in his heart had returned, it was gone, and he felt the emptiness once more.

I must be going mad. He rose from the step and started back toward town, shaking his head as he silently mocked himself. Anybody who talked to a woman who'd been dead more than six years probably belonged in an asylum somewhere.

But that didn't stop him from hoping she'd talk to him again, hoping she'd help him straighten out the mess he'd made of his life.

Sarah McLeod wasn't one to let the grass grow under her feet. Having decided that Jeremiah only needed an opportunity to discover he might love her, she set out to give him the opportunity that very day.

After the Christmas church service, she sent Tom home without her while she walked to the sheriff's office. She found Jeremiah behind his desk, just as she'd known she would. His surprise was evident on his face as he rose from his desk.

She closed the door behind her. "Merry Christmas, Jeremiah."

A lengthy silence stretched between them.

"I guess you know I broke my engagement to Warren."

He rubbed his jaw, saying, "So I heard."

"He came to see you, didn't he?"

"He came." Jeremiah scowled at her. "You shouldn't have done it, Sarah. You shouldn't have broken things off. You should have married him and gone to Boise. It would have been better."

She took several steps forward. "Why?"

There was another long pause.

As she looked at him, she felt the quickening beat of her heart, felt the love for him flowing through her veins. It was real and deep, and it wasn't going to go away. She was more sure of it now than ever.

"I'm not who you think I am, Sarah," Jeremiah said at last.

"Who are you then?"

He looked as if he might answer her question, but then he lifted his hand in an impatient gesture, raking his fingers through his hair. "Damn it, Sarah! We made a mistake. Let's leave it at that."

"Yes. It was a mistake. We were wrong." She drew a quick breath. "But what we felt was real. What I feel for you now is real."

"Go home, Sarah."

"I love you."

"You don't know me."

"You're wrong, Jeremiah. I do know you."

He swore softly. "Don't you understand what I did to you?" he asked, defeat and self-loathing in his voice.

Sarah moved to the side of the desk. She could have reached out and touched him. She wanted to touch him. Wanted it badly. "You didn't do anything to me that I didn't allow." She lifted her hand in petition, wanting him to hear her, to understand what she was saying.

"Go home, Sarah," he repeated in a harsh whisper.

How do I reach you? she wondered, sensing his inner turmoil, realizing how high the wall was he had erected between them.

She lowered her hand. "All right. I'll go home." She took a step backward. "I came to invite you to Christmas dinner. Grampa hopes you'll come."

"I can't."

"Jeremiah—"

"I *can't!*"

Sarah sighed as she turned and walked to the door.

As she reached for the doorknob, Jeremiah said, "Don't come in here anymore, Sarah. Don't bring me any lunches in a basket. It'll only cause gossip."

She looked over her shoulder and met his gaze. "If that's what you want, I won't come in. I won't bring your lunch. But it doesn't change anything. I still love you, Jeremiah."

She didn't bother to wait for a response. She was fairly certain there wouldn't be one.

Chapter Twenty-two

Tom was feeling discouraged and more than a little angry. Finding Fanny a job was going to be more difficult than he'd thought. He'd talked to Michael Rafferty at the hotel, to Leslie Blake at the mercantile, to Madeline Gaunt at the dress shop, to Zoe Potter at the restaurant, even to Felix Bonnell at the newspaper. Nobody needed to hire any help. At least, that was what they'd told him. Tom suspected it had more to do with Fanny herself. They didn't want to hire a young girl who served drinks and lived above the saloon.

What if he wasn't able to help her? he wondered as he walked along Main Street. What if he'd raised her hopes only to see them dashed?

There sure weren't many opportunities for a girl to work in this town. The sawmill was no place for Fanny, and he knew without asking that Vince Stanford would never give her work in the bank. The bathhouse was out, too. What places were left?

As if in answer to his unspoken question, he heard someone call his name. He glanced across the street and saw Rose Rafferty wave her arm and motion him toward her.

"Can I speak to you a moment, Tom?" she called from the veranda of the hotel.

With a nod, he started across the street.

When he reached her, she said, "Michael told me you were trying to find work for a friend."

He felt a spark of hope. "Yes, but he said he didn't have any need for more help just now."

"He doesn't, but I might. Let's go inside and talk about it, shall we?" She turned and led the way into the hotel restaurant.

The room was empty of customers at this time of the day, giving them a choice of tables. Rose selected one near the entrance, and Tom held her chair for her while she sat down, then moved to the chair opposite her.

"Tell me about this girl you wish to help," Rose said as soon as he was seated.

"Her name's Fanny Irvine. She's sixteen, and she has no other family besides her sister, Opal, who works in the saloon. When their mother died, Fanny came to stay with her sister. Mr. O'Neal gave her work to earn her keep." He waited for her to pass quick judgment, as others had, but Rose's expression didn't alter, so he continued. "She's real unhappy there, Mrs. Rafferty. I told her I'd try to find her work and a place to live so she could get out of there. It's no place for a young girl."

"Of course it isn't." Rose turned her head and gazed out the window. After a long silence, she softly said, "I've seen what drink can do to people." Another silence stretched between them.

Tom noticed the shadow of sadness that passed across her face. He remembered her brother, a ne'er-do-well who'd spent many a night in Homestead's jail, sleeping off the liquor. Her father had been even worse, a mean and ugly drunk with a dangerous temper.

Rose returned her gaze abruptly to Tom. "You bring Fanny over to see me. If it seems she'll work out, she can have a place to stay here. There's a room off the kitchen that could be made suitable for a girl to live in, if she had a mind to."

"But Mr. Rafferty said—"

"You leave Mr. Rafferty to me. I manage the restaurant, and Michael trusts my judgment. Mr. Penny, our chef, has been saying he needs more help in the kitchen. Maybe Fanny is the right person for the job."

Tom got quickly to his feet. He reached across the table to shake Rose's hand.

"Thanks, Mrs. Rafferty. I'll bring Fanny over just as soon as I can. Maybe this afternoon."

"Do you take sugar?" Sarah asked as she poured coffee into a cup.

Ethel Bonnell nodded. "Please. Two spoonfuls."

Sarah couldn't help wondering what had brought the woman to her house for a visit. It wasn't as if the two were close friends. Ethel was at least twenty years Sarah's senior and couldn't be considered an intimate. She'd lived in Homestead less than three years, and as the wife of the proprietor and editor of the newspaper, *The Homestead Herald*, Ethel considered herself somewhat above the rest of the inhabitants of the town.

"I can't tell you how sorry I am about your wedding, my dear," Ethel said as she accepted the cup from Sarah. She shook her head in a gesture of pity. "You must be heartbroken to have Mr. Wesley desert you this way."

So this was why she'd come. To dig for grist for the gossip mill. Sarah's blood began to boil, but she did her best to hide it, answering sweetly, "He didn't desert me, Mrs. Bonnell. We just decided not to marry."

The woman's eyebrows lifted in surprise. "But whatever for? He was such a fine, upstanding young man, and successful, too.

You'll not find better in these parts. Cowboys and farmers. That's all that remains. Why ever would you let a man like Warren Wesley go?"

Sarah wanted to tell her it was none of her business. "We both realized we were not suited for each other, Mrs. Bonnell. It's as simple as that."

"But it came about so suddenly. At the Christmas social, he said—"

"Warren was excited about his new business venture. It didn't seem the right time to announce we weren't going to marry." She knew her lies made little sense, but she hoped Ethel wouldn't notice.

"Well, I must say, you're taking it all very calmly." She sipped her coffee. "You are a remarkably strong young woman. I'll say that for you, Sarah McLeod. Your wedding plans have gone awry, your grandfather is in poor health, and now your brother has taken up with one of those floozies from the saloon, and still you're able to sit here looking as if you hadn't a care in the world."

Sarah stiffened. "What?"

Ethel smiled innocently. "I must say, I admire you. I wasn't nearly so self-assured when I was your age."

"What did you say about my brother?"

"Oh, my." The woman set aside her coffee cup and glanced at Sarah with a look of concern. "Don't tell me you don't know about Tom and that girl from the Pony Saloon?"

Sarah drew a deep breath, trying to calm her clanging nerves. "No, I'm afraid I don't. Why don't you tell me, Mrs. Bonnell?"

"Well," Ethel began with obvious relish, "he's been going to visit her in the saloon almost every day. I realize that young men must sow their wild oats, and I suppose there's little that can be done to change it, but now he's asking about town for someone to give her a job. He even came to the paper and asked Mr. Bonnell to take her on. Can you imagine? A girl like that. What respectable person would take her into their employ? I can tell you, I put a stop to any notion of such a thing happening at the *Herald*. Mrs. Varney was saying to me just last week what a terrible thing it is for our town to have a brothel right in our midst, and that's exactly what that place is. A place of sin. And now your brother wants to expose others to a girl of such low moral character. Let her at least stay inside the saloon where she belongs. That's what I say."

Sarah thought of the woman who had come for the doctor after church just after Tom's return from school. She remembered the purple shading on her eyelids, the heavy rouge on her cheeks, the bright red of her lips. She couldn't imagine her brother taking up with such a woman. Not Tom.

Fanny felt her heart skip a beat when Tom entered the saloon. Yesterday, on Christmas, he'd come to see her for only a minute. He'd given her a gift, a locket on a gold chain. He'd tried to say it wasn't much, that he'd just wanted her to know he was her friend. But it meant much more than that to Fanny. She'd gone to bed last night with the locket clasped in her hand, dreaming of the handsome young man who had given it to her.

Tom crossed the saloon to the table she was wiping clean with a damp cloth. "Morning, Fanny." He grinned at her.

Her heart did another tumble. "Mornin', Mr. McLeod."

He leaned toward her and said, "Don't you think it's time you called me Tom? After all, we're friends, aren't we?"

She didn't reply. She couldn't. Not even to save her soul. Her heart was thundering in her chest, and she felt all shaky inside.

He wanted her to call him Tom!

"I need you to come with me for a few minutes, Fanny. I think I've found you another job and a place to live."

"You have?" she whispered, finding her voice.

He nodded. "Over at the Rafferty Hotel restaurant. Mrs. Rafferty wants to meet you."

"She wants to meet me?"

Tom laughed gently. "Yes, she does. How else can she tell you she's going to put you to work?"

A door slammed at the back of the building, and Grady O'Neal came walking into the saloon. He frowned when he saw Tom with Fanny.

"You here again, McLeod?" he asked, his voice little more than a growl.

"I came to take Fanny out for a moment."

Grady's eyes widened slightly; then he barked a sharp laugh. "You don't have to take her nowhere. She's got a room upstairs that'll do you just fine."

Fanny flushed with mortification. She wished the floor would open up and swallow her whole, but of course, it didn't.

Tom's anger was evident in the flash of his lead gray eyes and the set of his firm mouth. He turned away from Grady and took hold of Fanny's arm. "Come on."

She wouldn't have thought she could feel worse, but she did as he guided her toward the stairs. He *was* taking her to her room. She wanted to die.

Opal was seated at her dressing table, wearing only her corset and frilly drawers, carefully applying her face paints, when Tom opened the door. Tom didn't even glance her way as he drew Fanny across the room toward her bed.

Maybe she *would* die.

"Get your things together," he ordered.

She looked up at him, wondering if she'd misunderstood.

His gaze fell to her dress. "Do you have anything else to wear? Something not so . . ." He left the sentence unfinished.

"Yes."

"Good. Put it on. I'll wait outside in the hall. Don't take long, and get everything you want now. You won't be coming back here."

In a moment, he was gone, the door closing soundly behind him. Fanny stood stock-still, unable to comprehend what was happening.

"What on earth is going on?" Opal demanded as she rose from her dressing table.

Fanny looked at her sister, looked at the once pretty face that had hardened through the years, looked at the bright, dyed-red coarseness of her once soft brown hair, looked at the figure that had been exposed for the pleasure of countless, nameless men. She looked and knew that if she didn't go now, this was what she would become.

"He's takin' me outta here."

"What do you mean, takin' you out?"

"Tom's found me another place t'work and a place t'stay." Tears pooled in her eyes as she stared at Opal. Despite everything, she loved her sister. Opal had taken care of her when she was sick. She'd seen that her little sister had a place to stay when Fanny had shown up in Homestead, an orphan with no place else to go. Opal had been as good to her as she knew how, and Fanny loved her for it. But she didn't want to be like Opal. She'd rather die first.

Opal seemed to read her thoughts. She

stepped closer and touched Fanny's cheek with her fingertips. "You go on then. You git out of this hellhole while you got the chance. You make somethin' of yourself. You be a real lady. I was wrong, what I said about you not bein' nothin' to look at. An' I was wrong about that fella, too. I hope he takes good care o' you." Suddenly, she hugged Fanny close against her, whispering in her ear, "You don't never have to speak to me again if you happen t'see me on the street."

"'Course, I'll speak to you," Fanny replied hoarsely, her throat tight with emotions. "You're my sister."

Opal released her as suddenly as she'd hugged her. "Now, git on outta here. It'll be a pure pleasure, not to have to chase you out when my visitors come callin'." She returned to her vanity, splashed on her lilies-of-the-valley cologne, then pulled on a dress that barely contained her ample bosom and left without another word.

Fanny glanced around the room, wondering what she would find beyond the walls of the saloon. It was scary, thinking about it. This was bad, but what if the other was worse?

A soft rap sounded; then the door opened, revealing Tom. "Are you ready?"

She swallowed the lump in her throat. "Not just yet. Give me another minute or two. I . . . I just got to change my clothes."

He nodded and started to close the door.

"Fanny?" He poked his head through the opening and looked directly into her eyes. "Everything's going to be fine. You'll see."

She smiled back at him. She was willing to believe anything he told her. After all, she loved Tom, even if it was impossible for him to love her in return.

Sarah was waiting in the entry when Tom returned home. He grinned broadly when he saw her, then hung his coat on the rack while humming softly to himself.

His good mood only served to make hers worse. "You're home early today. Did you and Doc go on many calls?"

"Nope. I didn't even see Doc today." He kissed her cheek as he moved past her on his way to the kitchen.

No matter how much she tried, she simply could not envision her brother with one of those hurdy-gurdy girls. Ethel Bonnell had to be wrong.

Following him into the kitchen, she asked, "So what have you been up to all day?"

"I was helping a friend."

That seemed to be all he was going to offer, but it didn't satisfy Sarah. "A friend? Who?"

Tom slathered butter on a thick slice of bread. "You remember when Doc and I went to take care of that sick girl over at the saloon?"

Her stomach plummeted.

"Well, she's feelin' better now, but she

needed different work and a place to live. Mrs. Rafferty's given Fanny a job over at the hotel restaurant."

"Fanny?"

"Mmm," he answered as he took a bite of his bread.

Sarah stared at her brother, uncertain what to do. He wasn't a boy any longer. He was a young man with a mind of his own. Still, she would be remiss if she didn't remind him he had to be careful about the company he kept. He had his career as a physician to think about.

"After she's had some time to settle in and get used to her new job, I want to invite Fanny over for supper. I'd like you and Grampa to meet her."

"Good Lord! You're not getting serious over some saloon girl, are you?"

He frowned. "Fanny's no saloon girl."

She didn't heed the warning in his voice. "Tom, you must think about what you're doing. You have a bright future before you, but doctors are expected to have high moral character. You can't be taking up with a girl like that. What would people think?"

"People are welcome to think whatever they want." He dropped the rest of his bread on the counter. "Fanny's a friend who needed my help. I didn't expect this from you, Sarah." He marched out of the kitchen before she could say anything more.

Sarah sank onto a straight-backed chair

near the kitchen table. Tom was right, she thought, feeling a spark of shame. But she was only trying to think of his career. If she were certain that all he wanted to do was help the girl, she would say nothing more. But there had been something about the way he'd spoken about Fanny that made Sarah think there was more to this friendship than he was letting on.

She hoped she was wrong.

Chapter Twenty-three

Jeremiah laid the slip of paper on the counter. "Here's my list. Oh, and give me a few of those licorice sticks, too."

Leslie grinned at him before pulling the jar off the shelf. "You're as bad as Benjamin Rafferty. Every time he comes in this store, he heads straight for the candy jars, too."

Jeremiah shrugged and returned her smile.

Bells jingled above the door as another customer entered the mercantile. Jeremiah glanced over his shoulder and watched Tom McLeod make his way toward the counter.

"Hello, Tom," Leslie greeted. "I'll be with you in just a minute."

"No hurry. I just came in to pick up Sarah's birthday present. Your husband sent word it came in on yesterday's train. I'd about given up hope it would get here in time."

"My lands. Is Sarah's birthday comin' up soon?"

"It's today," Tom answered. He looked over at Jeremiah. "Afternoon, Deputy."

Jeremiah gave a clipped nod in return, but his thoughts were on Tom's sister. Today was Sarah's birthday. He wondered what her brother was giving her as a gift. He wondered what he would give her if . . .

He cut off such thoughts abruptly. Buying gifts for Sarah wasn't something he ever planned to do. Shoot. Even if he wanted to—which he didn't—he needed every red cent of his salary just for essentials. Spring would be here before he knew it, and he had to have enough money put back to buy seed and another horse for plowing. There sure as heck wasn't anything left over for silly things like birthday gifts.

"Did you see what I'm giving her?" Tom asked Leslie as the woman continued to gather Jeremiah's supplies.

"No. George brought everything over from the depot and put it all in the stockroom."

"It's a bicycle."

"A bicycle? Land o' Goshen! That'll set a few folks on their ears." She glanced at Jeremiah. "Can you imagine Sarah McLeod riding down Main Street on such a contraption? Looks like Homestead is going to be forced into the twentieth century, like it or not."

Jeremiah merely nodded again and let the conversation continue without him, trying his best not to think of Sarah riding her bicycle down Main Street. Trying not to think of her at all. Trying but failing.

Sarah carried a tray with her grandfather's lunch up to his bedroom. When she opened the door, she found Hank sitting in a comfortable overstuffed chair near the window. Her heart ached when she looked at him. He seemed to have aged several years just since Christmas. It frightened her to think of losing him. He was her anchor. He always had been.

"I brought your lunch," she said cheerfully, putting a good face on her worries.

Grampa's gray eyes studied her as she walked toward him. As she set the tray on the table beside his chair, he said, "I don't understand the men in this valley. In my day, we'd've been flocking around your door. You're a beautiful young woman, princess."

"You're prejudiced, Grampa."

"No." He shook his head. "I've just got good eyes in my head. I may be old, but I'm not blind."

She kissed his forehead. "I don't want other men flocking around my door. I've got you."

"It's too blasted quiet in this house.

When your grandmother was alive, there was always a party for your birthday."

"Twenty-one is too old for such nonsense," she said as she sat on the stool near his feet. "I'm perfectly content to just be with you and Tom."

He peered at her, as if trying to see inside her soul. "You're really not grievin' for Warren." It was a statement, not a question.

"No, I'm not." She folded her hands in her lap and stared down at them. "Gramma Dorie wasn't wrong very often, but she was wrong about Warren and me. He's a good man and all. We just . . ." She shrugged helplessly, not knowing how to explain things.

"You just didn't love him," Grampa finished for her.

She glanced up, surprised by his quick understanding and easy acceptance.

"I loved your grandmother a good many years. I know what it is you're lookin' for." He sighed. "I'd like to see you married and happy before I go."

"You're not going anywhere for a long time," she insisted with some urgency, forcing a smile.

Grampa chuckled. "Not if I can keep from it. Not just yet anyway."

She wished she could tell him about Jeremiah, but of course she couldn't. She wished she had someone to confide in, someone who could advise her. She'd thought of talking to Rose, but was afraid of saying too much. Afraid someone would guess the entire truth, just as Warren had.

"Where's Tom?" her grandfather asked as he picked up a spoon and dipped it into the bowl of soup.

"With Doc, I suppose." Sarah hoped he hadn't gone to see Fanny, but she didn't say so. She didn't think Grampa knew about Tom and the girl from the saloon. She'd just as soon keep it that way.

Hank frowned. "You and your brother have a spat?"

She smiled weakly. "A little one," she lied. "Nothing serious."

"You two never could stay mad at each other for long. I remember when he was a baby; you were like a little mother, always watchin' out after him."

She nodded, her head filled with memories of Tom. She'd adored him from the first moment she'd laid eyes on him. They'd always been extremely close. Perhaps it was because they'd lost their parents at such a young age, but whatever the cause, they'd discovered a bond even distance hadn't weakened.

When she'd seen him this morning, she'd apologized for what she'd said the previous day. She hoped he'd forgiven her, but she couldn't be certain. He'd left the house, forgetting to wish her a happy birthday. It was the first time since they were small children that he'd forgotten. Was it because he was still angry at her?

She swore to herself she wouldn't listen to any more gossip from Ethel Bonnell, that she wouldn't poke her nose in where it didn't belong. Tom wasn't going to jeopardize his future by becoming involved with a saloon girl. He was too levelheaded to make such a mistake. Tom was the reasonable one. It was Sarah who had always had her head in the clouds.

Grampa was right. The two of them had never been able to stay mad at each other for long. Things would be fine between them. They just had to be.

Jeremiah had never been inside a lady's dress shop in his entire life, and he knew it was crazy for him to be there now.

"Well, hello, Deputy Wesley," Madeline Gaunt said as she entered the shop through the heavy velvet curtain at the back. "How can I help you?"

He lost his nerve. "I . . . I just thought I'd see if there were any problems you'd had lately that I should know about."

"Why, no." She cocked one eyebrow, as if she'd seen through him. "What sort of problem do you mean?"

"Nothing in particular. Just keepin' an eye on things."

She nodded. "Well, you're doing a very good job of it. We're all mighty glad to have you as our deputy. I shudder to think what might have happened to Sarah McLeod if you hadn't been there to rescue her."

Sarah. Sarah's birthday.

He glanced toward the shop window. "I . . . ah . . . I was wondering about . . . about that hat. The one in the window."

"Oh, yes. The Avery. It's a pretty bonnet, don't you think?" She bustled over to the display and picked up the blue and yellow hat, then turned to show it to him. "Just look how wonderfully it's made. Fancy straw braid and fine silk ribbons. See how real these velvet flowers look. Of course, it's not suitable for winter, but I just couldn't leave it in the storeroom a moment longer. The colors make me think of spring, and I'm so tired of cold and snow I thought others might like to see it, too."

The pale yellow ribbons were the exact color of Sarah's hair. The blue flowers were the same color as her eyes.

"How much is it?" he asked, unable to stop himself.

"Two dollars and seventy-five cents," she replied, looking at the tiny price tag pinned to the back of the bonnet.

"I'll take it." He reached into his pocket and pulled out the money before he could change his mind.

Madeline Gaunt was obviously dying of curiosity, wondering who the hat was for.

"This will make a very nice gift for your young lady."

He should have told her to forget it. He should have told her to keep the hat. He should have lit out of that lady's shop like a dog with firecrackers tied to its tail.

He should have, but he didn't.

Jeremiah paid for the bonnet and took it back to his dismal room above the jail. He sat on the side of his bed, staring at the straw hat with its ribbons and flowers and imagined it perched upon Sarah's head, all the while wondering why he'd bought a gift for a woman he wanted so desperately to forget.

With a slow shake of his head, he slid the bonnet beneath his bed, deciding it was one birthday present Sarah McLeod would not receive.

Tom let out an angry curse as the wrench slipped from the nut and banged him in the knee. "I swear, if my friend at the academy had told me I'd have to put this contraption together, he'd never have talked me into buying it from him."

Doc Varney chuckled. "Well, if you don't figure it out soon, your sister's birthday is going to be a thing of the past."

"I've nearly got it now." He squinted, trying to see better in the dim light of the doctor's barn. "I only need to tighten this one last nut and bolt. Then it's ready to ride."

"Hmmm. I'm afraid I put as much faith in

a bicycle as I would in one of those motor carriages I've read about."

Tom glanced up at the doctor. "Have you ever seen an automobile, Doc?"

"No, and that suits me just fine."

"But you can't imagine how important they're going to be to doctors in areas like ours. Imagine going twelve or fifteen miles an hour. Think how much more quickly we'll be able to reach our patients when they need us."

"If you don't kill yourself first," Doc Varney said with obvious disapproval.

Tom laughed. "You'll see. The automobile will be used everywhere before too many years go by."

"They'll never replace the horse and buggy. Can't trust a machine like you can the noble equine."

Tom shook his head as he rose to his feet and grabbed the bicycle by the handlebars. He knew it was useless to argue with Doc Varney about modern inventions. When it came to medicine, the physician was as learned as possible. He read all the latest medical journals and books and was willing to entertain new ideas and advancements in the science of healing. But when it came to anything else, he was as set in his ways as Tom's own grandfather. Perhaps more so.

"Stand back," Tom said as he swung his leg over the bicycle, "and let me show you how this thing works."

With a little coaxing, he thought, he just might convince the doctor that not all things new were destined to destroy civilization. And in the meantime, he knew Sarah would be delighted.

Tom was right. Sarah was delighted with his birthday surprise. But more importantly, she was relieved he'd forgiven her for the things she'd said. She didn't want anything to spoil the remainder of his holiday in Homestead.

In the weeks following her birthday, Sarah heard that Tom continued to drop in to see the new kitchen maid at the Rafferty Hotel, but Tom didn't mention bringing Fanny Irvine home for supper again and Sarah didn't remind him. She much preferred to be on good terms with her brother, and she continued to have faith in his good sense. Besides, he would be leaving for Boston by April first, and she was certain, once he was away from Homestead, he would forget the girl quickly enough.

With the arrival of the new year, her grandfather's health began to improve, which lightened Sarah's worries considerably. It wasn't long before Hank McLeod was enjoying visits with his old friends and holding long discussions on politics and the likelihood of Homestead becoming the county seat. Sarah suspected that Grampa even snuck into his office for an occasional cigar late at night, despite Doc Varney's strict orders to give them up.

With the rest of her life falling back into order, Sarah had more time to think about Jeremiah, but she was no closer to discovering a solution to her dilemma than she'd been weeks before. Since he'd forbidden her to bring him his lunch or come to see him at the sheriff's office, she became familiar with the hours he normally made his rounds about town and started taking a daily constitutional at the same time. It was surprisingly easy to meet up with him on the street. She always greeted him with a warm smile and love in her eyes, but he either couldn't see what she felt or refused to see it. She suspected it was the latter of the two.

But Sarah didn't give up hope, not even when it was so obvious that Jeremiah was doing his best to avoid her. Her heart told her that destiny had brought them together. She was certain that Jeremiah was the man she'd dreamed of all her life. Why else had she felt drawn to him from the moment they first met? She was determined to be patient. She was willing to wait, for years if necessary, for him to love her in return.

Chapter Twenty-four

"You're looking kind of pale and peaked this morning," Hank said as Sarah set a jar of jam in the center of the table. "Are you feeling poorly?"

She shook her head. "Just a little tired. I didn't sleep well last night."

"Well, eat a hearty breakfast." Her grandfather slid the platter of fried eggs toward her. "It'll put some color back in those cheeks of yours."

Sarah's stomach lurched, and she swallowed the bile that rose in her throat. "I think I'll just get some fresh air," she whispered before hurrying toward the back door. She grabbed an old coat off the hook near the door but didn't put it on until she was outside.

Rising temperatures had turned the snow to slush yesterday, but the frigid night air had frozen it again into a hazardous path of small hills and ruts. Sarah tripped and nearly fell twice as she rushed toward the outhouse. She barely made it inside before she emptied her stomach.

When the spasms ceased, she sank to the floor, her legs drawn up to her chest. She rested her forehead against her knees. She heard the rapping on the door but ignored it, not certain she could speak yet.

"Sarah?" Tom called softly. "You okay?"

She sniffed and wiped at her watering eyes. "I'm okay," she croaked.

Her brother opened the outhouse door and peered down at her. Mutely, he handed her his handkerchief.

"Thanks." She blew her nose. "I don't know what came over me."

"Maybe we'd better have Doc take a look at you."

"It's nothing. I'm feeling better already." She started to rise.

Tom grabbed her arm and helped her up. His gray eyes were filled with concern as he studied her. "This isn't the first time you've been sick, Sarah. I heard you yesterday morning."

"It's nothing," she said again as they stepped outside into the morning sunshine. "Really."

"I'd feel better if you'd let Doc—"

"For pity's sake, Tom McLeod. I'm not an invalid. I need nothing more than some cider and ash to calm my stomach, and I'll be good as new."

He peered at her a moment longer, then allowed himself a small smile. "Well, I must say, you're sounding a bit better."

She drew in a deep breath of crisp winter air and returned his smile. She didn't want him to see that even she wasn't convinced that what she said was true. He didn't know she'd vomited every morning this past week. She had no appetite, no energy, and every afternoon, she took a nap, just like her grandfather.

But she couldn't allow herself to be sick. Tom was scheduled to leave for Boston at the end of March. She didn't want to think about what would happen to his schooling, his career, if anything was seriously wrong with her. She knew her brother. He would feel compelled to remain in Homestead to take care of both her and Grampa.

With one hand still supporting her arm, the other around her back, Tom guided Sarah slowly toward the house. "Watch your step," he cautioned gently as they picked their way along the uneven path.

"Are you going to be this solicitous with all your patients, Dr. McLeod?"

"Only the ones as pretty as you, Miss McLeod."

By the time they reached the back door of

the house, Sarah felt significantly better. She decided she was silly to worry needlessly. It was nothing more than a mild stomach upset. She would have that cider and ash and be completely herself in another hour or two.

Gramma Dorie's old home remedy did make Sarah feel better. By late morning, she was filled with a restless energy. She dusted and swept and cleaned until the house was spotless. Finally, she decided to bake a cider cake, her grandfather's favorite dessert. As she set out the ingredients, she discovered she was low on both flour and sugar.

"Grampa," she said, looking into his study, "I'm going to the mercantile. Do you want me to bring anything for you?"

Hank lowered the book he'd been reading. "I don't suppose you'd bring me a couple of my favorite cigars."

She wrinkled her nose at him. "No. I wouldn't think of depriving your friends of the privilege of sneaking them in here for you."

She heard him chuckling as she walked away from his study, and she couldn't help her own soft laughter. Her grandfather was incorrigible, she decided, but she wouldn't change a single thing about him.

The afternoon temperature was almost balmy for January. The sun was a yellow ball in a crystal clear sky. Icicles dripped off the rooftops. The promise of spring seemed to be everywhere, but Sarah knew it was a false promise. Winter never relinquished its hold on the valley until well into March or sometimes April.

She followed the boardwalk the long way around to the mercantile rather than taking her usual shortcut down the alley, which was now a sea of slush and mud. As she walked, she pondered the ever present problem of Jeremiah Wesley.

How was she to make him love her if he continued to avoid her so successfully? This past week, she hadn't managed to run into him once while about town. Not even on Sunday. He'd taken to standing at the back of the church, and as soon as services were over, he slipped out the door before she could scarcely rise from the pew.

As she approached the mercantile, she glanced across the street at the sheriff's office. She willed the door to open and for Jeremiah to step outside, but it didn't happen. The door remained closed, and Sarah was denied even the briefest glimpse of him.

But only for a moment or two longer. When she entered the mercantile, she saw Jeremiah standing near the counter. Her heart began to race as it always did when he was near.

As if he sensed her standing there, he turned and their gazes met.

I love you, Jeremiah. Why won't you see how I feel?

Jeremiah did see, and he felt the familiar panic slice through him because of it. Why did she persist in seeing him as something he wasn't? An honorable man would have made her a respectable offer. Why couldn't she see he wasn't an honorable man? There was nothing worthwhile about Jeremiah. He could never be what she thought him to be, what she wanted him to be. She should have seen that by now. She should hate him by now.

"Good afternoon, Jeremiah." Sarah made her way toward him through the tables and barrels that cluttered the center of the mercantile.

"Miss McLeod."

She glanced toward the counter at George Blake. "Hello, George."

"Afternoon, Sarah. How's your grand-father?"

"Much better. He'd like some of those cigars Doc Varney forbade him to smoke."

George grinned. "Well, I've got a few put back for him."

"I'm sure someone will be by for them soon." She shook her head. "Just add them to my bill."

Jeremiah hadn't been able to tear his gaze away from Sarah as she talked. He was thinking how pretty that yellow and blue

275

bonnet, now gathering dust beneath his cot, would look on her. She glanced up at him, her smile warm and genuine.

"Grampa knows better. He just won't listen to reason, and I've given up arguing with him."

She was so beautiful. He remembered the feel of her, the smell of her, the taste of her. He remembered the way she'd clung to him in the dim light of his bedroom. He remembered the small cries in her throat. He remembered a great deal about Sarah that he'd tried to forget.

If things were different . . .

He caught himself before the thought could complete itself. Things weren't different. *He* wasn't different. He tore his gaze free of hers just as George held up the burlap bag holding the supplies he'd ordered.

"Here you go. Everything's in there."

"Thanks, George." He spared Sarah only the briefest of glances. "Miss McLeod."

She seemed unfazed by his curtness. "Good day, Jeremiah. Do come by the house and say hello to my grandfather. I'm sure he'd like to hear how things are going over at the jail."

"I'll try," was the most he would promise before leaving the store.

But her words and the look in her eyes stayed with him for many hours afterward.

*   *   *

Tom leaned against the work counter and watched as Fanny washed dishes in a big tub of hot, soapy water. Her brown hair was tucked up beneath a pristine white cap, and her shirtwaist and dark blue skirt were partially hidden by an enormous white apron.

"Mr. Penny taught me how to make a macaroni pie yesterday, and tomorrow he's expectin' oysters on the train. He says he'll show me how to fix them. Fit for a king to eat, he says. I ain't . . ." She glanced at him, then corrected herself. "I *haven't* never eaten oysters before. Have you?"

He smiled, enjoying her enthusiasm. "All the time when I was in San Francisco. And lobster and shrimp and crabs, too."

She wrinkled her nose in distaste. "I don't know about eatin' things that crawl up outta the ocean."

"You'd like it. Maybe you and I could have some of those oysters tomorrow."

She flushed as her gaze dropped to the dishpan again.

Well, I'll be damned, he thought, his eyes widening. He'd fallen in love.

He pushed off from the counter and stepped toward her. Her blush spread to her neck. The skin on her nape was bright red by the time he reached her.

"Fanny?"

She didn't turn her head to look at him.

Instead, she set another dirty pot in the dishpan and began to scrub it.

"Fanny . . ." He put his hands on her waist.

He heard her quick intake of breath, felt her stiffen, heard the pot drop to the bottom of the dishpan as her hands stilled.

Tom wasn't sure exactly what a man in love was supposed to do. He'd never felt this way before. He'd never even thought about feeling this way.

So he did what came naturally. He leaned down and kissed the back of her neck. Tiny wisps of hair tickled his nose. She smelled of lemon verbena, a pretty, clean scent, well suited to Fanny.

She twisted to look at him, neither one of them mindful of the water dripping from her hands onto the floor. "What'd you go and do that for?" she whispered.

He grinned. He'd never felt happier than he felt right then. "Because I just realized you're the prettiest thing I've seen in all my life."

Her blush brightened. "I don't think you ought t'be sayin'—"

"I love you, Fanny."

She gasped, and her large eyes grew even larger.

"I think I should kiss you. Don't you, Fanny?"

She shook her head.

He cupped her face with his hands. "Oh, yes. I think I should."

He could feel her quivering beneath his lips, but she didn't pull away from him, and he knew he was right. *This* was right. Tom McLeod was in love, and he'd fallen just about as hard as a man could fall.

He lifted his head slightly away from hers and stared down into her big brown eyes. "Will you marry me, Fanny?"

Again she gasped.

"I don't have anything to offer you now. I'll have to finish my training as a doctor before we can marry, but if you'll wait for me, I'd be real proud to have you for my wife."

She did no more than nod her head once before he was kissing her again. Tom figured his life was just about perfect at that exact moment. Nothing could spoil things for him now.

Sarah stared at her brother in open-mouthed surprise. When she found her voice at last, she could only say, "You must be joking."

His expression hardened. "No, Sarah, I'm not joking."

"But you're only eighteen. You still have your medical schooling to finish and—"

"I intend to go to Boston as planned. Fanny will wait for me here in Homestead. We'll get married when I return."

Sarah let out a quick sigh. At least he wasn't going to marry the girl immediately. He'd forget Fanny after a few months in

Boston. Perhaps it wasn't as bad as it had sounded at first.

"I won't forget her."

Heat flushed her cheeks as she knew he'd guessed her thoughts.

"I want to bring her over for supper tomorrow night to meet you and Grampa. It's her night off. I want you to welcome her, Sarah. You should get to know her before you judge her."

She turned away from him and walked over to the parlor window. The sun was resting just above Tin Horn Pass. In a matter of minutes, it would dip behind the mountains, and the valley would settle into night. Quiet would reign. Except at the Pony Saloon.

How many nights had her grandfather had to take men who'd imbibed too much to the jail to sleep things off? How many fights had he broken up in the saloon? How many times had she overheard women gossiping about the hurdy-gurdy girls? How many times had a pastor stood behind the pulpit and railed against the sins of strong drink and the sins of the flesh?

She felt her skin turn hot for a second time as she envisioned herself, naked, in Jeremiah's arms. *The sins of the flesh . . .* She wanted to be back in his arms. *The sins of the flesh . . .* She wanted to spend her life in his arms.

Just who was she to judge Fanny Irvine?

"Sarah?" Tom laid his hand lightly on her shoulder.

She turned and looked up into his eyes.

"Fanny isn't like the others. She's good and sweet. You've never been quick to judge people before, Sarah." His voice softened. "Give her a chance. For me?"

This was her beloved brother, her little Tommy. She wanted the very best for him. She wanted him to achieve everything he'd ever hoped for, ever dreamed of. He deserved the best wife in the world. She couldn't believe the best wife for him was a girl who'd worked in the Pony Saloon. But neither could she deny him what he was asking of her now.

"She'll be welcome at supper tomorrow, Tom." She placed her hand over his where it still lay on her shoulder. "But promise me you won't rush into things. You're still young. In time, you may find you want something very different from what you think you want now."

"When have you ever known me to change my mind once it's made up?"

Never. Tom McLeod had always been the most single-minded individual she knew. Even when he was a schoolboy, he'd gone after whatever he'd wanted and hadn't given up until he'd achieved it. Even if it meant falling out of an occasional tree and breaking an occasional arm.

"Now, let's talk about you a minute," he

said, changing the subject abruptly. "How are you feeling? You scarcely touched your supper tonight."

"I wasn't very hungry, but I'm all right."

"Is it because of Warren?"

"Warren?" She gave a half-laugh. "Good heavens, no." She almost told him then about Jeremiah, about how she felt about him. But she stopped herself. How could she tell Tom she'd fallen in love with Jeremiah so quickly and, at the same time, tell him his feelings for Fanny were no more than a passing fancy?

"If you're sick again," Tom said, breaking the ensuing silence, "I'm going to insist that Doc take a look at you." He frowned, but then the expression was softened by an upward tilt at the corners of his mouth. "I mean it, Sarah. I won't let you talk me out of it if you don't start acting more yourself. Agreed?"

She sighed dramatically. "Agreed."

It was easy to acquiesce. She wasn't feeling the least bit ill and was certain his worries were for nothing.

Chapter Twenty-five

Sarah watched Doc Varney remove his spectacles and clean them with a cloth as he leaned back in his office chair. The room was dreadfully silent. So silent she could hear the ticking of Doc's pocket watch.

Finally, Doc replaced his glasses, hooking the wire end pieces behind his ears, his gaze still lowered toward his desk. "Tom, I think you should leave me alone with your sister for the rest of the examination."

Her brother obviously wanted to protest. His concern for Sarah was written on his face. But in the end, he left without any argument.

As soon as the door closed, Doc Varney said, "Sarah, I'm afraid I must ask you what could be a rather embarrassing question."

He looked up, staring directly into her eyes. "Your symptoms seem to indicate you might be pregnant. Is there any possibility of that?"

"Pregnant?" She straightened, her hands gripping the sides of the examination table in Doc's office.

"Before I continue, I'd like to know if there is such a possibility."

Pregnant? But Rose had said she needn't worry, that it didn't happen every time.

"Do you realize what it is I'm asking you, Sarah?" He rose from his chair, stepped over to the table, and laid a fatherly hand on her shoulder. "You must tell me the truth, my dear."

Her throat closed on her, refusing to let out a single sound. She felt both hot and cold, and she wondered if she might be sick again.

Her silence seemed to answer the doctor's question. He sighed deeply. "Dear heavens," he muttered, his fingers tightening on her shoulder.

Jeremiah's baby. She was pregnant with Jeremiah's baby.

"Does Warren know?"

She glanced up and met Doc's gaze. "Warren?"

"Does he know you're carrying his child?"

She shook her head slowly. Of course, Doc would think it was Warren's child. Everyone would think it was Warren's child. But it wasn't. What was she to do? What was she to say?

"He must be told."

"No!" She grasped hold of the doctor's arm. "I . . . I don't want Warren told. We don't wish to marry. This isn't any of his concern."

"My dear Sarah, it most certainly is his concern. It's his obligation to return and marry you. You cannot—"

"It's not his baby!" she blurted out.

It was Doc's turn to be speechless.

More softly, she repeated, "It's not his baby." She dropped her gaze to her lap, unable to bear looking into his eyes another moment, knowing what he must be thinking of her.

"Whose baby is it, Sarah?"

She shook her head, tears pooling in her eyes.

"Sarah . . ."

She went on shaking her head.

Doc placed his fingers beneath her chin and forced her head up, forced her to look at him, although she couldn't see clearly through the blur of tears. "You have no choice, Sarah. You must tell me who the father of this baby is."

"I love him," she whispered as tears began to slide down her cheeks.

"I'm sure you do. Now, give me his name."

He would never love her now. He would

hate her forever. "Jeremiah."

"Jeremiah Wesley?" He took a step back from her.

Miserably, she nodded.

Doc removed his glasses with one hand and rubbed his forehead with the other. "The blizzard," he said to himself, but Sarah heard him clearly enough.

"It was my fault, Doc."

"Nonsense!" he exclaimed, his voice suddenly filled with anger. "He should be put in his own jail cell and left to rot." He took a sudden step toward her. "Did he force you, Sarah? By gad, if he did, we'll hang him."

She slid off the table, fear streaking through her veins. "He didn't force me, Dr. Varney. It was . . . it was me. It was all my own fault. I . . . I love him. I . . . he . . . he didn't force me. You mustn't say that he did. I . . . I wanted . . . I wanted him. It was me. All me."

The doctor stared at her for what seemed an eternity, but at last he appeared to accept what she was telling him as the truth. "Very well." He glanced toward the door. "Are you going to tell Tom or shall I?"

"Tell Tom?" She'd rather die.

"He has to know. And so does your grandfather."

Oh, why couldn't she just die?

Jeremiah tore a page from the seed catalogue. The premature thaw had him thinking more and more about the farm. He was anxious to return to his own land, anxious to plant the crop. He would put in wheat and alfalfa this first year. And of course he'd have his own vegetable garden. Corn, tomatoes, potatoes, beans, and peas.

Maybe next year . . .

The door flew open, banging against the wall.

Jeremiah jumped to his feet, automatically reaching for his rifle before he saw Tom McLeod stride into the office. His fingers relaxed, and he left the rifle leaning against his desk.

Tom stared at him for a moment, then turned and closed the door. When he looked at Jeremiah again, he said, "I came to invite you to a wedding."

Jeremiah cocked an eyebrow. Tom didn't sound like an overjoyed bridegroom. Besides, Jeremiah had understood that Tom was bound for medical school.

"It's Sarah's wedding," her brother said, taking a step forward.

Sarah's wedding?

He felt as if the floor had suddenly given way beneath his feet and he'd plummeted into a deep, dark pit. He shouldn't have felt that way. He'd wanted her to marry Warren. He'd wanted her to marry and go to Boise and leave him in peace. He was glad Warren had forgiven her. He was glad Warren was coming back to marry her.

Tom took another step forward. His eyes flashed with anger. "And *your* wedding, too."

"What?" His full attention jerked back to the young man opposite him.

"Sarah's pregnant with your bastard, Wesley, and you're going to marry her. Today."

"Sarah's pregnant?" Jeremiah whispered, then a breathless, "Oh, no." He dropped onto his chair.

"You take care of whatever paperwork needs to be done. We'll have the minister at our house this afternoon. You be there, Wesley. Two o'clock."

Sarah lay sobbing on her bed, her face buried in her pillow. She kept hoping she would awaken from some horrible nightmare, but she was afraid this was all too terribly real.

She remembered Tom's cold fury when Doc Varney had explained to him the exact nature of her "illness." Her brother had said some awful, hurtful things to her, calling her a hypocrite for judging Fanny for working in a saloon when she had done far worse. If that hadn't been bad enough, her grandfather's stunned expression when she'd told him what she'd done would haunt her forever. And in a very short while, she was expected to stand beside Jeremiah while the minister pronounced them man and wife.

Oh, please, let this be a nightmare. Let me

wake up and find this is all a nightmare.

She'd wanted him to fall in love with her. She'd wanted him to propose marriage. She'd wanted to be his wife. She'd been so hopeful he would discover how right they were for each other. But she hadn't wanted it to happen this way. She hadn't wanted him to be *forced* into marrying her.

She had failed them all. Jeremiah would resent her. Tom would despise her. Grampa would be ashamed of her.

Sarah was so distraught she failed to hear the bedroom door open.

"Princess?"

She stifled a sob as she sat up and turned toward the doorway.

Her grandfather closed the door behind him, then walked slowly across the room to Sarah's bed. He sat on the edge and folded her small hand inside his larger one. At first, he didn't look at her. Instead, he stared out the window of her bedroom toward the sawmill.

He can't even look at me, Sarah thought, her heart breaking all over again.

Hank squeezed her hand. "Sarah, my dear, you've always been led about by your heart, not your head. You'd see a lost kitten or a bird with a broken wing, and you'd cry as if it was one of your own family sufferin'." Slowly he turned his gaze upon her. "I worried about you plenty, hopin' life wouldn't hurt you too much."

"I'm so sorry, Grampa. I never meant to make you ashamed of me."

"Ashamed? No, princess, I'm not ashamed. I could never be ashamed of you. 'Course, I wish this hadn't happened. I wish . . . Well, I just didn't want you hurt, that's all." Again he squeezed her hand. "Tell me. What're your feelings for Jeremiah?"

She swallowed the lump in her throat.

"Be honest now. You tell me true."

She blinked away the tears that threatened so she could meet his steady gaze. "I love him, Grampa. I think I loved him from the first day I laid eyes on him." She sniffed. "That's why I couldn't marry Warren. That's why I broke our engagement."

Hank McLeod let out a long sigh. "I see."

"Grampa?" She leaned toward him. "This isn't Jeremiah's fault."

"I have a hard time believin' that."

One more reason Jeremiah would resent her. Folks would blame him, yet both she and Jeremiah knew it was Sarah who'd refused to send him away. He'd wanted her to. He'd *asked* her to, but she hadn't heeded him.

Her grandfather leaned forward and kissed her cheek. The tender gesture made her feel like crying again.

"Well," he said wearily, rising from the side of the bed, "it's time you washed your face and prepared to come downstairs. Rev.

Jacobs will be here any time, and so will Jeremiah."

Sarah nodded but didn't move to get up. She waited until her grandfather had disappeared, and the bedroom door was once more closed behind her. Then she flung herself back onto the pillow and wished once more she could die.

Feeling like a man going to his own hanging, Jeremiah visited Carson's Barbershop and Bathhouse. After a hot bath, he got a haircut and a shave. Then he dressed in his best—and only—suit and walked over to the McLeod house, arriving at two o'clock on the dot.

Hank McLeod opened the door in response to his knock. Jeremiah waited for the older man to say something, but all he did was step back from the opening and allow Jeremiah entrance. Jeremiah wished the sheriff would just go ahead and say what was on his mind, what was on *both* their minds.

"The reverend's already waitin' in the living room," Hank said at last, "but I think you'd best have a few words with Sarah before the ceremony."

He was surprised as much by the even tone of the older man's voice as he was by his words.

Hank pointed. "Up those stairs. Second door to the right."

He wasn't certain he wanted to talk to

Sarah before the ceremony, but it didn't seem that he had any choice. He headed up the stairs.

He rapped once on her door, waited, then rapped again. The second knock received a reply.

"Come in."

He opened the door.

Sarah was standing in the middle of a spacious bedroom, her hands folded tightly in front of her waist. She was wearing a dress of periwinkle blue, and her hair was swept up from her neck into a cluster of pale curls at the back of her head.

Finally, his gaze moved to her face, and he felt his heart skip a beat. Her eyes were puffy from crying. Her skin appeared ashen. But it was the look in her eyes he would never forget. Disillusionment. Shattered hopes and dreams. The death of innocence. It was all there for him to see—and all his fault.

"Hello, Jeremiah," she said softly.

"Sarah."

"I . . . I'm sorry. I . . . I never meant for this to happen."

He shifted his weight. "Neither of us did."

"Jeremiah, I . . ." She dropped her gaze to the floor. "I'll try to make you a good wife."

A wife. A pregnant wife who was depending upon him to take care of her. A piece of land that was buried under a foot of snow. Barely enough money to put in his spring crop and see him through to harvest. Failure loomed before him.

He felt as if he'd been dragged back through the years. Life was repeating itself, and there was no escaping it. He would fail, as he always had, and it would be his wife and baby who would pay for it, just as had happened before. It was happening again, and there was no escape.

Sarah looked up, her gaze meeting his. Gone was the disillusionment, the sorrow, the lost dreams he'd seen in her eyes when he'd first entered the room. And in their place was the look he dreaded far more.

"I love you," she whispered, acknowledging aloud what he'd seen in her eyes.

He stiffened, and his voice was harsh. "Let's go downstairs and get it over with."

Chapter Twenty-six

"What God has joined together, let no man put asunder." Rev. Jacobs closed his prayer book. "Jeremiah, you may kiss your bride."

He didn't want to kiss her. He was too afraid of feeling things he didn't want to feel. But Rev. Jacobs was watching him expectantly, and when he looked at Sarah, he knew he could not embarrass her by ignoring the invitation.

He bent forward and brushed her mouth with the faintest of kisses. When he pulled back, their gazes met. He saw the glitter of tears in her eyes once more, but this time they were accompanied by a smile. Despite himself, he felt warmed by it.

Was there any chance he could make her happy? Was there a chance he wouldn't fail her as he'd failed others so often in the past?

Simon Jacobs cleared his throat before saying, "Congratulations, Jeremiah, Sarah. I wish you both every happiness."

"Thank you," Sarah whispered, a faint blush in her cheeks, wondering if he'd been told the truth, wondering if he'd guessed.

The reverend stepped away from the newly married couple and shook Hank McLeod's hand, speaking a few appropriate words. Then Tom walked with him out into the entry hall and bid him farewell at the door.

The lingering silence in the parlor became suddenly awkward. Jeremiah wasn't certain what he should do next. He wasn't sure what he should say to Sarah or her grandfather or Tom.

Sarah's fingers lightly touched the back of his hand. "I . . . I've packed a few things. Shall I get them?"

He nodded. There was no point prolonging everyone's discomfort, no point in postponing the inevitable. They were married now.

She started to leave, then glanced up at him with a hesitant gaze. "Are we . . . are we going out to the farm?"

"We don't have much choice that I can see." He hadn't meant his reply to sound sharp, but he knew it did.

Sarah watched him, as if she expected him to say something more. When he didn't, she turned and walked away.

Jeremiah looked at the sheriff. "I think you should start looking for another deputy, sir."

"I've got no quarrel with the job you're doin'."

"I won't be able to stay in town. The room over the jail is no place for Sarah. Besides, as soon as spring gets here, I'll need to—"

"Let's leave things be for a day or two? I imagine Homestead can get by without a deputy for a few days while you settle in with . . . with Sarah. Then you come see me, and we'll see what we can work out."

There wasn't much Jeremiah could do besides nod in agreement. There was no getting around the fact that he needed a job, now more than ever, but he hadn't expected Hank McLeod to want to keep him on, not after what he'd done.

Sarah looked around her bedroom, memories flooding over her. The times she had sat in the window seat and told her grandmother all her dreams of traveling the world. The nights she had lain in bed and read books about exotic places and exciting people until the wee hours of the morning. Memories of a girlhood filled with warmth and love.

She smiled sadly as she bid the room—and her girlhood—a silent good-bye.

She promised herself she had shed the last of her tears. Marrying Jeremiah, leaving this house, her grandfather, her brother—it was all so bittersweet. She wished Jeremiah had wanted to marry her, wished he had proclaimed his love. She wished Grampa and Tom weren't ashamed of her. She wished things were different.

But they weren't different. She had given herself to Jeremiah in a moment of passion and now she was carrying his child. He had been forced into this marriage by her outraged brother. Nothing would ever change the circumstances surrounding this day.

Yet she *could* change the future. She could teach Jeremiah to love her. She clung to that hope tenaciously. She had to believe it. She would forget the bitterness of this day and remember only the sweetness.

She touched her lips with her fingertips, thinking of the kiss that had sealed their wedding vows. She would remember the touch of his mouth upon hers for the rest of her life.

Somehow I'll teach you to love me, Jeremiah. Until then, I'll love you enough for both of us.

She picked up her satchel off the floor and set it on her bed. It was a small bag. She had packed only what she'd thought she would need for a day or two. She could get the rest of her things later.

She opened the satchel and looked inside. In addition to a second dress, she'd packed a change of underwear, another pair of stockings, two bars of scented soap from the

Montgomery Ward catalog, her toothbrush, and a tin of saleratus. Her grandmother's silver-handled hairbrush and mirror and her porcelain hair receiver were tucked between the folds of her clothing. Her nightgown lay on top of it all.

She felt a flush of wanting as she brushed her fingers across the soft fabric of her nightgown. Ever since that morning in Jeremiah's farmhouse, Sarah had forced herself not to think about their lovemaking. But now she was his wife. It was his right to hold her, caress her, make love to her.

Swallowing quickly, Sarah closed the satchel and lifted it from the bed. Then she turned toward the door and left her room.

Tom was waiting for her at the bottom of the stairs. When Sarah saw him, she paused in her descent, afraid of what he might say to her, even more afraid he would never speak to her again.

She drew in a quick gulp of air, then went down the last few steps, her gaze never wavering from her brother's. When she reached the bottom of the stairs, she reached out and touched his shoulder. He continued to glower at her, but at least he didn't pull away. She took that as a good sign.

"Tommy," she said softly, "I know what I did was wrong, but I do love him. We're right for each other, Jeremiah and me."

"I hope you'll be happy, Sarah." He didn't

sound as if he meant his words, but it was a beginning. "The sleigh's all set and waiting for you."

"I know. I saw it."

"We put together some supplies we thought you might need. Flour, sugar, meat, some canned vegetables, a couple of frying pans, things like that."

"Thank you." She paused, then added, "Take care of Grampa for me."

"You know I will."

"Yes," she whispered, "I know you will."

Her grandfather and Jeremiah appeared in the parlor archway, ending the stilted conversation between brother and sister. Tom retrieved her cloak from the rack and brought it to her. Wordlessly, he helped her into it. She wondered if he would be glad once she was gone from the house.

At the door, her grandfather gave her a warm embrace and kissed her forehead, then whispered, "Make your own happiness, princess."

She found it impossible to reply, so she merely nodded and quickly turned away, hurrying out to the sleigh that awaited them. Jeremiah took her elbow and assisted her onto the seat.

She glanced one last time toward the house. Grampa and Tom were standing on the porch. She raised her hand slightly. Her grandfather returned the wave.

"Ready?" Jeremiah asked.

She turned her head to look at him. She felt once again the quickening of her heart and knew, no matter how hard it was to leave those she'd loved all her life, it would be far worse not to be with Jeremiah.

"I'm ready," she answered.

Hank watched the horse and sleigh pull away from the hitching post in front of the house. His gaze followed the sleigh as it turned the corner and crossed the bridge over Pony Creek.

"Come on, Grampa," Tom said as he took hold of the older man's arm. "It's time we got you back inside before you catch a chill."

"They're going to be all right, Tom. Mark my words. They're going to be all right."

The journey out to the Wesley farm was a silent one. Jeremiah felt Sarah glance his way occasionally, but he kept his gaze fastened to the road. He wasn't ready just yet to begin a conversation with Sarah. He hadn't had time to sort things through in his head, and he needed to do that before they decided what this marriage would mean to the two of them.

As the ground swished by beneath the horse's hooves and the runners on the sleigh, Jeremiah let his thoughts slip back across the weeks since he'd returned to Homestead. The memories that were most prominent were those of Sarah. Time and again, he envisioned her—at church, in her home, in his office, along the boardwalk, in the snow, in his bed, in his arms.

Reluctantly, he admitted to himself that he cared for her, cared for her more than he wanted to care, more than he should care. It would be far wiser for him to keep his heart closed to her. But he'd already proven he couldn't act wisely when it came to Sarah.

The farmhouse came into view, and Jeremiah shoved aside his troubled musings. He had to concentrate on more practical things for now.

A few minutes later, he drew the horse to a halt near the front door. "Here we are," he said, glancing at her for the first time.

She was staring at the house, as if seeing it for the first time. He wondered what she thought of it. It must seem tiny and crude after the house she'd grown up in. Would she grow to hate it here? To hate him for bringing her here? She could have gone with Warren to Boise. She could have had a fine home and an easy life with his brother. Did she already regret the decision she'd made?

Frowning, he hopped down from the sleigh, then helped Sarah to the ground after him, carefully avoiding looking into her eyes. He didn't think he wanted to know what she was thinking.

Jeremiah led the way to the front door. He pulled the key from his pocket and unlocked the latch, then opened the door and stepped inside. The house seemed even colder than outdoors.

"Keep your coat on while I get a fire going," he told Sarah, then went out to the log pile and filled his arms with firewood. When he returned, Sarah was standing in the middle of the small kitchen.

Again he wondered what she was thinking, and again he decided he'd rather not know.

He knelt beside the wood stove and dropped the firewood into the box. Then he set to work building a fire. It wasn't long before warmth began to drive the cold into the farthest corners of the house.

As Jeremiah stared at the flickering flames, he was reminded of his first night back in Homestead, less than two months ago. He'd sat in this room and stared at the fire in this stove and felt the loneliness of his life surrounding him.

He heard Sarah moving about and knew he wasn't alone anymore. He had a chance to put old things to rest. He had a chance to get on with his life.

It's time to let me go, Jeremiah.

"Millie," he said beneath his breath.

Let me go.

"Jeremiah?"

He turned abruptly to find Sarah standing not far away. Her blue eyes were filled with questions, and she was waiting for Jeremiah to answer them. Despite everything, he realized, she trusted him.

"We'll make out, Sarah." He hoped it was true. He knew it wasn't everything she wanted to hear, but it was the best he could offer for now.

Sarah's heart raced in her chest. "Yes. I know we will."

She watched as he raked his fingers through his hair and she thought how much she'd always enjoyed that gesture of his. He seemed to do it whenever he was troubled. She was what troubled him now.

"This isn't much." He motioned with one hand toward the three rooms that made up the house.

"I think it's nice."

He shook his head. "It's not what you could have had."

If I'd married Warren, she silently finished for him. *But I didn't want Warren. I wanted you.* She wondered if a time would come when he would believe her.

He broke his gaze away from hers. "I'd better take care of the horse. Feels like it's going to be another cold night."

Don't pull away from me, she wanted to tell him, knowing that was what he was doing and yet not knowing how to keep him from it.

"I'll bring your things in first so you can get settled. Clear some drawers in the bureau for your clothes. Just move things around however you want them."

"Thank you."

"Sure." He headed for the door.

She felt as if he were running away from her. "Jeremiah?"

He stopped and glanced over his shoulder.

"We're going to be fine," she promised him, hoping he would believe her, hoping he would hear the words behind the ones spoken, hoping he would accept what she was actually saying: *I love you, Jeremiah.*

He merely nodded and went outside.

Chapter Twenty-seven

Jeremiah released the horse from the traces and led it into the barn. Once inside, he removed the harness, hanging the damp leather on a nail that had been hammered into a nearby post. He rubbed the animal down with slow, gentle strokes, taking his time, not prepared to return to the house just yet.

When he was finished with the grooming, he took the horse into the nearest stall and removed its halter. Then he shattered the ice in the watering trough so the animal could get a drink. Finally, he tossed hay into the manger and put a couple of scoops of grain into a heavy tin pail.

As the horse buried its muzzle in the bucket, Jeremiah leaned his arms on the top rail of the stall and watched. The only sounds in the barn were the crunching of oats and an occasional *whish* of the horse's tail.

Let me go. Let me go.

He repeated the words in his head several times, and each time, he felt a little more sure he understood what they meant.

He'd shared something special with Millie. For the years they were married, he hadn't felt like a fool or a nobody or a failure. Millie had believed in him, and so he'd believed in himself. Those hadn't been easy years, but they'd been good ones.

Maybe . . . just maybe, Millie wanted him to find that sort of happiness again. Maybe he wasn't supposed to cling to memories from the past. Maybe it was time for him to let go and move on. Maybe . . .

He turned his head, staring at the barn door. Beyond that barrier was the house, and inside that house was Sarah. Sarah Wesley. His wife.

She wasn't anything like Millie. He didn't expect he would ever feel for Sarah what he'd felt for his first wife. No man could— or should—expect to experience love twice in one lifetime. In truth, he didn't want to feel the same way again. If he didn't love Sarah, he wouldn't be hurt if he lost her. And experience had taught him what it meant to lose someone he loved. He didn't want to feel that kind of pain ever again.

But perhaps he and Sarah could find

some measure of contentment together. He couldn't deny she had a way of filling his thoughts both day and night. He couldn't deny wanting her. Many marriages were based on far less than contentment or even the strong desire she stirred to life within him. Perhaps contentment and desire would be enough for the two of them.

Straightening, he checked the latch on the stall gate one last time, then left the barn and hurried through the gathering dusk to the house.

When he opened the door, he was met with delicious odors wafting from the cook stove, and his gaze was drawn toward the kitchen. Sarah was leaning forward, checking something in the oven. She had tied a faded apron over her blue wedding dress. Wisps of her pale hair had pulled free from the cluster of curls at the back of her head, falling forward in long, silvery-gold coils. As she straightened, she rubbed the back of one hand across her forehead, then pushed the wisps of hair away from her face with her fingertips.

She looked entirely too beautiful and completely incongruous in that setting. The kitchen of the house had been built with the simplest needs of a widower and two sons in mind. The shelves and cupboards were open-faced. The plates and cups were made of graniteware rather than fine porcelain. The wooden floor was worn and uneven.

Sarah deserved better.

She turned and saw him standing there. She smiled uncertainly. "It will be a while before supper's ready."

"No hurry." He removed his hat and coat and placed them on pegs near the door.

"I took the bottom two drawers of the bureau. I hope that's all right."

Hearing the anxiety in her voice, he looked at her again. Maybe it was because she'd said she loved him. Maybe it was because she was carrying his child. For whatever reason, he'd forgotten that this marriage had been thrust upon her, too. It hadn't been of her choosing. She'd never been given a chance to say she wanted to marry him. She was afraid and nervous, and he hadn't been making things any easier for her.

"That's fine, Sarah," he said gently. "Take whatever space you need."

She offered a tentative smile before turning back to the cook stove.

Jeremiah watched her a moment longer, then went into the bedroom, not quite sure what he should do with himself. It had been a long time since anyone had cooked him supper in his home.

He removed his suit jacket and reached to hang it on a peg. He stopped when he saw one of Sarah's dresses hanging there. He touched the yellow calico fabric, as if not quite believing it was real.

He remembered there had been a large

oak wardrobe in her bedroom at her house in town. The rich wood had been finished as fine as piano polish. It had been large enough to hold a dozen dresses or more. Certainly, he'd seen no dresses hanging on pegs in the wall.

All his uncertainties returned, taunting and accusing him. How would he give Sarah the life she deserved? How would he provide for her? How would he make sure she had everything she needed or wanted?

"Jeremiah?"

He turned toward the door to find her standing there.

"I filled the pitcher with water if you'd care to wash up before supper."

He glanced toward the plain white chamber pitcher with its chipped brim, sitting on the stand near the bed. There was a bar of soap in the large, empty bowl, and a towel had been laid out nearby. "Thanks."

"It's nice to have the pump indoors," she said. "So many women don't have that convenience."

Before he could think of anything to say, she disappeared from the doorway, returning to the kitchen and the meal she was preparing.

Jeremiah felt oddly comforted by the few words she'd said to him. With the hint of a smile playing around the corners of his mouth, he poured water into the bowl. He removed the tissue-paper wrapping from the bay rum and glycerine soap and couldn't help smiling when he realized she must have brought the bar of soap just for him. Somehow he knew Sarah's soap would be scented with lavender.

As soon as Sarah set the last item on the table, she removed her apron and sat down across from Jeremiah.

"It isn't much," she apologized, glancing first at her husband, then at the simple fare of chipped beef, biscuits, and gravy. She wished she could have prepared something better for their first meal as man and wife, but there'd been little to choose from and less time to prepare it.

"It looks fine," he assured her.

They ate supper in relative silence. Sarah searched for something to say, something witty or interesting, but her mind seemed like mush. She longed for the lively conversations that had normally gone on around the table at the McLeod home, especially when Tom was there. She was certain she could ease the tension if only there was something neutral or interesting she and Jeremiah could discuss.

As the minutes ticked by, she became more and more aware of the darkness beyond the window. Night had fallen. Before long, it would be time for bed.

She glanced across the table at Jeremiah and felt her stomach somersault, losing what little appetite she'd had to begin with. Suddenly, she couldn't think of anything except lying in Jeremiah's arms. She couldn't think of anything except having him touch her the way he'd touched her all those weeks ago.

Abruptly, she rose from her chair and reached for her apron. Jeremiah looked at her, his eyes questioning.

"I'll begin clearing up," she said. "You go on and finish eating."

With a folded towel to protect her hand from the hot metal, she carried a kettle of boiling water to the sink and partially filled the washbasin. She added cold water from the pump and mixed in some soap before placing dirty dishes into the basin. Then she began to scrub them for all she was worth.

"Here. Let me help you."

Her heart raced madly as Jeremiah stepped up beside her.

He moved her gently aside and took the scrub brush from her hands. "I'm not used to having anyone else doing for me. Why don't you take a moment to relax? It's late, and you've had a long day."

Was he telling her to get ready for bed? She felt a strange quiver in her belly. It was almost an ache.

"All right," she whispered. She dried her hands on her apron, then left the kitchen and went into the bedroom. After lighting the lamp, she closed the door, wondering how long it would be before he joined her there.

Sarah also wondered how any married couple ever understood each other when neither one said what they were really thinking. And she was as guilty as Jeremiah. There were so many things she wanted to tell him, so many things she wanted to ask him, but she kept them all wrapped up inside her, afraid to speak, afraid of his reaction.

But she needn't think about that right now, she told herself. At the moment, she need only think of the hours ahead of them. This was her wedding night, and no matter how unfortunate the circumstances that had brought about their marriage, Sarah wanted her first night as Jeremiah's wife to be perfect.

With the door closed, the room cooled quickly. Sarah shivered as she removed her clothes, washed, and slipped into her nightgown. Her skin was puckered with gooseflesh by the time she pulled a rough-hewn stool over near the washstand. She took her grandmother's mirror from the bureau drawer and braced it against the pitcher so she could see her reflection when she sat on the stool. Staring into the glass, she removed her hairpins and began brushing her hair.

She kept expecting the bedroom door to open, kept expecting to see Jeremiah standing in the doorway. But neither happened. As the minutes slipped away, her arm grew tired. She set the brush aside and twisted on the stool, staring at the still-closed door. She shivered, her nightgown little protection from the chill that had taken hold in the bedroom.

Surely it wasn't taking him so long to wash dishes, she thought.

As she rose from the stool, she was assailed by a horrible thought. What if Jeremiah didn't want to make love to her again? What if their lovemaking had meant nothing to him, just as he'd said?

On trembling legs, she walked to the door and opened it. She half-expected to find the front room empty.

But he was there, sitting near the fire, staring at the flames. Firelight and shadows danced across the handsome planes and angles of his face. She wanted to go to him, but uncertainty held her captive in the doorway.

He felt more than heard her. He raised his eyes and found himself looking upon perfection.

Soft lamplight from the bedroom surrounded her like a ring of moonlight, outlining her delicate shape through the light fabric of her nightgown. Her silky hair fell in soft waves over her shoulders, the ends brushing the gentle swell of her breasts.

He didn't know the moment he rose from his chair. Only suddenly he was on his feet, his gaze still locked on the angelic vision that stood before him.

"I . . . I thought you were coming to bed," she whispered.

Wanting seared through him. He'd almost convinced himself it would be better if he didn't make love to her tonight. She'd said she loved him, but only after he'd taken advantage of her. It would be better if he didn't add to her confusion, if he gave her time to adjust to living with him, if he . . .

She walked toward him, and he felt his mouth go dry.

"Jeremiah? Is something wrong?"

Unable to stop himself, he reached out and drew her toward him, pulling her close, allowing himself the sweet torture of having her pressed against the length of him, yet separated by thin layers of clothing. He cradled her face between his hands, tipping it back so their gazes could touch as well. In the dim light of the room, the blue in her eyes appeared a steely gray. He rubbed his thumbs over her cheeks. Her skin was as soft as rose petals.

He claimed her mouth with his. She tasted sweet.

Sweet, sweet Sarah.

His hands drifted from her face, along her throat, over her shoulders, and down to her breasts. Her nipples were hard. He teased them with his fingertips, brushing across the fabric of her nightgown with the faintest of touches.

He felt her knees give, and he pulled her

back against him, his arms wrapping around her back to hold her in an unbreakable embrace. His body throbbed with wanting, but he would not be hurried. Not tonight.

She sighed softly into his mouth. He drew her sigh inside of him like sustenance for a dying man. He ran the tip of his tongue along the contours of her lips, thinking once again how soft and sweet she was.

At last, he broke the kiss that had joined them for so long. He watched as Sarah opened her eyes, staring up at him in wonder. With quivering fingers, he untied the satin ribbon that closed the neck of her nightgown. When she made no sound of protest, no move to stop him, he slowly pushed the garment from her shoulders, easing it downward until his eyes could feast upon her.

Once again, he brushed his fingers across the peaks of her breasts, watching as the sensitive flesh puckered and the nipples stood even more erect. A low groan worked its way up from his throat as he kissed her mouth, her cheek, her throat, and finally, her breast.

Sarah couldn't think straight. Emotions stampeded through her like a herd of wild horses racing across the range. There was no stopping them, no controlling them. She could only let them stampede and enjoy their wild beauty.

She thought she'd understood about love-making. She'd thought it would be exactly like the last time. But everything was different tonight. His touch was unhurried, yet infinitely more potent.

As he continued to suckle her breasts—first one, then the other—she wove her fingers through his hair, unconsciously drawing him even closer to her. She was scarcely mindful of her nightgown falling into a puddle about her feet, nor did she mind the currents of warm and cool air caressing her bare skin.

She had no idea how long they remained so. It seemed no more than a second, no less than a lifetime. Then suddenly she was swept into his embrace, and he carried her into the bedroom.

Moments later, as he joined her on the bed, Sarah opened her arms and gave herself, heart and soul, to her husband.

For Sarah, her wedding night was pure magic.

With his body, Jeremiah showed her his gentleness, his strength, his passions. With his mouth, he whispered tender words and kissed her until she was breathless. With his hands, he caressed and stroked and lit flames of desire inside Sarah which she feared might consume her.

Only one thing marred the perfection of the hours of lovemaking that filled the night—the knowledge that he was holding back from her the one thing she wanted most. His love. She felt the protective barrier around his heart as surely as if she could touch it with her hands, and she wondered what she could do to break it down so she might enter.

In the wee hours of the night, Sarah lay nestled against Jeremiah, her head on his shoulder, her hand on his chest. Her desires were sated for the moment, although little thrills of rapture still sang through her veins. She was exhausted, but pleasantly so.

The room was dark. Jeremiah had turned down the lamp after going to the kitchen to bring her a cup of water. That had been just before they'd made love a second time.

"When I was a little girl," she said softly, not knowing if he was awake or asleep, "I used to pretend Grampa and Gramma were a duke and duchess and all the folks in Homestead were their subjects. When there'd be a barn dance, I'd make believe they were all lords and ladies of the realm and the barn was a wondrous ballroom with beautiful chandeliers and the men with fiddles and mouth organs were members of a huge orchestra."

His breath stirred the hair on the top of her head. She was certain now that he slept, but she continued, wanting to tell him even if he didn't hear her.

"I dreamed of traveling all over the world. I wanted to see the Eiffel Tower in Paris and the castles of England and the Waldorf Hotel in New York City." She closed her eyes. "I remember when Rose married Michael Rafferty. She'd had her plans all made to leave Homestead; then Michael came here and they fell in love. I remember thinking she was crazy not to go. I knew I wanted a whole lot more out of life than a husband and babies."

She turned her head until her lips touched the flesh over his collarbone. She took a deep breath, enjoying the scent of him. She could smell the lingering traces of bay rum mingled with a more masculine scent that was all his own. With a small sigh, she turned her head once more, fitting herself so perfectly into the curve of his arm.

"I was going to leave Homestead. I was going to see the world—Rome, Paris, London. I thought I might be an actress or an opera singer. And if I did ever marry, I planned on marrying a duke or some handsome, mysterious count . . . or even a prince."

She opened her eyes as she bent her head slightly backward, looking up in the direction of his face. She couldn't see him in the darkness of the room, but she could see him clearly with her heart.

"And look what happened to me," she whispered, her voice filled with awe. "I *did* marry a prince."

With another sigh, she closed her eyes and drifted off to sleep.

Chapter Twenty-eight

Sarah awakened to a splash of sunshine spilling across the bedroom floor through the open doorway. The place where Jeremiah had slept was empty, the sheets cool.

She sat up, drawing the blankets with her to cover her naked breasts, and looked about the room. Her nightgown was lying across the stool near the washstand, and she knew that Jeremiah had put it there some time this morning. Last night, they'd been too involved with each other to pick up the gown from the floor.

She felt flushed with pleasure as memories from the previous night washed over her. She was also filled with hope for their future.

Humming softly, she got out of bed. She washed hurriedly, then slipped into her clothes and left the bedroom. Jeremiah wasn't in the house, and his coat was gone from the peg near the door. She assumed he was busy with his morning chores.

In the kitchen, she found a kettle of water already heating on the stove as well as a pot of freshly brewed coffee. She took a cup from the shelf and filled it with the dark liquid. Next, she opened a jar of peach preserves and spread some on a biscuit. She realized, as she took a bite, that she was famished. For a change, she didn't feel the least bit queasy.

As she stood in the middle of the tiny kitchen, she wondered if Jeremiah had eaten anything before going outside to do his chores. She wondered what he liked to eat for breakfast. Was he satisfied with a cup of coffee and a slice of bread or did he like bacon and eggs or flapjacks with fresh-picked strawberries and thick syrup?

She washed down the last of her biscuit and jam with a swallow of coffee, set her cup in the sink, then walked to the window to look outside. What was keeping Jeremiah so long in the barn?

For a moment, she considered putting on her coat and going out to join him, but in the end she decided against it. If he wanted to be with her, he knew where she was. She could be patient. She had the rest of her life to love and be loved.

*   *   *

Jeremiah rubbed the soap into the leather harness, working it in deep with his fingers, then rubbing it with a soft cloth. But his mind wasn't on the leather or the business of cleaning it. He was thinking about Sarah, about last night.

It was hard for him to believe how different he felt this morning. He wasn't a stranger to the pleasures to be found in bed with a woman. He wasn't even a stranger to the pleasures to be found with this particular woman. But last night had been different from anything he'd known before.

So why, he wondered, was he sitting out here in a cold, musty barn when he could be in a warm house with Sarah?

The answer was simple enough. Last night had been *too* pleasurable. Last night he'd seen all the possibilities just waiting for him, tempting him to take another chance. But he didn't want to need Sarah, and he didn't want to be needed by her. He wanted to keep his distance. It was better for both of them that way. He couldn't be what she wanted him to be. He couldn't give her what she wanted him to give her.

He closed his eyes and felt the cold emptiness of his heart. From his earliest memories, he'd longed to earn his father's love and to love him in return, but Ted Wesley had rebuffed all of his oldest son's efforts to bring them closer. Not until he'd met Millie had Jeremiah known what love could mean. For a few short years, his world had been a warm and wonderful place to be.

He'd loved her—and then he'd lost her.

Now there was Sarah. Sweet, sweet Sarah with her summer blue eyes and her gossamer hair of silvery-gold and her heart-shaped mouth and her dreams. So many dreams. She was offering him love, but he could not love her in return. He couldn't, because to do so might mean he would lose her forever.

And that, he suddenly realized, he could not bear.

At noon, Tom McLeod knocked on the back door of the hotel kitchen. A moment later, the door opened, and there stood Fanny. She was wearing a simple white shirtwaist and a tweed skirt, and on her head was a hat of blue straw with a striped ribbon around the crown. Tom thought she looked quite fetching.

"Are you ready?"

"Maybe this isn't a good time, Tom," she answered quickly, her eyes anxious.

"Grampa wants to meet you. He's waiting for us at home." He held out his arm. "Come on. You've got the afternoon off. There's no point in staying here."

She sighed deeply, as if knowing it was useless to argue with him. "Come inside. I'll get my wrap."

323

The kitchen was hot and steamy. Several pots boiled on the stove, and judging by the delicious smells, something succulent was roasting in the oven. Mr. Penny, the hotel chef, greeted Tom with a wave of his spatula, then went back to the dessert he was crafting.

Fanny came out of the tiny, cell-like room off the kitchen, already wearing her coat. "I'll be back before suppertime, Mr. Penny."

Again the chef motioned with the spatula, this time without lifting his gaze.

"Whew," Tom said as they stepped outside. "How do you stand working in there in all that heat?" He was grateful for the cool air on his cheeks.

Fanny shrugged. "You get used to it." It was almost as if he could hear her say, *It's better than workin' at the saloon.*

He took her hand and placed it in the crook of his right arm, then covered her fingertips with his left hand. Walking slowly, they left the back of the hotel and followed the boardwalk along West Street.

Tom glanced over at her several times, wondering if now was a good time to tell her what he'd been thinking or if he should wait until after she'd met his grandfather. What would he do if she thought it a terrible idea? What if Grampa didn't take to her? What if she didn't take to him?

Indecision kept him silent until it was too late. Before he realized it, they'd turned the corner onto North Street and arrived at his home. As they left the boardwalk, Fanny hesitated, pulling back on his arm and forcing him to stop beside her.

She stared up at the house, her brown eyes seeming larger than usual. "Oh, Tom, I don't know. I don't think—"

"That's right. Don't think, Fanny," he said with an encouraging smile. "Just come inside. Grampa's waiting for lunch. You don't want to keep him from eating on time, do you?"

She shook her head.

"Good." Putting his arm around her back, he guided her along the path and up the steps onto the porch. As he reached for the doorknob, he smiled again. "Grampa's going to love you, just like I do." With that, he opened the door and called out, "We're here!"

By the time the door was shut behind them, Hank had appeared in the parlor doorway. His gray eyes flicked quickly from Tom to Fanny. He studied her with that intense sheriff's gaze of his, the kind that made both hardened criminals and mischievous boys behave. Tom knew that the look was mostly bluster, but he also knew how intimidating it could be.

"It's okay," Tom whispered in her ear as he helped her off with her coat. "He's all bark and no bite." Once their coats were hung on the rack, Tom took her arm once again, urging her forward with a gentle pressure. "Grampa, this is Fanny Irvine. Fanny, this is my grandfather."

Fanny held out her hand, her chin lowered toward her chest, her gaze downcast. "I'm pleased t'meet you, Mr. McLeod."

"It's my pleasure, Miss Irvine." Hank accepted her hand within both of his, holding on until she finally lifted her head and looked at him. Then he smiled at her. "I understand you've made Tom happy by agreeing to be his wife."

She blushed. "It's me who's happy, sir."

Tom breathed a sigh of relief as his grandfather turned, still holding Fanny's hand, and led her into the dining room. His confidence had been bolstered by Grampa's reception of Fanny. Now all he had to do was find the right moment to share his idea with the two of them.

Sarah spent the morning acquainting herself with every nook and cranny in the house. She sorted through the drawers in the bureau, touching Jeremiah's clothes, memorizing every article. She counted the pots and pans and dishes and made a list of all the food supplies they needed from the mercantile. She noted how many blankets they had and that they were in need of more sheets. She climbed the ladder to the loft, finding it full of dust and cobwebs but nothing else.

The most notable thing about the house, in Sarah's mind, was the lack of anything that said a family had once lived there. The house was plain, simple—and completely lacking in warmth. The necessities were provided for, but that was all.

She remembered the wild animals Warren had carved from wood. Surely, his father would have saved something like that. But if he ever had, it was gone now.

Late in the morning, Sarah found a small metal box beneath the bed. Kneeling on the floor, she opened it. There were several letters bound by a piece of string and some official-looking papers which she suspected was the deed to the Wesley land. Beneath them, she found two photographs.

One was of a young man and woman on what appeared to be their wedding day. She wouldn't have recognized the groom as Ted Wesley, except for his striking resemblance to Warren. The woman was small and delicate with dark eyes that were very much like Jeremiah's.

The second photograph had been taken near the lumber mill in Homestead. Ted Wesley stood in the middle, Jeremiah to his right, Warren to his left. She guessed Jeremiah would have been about fourteen when the photograph was taken. Almost a man and yet still a boy. He had already stood several inches taller than his father. But what was most striking about the photograph was the distance between each member of the family. They stood apart from each other, but she sensed that the separation was more emotional than physical, and looking at it filled her with melancholy.

She touched a fingertip to the photograph, placing it over Jeremiah's heart. "You don't have to be alone," she whispered. "I'm here."

With a sigh, she returned the photographs to the box, closed the lid, and slid it back under the bed.

How could she make him open up to her? she wondered as she rose from the floor. She wanted so desperately to know him, to understand him. Nothing she learned would ever change the love she felt for him, would make it weaker or stronger, but she wanted to know, all the same.

Jeremiah Wesley, she decided, was a very complicated man. She knew he cared for her, but he was holding so much back. If he wouldn't talk to her, how could she ever know why he held back?

She left the bedroom and walked to the window once again, staring off to the side of the house in the direction of the barn, looking for any signs of her husband. As luck would have it, she saw him approaching the house, his hands in the pockets of his coat, his head bent forward against the winter wind.

Not wanting to be caught at the window watching for him, Sarah stepped quickly away and went to the kitchen. She filled a cup with coffee, turning from the stove just as the door opened.

Fanny wasn't sure she understood what it was Tom was saying. He wanted her to live here, in this beautiful house, while he was away at school? Her? Fanny Irvine?

Hank McLeod nodded his head approvingly. "I think it's a darned good idea."

Standing beside the fireplace, Tom glanced at Fanny, waiting for her answer.

"But I got no right to live here," she said, looking from Tom to his grandfather and then back again. "I wouldn't be your wife. I'm not family. And you might change your mind while you're off to Boston about wantin' to marry me."

"And you might do the same," he countered.

"Oh, no. I wouldn't ever do that."

"Neither would I." He left the fireplace and joined her on the sofa, taking her hand in his. "Don't you see? With Sarah married and living out in the valley, Grampa's going to just rattle around in this big old house. If you were to come stay with him, he wouldn't be so lonely."

Hank chortled, then shook his head. "What the boy is sayin' is, I'm gettin' too old to be left alone. I'll make you very poor company, too."

"You're not too old, Mr. McLeod," she

protested, "and I bet I'd like stayin' here."

Tom squeezed her hand. "Then you'll do it, Fanny? You'll move in here when I leave for the institute?"

"I guess I will." She looked from one to the other, wide-eyed, still not believing this was really happening. A girl like Fanny just didn't have wonderful things like this happen to her. "If that's what you both want, I guess I will."

Jeremiah's gaze found Sarah the moment he entered the house. She was wearing the yellow calico today, and he was reminded of a meadow filled with wildflowers, bathed in a shower of sunshine.

She held out a cup toward him. "You must be cold after all this time. Here. This coffee will warm you." She brought the drink to him.

She smiled gently as he took the cup, then turned away and walked back to the kitchen, saying, "I've been doing some thinking, Jeremiah." She filled another cup with coffee from the speckled pot on the stove. "I don't know much about farming, but if I'm going to be a farmer's wife, I think I should learn." She turned around. "Don't you?"

Jeremiah tried to imagine her working in the fields with him, walking behind a plow or planting seeds, but he just couldn't put the two together. Sarah belonged in some fancy parlor, pouring tea from a china teapot for her guests.

"And I know you weren't planning on marrying and having to worry about food and clothes for more than just yourself, so I want to help out that way, too. I suppose I'll be limited in what I can do, what with"—she blushed—"what with a baby on the way."

He sat down on the chair across from her. This time he imagined her sitting in a rocking chair, her belly swollen with his child. In response, he felt an odd ache in his chest.

"I do think, if you'd build a coop, I could take care of some chickens for laying. We could have all the eggs we wanted for cooking and eating, and we could sell the extra ones to the mercantile. Ralph Evans has chickens he sells. I went to school with his wife, and she's told me they've got some of the finest laying hens in the entire state. I'm sure Belle would tell me what to do so I wouldn't kill them unintentionally."

Her enthusiasm and optimistic outlook were hard to resist. He supposed, if she really wanted to keep chickens, that he could afford to buy some. There was enough lumber in back of the barn to build a fair-sized coop, and he had plenty of straw up in the barn loft.

"And another thing. I'm a good seamstress. I've been sewing my own gowns since I was a girl." She touched her sunshine yellow skirt. "I made this one."

"It's very pretty." *You're very pretty.*

"I thought I'd offer my services to Mrs. Gaunt. I could do alterations and such here at home, and you could take them into town when they're finished. It probably wouldn't pay much but it would—"

"You don't need to work for Mrs. Gaunt."

"But I—"

"No," he said firmly.

He looked away from her, turning his gaze out the window at the snow-covered land. He wanted to take care of Sarah. If he could make this farm produce, if he could give Sarah the things she needed, if he could keep her and the baby healthy and safe, then maybe, just maybe . . .

He closed his eyes for a heartbeat, knowing what he wanted to feel, what he wanted to think, but afraid to feel it, afraid to think it.

"You won't need to take in sewing for others for us to get by." He took a deep breath and hoped what he said was true. "I'm going to take care of you, Sarah."

She was silent for a moment, as if considering his words. Then she leaned forward, reaching across the table to touch his hand where it rested around the coffee cup.

"I never doubted you'd take care of me, Jeremiah," she said, her gaze unwavering. "I never doubted it for a minute."

Perhaps Sarah didn't doubt it, but

Jeremiah did. He couldn't seem to help it. Sarah didn't know how many times he'd failed those he'd loved the most. She didn't know the price they'd paid because of his failures.

But Jeremiah knew. He knew all too well.

Chapter Twenty-nine

During the night, a chinook wind blew in from the west. When Jeremiah awakened in the morning, it was to the rhythmic sound of melting snow dripping off the roof.

Jeremiah tightened his arm, drawing Sarah close against him. Her breathing was slow and steady, and he knew she still slept deeply. For a moment, he allowed himself to enjoy the feel of her bare skin against his. He considered waking her with kisses before making love to her again. He knew it would be easy to remain in bed with her both day and night.

But as tempting as the notion was, he knew it wasn't to be. He'd already slept later than he should have.

He sighed as he softly kissed her forehead,

then slipped his arm from beneath her neck and sat up, lowering his feet to the rag rug covering the floor beside the bed. He stood up, stretching his arms above his head and yawning. Grinning, he reminded himself he wouldn't feel so tired if he'd spend his time sleeping when he was in bed.

He poured water into the washbasin and splashed his face. The shock of the cold water helped revive him, and he completed his ablutions with haste. When he turned to reach for his clothes, he found Sarah watching him from the bed. She was lying on her side, one arm braced against the mattress, her hand supporting her head. Her pale hair was mussed, her blue eyes still sleepy.

Caught staring at him, she blushed, and her gaze fell away. "You're a pleasure to look at," she admitted honestly but with obvious embarrassment.

Her words caused a bolt of desire to streak through him. Again he was tempted to return to the bed and spend the day there with Sarah. It took all his resolve to ignore the enticement she presented. "If we're going to town, we'd best get a move on." Before he could change his mind, he stuck first one leg, then the other, into his union suit.

She sat up. "We're going to town?"

"I need to get my saddle horse from the livery"—he slipped his shirt over his head—"and you mentioned we needed some supplies. Besides, I figured you'd want to get the rest of your things." He pulled on his britches, then picked up his boots and walked to the door. "I'll hitch up the sleigh while you get dressed."

"I'll hurry," she called after him.

He sat down on the chair near the stove and pulled on his socks and boots. He could hear Sarah moving around in the bedroom, and he wished he was lying on the bed, watching her as she'd watched him.

But when he closed his eyes, he could see her almost as clearly as if he were in the bedroom. The way she brushed her hair, tipping her head slightly to one side, a waterfall of pale hair hanging down nearly to her waist. The tender way she touched the silver-handled mirror before putting it back in the bureau drawer. Her legs, long and shapely, as she pulled on her stockings and white cotton drawers. Her breasts, round and firm, disappearing beneath a lacy chemise.

He opened his eyes again and stared toward the doorway of the bedroom. It seemed impossible he should have memorized so many things about her in so short a time. He knew it was a dangerous sign.

Rising abruptly, he stepped toward the door, put on his coat, and headed outside, hoping the Chinook wind would clear his head of thoughts of Sarah.

The trip into Homestead was as silent as their passage to the farm had been on their wedding day. Sarah sensed Jeremiah's unwillingness to speak and didn't attempt to start a conversation. Instead, she allowed herself simply to enjoy the passing landscape and the pleasure of being with Jeremiah.

The mild weather had already changed the appearance of the valley. Roofs were no longer covered with snow, making them easier to see from a distance. Trees stood bare and straight, like gray skeletons against a white background.

She knew winter was once again teasing the inhabitants of the valley. There would be more weeks of snow and cold. Spring was still many weeks away.

But when spring came, the stands of cottonwood and aspen would drape themselves in lush green robes, and from their branches, birds would welcome each day with song. The pastures would roll with long grasses waving in the fresh breezes of the season. Farmers would turn their fields, and the air would be filled with the earthy scent of rich, dark soil awaiting planting.

In the summer, the days would turn hot. Wildflowers in glorious shades of yellow, purple, blue, and white would spill across the valley like an overturned jar of jelly beans on the mercantile floor. Morning glories would crawl along the ground and climb banisters on front porches. In town, folks would sit in the shade and sip lemonade, gossiping about their neighbors and bemoaning the state of politics.

By late August, the days would already be noticeably cooler, the nights cold. Dust would roll in giant clouds behind wagons and buggies as they went to and from town. Autumn would come early to the valley, bringing with it the scents of harvest.

And then their baby would be born.

For the first time, she realized what it truly meant to be pregnant with Jeremiah's child. When she'd first found out, she had felt despair and shame and had tried to deny the truth. Then she'd thought only of the consequences—Jeremiah being forced to marry her without loving her, the unhappiness it caused her grandfather and brother. But now, in this instant, she became aware of the beauty and miracle of life.

She was carrying Jeremiah's child within her.

She felt aglow, her sudden joy warming her from the inside out. Closing her eyes, she folded her hands over her abdomen and began wishing the months away.

"Well, we're here," Jeremiah said, interrupting her pleasant musings.

Sarah opened her eyes, surprised to find that what he'd said was true. She glanced sideways at Jeremiah and found him watching her.

"Nervous?" he asked.

"No."

"There's probably been some gossip."

She smiled weakly and gave a little shrug. "There's always gossip in a small town." Gathering her courage, she slipped her hand into the crook of his arm. "But they can't help but see how much I love you. No one will be surprised I wanted to marry you."

He didn't scowl or pull away as she half-expected him to. Instead, he momentarily covered her hand with one of his and met her gaze with one of concern. "There may be some things said about you that—"

"Jeremiah," she interrupted quickly, leaning closer to him, "it doesn't matter what people say. Not as long as I'm with you."

Jeremiah thought Sarah was too naive for her own good. She was forever looking for the bright side of everything and everyone. But he knew that things didn't always turn out for the best. Everyone wasn't always pleasant and kind. He didn't want her hurt on account of him, but he was afraid she would be.

He guided the horse and sleigh to the mercantile. After they'd drawn to a stop, he glanced once again at Sarah. "You sure you don't want to go to your grandfather's and wait for me?"

"I'm sure."

He wrapped the reins around the brake handle and climbed out of the sleigh, stepping into a good two inches of slush. Turning to help Sarah, he placed his hands around her waist, then lifted her straight from the vehicle onto the boardwalk.

Despite her denial, he suspected that Sarah was nervous about facing the citizens of Homestead for the first time since her wedding. Hoping he'd be able to ease the way, he put his arm around her, his palm in the hollow between her shoulder blades, and together they entered the store.

Before the door had even closed behind them, Leslie Blake welcomed them. "Land o' Goshen! George, look who's here. It's Mr. and Mrs. Wesley." She bustled out from behind the counter, her arms outstretched. "You sure gave everyone a surprise." She hugged Sarah, then stepped back to look up at Jeremiah. "Quite a surprise," she added, a slight question in her voice.

He smiled evenly. "I couldn't take the chance of some cowpoke sweeping her off her feet. Marryin' her quick seemed like the smart thing to do."

Leslie's husband came out of the stockroom to add his congratulations. "Good thing you did," George said with a laugh as he grabbed Jeremiah's hand and shook it in an iron grip. "Sarah was the prettiest single gal in three counties, and don't think the young bucks hereabouts didn't know it. Come the spring thaw, there'd have been a herd of 'em hangin' about the McLeod house." He let go of Jeremiah's hand and looked at Sarah. "I wish you a world of happiness. Both of you."

"Thank you." Sarah's smile was breath-taking.

Jeremiah began to relax. Maybe he'd been unnecessarily worried about what others would say. Besides, George was right. Sarah *was* the prettiest gal in three counties.

"Well, what can we do for you?" Leslie asked expectantly.

Sarah drew a slip of paper from her pocket bag. "We need some supplies."

"'Course you do. I know what Jeremiah bought to take out to that farm of his. It's a wonder you both didn't plumb starve in the last two days."

Sarah glanced over her shoulder, and Jeremiah would have sworn he knew exactly what she was thinking—that neither one of them had given much thought to food in the last thirty-six hours.

Then Leslie took hold of Sarah's arm and led her away from the two men.

George patted Jeremiah on the back. "You're a lucky man. A very lucky man."

"Yes," he replied softly, "I guess I am."

Sarah fingered the soft flannel fabric, thinking it would be perfect for infant clothes. Of course, it was too soon for her to worry about such things, but in a few months she would want to begin making diapers and small shirts and tiny caps and nightgowns. She was vaguely aware of Leslie chattering on about her youngest brother, Loring, who was badly in need of a wife, but the other woman's words meant little to her as she thought about the baby in her womb—Jeremiah's baby—and the potent love she felt for it.

"Good day, Mrs. Bonnell," Leslie said in a loud voice, interrupting Sarah's musings. "I'll be with you in just a moment."

Sarah felt a sinking sensation in the pit of her stomach when she heard the woman's name. Jeremiah had been right. She should have gone to her grandfather's house while he did the shopping. She didn't feel ready to face Ethel Bonnell, the town busybody, just yet.

"My goodness! Sarah McLeod, is that you?"

Taking a deep breath to steel herself, Sarah turned around. "Good morning, Mrs. Bonnell."

"I thought that was your grandfather's sleigh I saw outside."

"Yes." She moved away from the bolts of fabric, afraid the woman would take one look at the flannel and know what she'd been thinking.

"Such a surprise you gave everyone, getting married without a word to a soul."

"It's the way we wanted it. Just the two of us and family."

Ethel's eyes had the gleam of a wily predator moving in on its quarry. "Such a shame

the groom's family couldn't be there, too."
She raised a hand to cover her mouth. "Oh
my! What a careless thing to say. Naturally,
Warren wouldn't have wanted to be there,
given the circumstances."

Sarah couldn't think of a response. The
woman had spoken nothing but the truth.
Was it possible she knew even more than
she was saying?

"What circumstances are those, Mrs.
Bonnell?" Jeremiah asked as he stepped
out from the storeroom.

Ethel's eyes widened as she turned. "Mr.
Wesley, I didn't know you were here."

"Obviously." He moved steadily forward.

Ethel Bonnell pressed herself against the
display table behind her, but Jeremiah
stepped past her without a second glance,
arriving at Sarah's side. He gave her a
look of encouragement, then turned to look
at Ethel.

"Just what circumstances were you refer-
ring to, Mrs. Bonnell?" he asked again.

Her color was high as she edged away from
the table which was pressing against her
ample backside. "Well, I just meant . . . Well,
certainly everyone knows . . ." She drew herself up in righteous indignation. "She *was*
engaged to Warren, after all."

"My wife broke her engagement to my
brother a month before we were married.
She was under no commitment to him or
anyone else." The tone of his voice dared the

woman to say something more.

Sarah couldn't have hidden her smile if her life depended upon it. Witnessing the way he'd defended her made any gossip that Ethel Bonnell might start a trifling matter.

Jeremiah glanced toward the counter. "Mrs. Blake, is our order ready?"

Caught staring, Leslie flushed with embarrassment. "Yes. Yes, it is."

He returned his gaze to Sarah. "I think it's time we went to your grandfather's."

Her smile broadened as she nodded wordlessly. *He does love me*, she thought in wonder. *He may not know it yet, but he does love me.*

Jeremiah was still seething as he helped Sarah into the sleigh a few minutes later, but his anger was directed at himself, at his own helplessness, not at the nosy, self-appointed guardian of Homestead's society. Sure, he'd stopped Ethel Bonnell for now, but when the baby arrived weeks earlier than it should, there'd be nothing he could do to protect Sarah. Everyone would know she'd been pregnant when they married. People like the Bonnell woman would do their best to hurt Sarah because of it.

As he got into the sleigh beside Sarah and took up the reins, he looked at her and found her watching him with that same beautiful smile still curving her attractive mouth.

"Don't you understand what she was

saying about you?" he snapped, frustrated by her seeming lack of comprehension.

"Of course I understand." She slipped her arm through his and slid close up against his side. "But you took care of me, just as you promised."

"Women," he muttered beneath his breath as he slapped the reins against the horse's rump.

And then, unexpectedly, he smiled, too.

Chapter Thirty

Sarah looked toward her grandfather's house as the horse and sleigh moved along North Street. Odd how she had spent her entire life in that house, and suddenly it no longer seemed like home. Home was three small rooms and a loft near the mountain range, a place surrounded by farmland and little else.

Arriving at their destination, Jeremiah drew the sleigh to a stop. He helped Sarah down; then the couple walked side by side along the pathway to the front porch. When they stopped before the door, Sarah found she was uncertain what to do next. Did she open the door and walk in, the way she'd been doing all her life? Or did she knock, as any visitor would?

The decision was taken from her as the front door opened from the inside. Tom, wearing his coat and hat, looked surprised when he saw them standing there.

"Hello, Tom," Sarah said, uncertain what his reception might be. He'd been so angry with her two days ago.

"Sarah." His gaze shifted to Jeremiah, and he acknowledged him with a quick nod. "I'm on my way to Doc Varney's."

"That's all right. We needn't keep you. I just came for the rest of my things." She heard the stiffness in her voice and was saddened by it. She wanted to share the joy of her love for Jeremiah with Tom, but she knew he wasn't ready to listen. Maybe someday but not now. "How's Grampa?"

"He's doing well. You'll find him by the fire." Again Tom glanced at Jeremiah, then back to Sarah. "I've got to get over to Doc's."

Sarah and Jeremiah parted, opening a path for her brother to pass through. She watched Tom as he swiftly walked away from them.

"He'll come around," Jeremiah said. "Just give him some time."

She turned to face her husband, wondering how something that could bring her so much joy—her marriage—could also bring her so much sorrow. She loved Jeremiah. She wanted to spend the rest of her life with him. Despite the circumstances, she was even glad to be carrying his child. She hoped there would be many more to follow. But she'd also hurt and disappointed others she loved, and her brother's continuing anger was painful to her.

"Come on," Jeremiah urged, "we're letting all the cold air inside."

Sarah nodded and moved into the entry hall. Without stopping to remove her cloak, she walked to the doorway of the parlor. Hank McLeod was seated in the overstuffed chair near the fireplace, an open book in his lap. His reading glasses were perched on the end of his nose, but his eyes were closed and his chin was resting on his chest as he dozed.

Moving silently, she crossed the room, then leaned forward and kissed his forehead.

"Hmm." His eyes opened as he straightened.

"Hello, Grampa."

"Princess."

She knelt on the floor beside him and took hold of his hands. "How are you feeling?"

"Like I'm seventy-five," he answered with a wry smile. "Question is, how're you?"

"I'm fine."

Her grandfather's gray eyes searched her face before he said, "Yes, I think you are." He glanced over Sarah's head. "Hello, Jeremiah."

"Sheriff McLeod."

"You decided what you're gonna do?"

Wondering what her grandfather meant, Sarah twisted around to look at Jeremiah.

"I've given it some thought, sir. I need a job, at least until I can bring in my first crop, but I'm not sure how much good I'll be as a deputy, living so far out in the valley. If I was working at the sawmill like my dad did, it wouldn't matter. Nobody needs lumber in the middle of the night. Same can't be said about a deputy."

"No . . . no, it can't."

"I'm willing to come into town during the day if that'll suit you and the rest of the town"—Jeremiah's dark gaze dropped to Sarah—"but I'll be spending my nights out at the farm."

Sarah felt warm all over. It was more than simply remembering what nights with Jeremiah meant—the kisses, the caresses, the soaring moments of passion. It was hearing something in his voice that said he wanted to be with her, he wanted to take care of her and cherish her.

I love you, Jeremiah.

Hank cleared his throat and leaned forward, drawing Sarah's attention back to him. "I guess that's clear enough, Jeremiah. You let me talk it over with the mayor. I think we can work things out to suit everybody's needs."

Jeremiah agreed, then told Sarah he was going to the stables and would be back for her in a short while.

When he was gone, her grandfather took her by the shoulders and drew her forward so he could kiss her cheek. "Tell me again how you're doing."

"I'm happy," she said, envisioning Jeremiah with her heart. "I love him."

Those three words didn't seem enough to express what she was feeling, and yet she didn't know how to tell her grandfather all that was inside her. How could words express her feelings, and if there were words, how could he understand? It was all too new, too miraculous. Surely no one had ever felt this way before.

When I'm with him, she wanted to say, *I know I'm whole, complete. When I'm with him, the sun is brighter, the air is sweeter. When he touches me, I come alive. Really alive. All my dreams . . . they were all fulfilled the moment I met Jeremiah. If I died tomorrow, I would die happy because of him.*

"I understand, princess," her grandfather whispered.

Looking into his gray eyes, she thought perhaps he did.

After leaving the livery, Jeremiah rode to the sheriff's office. He tethered his buckskin to the hitching post, then climbed the steps leading to the storage room above the jail. He stepped inside and looked around. Strange, the place seemed smaller and bleaker than he'd remembered. He wondered if another deputy would live here someday.

He knew he wouldn't be back. He would

be staying out at the farm—with Sarah.

Sarah, who'd made him begin to hope again.

Sarah, who'd made him begin to believe.

Sarah . . . the woman he loved.

He walked to the cot and sank down onto it, then braced his elbows on his thighs and cradled his head in his hands. He let out a long, defeated breath.

There was no point in trying to deny it any longer. He loved Sarah. She'd moved into his heart with the swift determination of a cavalry charge, and he'd been unable to stop her.

Yes, he loved her, but nothing else had changed. Nothing about him was different. He still had too little to give. There was no promise he'd ever have more than he had right now, no assurance he'd be able to take care of her any better than he'd taken care of Millie. It was his fault his first wife had died. If he hadn't married Millie, if he hadn't taken her away from Homestead, if she hadn't been pregnant with his child . . .

Take a chance, Jeremiah.

If he lost Sarah . . .

Take a chance, Jeremiah.

If they could make it through harvest, if they could make it through the safe delivery of their child . . .

Take a chance.

He closed his eyes and envisioned her. Sitting in the church pew, a bonnet of

351

feathers and flowers adorning her head. Walking along Main Street in her silver-gray cloak, her pretty face framed with white fur. In the kitchen, dressed in yellow calico, all points and ruffles and puffy sleeves, wisps of pale hair curling about her face. Lying in his bed, her skin so fair next to his own, her body so soft and willing and eager.

"I love you, Sarah," he whispered to the lonely room, and knew there was no going back.

The large trunk sat in the middle of the bedroom floor, filled to capacity with clothing and toiletries, dolls and books. Filled with everything that had made this room Sarah's through the years. Memories, like shadows, lingered in the corners of the bedroom, reminding her of the girl she'd been, of the people she'd loved.

Sarah sat down in the window seat and stared out the window at Pony Creek and the sawmill and, in the distance, the snow-covered mountains. The scene was so familiar, so much a part of her. If she closed her eyes, she could see the same scene in spring or summer or autumn. She could see herself as a small child, as a little girl, as a young woman.

"I remember, too," her grandfather said from the doorway.

Sarah turned and met his gaze.

He entered the room, moving slowly across to a chair near the window. "Room looks mighty lonely now."

"It does seem strange."

"Someday, I hope there's another little girl livin' in this house who'll spend her days in that window seat, dreamin' about faraway people and places."

She smiled at him, thinking of a little girl with ebony pigtails and rosy cheeks and eyes like Jeremiah's. "I hope so, too."

But it wouldn't be her daughter who would live here, she suddenly realized, and then she realized something else. She'd been thinking of no one besides herself for the past several days. It hadn't occurred to her until this moment what her moving out to the farm meant to others, what it meant to her grandfather.

"Grampa, what are we going to do when Tom goes back to school? We haven't an extra room out at the farm. The house only has one bedroom, and Jeremiah doesn't want to live in—"

"Tom's already thought of that, Sarah," he interrupted, reaching out to pat her knee. "His young lady, Fanny, is going to come stay with me until Tom comes back a doctor and they get married. I'll be in good hands. Don't you worry. You've got your own life now. You shouldn't be worryin' about a burdensome old man."

Sarah sat in stunned silence, unable even

to protest that her beloved grandfather wasn't burdensome. She was still trying to digest what he'd told her. Fanny—the saloon hall Fanny—living here? Staying with her grandfather? Maybe living in Sarah's old room?

"But, Grampa—"

"I like her, Sarah. And, more importantly, Tom loves her. Once you meet her, you'll understand."

Remembering her promise to Tom to give this girl from the saloon a chance and not to judge her too quickly, Sarah nodded, wondering at the odd twists and turns life had taken of late. It seemed that nothing was going to happen quite as she'd always imagined it would.

That evening, after Sarah had washed and dried the supper dishes, she joined Jeremiah in the front room. She sat on a chair near the stove, setting her sewing basket on the floor near her feet. As she mended a tear in one of Jeremiah's shirts, she thought about Tom and her grandfather and the girl named Fanny. She thought about how very much she wanted to be here with Jeremiah and how hard it was to let go of her room in the house on North Street. She pondered the confusion of her thoughts, not quite certain how she felt about any of it.

"Is something wrong, Sarah?"

She glanced up. The catalogue he'd been reading was closed, and he watched her with a concerned gaze that made her feel warm inside.

"You haven't said a word since we left your grandfather's. That's not like you."

She couldn't help smiling. "Do I talk so much?"

He smiled, too, even as he shrugged.

Looking down, she took a couple of stitches in the shirt before saying, "I was thinking about Grampa and Tom and . . . and the years I was growing up." Her hand stilled as she glanced at him a second time. "Tell me about when you were a boy. What was your family like?"

A shadow passed across his face. He turned his gaze toward the fire in the stove. He was silent for such a long time that Sarah thought he wouldn't answer at all.

"I got into trouble more than others," he said, more to himself than to her. "Mostly schoolboy pranks. Frogs in a girl's lunch pail. Firecrackers beneath Miss Pendroy's front porch. Locking the teacher in the outhouse." He shook his head. "I guess I was always trying to get my dad to notice me."

"To notice you?"

"Raising us boys alone was hard for him. Dad wasn't any good at showing what he felt. Unless he was angry. He showed that okay." Jeremiah smiled, but the expression was humorless. "It seemed I was always looking at other families and wishing we could be like them. We just never were. I

355

didn't measure up to what he thought a son should be, and Dad was always too . . . well, too remote, I guess. He just never warmed up to people. Folks liked him well enough, but he never let anybody too close. Maybe he wanted to. He just couldn't."

"Like Warren," she said softly.

Jeremiah's gaze darted back to her face. "Yes, I guess you're right. Warren is a lot like our dad."

"How sad."

She dropped her mending on top of her sewing basket and rose to her feet. She stepped forward, closing the distance between them. When she reached him, she took one of his hands and pressed its palm against her stomach. With her other hand, she brushed the dark hair back from his face, twining her fingers through it.

"You're not like your father," she said as she gazed down into his eyes. "Your son will know how much his father loves him."

My son, Jeremiah thought as he rose slowly. *Our son.*

He gathered Sarah into his arms, drawing her head against his chest; then he pressed his cheek against her hair, breathing in the lavender scent that was always part of Sarah. Sweet Sarah.

Lord, he wanted it to happen just that way. He wanted to be a good father, to raise a son who knew his dad loved him and was proud of him. He'd given up hope that such a thing would ever happen, but now here was Sarah, offering it to him with complete trust. He knew she believed it, that there wasn't a shred of doubt in her heart.

Sweet, sweet Sarah. She didn't see life as he saw it. Even after what he'd done to her—taking her innocence, impregnating her, opening her up to gossip and scorn—she still looked for the good in him and thought she'd found it.

Jeremiah had failed at everything he'd ever set his hand to. He didn't want to fail this time, if only because she believed in him.

He wanted her to be right. For her sake, he wanted her to be right. And for his sake, too.

Chapter Thirty-one

Fanny's fingers were shaking almost too much for her to poke her hat pin through the straw boater. She knew Tom would be arriving at the back door of the restaurant at any moment. She shouldn't have said she would go to church with him. It was too soon. She wasn't ready.

She wished she had someone to talk to about her fears. She couldn't talk to Tom. He'd just tell her not to worry. He'd say he knew what he wanted and folks would just have to accept her as his wife. But Fanny knew it wouldn't be that easy. Opal had warned her, but she hadn't wanted to listen to the truth.

Her hat in place, Fanny sat on the edge of

her bed, her hands folded in her lap, staring at the door and listening, waiting, as her anxiety increased.

Tom had said his sister would probably be in church today. That made Fanny even more nervous. Something told her Sarah wasn't happy about her brother's involvement with Fanny Irvine. It wasn't anything Tom had said. In fact, it was what he'd stopped saying that had warned her.

When she was sick and he was bringing her lunches from the restaurant, he'd talked about school and he'd talked about when he was a boy and he'd talked about his family. It had been clear to Fanny how much he adored his older sister. She remembered feeling envious, wishing she and Opal had been that close. Then, just after Tom found her the job at the hotel and moved her out of the saloon, he'd quit talking about Sarah altogether. Fanny sensed there had been a falling out between the two. She was certain she was the cause.

She grabbed the small, cracked mirror from the washstand and looked at her reflection.

Lord only knew why Tom wanted to marry her, she thought. Just like Opal had said, Fanny knew she wasn't anything special to look at. Thin and sharp-boned. Eyes plumb too big for her face. Her nose long and pointed. She glanced down at her chest and felt even more despair. She'd worked in the saloon long enough to know that men liked buxom women.

She felt the blood rush to her cheeks, thinking about why men liked buxom women. She knew all about what went on between the sheets. Opal had explained it to her in graphic detail. At the time, Fanny had been certain she'd never want any part of it, but lately, when Tom kissed her, she wasn't so sure. She almost wished he'd do more than kiss her. He never did. He was always a gentleman.

It just went to prove how ill suited they were to one another. Tom was a gentleman, but Fanny wanted him to treat her like . . . like men treated her sister.

She swallowed the lump in her throat as she dashed away tears from the corners of her eyes. She didn't want Tom to know she'd been crying. She didn't want to spoil any of the time they spent together. It wasn't all that long before he'd be leaving for Boston. She knew there was a good chance he wouldn't want to marry her when he came back. She wanted everything to be perfect now, just in case.

She heard the knock on the back door of the kitchen. Drawing a deep breath, she rose from the bed and went to answer it.

Opening the door and seeing his smile was like letting in the sunshine on a clear spring day. Her heart skipped a beat, and her spirits rose. It was impossible not to be happy when she was with Tom.

"You look mighty pretty, Fanny," he said as he stepped into the kitchen and closed the door behind him. Before she could move, he leaned down and kissed her on the lips, right in the presence of the hotel chef. "Doesn't my girl look pretty, Mr. Penny?"

Mr. Penny cocked one bushy eyebrow and studied her a moment. "Yup. That she does." Then he turned again to the stove.

Fanny suddenly felt pretty. Tom could make her believe anything, just by saying it was so.

"Better get your wrap. We don't want to be late."

"Tom, I don't know about—"

He kissed her again, a kiss so tender it brought the tears back to her eyes. When he drew back from her, he said, "Get your wrap, Fanny. We're going to church together, you and I."

With her heart beating a chaotic rhythm in her chest, she went for her coat, unable to deny him anything he wanted because she loved him so.

For the second time in two days, Sarah sat beside Jeremiah in the sleigh as they headed toward town, this time to attend church.

She tried not to feel nervous. She'd been attending services at the Homestead Community Church for as long as she could remember. The members of the congregation were her friends and neighbors. She knew them all. Knew them well.

But after her encounter yesterday with Ethel Bonnell, she knew there would be some who would judge her harshly for breaking her engagement with Warren and marrying his brother just a few weeks later. There might even be some who suspected the truth.

Slanting a glance at her husband, she wondered what he was thinking. She remembered the way he'd defended her in the mercantile, and she couldn't help smiling at the memory. He'd made it so very clear he wouldn't allow Mrs. Bonnell to gossip about his wife.

She felt again the wonder of her love for him—and she rejoiced in that secret corner of her heart where she knew he loved her in return. She longed to hear the words from his own mouth, but she was willing to wait.

The horse's hooves thundered across the bridge over Pony Creek. Jeremiah pulled back on the reins, slowing the animal to a walk as they approached the church. Once the sleigh was brought to a stop, Jeremiah wound the reins around the brake handle, then stepped down and turned to help Sarah do the same.

Just as her feet touched the ground, she saw her brother crossing the street from the hotel, a slender girl at his side. Sarah knew immediately the girl must be Fanny. Her gaze flicked quickly to Tom, searching his face. She wanted him to forgive her for her mistakes, and she knew he never would if she rejected this girl.

Jeremiah drew Sarah's hand through his arm. He squeezed her wrist against his side as he stepped forward, leading her toward the inevitable meeting with her brother and Fanny at the church.

They arrived at the base of the steps at the same moment. Both couples stopped and looked at each other. Sarah was afraid, for just a moment, that Tom wasn't even going to speak to her. He was still angry with her, for judging Fanny and for failing to live up to what he thought she should be.

They were much alike, she and Tom, Sarah thought as she met his gaze. As much as she hated to admit it, their reactions had been unflatteringly similar.

She looked at Fanny, trying to see her without prejudice. There was nothing extraordinary about the girl's appearance. She was young, no more than sixteen or seventeen, and plain-faced. Her brown eyes were wide and fringed with thick lashes. She was thin and fine-boned and looked as if a strong breeze would blow her away. She wore no face paint. Her coat was a dark wool, the skirt beneath it an ordinary blue fabric. Fanny looked little different from any other girl her age in Homestead.

"Hello, Miss Irvine." Sarah gave her a determined smile and held out her hand. "I'm Sarah Wesley, Tom's sister."

Fanny glanced quickly at Tom, then back to Sarah. Finally, she took the proffered hand.

"This is my husband, Jeremiah," Sarah continued.

Jeremiah nodded. "How do you do, Miss Irvine? It's a pleasure to meet you."

Sarah didn't have to look at her brother to know the tension had left him. She could feel it go. She wanted to stand on tiptoe and kiss Jeremiah for what he'd said, knowing that his words, combined with her own, had made a tremendous difference.

"I hope you'll sit with us," Sarah added to Fanny, realizing she meant it. If Tom loved this girl, she must be special. If Tom married Fanny, then Sarah wanted to be her sister. She returned her gaze to her brother, saying, "I guess we'd better go inside."

Tom didn't say anything. He didn't have to. Sarah knew they'd removed the first obstacle to their reconciliation. They would simply have to keep working at it until nothing else kept them apart. Given time, she believed they would succeed.

Rose heard Ethel Bonnell whispering to her husband as Jeremiah and Sarah Wesley slipped into a pew, followed by Tom McLeod and Fanny Irvine. She could tell by Ethel's tone that the woman meant no good for those four young people. Ethel Bonnell liked nothing more than a scandal to gossip about. If a scandal wasn't easily found, she would invent one. Rose had already heard what had happened at the mercantile the previous day and could imagine what else the woman might have said to Sarah had Jeremiah not been present to stop her.

She thought back to her own quickly arranged wedding. There had been a fair share of gossip because of it, too. She'd been forced by her father to marry a man who was hardly more than a stranger, and folks had wondered why.

Hers could have been a disastrous marriage, but God had blessed her with a wonderful husband. Michael had taught her how to trust enough to love with her whole heart, just as he loved her. She couldn't wish for anything better than that for all four of the young people seated in that pew.

The moment the final hymn was sung and the church service was over, Rose took Michael's arm and drew him with her toward Sarah and the others. She recognized Sarah's look of apprehension and understood it. She'd felt much the same herself not many years ago.

"Sarah, I'm so very happy for you," she said as she hugged the younger woman. She glanced up at the tall, handsome man at Sarah's side. "Mr. Wesley, you have extremely good judgment. You couldn't have chosen a better wife."

Jeremiah inclined his head in acknowledgment of her comment.

As Rose met Jeremiah's dark gaze, she couldn't help thinking Sarah had made the right choice, too. She sensed Jeremiah would love his wife as Warren Wesley never could have.

She turned back to Sarah. "The day Michael and I were married, we moved into the Pendroy house. That place had sat empty for a long time and was filled with dirt and dust. And here came your grandma, along with Emma Barber and Zoe Potter. That was sort of their wedding gift to me, putting a real spit and polish on that whole house. Your grandma was a special woman, and I know she'd be happy for you if she were still alive."

"I think she'd have liked Jeremiah," Sarah replied softly.

"She would have," Rose assured her, then turned toward the next couple. "Fanny, this is a nice surprise, seeing you in church. I should have thought to invite you myself. I know how shy you are and should have realized you wouldn't want to come alone. I'm glad Tom was good enough to bring you."

Out of the corner of her eye, Rose saw Ethel Bonnell speaking to Betsy Varney, a look of vindictive pleasure on her face. Rose could only imagine what Ethel was saying and how much trouble she was trying to cause.

In a voice loud enough to carry across the room, Tom announced, "Fanny's done me the honor of agreeing to be my wife."

Conversations ceased throughout the church, and all eyes turned in their direction. Even Ethel Bonnell appeared speechless.

Sarah was horrified by the terrible silence that followed Tom's declaration. She wanted to do something to protect Tom and Fanny from the censuring glances coming their way. She would prefer that everyone learned the truth about herself, about how she'd gone to Jeremiah's bed before they were married and how she was carrying his baby, rather than to have folks be cruel to her brother. Or Fanny either. But she didn't know what to do to help them.

Thank goodness Rose Rafferty was there. With nary the blink of an eye, Rose said, "How very wonderful," and leaned forward to kiss Fanny's cheek. "And how exciting for the McLeod family."

Michael Rafferty followed his wife's lead, shaking Tom's hand and slapping him on the back.

And then there were others crowding around them, congratulating Sarah and Jeremiah on their wedding and Tom and Fanny on their engagement. The Rev. and Mrs. Jacobs. Sigmund Leonhardt and his wife, Annalee. Chad and Ophelia Turner. Will and Addie Rider. Yancy Jones of the Lazy L Ranch and his wife, Lark. George and Leslie Blake. And more. Many, many more.

As the familiar faces filed past her, each

with their own words of affection and good wishes, Sarah felt a warmth flow into her chest, surrounding her heart. She glanced up at Jeremiah.

It's going to be all right, my love. We're both home. Whatever you were looking for all those years you were away was right here all the time. All those things I thought I wanted in all those faraway places are here, too. Right here in Homestead with you and me and my family and these friends. Can you see it, Jeremiah? Can you feel it?

Jeremiah had come to church today mostly for Sarah's sake. He knew that Mrs. Bonnell would not cease her gossip simply because he'd intercepted her barbs yesterday. He'd known her sort before. He'd hoped, if he appeared in church with Sarah, that others wouldn't believe whatever cruel rumors Mrs. Bonnell tried to spread.

He hadn't expected this warm reception, however.

This was different from simply being welcomed as the town's new deputy. It was different from being thanked for rescuing Sarah from a blizzard. This was being a part of something. This was . . . this was belonging.

He looked down at the woman at his side and found her watching him. He saw the happy glow on her face, saw the love in her eyes. She'd given him this. She'd made him belong.

Sarah, with her bright, optimistic view of the world and a smile that could outshine the sun, had pushed her way into his heart until now she filled it, and he knew he would be nothing, have nothing, without her.

In the days and weeks following that memorable Sunday, Jeremiah began to believe that things just might work out.

Hank McLeod announced his retirement, despite the objections of the loyal citizens of Homestead, and Chad Turner, who had run the livery and blacksmith shop for two decades, became the new sheriff. Jeremiah was kept on as deputy, going into town three days a week and always returning before nightfall.

Jeremiah built the chicken coop Sarah had said she wanted, and when it was finished, he rode over to the Evans place and bought six laying hens. Sarah acted as if she'd been given a priceless gift when she saw them, smiling and thanking him as she gave each of the hens a name.

As the snow continued its slow melt, Jeremiah repaired the plow, sharpening the blades and replacing parts that were worn with age and rotted by disuse. He repaired the harness. He cleaned the barn of moldy feed and mucked out stalls and built a new door for the hayloft.

In the evenings, he sat for hours at the table, poring over catalogues and deciding what he had to order to get by and what could wait until after harvest. He ciphered long columns of numbers and calculated how much he could afford to spend and when.

At night, he lay in bed and held Sarah close against him and longed for autumn and harvest and the baby's delivery. Then he would know he hadn't failed her. Then he would know he hadn't failed himself. Then he could tell her he loved her.

He wished he could tell her sooner. He wished he could tell her now. But he couldn't. He was afraid that if he did, he would lose her. He knew his fears didn't make sense—he wasn't normally a superstitious man—but he couldn't help feeling that way. He'd never succeeded before. Why tempt fate now? It might be just a silly superstition, but if his silence might keep Sarah safe, what could it hurt to wait?

For Sarah, this was a special time. Although impatient for Jeremiah's declaration of love, she recognized the many silent ways he told her of his feelings and treasured them in her heart. She was certain that whatever obstacle kept him silent would one day be removed and she would hear the words she longed to hear.

In the meantime, she busied herself making the little farmhouse into a home. She sewed lace curtains for the front window, and hung paintings brought from her grandfather's attic on the plain board walls. She used her sewing scraps to begin a quilt for the bed, planning a matching one for the baby's cradle. She took several of her older skirts and altered them, letting out the waistbands in anticipation of an expanding girth. She learned all about caring for her chickens, and three days a week she sent the extra eggs into town with Jeremiah to sell at the mercantile. When her husband returned to the house in the evenings, either from Homestead or from the barn, she always had a hot meal waiting for him.

Except for Sundays when they attended church and visited with her grandfather and Tom, she rarely left the farm. She was happy there. Just being with Jeremiah brought her pleasure, and there was always something new to learn about him. He still didn't open up much about himself or his past, but Sarah discovered there were things to be learned from a glance or an expression or an unfinished sentence.

And so the days and weeks melted away with the snow, and at night, when Jeremiah took her into his arms and held her close, she knew she was the most blessed of women on God's earth.

Chapter Thirty-two

Sarah was just removing a pie from the oven when she heard the rattle of a wagon entering the yard. She set the hot pie tin on top of the oven, then walked to the window to look out through the lace curtains. She was surprised to see Addie Rider drawing the wagon to a halt not far from the house.

Sarah hurried to the door and opened it just as Addie stepped down into the sloppy earth, mud splashing up onto her boots and the hem of her skirt.

"Mrs. Rider, this is a surprise," she called to her guest.

Addie smiled as she walked toward Sarah. "I thought it was time I came calling. Is your husband around?"

"No, he's in town today."

"Well, then I guess I'll just have to leave my wedding gift with you."

"A gift? But you shouldn't—"

"What do you think of her?" Addie interrupted, motioning toward the horse tethered to the back of the wagon. "She's yours."

Sarah couldn't believe what the other woman was saying. The mare was a beautiful sorrel with a flaxen mane and tail. Her coat gleamed with reddish highlights in the afternoon sunlight.

"She's one of our best mares. She'll give you a grand colt before long."

"Mrs. Rider, I couldn't possibly accept such a valuable gift."

"I want you to have her, Sarah." Addie shortened the distance between them. "If you've got a moment to spare, I'd like to share something with you."

"Of course. Do come in." She backed up and held the door open wide.

A short while later, after Addie had cleaned the mud from her boots and Sarah had made some tea, the two women sat down at the table.

While Addie sipped her tea, her gaze moved about the room, and when she set down her cup, she smiled and said, "You've been busy. This house never looked this way when Ted Wesley was alive. You've made it very warm and pretty."

"Thank you." Sarah glanced toward the window. "Mrs. Rider, about the mare, I really can't—"

"Please, Sarah. It's my way of repaying a debt."

"A debt?"

"You were just a toddler when I came to Homestead from Connecticut so you couldn't possibly remember what it was like then. I was the town's first teacher when school was still held in the church. I was homesick at first for the home I grew up in back in Connecticut, and for the ocean and everything familiar to me. But folks hereabouts were friendly, and that helped ease the loneliness. Then I fell in love with Will . . ." Her expression was as dreamy as a schoolgirl's. "After I accepted Will's proposal, your mother offered me the use of her wedding gown. I'll never forget the day she showed it to me. It was the most beautiful gown I'd seen in my entire life. Cream-silk faille and cotton sateen and Belgian lace. I felt like a storybook princess when I tried it on."

"I know. I tried it on, too. I thought I might wear it for my own wedding, but . . ." Sarah finished her sentence with a shrug, realizing for the first time that she hadn't wanted to wear her mother's gown because she hadn't loved the man she planned to marry. That was why the gown had never seemed right. And that was why the beautiful creation Mrs. Gaunt had made had gone unused for her wedding to Jeremiah. It wouldn't have seemed right, not when it had been made to wear for Warren.

Addie leaned forward, touching Sarah's hand with her fingertips, bringing Sarah's attention back to the present. "Your mother had no reason to be so generous with me. We barely knew each other. It's just the way she was. She was so much in love with your father, and she wanted everyone else to be equally in love and happy. She hadn't a selfish bone in her body." A frown drew two small lines between her eyebrows. "I never got a chance to thank her properly. Tommy was born just an hour or so after the minister pronounced Will and me man and wife."

Addie didn't have to say anything more. Sarah knew what she'd left unsaid. Maria McLeod had died that day, not long after giving birth.

"So, you see," Addie continued, "this is my way of saying thank you to your mother. Please. Don't refuse my gift."

Sarah shook her head, finding it difficult to speak around the lump in her throat. "All right," she whispered.

Addie grinned. "Good. Now, you put on your wrap and come out and have a look at her. The Rocking R raises the finest horses in the whole state, and Ember is no exception."

"Ember?"

"My youngest named her when she was born. Naomi has always liked naming our foals. She thought this little gal's coloring looked like embers in the fireplace. The name stuck."

"Ember. I like it." Sarah reached for her shawl as Addie opened the door.

Side by side, they walked toward the mare, which was tied to the back of the wagon. As they rounded the end of the wagon, Sarah saw the mare's swollen belly and knew Addie had not been exaggerating when she'd said it wouldn't be long before Ember gave birth.

"Oh, Mrs. Rider . . ." she said breathlessly. "She really is beautiful."

"I've always thought so. She's the granddaughter of the mare I bought from Will way back in 'eighty when I first came to Homestead."

"Are you sure you want to—"

"I'm sure. Now, let's take her into that barn of yours and get her settled." She untied the rope from the wagon, then led the mare across the barnyard.

Sarah fell back a ways, simply so she could look at the horse. When she was a girl, she'd had a mare of her own. Victoria, named for the Queen of England, had been small and old and not much to look at, but Sarah had loved her all the same. In the summer, she'd ridden the mare off by herself where she could sit and dream about the places she wanted to go, the things she wanted to see. Victoria had died when Sarah was seventeen. She hadn't owned a horse of her own since.

The barn smelled of clean straw and

leather. As they entered, Jeremiah's new workhorse thrust his big, black head over the stall rail and nickered to the newcomer. The mare answered the greeting.

Addie selected one of the two empty stalls and led the mare inside. "She could drop her foal any time, but I suspect she's got another week or two to go. Jeremiah knows what to do when her time comes. He helped us one spring at the ranch, and he's got good sense when it comes to horses."

"Jeremiah worked for you?"

"Yes." Addie removed the halter, then scratched the mare behind one ear. Ember bobbed her head up and down.

"What was he like as a boy?" It was a question that was never far from her thoughts.

Addie smiled. "Mischievous. Pulling pranks all the time. Not a lot different from your brother, actually, only he got caught more often than Tom."

Rose Rafferty and Sarah's grandfather had told her much the same thing when she'd asked them. Still, she kept hoping someone would give her another clue to her husband, something that would help her reach him.

Addie's smile faded. "Jeremiah was lonely, I think. He and Warren were like water and oil. They just didn't mix well. Never did. And Ted . . . well, Ted Wesley was a difficult man to know. He'd come to church and he'd play his fiddle at barn dances and such, but he never talked much, never let anybody I know of get close to him. I don't think he even let his boys get close."

"And Millie Parkerson?" Sarah asked softly. "What was she like?"

Addie considered her reply for a moment, her expression thoughtful. "Millie was shy and plain and very tiny. Rather fragile looking. And lonely like Jeremiah, I think." She shook her head, a wry smile touching her mouth. "It always seemed such an odd pairing, Jeremiah and Millie. He was a rough-and-tumble sort. She was so quiet she could fade into the background and not even be noticed. Jeremiah was as handsome as they come, even back then. I don't think other boys even noticed Millie."

Sarah tried to picture Jeremiah's first wife in her mind. "He loved her a great deal, didn't he?"

"Yes, I'm sure he did." Addie patted the mare one last time on the neck, then crossed to the gate and let herself out of the stall. "Maybe you should let him tell you about her."

"I've asked. He doesn't want to talk about her."

The older woman nodded. "Will is kind of like that, too. Hard to get him to open up. Give Jeremiah time. He'll tell you about Millie when he's ready."

Give him time. It seemed to Sarah that everyone had been saying those words to her. But it was hard not to be impatient, especially when she loved Jeremiah so. She wanted them to share everything. Every joy and every sorrow.

She met Addie's gaze. "I don't mind that he loved her."

Addie shared another gentle smile. "You're a wise young woman, Sarah Wesley." Then she turned toward the barn door. "I'd best be on my way back to the ranch."

Sarah fell into step beside Addie, thinking, *I don't mind that he loved Millie. Not as long as he loves me now.*

Jeremiah strolled slowly along the boardwalk, touching the brim of his Metropolitan as he greeted folks, checking to make sure all was right in Homestead. Not that he had any reason to expect it wouldn't be. One day was pretty much the same as another, except for the changing season.

And he, for one, was enjoying the springlike weather. The temperatures had hovered around fifty degrees for several days. The sky was so blue it almost hurt his eyes to look at it, and the air was fresh and clean. Most of the snow was gone. Soon, the light slick of mud would turn into a brown sea. Nobody would feel good about spring at that point, he conceded, not even him.

But after spring would come the warm days of summer. The grass would turn from brown to a brilliant green. Crops would sprout up through the rich brown soil. Colts and calves would trot after their mothers.

He suddenly thought of Sarah, out in the barnyard, feeding her chickens, the sun catching the golden highlights in her pale hair. He imagined her hanging out laundry to dry as wildflowers bloomed on the hillsides. He envisioned her with her belly large with his child and felt the familiar urge to go home, take her in his arms, and kiss her until she was completely and utterly breathless.

Loud laughter brought him out of his pleasant reverie. He saw six men walking toward him. They were strangers, all of them, their hair long and shaggy, their faces bearded, their clothes unwashed. One man slapped another on the back and shouted a rude expletive at the fellow behind him. The leader of the group pushed open the slatted doors of the saloon and they disappeared inside. The others followed.

Jeremiah frowned. He didn't like the look or the sound of them. He wondered what they were doing in Homestead.

Just then, Sheriff Turner hailed him from the steps of the Rafferty Hotel. Jeremiah glanced once more toward the saloon, then crossed the street to join Chad on the hotel veranda.

"Loggers headed up to the camps," the sheriff said, as if he'd known what Jeremiah was thinking. "They got off the train from Boise today. There'll be plenty more comin' through Homestead for the next month or two. A steady stream of them. Keep a close eye on the saloon. That's where trouble usually starts."

Jeremiah nodded.

Chad Turner tipped his Stetson back on his head. "Spring's here early this year. Won't be long before you're able to put in your crops. Imagine you're eager to get started."

"It's been a long time since I stood behind a plow and worked my own land."

It was Chad's turn to nod. "I understand. There's some things a man's just born to do. I've always liked workin' as a smithy myself. Don't know why I let Rafferty and McLeod talk me into takin' this job as sheriff." He stepped off the veranda. "But since I did, I think I'll just wander on over to the saloon. Let those fellas know there's law in Homestead. I'll see you in church on Sunday."

Jeremiah watched the sheriff saunter across the street before heading off in the direction of the jail. It was time he returned to the farm . . . and Sarah.

As quickly as that, thoughts of the troublesome loggers and his work as a deputy disappeared from his mind. All he ever had to do was think Sarah's name, and everything else faded into obscurity.

And with each passing day, he believed a little more strongly in the future. He began to imagine the two of them growing old together. He began to imagine a son of his own working beside him in the fields.

If they could make it through harvest . . .

Chapter Thirty-three

Tom watched as Doc Varney removed his spectacles and rubbed his eyes. "Mr. Johnson, I suspect you have the grippe. I recommend you remain in bed for the time being." He slipped the eyeglasses back into place, hooking the curved end pieces behind his ears.

The patient looked up at the doctor through feverish eyes. "But we're leavin' for the camps tomorrow mornin'."

"You would be very foolish to attempt such a trip before your fever has broken, sir. In fact, I suggest you remain here for at least a week."

Johnson rolled onto his side as he began to cough harshly.

The doctor reached for his black leather

bag and opened it. "I'll send over a prescription of phenazone and ammonium carbonate. It will help bring down your temperature and ease your breathing." He dropped his stethoscope into the bag. "I'll be by to check on you tomorrow, Mr. Johnson."

"I'll be on my way to the loggin' camps by then."

"I sincerely doubt it, sir," Doc Varney replied dryly as he turned toward Tom, his medical bag in hand.

Tom sprang into action, turning the knob and opening the door for the physician, then followed him out of the room. As they traversed the hotel hallway, Tom kept his gaze on Doc Varney, noting the deep furrows in his forehead and the tightness of his mouth. Finally, unable to keep silent a moment longer, he asked, "Is it serious, Doc?"

"Influenza can be very serious. More serious than it at first appears."

"But you said it was the grippe."

Doc Varney shrugged as the two men started down the stairs, the older leading the way. As soon as they reached the base, Tom stepped up beside the physician again.

Doc met Tom's curious gaze. "I've been reading the papers of an eminent British epidemiologist, Dr. Charles Creighton. He disputes the theory of contagion in regard to influenza and prefers the concept of a miasma spreading over the land."

Tom listened closely. He knew Doc would

ask for his opinion before he was finished. Doc always forced Tom to come to his own conclusions. In some ways, every patient was a test, and Tom never wanted to fail one of Doc's exams.

"Dr. Creighton sites the epidemics of 'thirty-three, 'thirty-seven, and 'forty-seven as proof of his point of view because the outbreaks affected the population almost at once. He asserts these are not the marks of a disease that passes from one person to another."

They stepped outside. Doc Varney blinked several times and glanced up at the sky, as if surprised to find the sun shining. He removed his glasses again, cleaned them with his handkerchief, then turned and started forward along the boardwalk, setting the spectacles back in place as he went.

"But I can't agree with Dr. Creighton. I think the germ theory of infectious diseases is more accurate, and certainly the research that followed the influenza pandemic of 'eighty-nine and 'ninety seems to substantiate the theory. There's an article in one of my journals by a German who claims to have discovered a particular bacterium present in great numbers in the throats of patients with influenza."

Doc Varney stepped off the boardwalk and crossed the muddy thoroughfare. When he reached the boardwalk on the opposite side of the street, he stopped and looked at Tom with a raised eyebrow.

"So tell me, young man, if you were in charge of our patient, Mr. Johnson, what would be your opinion?"

Tom frowned thoughtfully as he considered what Doc had told him. "Well, no matter how Mr. Johnson became ill, his treatment should remain bed rest. If influenza is a contagious disease, spread by germs, then the appearance of one case could certainly mean we could see more of them soon, and we could attempt to control the spread by quarantine." He shook his head. "But I'm still not sure why you're concerned. When I was at school, we had an outbreak of influenza. Boys were sick for a few days, maybe a week. They felt poorly, but it didn't seem to have any lasting effects."

Doc nodded slowly, rubbing his chin between thumb and forefinger. "We'll hope it's nothing more than that." Abruptly, he turned and strode east again, Tom hurrying to keep up. "Now I'm going home for supper. Mrs. Varney promised me a nice roast beef and yams, and I'm hungry. Are you coming with me tomorrow out to the Evans place? I'll be removing the stitches from Mr. Evans's arm."

"Yes, sir. I'll be there."

"Good. See you at nine sharp."

Tom stopped and watched as the doctor

walked away. He felt an odd sense of foreboding, but shook it off. Surely there was nothing to worry about.

He spun on his heel and headed for home, cutting between the saloon and the barber shop, mindless of the mud that quickly caked his boots. Tonight was Fanny's evening to cook supper at the McLeod house, and he was as eager as always to see her.

As Jeremiah cantered toward the house, he saw the door open and Sarah rush outside. At first he thought there must be something wrong. Then he saw the smile lighting her face.

Arriving near the front of the house, he drew his big buckskin to a halt. She hurried forward, laying her hand on his thigh as she gazed up at him with sparkling blue eyes. "You'll never guess what happened today. Mrs. Rider came to visit, and she brought us a wedding gift."

"From the look of you, it must be some gift." He stepped down from the saddle.

"It is. Just wait until you see it." She took hold of his hand and pulled.

He held his ground. "Let me put up my horse first," he said with a laugh, enjoying the way she looked, enjoying her excitement, wanting to prolong the moment.

She laughed with him. "I was taking you to the barn anyway."

"The barn?"

"Come on." She pulled on his arm again, and this time he went with her, leading his horse behind him. "I couldn't believe it. You won't either. Wait till you see."

Jeremiah's interest was definitely piqued.

A few yards away from the barn, Sarah dropped his hand and hurried forward to open the door. As he approached, she motioned him inside.

At first, he saw nothing out of the ordinary. The workhorse he'd purchased from Chad Turner's livery thrust his head over the stall railing and snorted as he bobbed his head. The big black did the same thing every time Jeremiah entered the barn.

Then another equine head appeared from what, that morning, had been an empty stall. Jeremiah stopped and stared at the animal before glancing over his shoulder at Sarah.

"Isn't she wonderful?" his wife asked, her smile even brighter than before. "Her name's Ember. And she's going to have a foal. Any time, Mrs. Rider said."

He moved to the edge of the stall for a better look at the horse. "But why?" he asked, noting the mare's intelligent eyes and fine conformation which was evident despite her advanced pregnancy. "This mare isn't a ten-dollar saddle horse. Why would the Riders give us such a gift?"

"Mrs. Rider said it was a debt she owed to my mother." Sarah stepped up beside him. "She said you've got good sense when it comes to horses. She told me you worked at her ranch one spring."

"Yes."

"Tell me about it."

Jeremiah smiled to himself. How often since he'd returned to Homestead had Sarah said those very same words to him? *Tell me about it.* She'd wanted to know about his travels, the places he'd been, the things he'd seen. She'd wanted to know about his father. She'd wanted to know about his brother and what their childhoods had been like and why they weren't close like she was with her brother. She'd even wanted to know about Millie. She'd always wanted to know everything about him. She would always want to know. Sarah was like that.

His smile faded as he turned to look at her. He reached out and touched her cheek with his fingertips, then flattened his palm against the side of her face. She tipped her head to the side, pressing closer to his hand. Warmth seemed to flow from her skin and up his arm. It flowed through his veins, directly to his heart.

He had no right to the love he saw in her blue eyes. When she looked at him, she saw something that wasn't there, that had never been there. She saw a man worth loving, a man who was somehow perfect in her eyes. Jeremiah Wesley wasn't a hero, and he sure as heck wasn't anybody's idea of a saint.

I'd rather give you up forever, Sarah, than

*have anything happen to you because of me.
I'd rather leave this farm and go away for
good.*

He gathered her into his arms, pulling her
close against him, resting his cheek against
the crown of her head.

*God, don't let me lose her. Let me stay right
here and love her till we're both old and gray.
Don't make me go.*

His heart skipped a beat.

*But I'll go away if I have to. Just don't let
anything happen to Sarah because of me. Send
me away first.*

He held her for a long time, not moving,
not talking, just holding her, breathing in the
soft lavender fragrance of her hair, feeling
the gentle curves of her body that fit so well
against his own.

If they could just make it until harvest . . .

Harvest. That was the sign he was waiting for, the sign he could stay for good. If
they could make it until harvest, everything
would be all right for them both.

And then he could tell her he loved her.

His silence frightened her. There was
something about the way he held her that
made her think he would disappear at any
moment, as if he were preparing himself to
say good-bye. It was nothing tangible, yet she
felt it in her heart.

"Well . . ." He stepped back from her. "I'd
better have a closer look at our new mare.
She looks about ready to drop that foal."

Sarah didn't reply. She couldn't. Her heart was still racing with fear.

Jeremiah opened the gate and stepped into the stall. He hunkered down and looked at the underside of Ember's belly. "She's not waxing yet. We'll keep a close eye on her." He stood and ran his hand over the mare's fuzzy winter coat. "Pretty miserable, huh, girl?"

Sarah let out the breath she'd been holding, silently chiding herself. Jeremiah wasn't going anywhere. He wasn't saying good-bye. He was going to be there to help with Ember's foal and to till the soil and plant their first crops. He was going to be there when their baby was born and for the rest of their lives.

She was being silly to read something into his embrace that wasn't there. Jeremiah wasn't going to leave her. She'd already bet her heart on it.

Chapter Thirty-four

Fanny paused on the boardwalk outside the Pony Saloon. Inside, Quincy was pounding out a tune on the tinny-sounding piano. The stale odor of smoke, beer, and whiskey drifted through the open doorway, bringing back more than a few unpleasant memories.

Fanny turned around. It would be so much easier to just go back to the hotel and forget the whole idea. She hadn't set foot in this awful place since Tom had led her out of it more than two months ago. She didn't have to go in there now.

She faced the saloon again. Opal was in there. Her sister, who'd made certain Fanny had a place to stay and food to eat after their ma died. Her sister, who'd gone for the doctor when Fanny was sick and helped take care of her. They might not be close like Tom was with Sarah, but Opal was still her only surviving flesh-and-blood relative.

Fanny drew in a deep breath for courage, then held herself straight and walked into the saloon.

The smoky room was filled with the loggers who'd been arriving in Homestead over the past few days, men on their way to the logging camps in the mountains east of Long Bow Valley. It took Fanny a minute to find her sister. Opal was standing behind a man at one of the poker tables, her arm draped over his shoulder, her breasts pressed against his back as she leaned low and looked at his cards while whispering something in his ear.

Fanny felt several pairs of eyes turn in her direction. The brash gazes left her feeling nervous and vulnerable. She wanted to turn and run out of the saloon, but she was determined to talk to Opal, if only for a few minutes.

"Well, look who's back," Grady O'Neal called from his place behind the bar. Then he laughed, as if mocking her.

She felt more heads turn and look her way, but she kept her gaze trained on her sister, determined not to let anyone cow her. Holding her head high for courage, she started across the room.

Fanny had nearly reached the poker table before Opal glanced up. A look of surprise flitted across her painted face. The look was replaced by the smallest of frowns as she straightened.

"Opal, can I talk to you?"

Her sister glanced toward the bar. "Now's not a good time, Fanny. We gotta lot of customers t'see to."

"I know, but I only need a minute or two. We could step out onto the boardwalk. I wouldn't keep you long."

Opal's gaze ran down the length of Fanny's plain white shirtwaist with its high collar and puffy sleeves and the simple brown skirt that hid all but the toes of her sturdy leather shoes. When she brought her gaze back to Fanny's face, she said, "I don't think it'd do you no good t'be seen with me. You better go on back to cookin' hash or whatever it is you do over at that restaurant."

Fanny felt a sting of disappointment and fought the tears that rose to her eyes. "I . . . I wanted you to know Tom McLeod's asked me t'marry him."

Opal stared at her as if she'd suddenly sprouted an extra head. Then she turned abruptly and walked toward the back door of the saloon. Fanny followed after her.

The moment they stepped outside into the passage between the saloon and livery, Opal whirled to face her little sister. "You sure he means to marry you? You ain't been givin' him somethin' for free he should be payin' for?"

"No." Fanny stiffened. "Tom's always a proper gentleman. He loves me, and I love him. We're gonna get married when he comes back from Boston. He's goin' t'school to finish becomin' a doctor, and I'm gonna live with his grandfather while he's gone."

Opal's expression immediately softened. "Livin' with his grandpa? Well, I'll be. I guess he really is serious about you." Her smile was somehow sad. "I'm happy for you, Fanny. Really I am."

"Maybe, after we're married, you could—"

"Don't!" her sister said sharply. Then, lowering her voice, she continued, "I am what I am, Fanny. I don't reckon I'm likely to change, not even for you. You're a sweet kid. I'm glad you came t'me when Ma died. I'm glad I could help you out. But you've got a chance at a better life. You grab on to it. You grab hold with both hands and don't you never let go. You hear me?"

Fanny nodded, her throat too tight to speak.

Opal took hold of Fanny's shoulders. "Look at you. You look like a lady, all neat and tidy. And pretty, too. I imagine folks in this town have taken right to you. And those that haven't . . . Well, to hell with 'em. You know you ain't done nothin' wrong."

"Opal, I—"

"You go on about your business now, Fanny, and don't be comin' back to the saloon. Not ever again. It won't do neither of us any good. This place"—she waved at the saloon—"it's a whole other world from the rest of the town. You let me live in my world, and you go on and live in yours. And when I hear how well you're doin' with that doctor o' yours, I'll be happy for you."

There seemed nothing else for Fanny to do but nod in agreement. She couldn't change Opal's mind. She couldn't make her sister something she didn't want to be.

"And, Fanny, just 'cause we don't see each other don't mean we don't care. I'll know that. You know it, too."

Opal turned abruptly and went back inside, leaving Fanny standing in the shadows between the livery and saloon. For a long while, she didn't move. She felt lonely, abandoned, cold. She shivered and hugged herself.

Just 'cause we don't see each other don't mean we don't care. I'll know that. You know it, too.

Fanny's eyes filled with tears. Opal had been telling her she loved her.

"I love you, too," she whispered. "Maybe someday you can be happy like me."

Without speaking, Tom and Doc Varney left the small farmhouse and climbed into the buggy. They had nearly reached the summit of Tin Horn Pass when Doc pulled back on the reins, drawing the horse to a halt.

The older man lowered his head as if in

weary defeat. "Influenza."

The word, the way Doc said it, sent an ominous chill up Tom's spine.

Doc Varney lifted his gaze toward the canopy of cerulean blue. "Lord, I hope I'm wrong," he said softly. Then he clucked to the horse, and they started forward again.

While Sarah prepared lunch, she listened to the sounds of Jeremiah working outside. She could hear the saw as it cut through wood, the rhythmic smack of the hammer. And in her mind, she imagined the barn as it would look when Jeremiah was finished.

Maybe next year we could afford to add onto the house.

She lowered a hand to her abdomen. She could feel the slight change in her physical appearance, although it would be some time yet before others would notice. More importantly, she felt different inside.

Jeremiah's son.

She smiled, feeling the familiar sense of joy spreading through her, warming her. It was so easy to imagine their little boy, toddling after his father, following him around the barnyard. It was so easy to imagine holding her son close to her breast, rocking him to sleep at night. He would have his father's midnight black hair and sooty eyes and handsome smile.

She opened her eyes and began chopping onions again, but her thoughts lingered not only on the baby she carried in her womb but on others that would follow. She hoped there would be many. She wanted a home full of Jeremiah's children.

Yes, they would need to add on to the house before too many summers had passed.

The door opened behind her. "Sarah . . ."

She turned.

"Ember's having her foal."

Sarah set down the knife and wiped her hands on her apron. "What do we need to do?"

"Nothing, if all goes well. I just thought you'd like to know."

She removed her apron and laid it on the counter, then hurried toward the door. She lifted her shawl from the peg in the wall, draping it over her shoulders. When Jeremiah didn't move, she met his gaze and asked, "Hadn't we better get out to the barn?"

"Are you certain you want to be there?"

"Of course I do. She's my mare, too." She smiled, realizing suddenly why he'd asked. "I'm not the least bit squeamish, Jeremiah. I won't swoon or any such nonsense."

He nodded as he took hold of her arm, and together they headed toward the barn.

The moment Sarah stepped inside, she felt something different. A breathless waiting. An air of expectation. Neither of the two geldings whickered in greeting as they normally did when someone entered the barn. Even they seemed to know that something out of the ordinary was happening.

Sarah hurried to the stall and looked inside. Ember was lying on her side. Her breathing was labored. Once, she lifted her head and reached back to nip at her side, as if angered by the pain.

"Isn't there anything we can do to help?" Sarah whispered.

Jeremiah shook his head. "No. It's best to let her do it on her own." He closed his hand around her arm, pulling her gently. "Come on over here. Sometimes it makes a mare nervous to have humans present."

He led her into a shadowy corner and motioned for her to sit on a three-legged stool; then he sat beside her on an upended barrel. Brilliant March sunlight spilled through the open doors in the hayloft and spotlighted the stall, as if even the heavens knew this was a special occasion.

For a long time, they sat in silence, watching the mare. The quiet intimacy of the barn seemed to surround them. Sarah felt the need to share her thoughts with Jeremiah, to tell him the many things that were in her heart, and yet she couldn't seem to speak. She waited without knowing what she waited for.

"Last time I did this was with Millie."

Sarah's heart nearly stopped. She turned to look at Jeremiah, knowing she'd been awaiting exactly this.

"We lost that mare. She was the only horse

we owned. A big, ugly plow horse Millie had named Twinkles. But Millie managed to save the colt. She fixed up a bucket with a nipple and fed that colt day and night for weeks. Months, I guess." He paused, then added, "I sold him after Millie died. Couldn't stand the sight of him."

Her heart began to race in her chest. *Go on, Jeremiah,* she wanted to say, but she managed to remain silent, waiting, hoping, wanting to know, wanting to understand, yet dreading it, too.

"Millie was . . . special," he said softly. "You would have liked her, Sarah."

She heard the pain in his voice and ached for him.

"She was just sixteen when we ran off together. My dad was against us marrying. He wanted me to go to college. He'd never said a word to me about it before, but when I told him Millie and I wanted to get married and help him work the farm, that's when he told me he'd been puttin' money back for my schooling. All my life, he'd told me I wouldn't amount to much, and then he says I should go to college. But it wasn't what I wanted." He paused. "That was probably the angriest I ever saw my dad. He tried to tell me I couldn't ever see Millie again. He accused her of trying to ruin my life." He drew in a deep breath. "We said some mighty ugly things to each other that day."

Sarah touched his knee with her fingers,

but he didn't seem to notice.

"I never should have taken Millie away from here. She didn't want to run off. She wanted us to wait, to try to talk my dad into giving us his blessing. Only I knew Dad never would, so I made her go away with me. I didn't know where we'd live or what we'd do, but I thought I could take care of her."

Again there was a lengthy silence.

"We didn't have much when we left Homestead. Just the money I took from the savings my dad had put away for me to go to college. Just enough to get us to Ohio where her grandma lived. If it wasn't for Grandmother Ashmore, we'd have both starved. Even so, I guess there wasn't ever a year that went by without us doin' without something we needed."

Again he fell silent, and again she waited.

"But Millie never complained. Not once."

"She loved you very much," Sarah whispered, her throat tight with emotion. "And you loved her."

Jeremiah didn't reply, but she knew it was true. In a dark corner of her heart, she resented the love he'd felt for Millie, resented it because he was so afraid to love again. So afraid to love her.

"I never did right by her, Sarah. I never took care of her the way I should've."

"Lots of people go through hard times, Jeremiah. It wasn't your fault. You were young."

"There wasn't any money for a doctor when she took sick. Wasn't one I could send for even if I could've paid. The farm was out in the middle of nowhere. Wasn't a doctor in a half-day's ride. If there had been, maybe . . ." His head sagged forward. "I couldn't take care of her. I couldn't help her. If I hadn't made her go away with me, she'd still be alive today. It's my fault she's dead."

For the first time, Sarah had a real understanding of the blame he'd heaped upon himself all these years. She searched her mind and heart for the right words to say but found only platitudes.

She took hold of his hand, squeezing until he lifted his gaze to meet hers. "You can't know that, Jeremiah. Perhaps Millie would have died even sooner here. We can't know what might have happened if we'd chosen a different path. We can only do the best with where and who we are right now." She leaned toward him. "You loved her, Jeremiah. That was all she wanted from you."

Sarah didn't have to wonder if what she'd said was true. She knew because that was all she wanted from him, too. She didn't need his promises that she would never be in want or that he would be able to buy her pretty gowns and hats or that he would make her life perfect or take her to faraway places. She didn't need anything from him except his words of love.

And those were the words he was most afraid to say.

Ember squealed, breaking the silence. Both Jeremiah and Sarah turned toward the stall.

"It's coming," Jeremiah said as he rose from the barrel and moved across the barn, leaving Sarah in the shadows.

For the first time, she wondered if she might never hear him say he loved her. For the first time, Sarah was afraid for their future.

Chapter Thirty-five

Doc Varney knew even before he examined Felix Bonnell what he was going to find. Within a matter of days, he'd already seen five cases of influenza. The sickness had spread with its usual swiftness, boding ill for the people of Long Bow Valley.

Epidemic!

The word echoed with an ominous ring in Doc's head.

After seeing to his patient and leaving instructions for Felix's care with Ethel Bonnell, Doc went directly to the McLeod home, ignoring the earliness of the hour. His knock was answered by Tom.

"Doc?" The young man pushed the door open wide.

"We've got another case, Tom. Felix Bonnell. I just came from his house."

Tom stepped back. "Come inside. I've just made some coffee."

"Thanks." Doc entered the house. He didn't wait for Tom to show him the way to the kitchen. He knew the McLeod home as well as he knew his own.

"Sit down, Doc," Tom said behind him. "I'll get your coffee."

Doc pulled out a chair from the table and sank onto it. Exhaustion pressed down upon his shoulders, and he felt every one of his sixty-four years. Maybe more like a hundred and sixty-four.

"Felix has been sick for several days." He removed his glasses and rubbed his bleary eyes with the pads of his fingers. "I think he's developing pneumonia," he said as he reopened his eyes.

Wordlessly, Tom set the coffee cup on the table, then sat down across from Doc.

"It's the young and the old who are most at risk. I think it's time we dismissed the schoolchildren. Parents should keep them at home. I want you to tell your sister to stay out at the farm. She shouldn't come into town. Influenza can be very difficult on pregnant women." He lifted the cup and sipped some of the hot, dark brew. "We'll make the school a hospital. That way we can see to our patients without delay."

"What do you want me to do first?"

"We need to spread the word. Any sign of illness, folks should come stay at the school. Otherwise, tell them to stay away from town. Tell them not to mingle with other folks till this is past."

Tom rose from his chair. "I'll get started right away."

"Meet me over at the school when you return." Doc took another gulp of coffee, then stood. "Let's just hope we've already seen the worst."

Egg basket in hand, Sarah stood beside Ember's stall and gazed at the leggy filly who was sucking noisily on the mare's udder. Even now, two days later, Sarah was still awed by the miracle of birth she'd witnessed, but her smile was bittersweet as she remembered other things about that same afternoon in the barn.

It seemed she'd waited a long time for Jeremiah to tell her about Millie, only now she wished he never had. Millie's specter seemed to stand between them, holding them apart, keeping Jeremiah from speaking the words Sarah most needed to hear. She had thought, once he trusted her with his memories from the past, that he would also trust her with his future. It seemed she'd been wrong again.

She set down the basket, then opened the stall gate and slipped inside. Startled by Sarah's sudden presence, the filly jumped and nearly fell, then hid behind her dam.

"Don't be afraid," Sarah said softly. "I'm not going to hurt you."

Don't be afraid, Jeremiah. I won't hurt you either. I love you. I'm not going away. Nothing's going to happen to me.

The filly poked her head forward and eyed Sarah with a look of distrust.

"It's okay. You can trust me."

You can trust me, Jeremiah.

"How do I reach you?" she whispered, but she wasn't speaking to the skittish filly.

The clatter of galloping hooves drew her eyes toward the barn door. Her eyes widened as she wondered who could be calling at this early hour. She slipped quickly from the stall, picked up her egg basket, and hurried toward the door. She arrived just in time to see her brother raising his hand to knock on the front door, his winded horse standing behind him.

"Tom?"

When he turned, she saw the concern written on his face.

Grampa!

Tom strode toward her. "Where's Jeremiah?"

"Inside. Why? What's wrong?"

"I need his help."

"What's happened? Is it Grampa?"

Tom grasped her upper arms. "No, it's not Grampa. He's fine. But we may have the start of an epidemic."

"An epidemic? What—"

"Influenza. We're closing the school. We think folks should keep away from town until it's over."

"But what about you and Grampa? Are you coming here to stay with us?"

Tom shook his head. "I'll be helping Doc. Grampa'll be fine. He'd rather stay in his own house, he says. I'll make sure he keeps inside, away from anybody who's sick."

"But I should be there."

"No. Doc said for you to stay here at the farm. We don't want you taking sick, too."

"But—"

Her brother's hands tightened around her arms. "Don't argue, Sarah. Just do what Doc says. I'll make sure Grampa's okay."

Sarah swallowed the panic rising in her chest and tried to quiet her pounding heart. She drew in a deep breath to steady her nerves. "You'll send for me if I'm needed?"

"Yes."

She let out the breath in a sigh. "All right. I won't argue with you." She stepped around him. "We'd better tell Jeremiah."

Fanny stood on the boardwalk and watched the Rafferty carriage drive away, taking Rose and the children to stay with her friend Lark Jones at the Lazy L Ranch. When the carriage had disappeared beyond the bend in the road, Fanny let her gaze move slowly along Main Street. It looked deserted, like a ghost town. No one walked along the boardwalk. No horses were tied to posts outside the saloon or the barber shop or the restaurants. No dogs barked. No children laughed. Everything was absolute silence. She felt as if she were completely alone in the world.

Except she knew there were already a number of sick people over at the school. Tom was there, helping Doc take care of them. Fanny wanted to help, too.

And there was no reason she shouldn't help, she decided as she turned and walked in that direction. She sure as shootin' wasn't going to be needed to help cook meals at the hotel restaurant. There wouldn't be any customers to feed, not if everyone did what Doc had told them to do and stayed home.

She entered the schoolhouse. In a glance, she found Tom, leaning over an old woman. He wore an expression of gentle concern as he held a cup to the woman's lips and watched as she drank. As he lowered her head back to the pillow, he spoke to her softly.

Fanny remembered the way he had cared for her when she was sick. He'd always been gentle and patient with her, no matter what. It was just one of the many things she loved about him.

Tom raised his eyes and saw her standing there. A small frown wrinkled his forehead as he skirted the sick woman's cot and crossed the room.

"What are you doing here?" he asked when he reached her.

"I came to help."

"I don't want you exposed to—"

"You're here. I want to be here, too."

He hesitated, but she could see he meant to continue to argue with her.

"Tom, if I'm gonna be a doctor's wife when you come back from Boston, then I'd better learn how t'help you in your work. Hadn't I? Isn't that what a wife's supposed t'do? Be a helpmeet for her husband, like Rev. Jacobs says. I'm not afraid of hard work. I've been doin' it as long as I can remember."

"Fanny—"

"I'm not goin' away, Tom McLeod." She raised her chin in defiance and met his gaze with an unwavering one of her own. "Now, you'd best tell me what t'do."

His smile was weary but earnest. "Fanny Irvine, I love you." Then he kissed her square on the mouth.

Late that night, overtaken by weariness, Doc sank onto a chair in the corner of the schoolroom. He removed his glasses and rubbed his eyes, wondering if he would find the strength to get to his feet again. His head and back ached, and his eyes felt hot. If he could just get some sleep . . .

Replacing his eyeglasses, he looked around the room. The lamps had been turned low and cast only a pale yellow light across the cots lining the walls. All was quiet for now. No one coughed or moaned. Doc knew it was a temporary respite.

Fanny sat in a rocking chair someone had brought here earlier in the day. In her arms was a toddler, the little Evans boy, sleeping at last. The child's fever had raged high for hours. If it didn't come down soon, Doc didn't think the boy could survive another twenty-four hours.

Doc moved his gaze across the room until he found Tom. The young man squeezed water from a rag over a porcelain bowl, then laid the cool cloth across old Mrs. Percy's forehead. Despite it being the middle of the night, Tom didn't seem the least bit fatigued. Doc tried to remember what it was like to be young with boundless energy, but he failed. He couldn't remember what it was like to be young. At the moment, it seemed he had always been old and tired.

His gaze moved on, touching on each of the twelve patients in the room. The cases ranged from light to severe. Felix Bonnell was the worst thus far, but Doc feared there would be many more needing his attention before the sickness had run its course.

He leaned back against the wall and closed his eyes again. Tomorrow he would send a telegram to Boise City, asking for another physician to assist him. He was an old man. Perhaps there was someone younger who had studied influenza, a doctor who was more knowledgeable about curing the disease. As it was, Doc felt helpless. He was doing nothing more than trying to relieve their symptoms. He wanted to know how to protect them, how to make them well again.

A racking cough broke the silence. With a sigh, Doc pushed himself up from the chair and made his way toward Mrs. Fremont's cot, knowing this was just the first of many long nights to come.

If only his head would stop aching . . .

Chapter Thirty-six

Jeremiah told Sarah very little, only that the town was quiet, that people were staying home, that the train had curtailed its route up from Boise until the epidemic had run its course. She sensed there was more to tell, but she hadn't the courage to ask. To keep herself from wondering what was happening to her friends and neighbors, she kept busy sewing a layette for the baby, washing and mending clothes, cooking meals.

And waiting. Always waiting.

A week after Tom had ridden out to the Wesley farm with news of the epidemic, Jeremiah returned from Homestead in the middle of the day. He hadn't returned before dark once since the sickness had begun, and Sarah knew the moment he walked into the house that something terrible had happened.

She laid aside the small nightgown she'd been working on and rose from her chair. Jeremiah met her gaze only briefly before turning away. He removed his hat and placed it on one of the pegs in the wall. Then he shrugged out of his coat. She couldn't help noticing the way he moved, as if the weight of the entire world were resting on his shoulders.

When he turned around and she saw his face, dread turned her blood to ice water in her veins. *Is it Grampa?* she wondered. *Is it Tom?* Yet she couldn't seem to ask, couldn't seem to make her mouth work.

Jeremiah stepped toward her, stopping just an arm's length away. "Hank and Tom are fine." He paused, then added, "Doc Varney died this morning."

Relief warred with sorrow. It wasn't her grandfather. It wasn't Tom. They were alive. They were all right.

But Doc was dead. Doc Varney. He'd been like one of the McLeod family. It was Doc who'd mended Tom's broken bones and treated Sarah's skinned knees. It was Doc who'd cared so tenderly for Gramma Dorie before she died, and it was Doc who'd nursed Grampa back to health. She hadn't even known that Doc was sick. She wasn't prepared for this.

Jeremiah's hands alighted on her shoulders. "Tom doesn't expect Mrs. Varney to make it through the night."

She met his gaze. "Both of them?" How could this be happening? Doc had always been so spry, so lively. He hadn't seemed old. And Betsy Varney . . . She was twenty years younger than her husband.

Jeremiah pulled Sarah into his embrace. There was something almost desperate in the way he held her.

"There's more," she whispered against his chest. Then she pulled back, tipping her head to look up at him. "There's more you have to tell me. What is it? Don't keep it from me."

"Tom says there'll be no doctor coming up from Boise City to lend a hand. They've been hit just as hard to the south as we have. We're going to have to get through this without a doctor. Tom's doing everything he can, everything he knows how to do."

She closed her eyes as she pressed her cheek against Jeremiah's chest once again. "Poor Tom." Losing Doc Varney was a blow to the town, but it had to be devastating for her brother. Doc had been Tom's inspiration, his mentor, his tutor. Now the folks of Homestead would be looking to Tom to care for them, and he hadn't even begun his official medical studies. He was only eighteen, for all his seeming maturity. "I should go to him. He'll need my help."

"No!"

The gruffness of Jeremiah's voice startled her. She took a step backward.

"I won't have you going into town. It's too dangerous."

"But, Jeremiah, I—"

"No, Sarah. Your brother has plenty of help. Fanny is there and so are several others. You must stay here, where you're safe."

She stared at him for a long time, seeing beyond what he was saying, understanding what went unsaid.

He was thinking of Millie.

Lord help him! It was happening all over again. Sarah was pregnant. There was illness all around them. And the town was without a doctor.

He remembered Millie lying on their bed, her face pale and drawn, her eyes glassy, her lips cracked with fever. She'd been so frail, so painfully thin except for the roundness of her belly. And Jeremiah had had no way to get help for her. There had been no doctor to send for. There had been no way to take her to a physician even if he'd known where to go, and no money even if he'd had a way to take her there. Millie had died because Jeremiah could do nothing to save her. He'd been helpless.

And now there was Sarah. She'd brought warmth back into his life, into his heart. She'd made him feel more alive than he'd ever felt before. She'd given him hope. She'd taken away the loneliness that had been his constant companion for so many years. He loved Sarah as he'd never loved before, as he'd never hoped to love. She had become like the very air he breathed, necessary to sustain life. If Sarah were to take sick . . .

"I'll stay, Jeremiah," she said softly. "As long as Tom and Grampa don't need me, I won't go into town until the danger is over. But if either of them need me, I'm going."

He closed his eyes as relief washed through him. Harvest . . . If he could keep her safe until harvest . . . Then he could dare to love her, really love her.

"Jeremiah." Sarah touched his arm, drawing his attention back to her. "Don't shut me out, Jeremiah. I'm your wife. I love you. Please, don't shut me out."

He wanted to say what she longed to hear. He wanted to tell her he loved her, too. But he couldn't. Not yet. It didn't matter that it didn't make sense. Logically, he knew that telling Sarah he loved her could not endanger her.

Logic and reason be damned! He couldn't take the chance. He couldn't risk anything happening to Sarah.

"I'd better take care of my horse," he said abruptly, then turned and left the house.

Sarah sank onto the nearest chair as the door swung closed. Her throat was tight. Her stomach ached. She felt as if the wind had been sucked from her lungs.

Maybe Jeremiah didn't love her. Maybe he

would never be able to love her. Perhaps
Millie Parkerson had taken everything he
had to give and left nothing for Sarah.

*What are you so afraid of, Jeremiah? How
can I reach you? What must I do? What can
I say?*

If only she could talk to her grandfather.
He would be able to help her. He'd always
been able to help her.

But she couldn't talk to her grandfather.
She'd promised Jeremiah she would stay at
the farm. She was going to have to work this
out herself.

In her mind, she began to carefully piece
together the things Jeremiah had shared
with her since his return to Homestead. It
wasn't an easy task, making sense of his life.
Jeremiah was always so careful about what
he said. And yet, she realized, he'd revealed
himself to her in countless ways.

She straightened in her chair and turned
her gaze toward the window. Her heart began
to race.

*If it wasn't for me . . . It was all my
fault . . .*

How many times had she heard him say
those words? When he'd talked about his
father. When he'd talked about his brother.
When he'd talked about Millie. Suddenly, she
understood the meaning behind those words.
Jeremiah blamed himself for whatever ill had
befallen those he loved.

He thinks if he loves me, he'll lose me.

Sarah rose from her chair. How could she show him he was wrong? How could she help him to open his heart and take the risk?

She walked to the window and looked out, turning her gaze toward the barn.

"I don't know how, Jeremiah," she whispered, "but somehow I'll make you see."

Overhead, wispy clouds were strained pink and lavender by the setting sun as Tom made his way home. He'd never felt more bone-weary than he felt today, but it was the heaviness of his heart that caused his feet to drag. He wasn't sure how he was going to tell his grandfather about Doc Varney. Even Tom found it hard to believe, and he'd been the one who had closed Doc's sightless eyes for the last time.

Pausing on the boardwalk, he looked up at the two-story house. He wondered if he should have insisted that Grampa go to stay with Sarah and Jeremiah at their farm. Doc was more than a decade younger than Hank McLeod, and he hadn't survived his bout with influenza. If Grampa were to take sick . . .

Head bowed forward, Tom started up the walk to the front porch. Just climbing the steps seemed a monumental task, and he found himself hoping his grandfather would be asleep so he could wait until morning to tell him about Doc.

He wasn't so lucky. Before he'd even closed the door behind him, Hank appeared at the top of the stairs. Tom met the old man's watery gaze for a moment, then shook his head slightly and turned to hang up his coat on the rack.

"Have you eaten, boy?" his grandfather asked.

"I'm not hungry."

"You need to keep up your strength. At least have a bit of cheese and bread."

Tom turned to face him. "Grampa . . ."

Hank started down the stairs with that slow, careful gait of his.

"There . . . there's something I need to—"

"I already know."

Tom found himself fighting tears. He hadn't cried, really cried, since Doc had set his broken arm when he was nine years old. But now it was all too much. He'd enjoyed Doc treating him as if he were already the older man's equal. He'd liked having the townsfolk giving him the sort of respect usually reserved for men of greater years and education. He'd begun to believe he'd earned it, that he was darned near a doctor already.

But he wasn't. He didn't know what to do for all these people. He didn't know how to care for them. He didn't know how to cure anyone. He was tired and afraid.

"Here now," Grampa muttered as he reached the bottom step. "Let's get some food in you and get you off to bed. You're plumb tuckered out." With a hand on Tom's back, Hank steered him toward the kitchen.

Tom didn't want to eat. He just wanted to go to bed. He wanted to go to sleep and stay that way until the epidemic was over.

"They brought a woman in today from the logging camps. She miscarried her baby. I don't know if she's going to pull through."

He thought of Sarah. What if Sarah took sick? What if she lost her baby? He'd been so angry with her, so infuriated that she was pregnant with Jeremiah's child before they were properly wed. But if she should lose it because he couldn't help her . . .

In the kitchen, he sank onto a chair and cradled his face in his hands, his elbows braced on the table. If only his head would quit pounding. If only his muscles didn't ache and his eyes burn.

"Here. Drink this." His grandfather held out a glass of cooled milk from the ice chest.

Tom didn't feel as if he had the strength to reach out and take the glass, but somehow he did as he was told. He gulped the milk down, then set the glass on the table and wiped the white mustache from his mouth with his shirtsleeve. His head dropped forward, with his chin nearly resting on his chest. It took too great an effort to hold himself erect.

"Eat some bread. Fanny baked it yesterday."

When did Fanny have time to bake? She was always at the schoolhouse, helping him. Wasn't she?

"Tom?" His grandfather's voice seemed to come from far away. "Tom?"

He tried to look up. The light from the kitchen lamp had weakened. Shadows pressed in from all corners of the room, drowning the light. There was a strange roaring in his ears, like the sound of a gale at sea.

"Tom?"

Grampa?

He tried to speak but couldn't find his voice. The roar in his ears became deafening. The room began to spin as the light around him narrowed to a pinpoint. Then the light blinked out, leaving him in utter darkness.

Sarah lay nestled against Jeremiah, her head on his shoulder. She drew in a deep breath, enjoying the scent of him. He had become so much a part of her. He had given her new eyes with which to see the world and everything in it. If she died tomorrow, she would die happy because she had known and loved him. She couldn't imagine her life without him.

"Jeremiah," she said softly as she slid her hand across his chest. "Are you awake?"

"Hmmm." He brushed his lips against her hair.

"Jeremiah, there's something I want to say to you. There's something I want you to understand. I know I haven't seen the things you've seen or traveled the places you've been. I know my life has been an easy one. I've been cared for and looked after for as long as I can remember. But I have learned some things in my life. I've learned some things about love."

She closed her eyes. *Please hear what I'm saying, Jeremiah.*

"It wasn't your fault your dad was the way he was. It wasn't your fault I didn't want to marry Warren. And it wasn't your fault Millie died."

She felt him stiffen, but she stayed close, didn't let him pull away.

"Bad things don't happen to people because you love them. Bad things happen because it's a part of life. Bad things happen to the just and the unjust, just like the Bible says. It's the way the world is. But love makes life worth living, no matter what else happens. Millie married you and went away with you because she loved you. She was going to have your baby because she loved you. But she didn't die because she loved you. She died because she got sick." Sarah took a deep breath, then added, "You can't make yourself safe from hurt by trying not to love people. You'll get hurt anyway."

He didn't move. He didn't even seem to be breathing. She wasn't sure he heard what she was saying. She wanted him to hear. She prayed that he could hear.

"I'm your wife, Jeremiah, and I love you. I'm going to love you till the day I die. Maybe

422

I won't live to be old and gray. None of us knows the number of days we've been given to live on this earth. But as long as I am alive, I'm going to be with you. I'm going to love you. I can promise you that, Jeremiah."

She held her breath for a moment, hoping he would respond, hoping he would tell her he understood, hoping he would tell her he loved her at last. But the room remained silent. The only sign she had that he'd listened was the tightening of his arm around her shoulders as he drew her closer against him.

Maybe, she thought. Maybe he heard me.

Clutching hope close in her heart, Sarah drifted off to sleep.

Chapter Thirty-seven

Jeremiah drove the pick into the earth, loosening the soil around the old tree stump. Sweat trickled down the sides of his face, but he ignored it.

But try as he might, he couldn't ignore the memory of the things Sarah had said to him last night.

Bad things don't happen to people because you love them.

If only he could believe it with his heart.

I'm going to love you till the day I die.

But that was exactly what he was so afraid of. Sarah dying.

Jeremiah had come back to Homestead with no dreams left. The years had killed the dreams he'd had as a young man. When he'd returned, he'd wanted nothing but a place of peace where he could exist. Where he could hide from the emptiness of his life.

But Sarah had been here, waiting for him. Sarah had made him feel again. Sarah had taught him how to dream again. Sarah had made him want things. Sarah had shown him what a life with her could be like, and he wanted it. He wanted to make her dreams his. He wanted to grow old with her. He wanted to tell her he loved her, to make her smile, to hear her laugh.

She wanted him to tell her he loved her, and he wished he could. But he couldn't. Not yet. If he said the words and then lost her . . .

"I love you, Sarah," he said softly. "God help me, I do. Only . . ."

Across the acres separating him from the farmhouse, he heard the sounds of a cantering horse and the rattle of a harness. He straightened and turned. He saw a man— he couldn't tell whom from where he stood— draw back on the reins, bringing the horse and buggy to a halt in the yard. He saw Sarah step outside and shield her eyes from the bright spring sunshine as she looked toward the driver of the buggy. After only a moment, he saw her turn and disappear into the house.

Who was it? he wondered. What did he want?

But Jeremiah was afraid he knew. Dropping the pick, he broke into a run. Before he reached the yard, Sarah was outside again, a shawl around her shoulders, a small valise in her hand. She started toward Jeremiah, stopping when she saw him running in her direction.

"It's Tom," she called to him as he drew closer. Her expression was tight with worry. "He's sick. I've got to go to town."

"You can't go, Sarah. It's too dangerous."

"I don't have any choice. Grampa can't take care of Tom alone, and there's no one else who can do it. Too many others are sick." She glanced over her shoulder toward the horse and buggy. "Rev. Jacobs said he'd give me a ride back to town." She started to turn.

Jeremiah grabbed her by the arm, spinning her back to face him. "You can't go, Sarah. I forbid it."

Her eyes widened with surprise.

He drew a quick breath and tried to soften the tone of his voice. "It's too dangerous," he repeated. "You could get sick."

"He's my brother. He needs me. And Grampa needs me, too. He's not strong enough to care for Tom all by himself. It wouldn't be right for me to stay out here. This is something I have to do."

"No." He felt the panic growing in his chest. "I won't let you. I'm your husband, and I'm telling you not to go."

"Jeremiah, you don't understand. This is my family. I can't *not* go to them when they're in need. If you love me, you won't forbid me to go."

A door slammed closed in his heart. "When did I ever say I loved you?"

She staggered back as if he'd hit her, and he dropped his gaze to the ground, unable to look at the pain in her beautiful blue eyes.

He'd known it wasn't safe for her to love him. He'd known it wasn't safe for her to be loved by him either. He'd known he would lose if he dared to love her. He should have stayed clear of her. For Sarah's sake, he shouldn't have let himself care.

"You're right, Jeremiah," she whispered, pulling his gaze back to hers. "You never did say it." She drew herself up straight and held her chin high. "And I can't force you to. Good-bye, Jeremiah." With that, she turned and walked resolutely toward the buggy.

"Sarah!"

She ignored him, climbing into the buggy without so much as a glance behind her.

Rev. Jacobs met Jeremiah's gaze for a moment, then clucked to the horse and drove away.

When did I ever say I loved you?

Sarah closed her eyes as she pressed the palms of her hands against her stomach.

Never, Jeremiah. You never have said it. Maybe you never will.

Sarah refused to think about Jeremiah in the following days. If she thought about him, if she thought about the way he held

427

her at bay, she would have cracked and shattered into a thousand pieces. Instead, she thought only of tending to her brother's needs. And when Fanny fell victim to the influenza, she brought her into the McLeod home and cared for her, too.

Sometimes her grandfather asked her about Jeremiah, about why he didn't come to see her, but Sarah only said he was busy at the farm and no more. She didn't want to think what his absence might mean. She didn't want to think that Jeremiah might truly not care.

When did I ever say I loved you?

Never. He'd never said it.

The hours of each day seemed endless to Jeremiah. The nights were even worse.

You're a fool, Jeremiah. You'll never amount to anything. . . . You can't provide for a wife. You'll probably both die. . . . You're a fool, Jeremiah. . . . You're a fool . . .

In the darkness of night, he wandered through the house, touching the lace curtains at the window that Sarah had made, standing in the center of the small kitchen where she'd so often stood. Even with her gone, her delicate lavender fragrance seemed to permeate the air, reminding him of all the things he loved about her. He remembered the many different ways she'd made him feel—happy and hopeful, strong and tender, even angry and frustrated. But above everything, he realized how she'd made him start to believe in himself again.

But he'd rejected her. He'd sent her away, cruelly withholding the one thing she wanted from him—his love. He remembered the look on her face, remembered the sound of her voice.

You're right, Jeremiah. You never did say it.

Would she ever be able to forgive him? Would he ever be able to make it up to her?

You're a fool, Jeremiah. You'll never amount to anything. . . . You can't provide for a wife. You'll probably both die . . .

All his life, his father's words had followed him. All his life, he'd waited expectantly for the failure that was sure to come. And it had always come.

Now, Jeremiah wasn't willing to accept failure as his certain fate. He wanted to be the man Sarah believed him to be. It wasn't enough that Sarah had been forced to marry him because she was pregnant with his child, a child created in one reckless moment of passion. It wasn't enough that she hadn't had a choice but to become his wife. And it wasn't enough that she was stuck on this farm with nothing but struggle and hardship before her.

But how could he make things different? His wages as a deputy were low, and his farm would do little more than break even with the best of harvests, at least for the next few years.

That was when Jeremiah made up his mind. He would leave Homestead. He would go out and make something of himself. He would become the man Sarah wanted him to be, the sort of man she deserved. Then he would return.

And when he returned, he would tell Sarah he loved her. When he returned . . .

Sarah was scrambling eggs in the large skillet on the stove when Tom walked into the kitchen. She smiled when she saw him. He'd lost a good ten pounds and looked too thin for his height, but there was color in his face again and light in his gray eyes.

"Leslie Blake stopped by this morning. Mr. Bonnell is going to pull through, and the Morton twins went home yesterday."

"Good," Tom said with a sigh. He pulled out a chair and sat down. "Any new patients?"

Sarah shook her head. "No. It looks like the worst is over." She pulled the skillet off the stove and set it on the counter. "Have you been in to see Fanny this morning?"

"Yes."

"She's looking much better." Sarah dished helpings of scrambled eggs onto several plates. "I believe she'll be up and about in another day or two."

"I think so, too." He paused, then said, "Sarah?"

She glanced over her shoulder.

Tom pointed to the chair opposite him.

"Could you sit down a minute? I need to talk to you."

She felt a shiver of fear as she wiped her hands on her apron. His expression was so serious. Was she being too optimistic? Was Grampa sick? He hadn't been down yet this morning. Was he—

"Sarah, I think it's time you went home."

She sank down onto the chair. "I can't."

There was a lengthy silence before Tom asked, "Why not?"

She didn't know how to explain it to him. How could she tell him what kept Jeremiah and her apart when she didn't understand it herself? She had told herself for weeks that Jeremiah loved her. It was only that he couldn't say the words. But now she wasn't so certain. If he loved her, wouldn't he have understood why she needed to take care of her loved ones? Wouldn't he have come after her, at least seen that she was all right?

"Why not, Sarah?"

She shook her head. "I just can't."

"But you love him." He covered her folded hands with one of his own.

Tears swam in her eyes as she continued to shake her head, feeling the despair she had steadfastly refused to feel since the day she'd told Jeremiah good-bye.

"Is there anything I can do?"

"No," she whispered hoarsely. "No, there's nothing you can do."

431

Chapter Thirty-eight

Shopping basket on her arm, Sarah opened the front door just as Jeremiah stepped up onto the porch. Both stopped dead-still and stared at the other in silence.

Sarah drank in the sight of him, noting the etched lines around his eyes, the golden hue of his skin from working under the March sun, the wrinkles in his unironed shirt.

The carpetbag at his feet.

She lifted her gaze to meet his. Each beat of her heart was like the pierce of a knife. He was leaving. He was going away.

When did I ever say I loved you?

Never. He'd never said it. Now, he never would.

"You're leaving," she said woodenly.

He glanced down at the carpetbag, then back to her. "Yes. I'm catching the noon train."

"I see."

Was this pain what he'd felt when Millie died? she wondered. If so, then she finally understood why he hadn't wanted to love again. The pain was too great. It hurt too much. It was unbearable.

"Can we sit down?" He motioned to the far end of the porch.

Stiffly, she turned and walked to the porch swing. Jeremiah followed her, waiting until she sat down. Then he leaned against the railing, purposely, she thought, keeping some distance between them.

He cleared his throat. "I hear Tom and Fanny are both well again, and your grandfather came through all right."

"Yes."

A weighty pause stretched between them.

"Sarah . . . I've been doing a lot of thinking while you've been in town. Being alone gave me time to take a long, hard look at myself and my life."

"Jeremiah—"

He raised his hand. "Let me finish."

She clenched her hands in her lap and bit her lower lip.

"I never have been very good at expressing my thoughts or my feelings, Sarah, and I'm sorry for that. I know these past weeks have been hard on you. You're so full of life. So free to give love, and I don't know how to accept it."

He pushed off from the railing and turned his back toward her.

"I've known from the first moment we met that I wasn't good enough for you, Sarah. I can't give you the sort of things you deserve. My dad always told me I wouldn't amount to anything, and I haven't. Ever since I left that farm in Ohio, I haven't wanted anything more than to keep a roof over my head and some food on the table." He paused as he shoved his hands into his pants pockets. "But, Sarah, you made me want more. More for myself and for you. You made me want to give you something better."

Her heart quickened.

"When you look at me, you make me want to be the sort of man you thought I was, back at the beginning." He turned to look at her again. "That's why I've got to go away. Somehow, I've got to prove I can be something more than what I am now."

Slowly she rose from the swing.

Again he raised his hand. "This is something I've got to do. I can't find out who I am or what I want here, living in my father's house, scraping by and hoping it'll be enough, always waiting for some disaster to strike, always wondering . . ."

Wondering what? she wanted to ask but didn't.

Two quick steps brought him to her. He

drew her into his arms and kissed her. It was the poignant kiss of farewell.

Finally, his mouth parted from hers. He lifted his head mere inches away. "I won't blame you if you can't forgive me. I won't blame you if you don't want me when I come back." He stepped away. "I'm sorry." He spun on the heel of his boot and walked away, grabbing his carpetbag off the porch before descending the steps.

Sarah watched him go through a sea of tears. Confusion, bewilderment, uncertainty warred within her. What was she supposed to do now? She sank onto the swing, grasping hold of the side until her knuckles turned white.

She didn't hear the door open, wasn't aware of her grandfather's approach until, suddenly, there he was, seated beside her. He took hold of her hand and squeezed it, then set the swing to rocking gently as he placed an arm around her back and drew her head onto his shoulder.

"Sarah, remember how you used to dream about going to all those foreign places? I'll bet you knew more about those cities than the folks who live there." He stroked her hair with a gnarled hand. "Well, I think you know more about that husband of yours than he knows about himself."

She straightened and looked up at her grandfather as she dashed away her tears.

"Most dreams don't come true just from

wishin', princess. They come true 'cause you go after them. You have to want them bad enough." He cupped her chin with his fingers. "I never thought you really wanted to go off, 'cause if you had, you'd have found some way to go. You wouldn't have settled for an engagement to Warren or stayin' in Homestead. But I reckon this is different. Am I right? Just how bad do you want Jeremiah, Sarah?"

Hissing and steaming, the train rolled into the station. With a final gasp, it stopped in front of the depot platform.

Jeremiah picked up his carpetbag and stepped aboard. He made his way to the first empty seat and sat down, turning his gaze out the window and staring south across the valley. He was glad he hadn't chosen to sit on the other side of the car. He didn't want to look at Homestead. He didn't want to think about Sarah or the McLeods or the Raffertys or any of the other townsfolk. He didn't want to think about how long it might be before he returned.

Above all, he didn't want to wonder if he was making a mistake.

Sarah . . .

He looked down at the blue and yellow bonnet in his hands. He'd stopped by his old room above the jail and retrieved the hat from beneath the cot. Heaven only knew why.

No. He knew. Sarah was why. He'd bought
it because it made him think of Sarah. He'd
brought it along for the same reason.

Sarah . . .

He'd come back to Homestead with a heart
as cold and empty as the old farmhouse in
winter. Sarah had moved in, building a fire
that had warmed the darkest corners. Sarah
had loved him despite himself. Sarah had
looked at him and seen someone worth
loving. Sarah had forgiven him for what he
was, for the mistakes he'd made.

Sarah . . .

Lord, if he couldn't find something good
within himself here with Sarah, where could
he find it?

With a burst of steam, the train jerked forward just as Jeremiah jumped to his feet.
He grabbed hold of the seat back to gain
his balance.

Chug . . . *chug* . . . *chug* . . .

He reached for his carpetbag and
turned . . .

And there stood Sarah, holding a carpetbag of her own.

"Sarah," he whispered, her name drowned
beneath the noise of the moving train.

"Where are we going first, Jeremiah?"

She was wearing blue, the same color as
her eyes.

"I've always wanted to travel and see the
world," she said.

Her milky complexion was highlighted

with splashes of pink in the apple of her cheeks, and there was a slight quiver in the lower lip of her heart-shaped mouth.

She took a step toward him, holding on to the back of the seat, her hand mere inches from his. "Grampa says the dreams you want bad enough come true because you go after them." Her voice lowered, but her eyes held his. "All the things I ever dreamed about . . . It turned out they all came true in you, Jeremiah. So I'm going with you. I want to be there when you find what it is you're looking for."

He reached out and touched her cheek. "You *were* there, Sarah. I just didn't know what I was looking for." He drew her to him, framing her face with his hands. "I was looking for you."

Sarah stared up into his sooty-black eyes. Her heart hammered wildly in her chest, and her throat was thick with repressed tears of joy.

"I almost let you slip away," he whispered.

"No," she managed to respond. "No, you didn't. I'll always be right here with you."

"I love you, Sarah. I'll never hesitate to tell you that again. I love you."

Then he kissed her, the words she'd longed to hear still echoing in her heart.

Epilogue

September 1899

The sun rested like a giant orange ball atop the purple-shaded peaks, then began its slow descent down the far side of the mountains, casting long shadows across the valley floor. The evening air cooled quickly, and a gentle breeze carried with it the fragrances of autumn.

Wrapped in a shawl, Sarah stood in the barnyard, watching the sunset and marveling at its beauty.

She heard the shrill whinny of Ember's filly and turned to watch Little Blaze race across the enclosed pasture toward her dam. In the neighboring pasture, the Wesleys' new milk cow grazed peacefully.

She rubbed her back with the fingers of one hand, knowing that soon there would be one more blessing to add to all the ones already surrounding her. Jeremiah's son.

Her joy seemed endless.

The barn door moaned as it swung closed, drawing Sarah's gaze across the yard. She smiled as she watched Jeremiah striding toward her.

He looked different from the man she'd first seen, standing in her grandfather's doorway nearly ten months before. His face had been bronzed by an entire summer in the sun. His muscles had been honed and his hands callused from weeks of backbreaking labor. His limp had disappeared entirely. But what was truly different about him was something that came from inside.

Jeremiah Wesley was at peace, with himself and with the world.

He grinned as he drew near, and she couldn't help laughing aloud in response. "I suppose it's safe to assume your trip to Boise was a success."

"Best prices in years, according to Norman Henderson." He drew her into his arms and hugged her as tightly as her distended abdomen would allow. "We'll be able to add that extra room onto the house."

She met his gaze. "And the rest of your trip?"

Jeremiah nodded as his grin faded. "I saw Warren." He drew a deep breath. "It was awkward at first, but I think it's going to be all right, Sarah. You were right about me going to see him. We . . . I think we're going to work things out between us." He kissed her forehead, and his smile returned. "He's courting Mr. Kubicki's niece. It seems to me he's quite smitten. I think we may get an invitation to a wedding before next spring."

Sarah felt her heart lighten. "Oh, I'm glad," she said softly. "I'm so glad."

Slipping his arm around her back, he turned them both to face the last glimpse of the setting sun. "Thank you, Sarah."

She didn't have to ask what he meant. She simply knew, just as she always knew what was in Jeremiah's heart.

She closed her eyes as she laid her head against his shoulder, remembering when she'd dreamed of finding her heart's desire in Philadelphia or New York, London or Paris. Remembering when she'd dreamed of her mysterious European count. And remembering when she'd discovered that everything she'd wanted, everything she'd dreamed about, could be found right here in Homestead.

"I love you, Sarah."

She smiled as she drew closer to her husband, knowing that no mysterious European count could hold a candle to Jeremiah Wesley when it came to making dreams come true.

Dear Reader:

I hope you have enjoyed our three visits to Homestead, Idaho (*Where the Heart is; Forever, Rose;* and *Remember When*). I know I've had fun, getting to know the many families of Long Bow Valley, watching Addie and Rose and Sarah (and others) fall in love. I've come to think of these characters as friends. I hope you have, too.

As I drew near to the completion of *Remember When,* I began to toy with the idea of a fourth novel in the Americana Series. There are a couple of young people in Homestead who just might be suited to each other, given a little time to convince them.

But deadlines being such as they are, I can't tell you in this note if I'll return to Homestead or if I'll take my readers to another location with my next book. If you would like to receive an autographed bookmark and newsletter (which will include the title and release date of my next novel), please send a legal-size, self-addressed, stamped envelope to the address listed below.

Wishing you love and luck,

Robin Lee Hatcher
P.O. Box 4722
Boise, ID 83711-4722

Heart's Landing
Robin Lee Hatcher

Winner Of The *Romantic Times* Storyteller Of The Year Award.

Vivacious Brenetta Lattimer is as untamed and beautiful as the Idaho mountain country where she has been raised. Only one man can tame her wild spirit—handsome Rory O'Hara, who has grown up with her on Heart's Landing ranch.

But fate has taken Rory away from Brenetta, and when they are brought together again, she feels her childhood crush blossom into an all-consuming passion. Brenetta thinks she will never allow another man to kiss her lips as Rory has so hungrily done, until her scheming cousin Megan plots to win Rory for herself.

Despite the seeming success of Megan's ruthless deception, Brenetta continues to nourish in her heart a love for the man who has awakened her to the sweet agony of desire.

__3621-5 $4.99 US/$5.99 CAN

A FRONTIER CHRISTMAS

Madeline Baker, Robin Lee Hatcher, Norah Hess, Connie Mason

Discover the joys of an old-fashioned Christmas with four stories by Leisure's most popular historical romance authors.

LOVING SARAH
By Madeline Baker

A white woman learns the true meaning of Christmas from the Apache brave who opens her heart to love.

A CHRISTMAS ANGEL
By Robin Lee Hatcher

A little girl's wish for a Christmas angel comes true when a beautiful stranger arrives at her father's Idaho farm.

THE HOMECOMING
By Norah Hess

An innocent bride finds special joy in the Christmas homecoming of a husband who married her on the rebound, then marched away from their Kentucky homestead to fight for his country's independence.

THE GREATEST GIFT OF ALL
By Connie Mason

A lovely young Colorado widow rediscovers the magic of love when her two children befriend a traveler who resembles St. Nicholas.

_3354-2 $4.99 US/$5.99 CAN

LEISURE BOOKS
ATTN: Order Department
276 5th Avenue, New York, NY 10001

Please add $1.50 for shipping and handling for the first book and $.35 for each book thereafter. PA., N.Y.S. and N.Y.C. residents, please add appropriate sales tax. No cash, stamps, or C.O.D.s. All orders shipped within 6 weeks via postal service book rate. Canadian orders require $2.00 extra postage and must be paid in U.S. dollars through a U.S. banking facility.

Name _____

Address _____

City _____ State _____ Zip _____

I have enclosed $_____ in payment for the checked book(s).
Payment <u>must</u> accompany all orders.☐ Please send a free catalog.